Seven Summer Nights

Harper Fox

FoxTales

Seven Summer Nights is dedicated,
with enormous love and thanks, to Jane.

FoxTales Publications
www.harperfox.net

Seven Summer Nights
Copyright © 2016 by Harper Fox
978-1-910224-60-1

Cover art by Jay Aheer

This is a work of fiction. Any resemblance to persons living or dead is entirely coincidental.

Acknowledgements / Author's Note

In this book, I have quoted from WH Auden's prophetic poem *A Summer Night*, written in 1933, six years before the outbreak of the Second World War. I have also made use of *The Charge of the Goddess*, by Doreen Valiente. The earliest version of the *Charge* does not appear until the late 1940s, after the action of the book. However, Valiente drew on deep roots, and I like to believe that Drusilla was something of a prophet, too.

"It is a confusing path, hard to follow without a thread,
but, provided the traveller is not devoured at the midpoint,
it leads surely, despite twists and turns, back to the beginning."

- Plato, *Euthydemus*

Book One
(Into the Labyrinth)

Chapter One

Sabros: nothing but a speck in the Mediterranean, a few miles of rock made important by its location halfway between Libya and the southern shore of Crete. Voices beating like dove wings under a hard blue sky.

Rufus Denby made his way through the shouting and the dust. On top of the most recently opened tomb, Professor Hargreaves was locked in argument with the Sabrian minister, arms waving, face brick-red in the heat. Ready to blow a gasket, by the look of things. The minister, by contrast, was cool in his djellaba, expression growing haughtier by the second.

Hargreaves spotted Rufus. "Denby! Up here, man, quickly. You speak these blasted people's lingo, don't you?"

"A little. It's an interesting hybrid of Cretan Greek and Arabic, actually, confined to this island and—"

"Never mind that. Tell this—this *gentleman* that all our rights to excavate here were cleared in advance by his own government. They can't bloody well change their minds the moment we find something worth digging for in this godforsaken desert."

Rufus's grasp of the Sabrian dialect wasn't quite up to that. As far as he remembered, the minister spoke decent English. "*Masa al-khayr*, Minister Belesh. Is there a problem?"

"Yes, Dr Denby. Bad problem. This tomb is *agapomenu*."

A hot gust blew up from the bronze-glitter sea beyond the village rooftops. The minister's robes fluttered. Rufus turned over his inadequate supply of Sabrian terms. *Agapomenu* sounded like one of the words for a no-go area, familiar to everyone from the fences around the military camps. There was a nuance to this word, though. "Forbidden?" Rufus tried. "No. More like *sacred*."

"Forbidden." Belesh accorded him a nod. "Sacred. Yes."

Hargreaves snorted. "Sacred? Isn't that the whole bloody point of a temple complex? Tell him, Denby!"

Rufus was Hargreaves' professional equal, in joint charge of the dig. He should have been annoyed that the old fool was using him as a translator and diplomat. But Rufus cared about very little these days. "Minister, everything's agapomenu here. What's different about this tomb?"

"No tomb, *sayyid*. The entry to *tih. Lavyrinthos*."

Hairs rose on the back of Rufus's neck. He turned to Hargreaves. "He says—"

"I heard him, for God's sake. Lavyrinthos—the labyrinth?"

"Well, some of the legends do point to—"

"Don't lecture me about the legends, Denby!" Hargreaves made a frustrated grab for his hat, sending it flying. He pointed to a skinny lad wheeling a barrowload of sandy earth across the site. "You, boy! Fetch that before it blows away. Lavyrinthos... Imagine, if that fool Arthur Evans was wrong, and this is the real site of Knossos!"

Rufus repressed a groan. Hargreaves' theories about the island of Sabros swung like a compass needle five times a day from scorn to grandiose delusion, ancient Cretan castles in the air. "I'm fairly sure that Evans has safely located Knossos at Knossos. Also that the labyrinth is no more than an attractive myth."

"Is it? Even Evans managed to bungle his way to a maze-like structure in the lower levels of the streets."

"Which is probably just what they are. Maze-like streets, I mean."

"And how do you propose to dismiss the coins?"

Rufus didn't propose to dismiss anything. He didn't have the energy. Belesh's robes were very white and pure, a peaceful blaze like that of the whitewashed village domes against the sky. His muscular nephew, clearing rubble from the tomb wall along with the other Sabrian lads, had a warm, bold stare, its message for Rufus unhidden, if he'd chosen to receive it. In preparation for this dig, Rufus had studied the Roman coins until he could have drawn their patterns in the dust—on one face a beast, half man and half bull, an undeniable Minotaur: on the other a series of nested lines that looped around and cupped their overall circular design. "If I had a savage beast to contain," he said mildly, "I wouldn't do it in a structure that had only one route in and one route out."

"Did you just explain the difference between a maze and a *labyrinth* to me, Denby?!"

"Maybe. More importantly, we need to understand why Minister Belesh doesn't want to let us dig here."

Bad choice of words. Rufus knew it as soon as they were out of his mouth. "*Let* us?" Hargreaves thundered. "Let? Belesh and his fragile bloody ministry have so far *let* us excavate six of these so-called sacred tombs, using resources and expertise the Sabrian state would never have been able to muster if they had another three thousand years to do it. Every one of them empty! If he proposes to balk just as we reach our last possibility for a worthwhile return from this dig, he and his shiftless, degraded bunch of puppet politicians can forget about support from the

British government for any kind of post-war rebuild on this damned island."

He ran out of breath. Belesh, picking out one word in ten, had a big enough collection now to get the gist. He frowned like the mythical Bronze Age royalty whose remains Hargreaves and Rufus had come here and failed to find, set his fists on his hips and began to bellow back in rapid-fire Sabrian.

Rufus walked away. His head was aching, the clattering dove-wings filling his skull. This was the hottest part of the day: no-one would mind if he went and lay down in his tent. The minister's nephew watched his retreat, his handsome face thoughtful, a strange trace of compassion in his eyes.

***

Late that afternoon, Hargreaves opened up the seventh tomb with a mechanical digger. Whether he'd have been more gentle in his approach had Belesh not opposed him, Rufus didn't know, but by the time the hired mainland driver had begun his work, it was too late anyway: most of the Sabrian labourers on the site had downed tools and walked off, some clutching the blue-glass amulets they wore against the evil eye.

Rufus stood watching the rusted machine from a few yards away, unbothered by the racket and flying grit. He was distantly ashamed of himself. Professor Hargreaves was ten years his senior, much revered, and a good academic when he could steer clear of intellectual hubris and the conviction, vigorously bolstered by the events of the last six years, that every foreign national on earth was inferior at best and at worst an outright threat. Maybe if Rufus had supported him, he wouldn't now be tearing down the entrance to the last Sabrian tomb with a bulldozer.

The sleep had done Rufus good. He barely closed his eyes at night anymore, and sometimes after a daytime rest, he could see the world as he had used to see it, his fellow human beings as real. "Hargreaves," he called over the roar of the digger. "Are you sure about this? If you just explain to Belesh that you don't mean any harm here—that we'll hand over all our finds to the Sabros museum, as we promised—maybe he'll persuade the workforce to come back. Then we won't have to take this place by storm."

"Quiet, Denby." Hargreaves hunched his shoulders and glared at the blocks of tumbling stone. "It's too bloody late for that now. If I had my way, I'd round up the cowardly, bone-idle lot and shoot 'em. Line 'em up against that wall and bang, bang, bang."

Rufus's ears sang. He folded his arms across his chest and fought the desire to lie down and bury his face in the forgiving Sabrian soil. Hargreaves was all talk. He'd sat out the war in a bunker in Kent and, as far as Rufus knew, had never fired a shot in anger. "We still have time. The ministry renewed our permits, didn't they?"

"Oh, yes, we have time. What we don't have anymore is money. I had a cable from London this morning—yet another one of our damn backers has pulled out."

"Which one this time?"

"Hunter & Co."

"What? Why?" The digger drowned out his questions, but the answer would likely be the same as for all the support they'd lost: those few businesses with money to spare were spending it, prompted by conscience, on the devastated daily world around them, not ruins three thousand years old.

The Hunter chain had been sponsoring Royal Museum expeditions for years. Without them, the Sabros dig was lost. Rufus looked around the valley he and Hargreaves' team had painstakingly excavated over the past two months. His indifference melted. This *could* be the fabled labyrinth, at a far stretch of imagination, a discovery to equal Minoan Knossos or Troy. "Come on, then, old fellow," he said, patting Hargreaves on the shoulder. "Let's go and see what we've dug up."

***

Unlike the other tombs, this one didn't end in a pile of plundered rubble a few yards inside. The roof was intact, corbelled limestone daubed in torch beams as Rufus left daylight behind. There were paintings on the walls, but not like the formal iconography of Egypt or the dancers Evans had found in Crete. These were abstract shapes, sinuous, leaping with the torch from side to side of the passage. A sense of discovery leapt with them in Rufus's heart, from a depth he'd thought long dead. He could still do this. He was an archaeologist, one of his country's finest. Despite the mud and chaos that haunted his dreams, he still had a place in the real world, in his chosen domain.

"Denby! Slow down, blast you."

Hargreaves was struggling along in his wake. With him was the driver of the digger, now pressed into service to carry equipment and lights, and Minister Belesh's handsome nephew. Rufus hadn't noticed the young man's return. He was picking a cautious path through the fallen stones, eyes wide. "Denby *sayyid*!" he whispered, approaching Rufus. "Lavyrinthos!"

"Maybe it is, Zadi. Maybe it is."

A pebble dislodged itself from high in the wall. It hit the ground and bounced, bringing another handful after it. They rattled in the tunnel's strange acoustics, echoing, a chatter like machinegun fire. What had Hargreaves said he would do to the men he thought of and treated as *natives?* Line them up against the wall, and...

Bang, bang, bang. More pebbles fell. The roof dissolved from over Rufus's head—opened up to a pale grey sky. He blinked in the sudden rain. His eyes were full of it, his mouth. It soaked his eyelashes through and blinded him. His heartbeat rose out of his chest and became the thump of anti-tank guns in the west. The walls of the passage turned to mud. There was mud underneath him, mud beneath his hands. When he clenched them, blood oozed out of the clay.

His enemy was in the trench with him. Rufus whirled to find him, lashing out. Bang, bang, bang... He could stop the gunfire if only he could close his grip round the neck of the devil down here in the mud. If only he could reach him, squeeze the life out from the demon's throat...

***

Belesh's nephew carried Rufus into daylight, cradled like a child. He set him down in the shade of the biggest stone the digger had displaced. Propped against the sun-warmed rock, Rufus listened to his running footsteps retreat. To the tangle of voices in the distance, angry skeins braiding and tearing apart. Fear as well as rage came rippling through the hot air. The effort to understand this—to care about it—was exhausting. Rufus let his head fall back, closing his eyes.

"Denby sayyid?"

Zadi was kneeling at his side. He was holding a pitcher in one hand, a tin mug in the other. Rufus watched passively while he poured water. "*Efcharistó.* Er ... *shukraan.* Thank you."

"I speak some English, sayyid. I learn from my uncle."

"That's good." Rufus frowned, taking the mug, trying to stop the tremor of his hand. Why was it good? So that the boy could lose touch with his family in the village, go off to Athens like Belesh and learn to be bullied by a faceless bureaucracy there? "What happened in the tunnel? Was there a rockfall?"

"You don't remember?"

"Only the pebbles coming down, and... a lot of mud. How can there be mud in soil this dry? It was red, too, like..." He shivered. "There must be more iron in the ground than I thought."

"There was no mud, sayyid."

Rufus tried to think it through. Instead he became sidetracked by the dark eyes on his. Hargreaves called Zadi *boy*, but he looked to be in his late twenties, barely five years younger than Rufus himself. The label was just an Englishman's haughty bark to every foreign male on site, from the children they used as messengers to fine, full-grown creatures like this.

How would it have been? The dig was finished now, no marvels waiting in the seventh tomb to save them, so Rufus felt free to speculate. One evening at dusk, perhaps, he'd have met the suggestive glance instead of evading it. He'd have waited until the camp was still, and then he'd have followed a fluttering white robe down into the village. There were places for men like him, he'd learned, on the edges of settlements like this, in Egypt, Morocco and the wilder parts of Greece. Yes, here in Greece—where men like him had once ruled nations—he could be sure of a shag against a wall. "Good God," he said, when the background racket grew so loud that he could no longer ignore it. "Is that Hargreaves, bellowing like a bull?"

"Drink some more water. Yes."

"What on earth's wrong with him?"

Fear in Zadi's eyes, not lust. His hand was resting on the hilt of the knife tucked into his belt. "Sayyid, you tried to kill him."

Chapter Two

A year on from VE Day, London was still in ruins. The Royal Museum had taken several direct hits, among the worst of them an incendiary bomb to the famous Assyrian gallery. Despite this, the vast, handsome structure had remained largely intact. It was open to the public once more, shored up and sandbagged where necessary. Deputy Director Taylor's office looked out over Monmouth Place. Underneath the plane trees, the ordinary processes of peacetime life were beginning once more, parties of schoolchildren being herded between buses and bakers' vans. Sunshine fell in dusty bands through the taped-up panes. Rufus raised his face to it. His pupils tightened painfully but he felt no need to blink, as if he'd become transparent to its brilliance and would cast no shadow. As if he wasn't really there at all.

"Dr Denby?"

Rufus sat up. Taylor had asked him a question. He was still able to analyse some of his lapses, and he turned over the contents of the last minute or so in his mind. *Take a seat, Doctor*, she'd said. *How are you feeling this morning?*

She was still watching him, eyebrows raised. She was a nice woman, the first female to be appointed to the deputy's role. She'd held her position with dignity amid the machinations of the museum's administrative hierarchy. Rufus wanted to help her out. "I'm well," he said mechanically. "The medications I'm taking make me a little sleepy, but they seem to be effective."

"Good. That's very good. And the hospital in Finchley?"

"Excellent. In fact they discharged me this morning."

"Already?"

"Er... yes, ma'am. Perhaps it was time off for good behaviour." The joke fell flat. Rufus cleared his throat and watched the sunlight making gargoyle faces out of the innocent caryatids on the building over the road. "Thank you for covering the costs of my stay."

"Well, the museum trustees did that. You've been a tremendous credit to us."

Her choice of the past tense fell like a shadow over the room. "Thank you," Rufus repeated dully. "Have you heard at all from..."

Now it was her turn to prompt him. "The Sabros dig? Professor Hargreaves? Yes. In fact I just received his full report this morning." She turned over the pages of the file laid out on her desk. "Do you mind if I go through this with you? Some parts of it seem a little... fanciful, that's all, and I know the professor can be..."

"Go ahead, please. I should think it's all true."

"All right." She steepled her fingers, cleared her throat. "Well. It appears that, on the second of May—just over a week ago now—the professor, actuated by fears of a loss of funding for the excavation, decided to enter the one remaining intact tomb. Rather abruptly, I might add, even by his standards. I believe a mechanical digger was involved."

"He was upset, ma'am."

"So it seems. You both entered the passage, which showed promise of leading to a chamber of considerable interest."

"Yes. There were some remarkable paintings."

"Indeed. I have a photo here." She extracted it, but showed no sign of handing it to Rufus, who restrained his hungry need to see once again the marvellous patterns and swirls. "Then there was a slight subsidence within the passage—nothing serious, just some loose stones. But it seems to have upset you, because—this is where I begin to doubt the professor's story—you apparently turned on him, knocked him down and attempted to strangle him."

One of the caryatids had a brood of pigeons nesting on her noble head. The silence in the office became intense. "I don't remember," Rufus said carefully. "But as I have no clear memories after the paintings, and Zadi said the same, I can't deny it."

"Zadi?"

"One of our site workers from Sabros. All the others had gone."

"And... you're on familiar terms with this person?"

She hadn't meant to sound cold. Rufus was certain of that. She was a true spare-boned bluestocking, never seen in male company in all his time at the museum. Maybe she'd found abstinence the better part of valour, or had learned to keep her head low. The world would sometimes turn a blind eye to her kind.

Not to his. "Not really. But he's a good man, a good worker." If Rufus could have transported himself back across space and time, he'd have done it, not for the shag against the wall but purely for the crush of strong male arms around him. He remembered being carried from the tomb. His body ached and yearned. "I accept his corroboration of Hargreaves' report. I accept the report itself. I don't know how to begin making amends to the professor. Did I hurt him very badly?"

"It seems not. Mr Zadi and another worker dragged you away, and Hargreaves was well enough to continue with the dig after you were shipped home, and to write me this..." She sighed, flicking through more pages. "This extremely long report. The gist of it is that he was shocked, but aware that the balance of your mind was disturbed, and he's elected not to press charges."

"That's good of him. Er... the excavation's going on?"

"Very much so. All our funding worries have disappeared in the light of the discoveries Hargreaves made in that last tomb."

"Oh." There were other photographs in the file. Even their monochrome edges were tantalising. "Did he find the labyrinth?"

"Labyrinth? No—the Bronze Age burial we'd hoped was there all along. It's a royal one, with grave goods and treasures enough to keep a whole department going for years. We'll be mounting an exhibition here as soon as he's brought them home."

Oh, what did he find? Was it drinking cups and arm bands, little goddess images in bronze and gold? A breastplate or a coronet, a torc, a mask like Agamemnon's? Rufus was almost glad of the backwash of apathy that wiped his envy away. "Didn't we agree with the Sabrian ministry to leave any finds on the island?"

"Not finds like these, I'm afraid. Ethics aside, the cultural importance of such a burial exceeds the Sabrians' ability to curate it." Taylor closed up the file. She set it aside, and with it her formality of manner. "Denby, I know you don't care to talk about your wartime experiences. You were caught behind the Maginot Line, though, weren't you?"

"Yes, ma'am."

"Before and during the Battle of France, for... rather a long time."

"Yes."

"We could have kept you here, you know. As I recall, we tried."

"Archaeology isn't one of the Reserved Occupations."

"But there were ways and means. We could have listed you as essential museum personnel. Irreplaceable."

"If there's one thing my experiences in France taught me, ma'am, it's that no-one is irreplaceable. Forgive me—I really don't wish to discuss it."

She sighed. "I respect that. From what I've been able to observe over the last year or so, the ones who talk loudest are the ones who suffered least. And memory lapses and blackouts are not uncommon in returning soldiers, but yours are severe. The museum trustees would be happy to help defray the costs of any further treatment you need. Your sister's father-in-law's a medical man, isn't he?"

"Yes. I'm going to visit them both this afternoon. But— Caroline, please. I just need to get back to work. If the Sabrian dig's going on—"

"Out of the question, I'm afraid. Our foreign expeditions are of great political importance just now. Many smaller nations affected by the war are likely to open their boundaries to academic-research teams, in consideration of aid, good relations, assistance with rebuilding. In that sense, the museum's archaeologists are our ambassadors, and we must have team leaders who will act accordingly."

"The hospital assured me that the medicine I'm taking will prevent any more violent outbursts."

"Nevertheless."

She was back in her buttoned-up skin. Rufus did his best to button up his own. "Are you dismissing me, ma'am?"

"Yes. You may not take part in any further expeditions, or indeed set foot on museum premises, until you've received whatever treatment you need to prevent you from assaulting other members of staff. Surely my position is clear to you."

He got to his feet. Automatically he tried to brush sand off the knees of his trousers, but there was only a little London dust to dislodge, the grey, gritty demolition pall that hung over everything now. "Yes. It is. When you reply to Hargreaves, will you tell him how sorry I am? I've written myself, but..."

"Don't go yet, please. I have a suggestion for you, though you may not find it worth your time. My cousin is the vicar of a village down in Sussex, a tiny place called Droyton Parva. Wait a minute while I find his letter... Ah, here." She took out an envelope from her desk drawer. "His church—a gem of a place if a bit tumbledown, late medieval—is due for restoration in a few months' time. He'd like any important archaeological features of the site to be recorded before the work starts, and he wrote to me to ask if I knew anyone who could undertake the work."

"That's kind of you, but churches of that era aren't my speciality."

"I know. And my cousin won't be expecting the famous Dr Denby to come and look at his woodwormy pews. All the same..."

"I thought I was fired."

"You are. This would be a private commission, though the parish could provide a small stipend, which—forgive me if I'm wrong—I rather feel you need."

Rufus stared at the floor. He had funds in his bank account for one last rent payment—just—and then he was cleaned out. There was a disgrace attached to his poverty he could never share with Taylor, kind as she was. "May I think about it?"

"Yes, of course. Here, take my cousin's letter. It explains everything he needs, and the address is at the top." She attempted a smile. "There's an inn where you can stay. I'll write and let them know you're coming. This might be just the thing for you, Doctor—rural scenes, fresh air."

She showed him to the door. Opening it, she glanced anxiously up and down the corridor, and Rufus wondered how much of a *persona non grata* he'd become in these hallowed marble halls. She laid her hand on his sleeve. "I never seem to find the opportunity," she said, her voice a dry whisper, "of condoling with you over Henry."

Rufus twitched. He couldn't help his recoil, though it dislodged her kindly grasp and made her flinch in turn. "It's all right. That is... Thank you. I should go now."

***

Most of the museum's treasures had been returned to the galleries. Only a handful of curators had known the location of their wartime hiding places. The deepest Tube tunnels, a fabled vault in Wales which would have withstood a strike even from that bomb whose cold fires were supposed to have put an end to all wars...

The last sandbags were being removed from around the clawed feet of the colossal winged-lion gatekeepers in the Assyrian room. Surely that was a token of faith in lasting peace. Rufus paused by the cordon. Perhaps his infamy hadn't spread this far. Joe Perkins, the overseer in charge of the work, grinned at him and touched his cap as usual. "Morning, Doc."

"Morning, Joe. Reckon we won't be needing those anymore?"

"Not this time round. And if there's ever another one, sandbags won't help us. It'll all be over in one big boom. That's what the papers and the wireless say."

Boom. Bang, bang, bang. Rufus retreated a step, suddenly drenched in cold sweat. He backed into the thin crowd gathering to see the lions' talons reappear. Thin in more ways than one, these weekday visitors, the shopgirls and elderly gentlemen.

Rationing had worked—no-one had starved—but the weeks and the years of the Blitz, night after night huddled in air-raid shelters, had stripped London's people to the bone. "Sorry," he muttered, stumbling away. "Sorry."

Joe's voice followed him, bouncing off the marble. "We heard about you and old Huffy Hargreaves, Doc! Good on yer, that's what I say. Probably have throttled him myself if I'd got the chance."

The workmen broke into laughter. The sound of it clattered up to the Assyrian room's high ceiling, bouncing off the glass. Voices like wings clapping, a throbbing disturbance in the depths of Rufus's brain. He pushed through the doors into the sunlight, ran down the steps and onto the flagstones of the courtyard. He composed himself fiercely. The hospital had laundered the clothes he'd come home in and sent him forth looking decent: he wanted to stay that way. He was crushing his hat in one fist. Taking shelter by the pediment of one of the vast gateposts, he punched the trilby into back into shape and put it on. He arranged the strap of his leather satchel neatly over one shoulder, so that it crossed his body and gave him the same feeling of security as his Sam Browne belt had once done.

That was better. He took a deep breath. He could still hear pigeons, but they were real enough now, swaying up and down on the branches of the plane trees and peering at him sideways to see if he had sandwiches. He glanced at his watch. There was still half an hour before his appointment with Rosemary, so instead of setting out for the Tube station, he began the journey on foot.

So much of his city was untouched. In Bloomsbury, the damage was mostly single-site strikes instead of whole demolished warehouses or streets. He could walk down Leonard Street and back through six years to 1939, when Henry would wait for him after work in a nearby coffee house. On summer evenings, they'd walk together to their Piccadilly flat. Rosemary and the brigadier lived further west, in the refined reaches of Mayfair. On a beautiful day like today, he might as well avoid the Underground's thundering dark. He could make his way down Shaftesbury Avenue, ignoring the diversion into the small streets that had once led him home. God knew he needed time to think.

He rode the tide of time as far as Dove Street, where a bomb had punched a neat hole in the line of Regency redbricks. Any thought processes he might have begun faded off into babble and smoke. His memory sank down to the soles of his shoes and bore him, eyes downcast, straight to Ashdown Mews.

He was tired when he got there, very thirsty, and he seemed to have lost all the mechanics of his pre-war life, the simple solutions of going into a pub or an ABC. Instead he sat down on a pile of bricks at the edge of the ruins. Here, as in many parts of the city, the damage had been eerily selective. Half the block was still standing, though propped with scaffolds, the windows vacant eyes. Fading paper hung in strips from an exposed interior wall. Rufus could see a fireplace, the shadow of a painting that once had hung above it.

A dog was running about in the debris. At first its movements seemed random. It stopped and snuffled round the barbed-wire barricade erected by the demolition crew, then crawled underneath it and trotted to a clear patch a few feet away. After scratching there for a minute, it jumped back over the piles of brickwork and rubble and returned to its starting point outside the barricade.

It was an ugly brute, little more than a skeleton covered in mangy hide. With a shock Rufus recognised his downstairs neighbour's dog. The tides of time shifted again and the building leapt back into existence. The clear patch had been his neighbour's yard, the place beyond the barricade her front steps.

Her dog—back then a fat mongrel, lazy and spoiled—was hopelessly trying to get back inside, scraping and whimpering first at the place where the front door had been and then at the back.

The wallpaper and fireplace on the first floor were Rufus's own, in the room he'd shared with Henry. As the dog trotted past him again, he reached out and grabbed it by the collar still hanging round its emaciated neck. "Hush," he said, pulling it close to his knees. It struggled and snarled but he held on. The bomb had hit Ashdown Mews in the early hours of June the third, almost a year ago. Suddenly the dog went limp and leaned into him: exhaustedly laid its muzzle on his lap.

***

Rufus found a piece of string in his satchel. The brigadier's mansion wasn't the kind of place where you turned up with a stray dog on a string, but that couldn't be helped. He was strangely reluctant to tie the beast. He instructed it to sit, hardly expecting to be obeyed. The dog settled at once beside the garden path, watching him emptily. Rufus had seen the same look in the eyes of shellshocked squaddies. They'd obeyed him with the same passivity. He straightened his hat, brushed his sleeves clear for the hundredth time of brick dust, then climbed the portico steps and knocked on the door.

The brigadier's major-domo politely ushered him in. Even when dressed up on Rosemary's wedding day, Rufus had felt scruffy in this house. Brigadier Spence liked order, gleaming surfaces. What Mrs Spence might have liked had never been an issue: she'd faded and died within a few months of her transplantation to the city. Rosemary was sitting alone by the fire in the immaculate drawing room. She rose and greeted Rufus with outstretched hands. "Oh, my darling. It's been such a long time."

Rufus wasn't sure what to do with her airy cheek-to-cheek kiss. He met her embrace clumsily. "Yes. Er, sorry. How have you been?"

"Dreadful. You can't imagine. Every day older that little Charlie gets, he reminds me more of Charles. Come and look at him. Come here."

She put out a trembling hand. Rufus let her tow him across to the cradle in the corner of the room. Involuntarily he glanced at the painting over the mantelpiece, a magnificent portrait of Major Spence in full dress uniform. He couldn't see much resemblance between Charles and the infant in the cradle, who like so many others was paying tribute to the war effort by looking like Winston Churchill. "Fine little chap," he said awkwardly. "Did he get over his bout of croup?"

"Oh, yes. He's very strong, even if he does seem small. The Brigadier says Charles was small at this age, too. He thinks I fuss too much."

Rufus would have been inclined to fuss too, as the parent of such a puny child. He wondered if he should pick the baby up. But the prospect of handling such a frail body was repellent to him, frightening. "I know the brigadier can be overbearing, Rosie. You're the child's mother. If you'd rather live somewhere else—"

"Oh, no. He's been so good to us. After Charles was killed, he managed everything. He says this is my home now, my home and Charlie's."

That was good. This was a good house for a war widow and her child to take refuge in. Maybe it was the scent of beeswax from the gleaming parquet floor that was making the air hard to breathe. Rufus nodded. He turned back to look at the portrait, trying to forge a connection between the major's haughty image and the face of the boy who had played with him and Rosie in the fields. The brigadier had disliked the connection from the start—

his only son, running around with the greengrocer's children. If he'd overcome his dislike for the girl who'd so disgraced his family by scrambling up into its majestic ranks, that too was good. "I'm glad. I wish I could have helped you more, but—"

The door swung open. Rufus wished he hadn't heard his sister's frightened gasp. The brigadier strode into the room as if it had been a parade ground. "Captain Denby," he boomed, catching sight of Rufus. "About time you honoured us with your presence. Been hearing all kinds of nonsense about this latest dig of yours. Rosemary, why on earth is the baby here in the drawing room? I'll ring for the nurse at once."

"It was just till it was time for his lunch," Rosemary pleaded. "He's been so fretful, and—"

"No wonder, if you coddle him down here. Come along, Jemima," he admonished the young woman who had scuttled into the room before the echo of the bell had died. "Take him upstairs. Babies thrive on routine, Rosemary. That's how I brought up..." He hung fire for just an instant, and his face changed. Then he continued, firmly, "That's how I brought up Charles."

Rosemary watched her child being borne away. "May I ring for some tea for Rufus? He looks tired."

"I've told you, you don't have to ask. You're mistress of this house now—don't treat the servants as if you were afraid of them. Take a seat, Captain. I want to talk to you."

Rufus sat down in a stiff-backed chair by the table. No-one but Spence called him *captain* anymore. He'd tried to not to disgrace the rank, but it had come as a field promotion—too sudden, too strange, and he'd gratefully reverted to his academic title as soon as he'd been demobbed. "Is there something I can do for you, sir?"

"I hope so. Rosemary and I most sincerely hope so." Spence drew out a chair for her and took up position behind it, resting a hand on her shoulder. She blushed, then looked pleased with herself in a vacant, silly way she'd acquired since her marriage. "A vile and slanderous rumour has arisen concerning Charles, and we're certain you can dispel it."

Once more Rufus looked at the portrait. This time it looked back. A furrow appeared in its brow. Horns sprang from its handsome head, and it butted the air and snarled at him. He shrank back. "A rumour about Charles?"

"Yes." Spence frowned. "What the devil is the matter with you? Your hands are shaking."

"Nothing. I'm fine."

"Good, because I'm getting damn tired of soldiers coming home without a scratch on them and complaining of nervous breakdowns. You were with Charles at the battle for Fort Roche, weren't you?"

"Fort Roche?" Rufus blinked flickers of the Minotaur out of his eyes. "Yes, I was."

"It appears that some nancy-boy of a corporal woke up in the military hospital at Farley Cross and claims that Charles—my boy, my only son—acted with cowardice during the assault. Cowardice, Denby!"

"I'm sure the lad's shell-shocked. You said he just woke up?"

"Yes, after occupying a perfectly good bed for more than a year. They thought he was going to die, and so he should have done, rather than spread such lies."

"His memories are probably scrambled. Was he with my company at Roche?"

"One of the handful that came out of that debacle. The rest are dead, apart from you."

I came out of it. I'm not dead. Rufus turned these ideas around and found them unconvincing. He stopped the tremor in his hands by clenching them together on the table top. "My report after that battle is on file. I couldn't give much information. As you know, I was hit by shrapnel at the beginning of the assault, and—"

"That's not what this wretched corporal says. He insists you were with him throughout. So you must have been present when Charles..."

The brigadier's grip on Rosemary's shoulder had tightened, hard enough to hurt her. She patted the back of his hand. "Philip?"

"Yes, dear. Forgive me."

They looked like husband and wife tableaued there. Rufus hid a shudder. Rosie wasn't built for survival on her own. What price was she paying for Spence's protection? "I'm sorry. I want to help. But I'm afraid my first memory after Roche was waking up in the field hospital at Saint Etienne. What does the corporal say Major Spence did?"

"It's unthinkable. The ravings of a lunatic. I should think that, given your friendship with Charles, you'd have no scruples in standing before the officers charged with investigating this matter, and setting the record straight."

Rufus had been friends with a tow-headed boy who had grown up all too soon into his father's son, leaving cricket and picnics behind him in the dust. "I've told you, sir. I have no memories of that day."

"Invent some, then, man! Think of what you know of his character, and stand up and tell the truth—what you know must *be* the truth, whether you remember it or not."

Rosemary was dabbing at her eyes with a lace-edged handkerchief. "Oh, yes, Rufus. Please do. They'll listen to you, with your war record, and you're a famous doctor of archaeology too. We heard how you discovered that marvellous tomb in Sabros, and—"

"I'm afraid you heard wrongly." Rufus got up. Shrapnel scars that hadn't bothered him in months ached and strained, as if they wanted to tear apart again and let him bleed. The ethics of lying to a military board ought to have bothered him, but all that mattered to him now was telling his own sorry truth. "I'm not involved with the Sabros dig anymore. I had what I suppose the brigadier would call a nervous breakdown, and I'm going down to Sussex to work on a village church."

"A church? You, Rufus?" Disappointment clouded Rosemary's face. Rufus knew the look well. Thwarted ambition, shame at the thought that anyone connected with her could fail. She'd done so well for herself, and what would the brigadier think of a relative who grubbed around in Sussex graveyards instead of opening up the treasures of the ancient world? "It's only for a short time, isn't it? Until you're better?"

"I don't know."

"It doesn't have to alter things, does it?" She clutched at Spence's hand and twisted round to look up at him. "We don't have to tell the investigators. As far as they know, Rufus is still..."

"Rufus is a neurasthenic coward!" Spence tore his hand free and came to stand in front of her, face reddening. "To think that creatures like him are still alive and walking around, when my son... Very well, Denby. Your sister and I will defend Charles' memory without your assistance."

Rufus braced himself not to sway. His dry mouth shaped itself round empty air. What was the harm in telling a handful of generals that Major Spence had died a heroic death? Then his sister could be the kind of war widow she wanted to be, and Rufus would not have men like the brigadier spitting words like *coward* and *creature* in his face. He drew a breath to agree.

The portrait contorted again. The room faded out. In a hospital he'd never seen, Rufus stood by the bedside of a boy whose face he couldn't remember and listened to his frantic, disconnected tale. The boy grabbed his sleeve. *You believe me, sir. You believe me, don't you?*

"Rufus! How dare you just walk out?"

He hadn't meant to. He was standing in the garden, and he'd forgotten about his dog. His sister had seized his jacket sleeve and was tugging it frantically. The mongrel, reading her action as an attack, shot out of the bushes, gave a yowling bark and sank its teeth into her leg.

"Denby!" the brigadier bellowed from the top of the garden steps. "Denby, grab that brute." He leapt down to the lawn and charged towards Rosemary and the dog. She was screaming, dancing away from the animal, which now seemed bewildered, jerking its head back and forth between her and the oncoming man. A scrap of skirt was hanging from its mouth. Without thinking, Rufus pushed the snarling creature behind him. "Spence, stop. The dog didn't mean any harm."

"*Spence?* How dare you address me—"

"Because it's over," Rufus interrupted him passionately, hanging on to the dog's scruff. "You're not *brigadier* to me now. It's over, Charles is dead, and if I could bring him back by dying myself, I'd let you shoot me here."

The brigadier gesticulated at the little group of servants who'd gathered in the portico. None of them seemed too upset at the sight of their mistress still shrieking and hopping, blood trickling down her calf. "Wilson! Fetch me my pistol from the study. I wouldn't waste a bullet on you, Denby. I *will* kill this vicious cur."

Wilson had broken into an irrepressible grin at the performance. He straightened his face but held his ground, only staring at his master in amazement. Spence repeated the order, voice cracking with rage.

His words lost power and dropped to the ground like dead pigeons. The dog left off growling. Rosemary ran out of breath for her screams, and a clanging silence settled over the gardens, the house, and the whole suffocating world where little men and women went about their little lives like ants on an overturned anthill. "For God's sake," Rufus whispered. He took hold of the dog's collar, and let the beast lead him like a blind man back onto the street.

Chapter Three

The dog sat at his feet in the railway carriage. Beyond the window, bombed-out suburbs were giving way to green. Sunlight flashed between houses, a dazzling broken rhythm to match the thud and the thump of the wheels. Cow-parsley streaked by on the embankments. Rufus had taken a third-class ticket, close enough to the engine that scraps of steam were flickering past, white against the flowers' ivory.

He'd walked straight from the brigadier's house to Victoria station. He'd meant to stop at his lodgings, but even that had felt impossible, a detour via the moon. Everything vital was in his satchel anyway: his notebook, favourite trowels, brush for delicate artefacts. Shaving kit, comb, prescription of Veronal barbitone. His wallet, containing the last of his funds from the Sabros expedition, enough for his ticket and a few nights' accommodation in Droyton. Whatever happened after that—when he needed a change of clothes, when the money ran out—belonged to a hazy future he no longer quite believed he would reach.

The dog whined and laid its head on his knee. The compartment was empty, a blessing since the poor beast was beginning to stink in the heat. Cautiously Rufus scratched one ragged ear. "Should have left you where you were, shouldn't I, old..." He lifted the dog's skinny hips and checked. "Old girl. You'd have scavenged yourself something to eat by now. We'll both have to hang on and see what Droyton brings us." He'd let her go when they got there, he decided. If she'd stayed alive for this long on a London bombsite, she ought to thrive in the country with rabbits to catch. It was better to be homeless in green fields.

He sat back on the unyielding bench seat. He hadn't travelled the Downlands line in years, and was distantly pleased that the electrification of the network hadn't reached this far. The stops unspooled themselves like beads on a thread. The dog yawned, and he caught the infection of sleepiness, biting back a gape of his own. He pulled out the letter Caroline Taylor had given him and scanned the address, printed in clerical black. The Rectory, Pilgrim Lane, Droyton Parva... Then a clear copperplate hand taking over, filling the page with energetic strokes. Speculation and concerns about the church. Enquiries about the health of someone called Matilda, and that lady's cats, and then—*so, dear Caroline, as we discussed, if you can see your way clear to loaning me one of your gentleman moles—just a small one, with nothing better to do—I'd be most grateful. I rather fear these restoration chaps will run roughshod over my murals. I'd only need him for a fortnight or so. Well, I must close now and take this to the post office. Drusilla is no better, I'm sad to report. The gamekeeper brought her back in a hessian sack last week. Yours affectionately, A.*

Rufus folded the paper up. It gave off a faint scent of good tobacco, and made him think for some reason of apples and yellow roses. The scent, and the rhythmic jolt of the train, were a powerful soporific. He resisted for a while. Sleep was an expensive risk, and he didn't want to wake up screaming here. Drusilla must be a cat, he decided. Gamekeepers tended not to like them. Maybe this chap was kind-hearted, and rather than shooting the creature when he found her among his young pheasants, had bagged her and brought her home. Having settled this, he began to wonder what A stood for. *Andrew, Alan, Alphonse, Aloysius. A is for apple...* His thoughts wandered off into an orchard of possibilities, and his eyes closed.

***

"Sir? Come along, please, sir. You can't sleep here."

He was lying underneath a tree in the stricken remains of Roche forest, and the vicar was coming to take him away in a hessian sack. As dreams went, it was so absurd—so benign, by contrast with his usual circus of horrors—that he woke up smiling. The railway guard standing in the doorway to the compartment smiled in his turn, and the dog left off snarling at him. "Sorry to wake you, sir. But this is the end of the line—Droyton Parva."

Rufus stood up stiffly. "Yes. Thank you. Come here at once, Pippin."

The platform was empty. It must have taken the guard a while to find him. In the narrow road beyond the station gate, his fellow passengers were dispersing. The gate was an arch, weighted down by untidy swags of honeysuckle. A few efforts had been made to contain and direct the oncoming summer, but platforms, sidings and signal box were under siege by the green. Grass bursting up between flagstones, ivy ramping over every wall...

Disoriented, Rufus settled his satchel into place. "Pippin. What a bloody stupid name for a dog. I dreamed I was lying under an apple tree." The dog spared a moment from anxiously sniffing the scent-laden air to glance at him. She looked even worse here than she had in the brigadier's garden, the sores on her spine standing stark, her scruffy vigilance an affront to the beauty and peace all around. If he let her go, she would disappear into the forest of willowherb that lined the track, severing their connection, which after all amounted to no more than a piece of string and a name. "Pippin," he repeated uncertainly, and she whined, wagged her tail, and set off towards the gate.

Rufus let her choose the direction. There was no-one to ask in the deserted street, which consisted of one row of flint-built cottages, their trim lawns long since sacrificed to dig-for-victory vegetable plots. In the distance was a crossroads with a cluster of larger buildings around it. Rufus identified them through a shimmering heat-haze as he approached: a post office, a tiny branch of the Westminster bank. A public house which looked older than all the rest combined, stuccoed and timbered, bearing a sign with a green-painted circle and the name *The Maidens' Dance*.

The dog towed him closer. One green circle on the sign enclosed another, and a third and a fourth, concentrics faded by time. Only when he was standing outside the tavern door did he see that the rings were incomplete, each of them pierced by an inward-leading path.

Inward or outward. If Rufus had a monster to contain, he wouldn't put it in a labyrinth. That's what he'd told Professor Hargreaves on the hot sands of Sabros. A labyrinth had only one way in and out, and who was to say which was which?

His head spun. He hadn't had anything to eat or drink since dawn, and he'd forgotten the power of oncoming summer on the South Downs. The chalk hills with their thin covering of turf could blaze sunlight back into the air, making the flocks of tiny blue butterflies spiral on the updrafts. Most probably this sign was the memory of some local squire's topiary garden. Those had been all the rage in the grounds of stately homes a couple of centuries ago. As for the Maidens, they danced everywhere, from Scotland to Cornwall, frozen into legends and circles of stone. The sign tin-tacked to the doorpost was much less cryptic: *No Dogs Allowed.*

Nowhere to tie one up, either. Rufus leaned over and unfastened the string from Pippin's collar. "Sorry, old girl. This is your chance." He patted her on the rump. "Go on with you. Go on."

He turned away before he could see her run. The tavern door was standing open. He entered hesitantly, eyes adjusting to the dusty shade. At the end of the hallway, a tall, rangy woman in a pinafore stopped arranging a vase of flowers and stared at him. "Yes?" she demanded. "Can I help you?"

"Good afternoon. Could I speak to the landlord or landlady?"

She unfastened the pinafore, whipped it off and retreated behind a small wooden desk. "You can speak to me. We don't take door-to-door trade here, though."

"I'm not a..." Rufus let the angry denial die. God alone knew what he looked like, sweat-stained and smudged with London dust. "I was told the inn has rooms to let. Are there any vacancies?"

Her mouth began to purse up into a *no* despite the row of keys hanging on the wall behind her. "My name is Dr Rufus Denby," he said experimentally. Sometimes the name opened doors for him. "Deputy Director Taylor at the Royal Museum may have told you about me."

"No, sir. I can't say as he did."

Rufus was a borderline case, he could tell. She was weighing up the chances of admitting a tramp into her respectable establishment against the prospect of funds. Of course she wouldn't have heard from Caroline yet. His London morning felt like days ago, but that letter wouldn't have been written yet, much less sent. "I can pay in advance," he said tiredly, "if that would help."

"Well, I'll have to check and make sure..." She put on a pair of spectacles from a chain around her neck and opened a leatherbound book. Then she glanced up, sniffing. "What's that horrible smell? Is that animal yours?"

Rufus too had registered the smell, but for him it had become somehow comforting, a touch of companionship in a hostile world. The dog was sitting at his feet. Her face was rucked into a terrible rictus of fear and rage. *No, just a stray. Some cur that's following me around.* She was eyeing up the landlady's well-muscled calves beneath the desk. Rufus put a restraining hand on her collar. "Yes, I'm afraid she is."

The verdict swung against him. The landlady banged the registration book shut. "There's no dogs allowed," she said ominously, "and anyway, we're full. There's a hotel in Ashfield, ten miles down the road. They might be able to accommodate you."

Rufus didn't have ten miles left in him. He was so tired that he could have lain down in the gutter. Back out on the pavement, he fastened the string to Pippin's collar again. "See what you've done? You've made the place too hot to hold us, and we've only been here half an hour." She panted up at him, big mouth gaping in every appearance of a grin. "That's all very well for you. You're used to sleeping rough. Where am I supposed to stay?"

She trotted around him twice. He turned with her, the movement making the sunny street waltz and lurch. When she stopped, they were facing the third arm of the crossroads, a lane so narrow that Rufus hadn't noticed it. In the far distance, floating in heat haze over the trees, a church spire broached the sky.

***

"The Reverend Archibald Thorne." Rufus straightened up. The sign on the gate was hard to read, half concealed in moss. The name was redolent of Sunday schools, village fetes and jumble sales. A was for Archibald, then. Rufus imagined a short, balding man in his sixties, fussing about the flowers in his church. "He sounds like a lot of fun, doesn't he?"

The dog whined in answer and beat her stringy tail off his leg. Other than her guidance and the name on the gate, he had no belief that he'd come to the right place. If this was Pilgrim Lane, it wasn't marked. He'd passed only three or four other houses on the quarter-mile walk from the main street, and this was the shabbiest of them all, set so far back from the roadside that it all but disappeared amongst rampantly growing laurels and oak. It must have been beautiful once. Knapped flint was still visible under the ivy and honeysuckle, and tall sash windows reflected the chalk escarpment beyond the sweeping valley. Only the third storey had escaped the hungry tendrils, and up there half the panes were broken, giving the elegant lunettes a vacant look. Maybe this had been the rectory once, and Thorne now lived in a cosy cottage nearer to his church. The spire Rufus had seen was at least another half mile down the track.

There was only one way to find out. The wrought-iron gate had swung down off its top hinge. He lifted it aside. Roses were growing wild around the pergola that led from the lane to the front door. Almost convinced the place was derelict, he edged past the thorn-covered shoots to the front door.

His knocking brought no response. Belatedly he noticed a bronze bell with a clapper on a chain, and rang that instead, eliciting a startlingly deep, sweet tone. But the shadowy porch beyond the door's one blue-glassed pane remained vacant, and after a moment he turned away.

He had a sense of having passed a point of no return—as if, when he'd left London, he'd been an arrow whose flight could only carry him so far, and in one direction. To retrace his steps to the village, find a telephone or ask to send a cable from the post office—these simple actions seemed huge, and even if he succeeded in getting Caroline to cable back and vouch for him, the idea of re-entering the Maidens' Dance was repellent. At least out here he could walk unseen down a long green lane and witness—as he'd never thought to do again—the beauty of an English spring untouched by war. He would go and take a look at the church. Probably the vicar had discovered some Victorian scrawls covered with whitewash, imagined they were ancient and called on his cousin's services. Rufus could probably discount the possibility of anything interesting within a couple of hours, which would still leave him time to return to the village and...

What? He laid the question aside. Pippin was romping around at the end of her string. He unleashed her, not with a view to losing her this time but just so that she could run. The gate squealed as he closed it, and then there was nothing but birdsong silence in the lane.

***

Immediately he saw why the rectory hadn't been built close to the church—why no other building stood near it. A mound rose out of the meadow, verdant and sudden. Surveying the scene with the geologist's eye all good archaeologists developed over time, he noted the ridge and the flat sweep beyond. The meadow was floodplain, embraced by a river to the west, to the east wide open to the downlands sky. If the river burst its banks, only the mound would remain above water. The church and its graveyard occupied the whole site.

A lot of nonsense was talked about such places these days, largely due to a misunderstanding of Alfred Watkins' work on landscape alignments. The mound was far more likely to mark the remains of a Norman castle than a site of ancient Druidical worship. Those pragmatic Frenchmen, arriving in the late eleventh century, would have perused the land just as Rufus did, appreciating the water supply, the rich valley soil and the defensibility afforded by a single approaching trackway. Here they would have set to and built first their great circular earthwork or motte, fenced it round with a bailey courtyard, and erected on the top anything from a simple stone tower to the most elaborate of castle keeps. The mottes outlasted their buildings by centuries, leaving enigmatic bumps to be misinterpreted by visitors who preferred a mystical explanation to a real one.

A motte was an unusual site for a church. That was the first point of interest. Rufus set out through the long meadow grasses, Pippin plunging between clumps of rushes and buttercups. Military strategists had different needs to soldiers of Christ, although there were areas of overlap. If Rufus had been building Droyton church, he'd have placed it by the crossroads in the village, not a mile down an unpaved track that must be all but impassable in winter. The Reverend Thorne must have a hard time persuading his flock down here every Sunday.

Perhaps he was preaching elsewhere. Unlike many early churches, this one had never lost its huge stone roof tiles. They were from Horsham, very beautiful, probably a match for the greensand stone of the corners and buttresses, but their weight would eventually bear down the sturdiest of structures. The porch was sagging, the north side of the nave ready to fall. Flint buildings stood the test of time remarkably well, and the subtle shine of their colour range was unsurpassed, especially in the rain or on an afternoon like this when sunlight could call out a spectrum of blue, bronze and brown from the well-knapped walls.

Removing the tiles could be Rufus's first suggestion to the vicar. If Thorne was a purist, the restoration team might have a battle on their hands, but red clay replacements looked well and would swiftly weather out to a pleasing moss-daubed rust. Rufus could cite Alfriston church, the so-called cathedral of the Downs, to support that. He had no idea why he was already marshalling such ideas and arguments in his mind. The process was so much less painful than the usual transactions in there that he let it continue as he neared the edge of the mound: reinforcing a buttress here, renewing stone window tracery there to protect what looked like precious pre-Reformation stained glass. He emerged from the meadow onto a turf path, and climbed the steep flight of greensand steps up to the south-side door.

Only the swallows were at home in this place. The iron-banded oak was ajar: gave easily to his push, startling a flight of youngsters out of the porch. Rufus watched them peel away across the field. A dreamlike peace descended on him. Perhaps he'd come to the wrong church. Maybe the Reverend Thorne had a sensible Victorian redbrick in the village, with central heating and a damp course. Rufus couldn't imagine a congregation gathering here. He couldn't imagine anyone at all—not even himself, and he dropped into his recurring fantasy that his heart had stopped at Fort Roche, and all his experiences since had been a kind of afterlife, a haunting.

Sunlight fell softly in dust-moted shafts in the nave. Yes, the glass was ancient. No system of metallic oxides invented since could reproduce that cobalt blue, gold-ruby red and delicate, spectral silver. Rufus stepped carefully through the painted light. He would once have been at home in such a place, created by skilled hands in the name of something beyond human understanding. Now he felt like an infection. He kept his hands away from the pews, though his palms craved the silky dark wood, and he walked a steady track down the aisle.

The dereliction wasn't so obvious inside. Someone had been hard at work, more with a handyman's touch than a craftsman's. The sagging roof was propped by timbers, an ugly but functional scaffold. Only a day's worth of feathers and droppings from the swallows marked the terracotta floor-tiles. Someone had swept them clean, and placed a vase of glaring orange chrysanthemums on the otherwise bare wooden altar. Rufus stopped in front of it. Automatically he'd removed his hat on his way in. His family had been typical Anglicans, darkening church doorways only for baptisms, marriages, funerals and the occasional midnight Mass. Even alone here, he wasn't quite sure how to behave. Was some gesture necessary, some acknowledgement of deity?

He lifted his face instead and let the filtered light penetrate his eyelids, making his pupils ache and contract. The handyman had been busy here too. Like many churches of the era, this one had suffered an outbreak of white plastering. Someone with more patience than skill had begun the work of chipping it away, with a very small chisel from the look of it. Almost half the eastern wall above the window was exposed, and other places too, giving the interior a mottled, untidy look. No one section had been completely stripped, as if each wall had been checked in the search for something and then discounted.

I rather fear these restoration chaps will run roughshod over my murals. The bold sweeps of the Reverend Thorne's writing, so at variance with Rufus's vision of him, danced in the air. He took a few steps back and looked again at the eastern wall.

There were marks on the bare stone, broad ochre brushstrokes. Another step back, and they resolved into a human figure. She was female in outline, her face a blank oval. Only her head, shoulders and one upraised arm could be seen, but she had to be vast, occupying the whole east end.

Medieval murals weren't unheard of in churches of this age. Earth pigments such as red and yellow ochre were relatively cheap to obtain, and many an impoverished fifteenth-century parson had turned to them to decorate his church. Then had come the Reformation, smashing stained glass out of windows, purging idolatrous imagery under a tide of plaster and white lime—ironically, preserving it from fading and erosion. The artwork was usually exquisite. Stiff-limbed saints would stare blankly back at their discoverers, bearing keys and scourges, their robes elaborately detailed. Who had decided to daub a whole wall with this crude outline?

He followed the upward gesture of her arm. The fingertips vanished behind the curve of the roof. Retreating a few steps down the aisle to gain perspective, he belatedly noticed the beautiful rood screen separating chancel from nave. The lower part had been removed, but the top portion shielding the choir loft was intact, a riot of carved leaves and woodland creatures. No sign of the usual Biblical themes, martyred saints and fat little medieval demons prodding errant souls with pitchforks... Intrigued despite the hunger pains beginning to gnaw at his guts, Rufus glanced around for access to the loft.

There were no interior stairs, but the church had a small north door. Legends abounded over these. He'd heard them called the devil's doorway, read that social outcasts—lepers, maybe, or the village prostitute—might be allowed to come and go that way rather than amongst their betters through the southern porch. The wall looked thick enough at that point to conceal an inner passage. Rufus gave the iron handle a tug. The door gave easily, as if in regular use, or as if the north side had recognised one more recruit to its outcast ranks. He had to duck his head to enter. Immediately in front of him was another dark-oak door, this one firmly locked. In the narrow space between the two, a stone staircase curved up out of sight.

The Droyton choir must have been composed of skinny fellows. Once Rufus would have struggled with the tiny space himself, but the war had stripped him down to bone and sinew, and he climbed the stairs slowly, feeling his way with his hands. He emerged into a peaceful space, washed by sunlight and oak-leaf shadows from the screen. The only furniture was one long bench. He set down his hat and his satchel and looked around.

The plaster had been chipped away here too. At floor level, the hand of the first figure reached past the boards, index finger raised. A second ochre drawing, as potently male in outline as she was female, bent gracefully beneath the rafters to point down.

Rufus stretched out on the bench. He was very hungry now, but he could wait. He tucked the satchel under his head as a pillow and considered the two figures, mentally wiping away the interruption of the choir loft and seeing the wall as a whole. The woman pointing up, the man down... They didn't seem to be reaching for each other. Graciously indicating directions, maybe, sky and earth and the connection between them, a link for the viewer or pilgrim to consider, if he so pleased.

As above, so below. In the flat he'd shared with Henry, Rufus had kept a replica of the Emerald Tablet of Hermes Trismegistus, a fantastical jade reconstruction. *That which is below is like that which is above, to perform the miracles of the one true thing.* Such was the basis of alchemy—the indivisible nature of creation, everything knit to everything else with invisible gossamer tendrils, a breathing, pulsating whole. The replica had been a cheap toy he'd picked up on a dig in Anatolia because he'd liked the idea. He'd been wrong, of course, and so had the thrice-greatest Hermes. All it took was a

V2 bomb to smash men and their trinkets back to dust. Dissolution was the law of this world, not joining.

Claws scrabbled on stone. Rufus sat up, choking on a gasp. His memory worked erratically now, recalling legends learned in childhood with glittering detail, blanking out such ordinary things as the existence of a dog. She shot out of the stairwell and reminded him, leaping onto the end of the bench and dropping a dead rabbit at his feet.

Rufus was disproportionately pleased. He ruffled her mangy ears. "I told you," he said. "Told you you'd be better off down here. No, I won't have any, if you don't mind. You take it off and eat it outside."

She gave him a disappointed glance, but picked up her prize and trotted away. A minute or so later, crunching sounds echoed gently up through the nave's acoustics. The alleviation of her hunger passed through Rufus like a soothing wave. He unlaced his boots and settled back down on the bench. He had only meant to close his eyes, but the red ochre lady pointed at the sky, which opened up and ate him in one painless bite.

Chapter Four

He woke in the Fort Roche trench. His enemy was near him in the
dark. He stumbled through the mud and bodies, and the trench
became the tunnel on Sabros then a narrow flight of stone steps in
a church. Pigeons burst up like fireworks around him. Rufus
grabbed for his gunbelt. This was his chance at last. He could
corner the bastard, take him out of action before the shrapnel hit.
This time it would work.

All he had at his waist was a civilian's belt. His gas mask was
gone too, his helmet and rifle. In panic he hauled at the oak door
in front of him, which turned out not to be locked after all, only
stiff on its hinges. It flew in towards him. He recoiled from it and
staggered outside.

The north side of the church was brushed by moonlight. One
gigantic yew towered over a marble tomb. Other than that, the
grave markers were small. Suicides and paupers... Rufus grabbed
the door frame and hung on, gasping. Cool night air filled his
lungs, rich with the scents of meadowsweet and the river. A
growing May moon, just off first quarter, hung poised between
spires of dark cypress. Gradually his breathing calmed and the
pounding in his chest slowed down.

He was awake. He'd come out here, reached the end of his road—the furthest he could travel, he now realised, all his momentum spent—and fallen asleep on the bench. As his night-terrors went, this one had been tame. Yes, he was awake, and yet still he could hear a woman laughing, and see her running barefoot over the grass.

She was more than barefoot. Rufus rubbed his eyes. He'd taken the weird radiance around her for some kind of nightdress, but she was naked from top to toe, only the moonlight painting her pale skin.

Even in the days when he'd still had pleasant dreams, they'd never featured naked women, so he held on to the concept of her reality. She leapt gracefully onto the yew-tree tomb and flung her arms open wide.

"Drusilla!"

She whipped round in the direction of the voice, dark hair swinging. Another peal of laughter broke from her, then she sprang down and ran on.

A man was in hot pursuit. All Rufus could see was that he was tall and dressed in black. He pelted through the graveyard, clearing the little tombstones as if they'd been fences in a steeplechase. At the very last instance before he disappeared into the woods, Rufus caught the flash of his white dog-collar.

He subsided onto the step. Here he was at Droyton Parva, where the clergy chased naked women through the moonlight. Drusilla's laughter drifted back to him on the breeze. This early-summer night—dew-drenched long grasses, the rustle of riverside oaks—was so far removed from the scenes of his recent waking that the mud walls dissolved from around his mind. His dog, returning with bloodstains round her snout from another hunt, looked curiously in the direction of the departed figures.

Then she came to sit beside him, and tried to lick away the tears that his own brief bout of laughter had stung onto his face.

***

The Reverend Archibald Thorne. He really didn't sound promising at all. Rufus discounted the idea that he was the clergyman from the night before. Perhaps he kept a curate, a troublesome fellow unsuited to his calling, who drank and smoked and chased the village maidens through the dark. Rufus already had his ideas of the Reverend Thorne. He added a pair of spectacles to the squat, fussy image, and an air of harassed fatigue. He even began the Reverend's next letter to his sister. *My dear Caroline, I really am going to have to do something about Fothergill. He's taken to running after naked women by moonlight.*

The sign on the gate was just as faded today, but the gate itself was standing open. So was the door to the porch. The birdsong was having to contend with the roar of an engine from somewhere behind the house. Throaty revs built up and died in a clatter of backfire. After a brief silence and a burst of hammering, the roar came again, making Pippin snarl in fearful response. She'd followed him back through the fields to the rectory without any need for her string. She looked much better this morning. Her coat was drying in curls and her scabs were less apparent. Rufus wished he'd taken time for a wash in the river himself. "Hush," he commanded. "We're on our best behaviour today. Going to see the vicar."

Maybe no more than that. Rufus was beginning to think he'd made a mistake in coming down here. Probably the murals were some passing fad of the Reverend's, forgotten as soon as he'd posted his letter. Rufus owed it to Caroline to introduce himself, but after that...

After that, what? He had no idea. When he tried to think of the future, any broad-scale continuation of his own life, his head filled with wing-claps and dust. He made his way down the rose-covered path, whose thorns seemed worse this morning, though the scent of the heavy-blossomed flowers—gold, with tender coral-blush hearts—was exquisite. The dog followed tamely at his heels: sat beside him, tongue lolling, while he rang the bronze bell. No response. That was hardly surprising, given the racket of the bike. After a moment, Rufus opened the door all the way and stepped inside.

He liked the porch. It was wide, a sensible space for the removal of boots and outside clothes. Against the back wall stood a boot-rack and coat-stand combined, battered and scuffed but solid. The floor was greenish-grey slate under sisal matting. Having grown up in an ordinary rural home, Rufus had thought that one day he'd have furnishings like these around him. But Henry had loved gaudy oil-cloths and bright new plastics and stainless steel, and Rufus had been glad to acquiesce. The plastic would probably last longer anyway. He remembered now seeing an undamaged sheet of it—the cover for a kitchen door—in the ruins of Ashdown Mews. The Reverend's slates smelled of damp, and the coat hooks were rusting. Hairline cracks marked the stained glass. One pane was missing entirely from the quiet pattern of amber and pale blue. Charming on a summer morning, the scent of roses blowing through, but come November...

Come November, scudding grey clouds and the winter's first sleet pattering onto the leaf-mould. A corner of Hyde Park, and Henry walking away. Rufus blinked the images out of his memory's eyes, wondering at the force with which they'd surfaced. He tapped on the inner door, and when the shadowy hall beyond it remained vacant, cautiously let himself in. "Hello?" he called, padding along the sisal runner that covered the length of the hall.

The roses had made it in here too, a pattern of them just discernible on the faded wallpaper, with brighter patches where pictures had once hung. A broad staircase curved up to his right in a generous sweep. Ahead of him was a door, its paintwork scratched and worn down to a kind of dove grey, and like the doors to the porch and the outside world, standing halfway open. "Reverend Thorne? Sorry to intrude like this. Is anybody home?"

The room beyond the door was large, and seemed to be doing service as a kitchen, living room and laundry combined. A huge oak table occupied the central space. Bedlinen was piled up on it. Beside the trough-like porcelain sink, several shirts were awaiting the attention of whoever had been using the scrubbing board and soap flakes. The water in the sink was gently steaming. On top of the range, which looked as if it had been fitted along with the house's foundations, a kettle was wisping towards the boil.

Rufus would have loved a cup of tea. His griping hunger pains had settled to a dull ache, but he was desperately thirsty. He took hold of the top rung of a shabby ladderback chair. "Reverend Thorne?"

There was no chance of anyone hearing him over the growl of the engine. It was coming from a shed in the wilderness garden beyond the kitchen windows. Someone was winning their fight with the bike by dint of sheer willpower, from the sound of remorseless revving—winning, then abruptly suffering total defeat as the motor cut and died. No struggle or backfires this time: just a cessation, filled immediately with the sweet, massive hush of an English country morning. Birdsong, and the rasp of honeysuckle tendrils at the window. Bees in the blossoms of the stately linden tree that shaded the lawn. Then came the clatter of a metal tool hitting a concrete floor, and the roar of a male voice, deep and almost musical with frustration: "Blast! Blast and damn you! That was your last chance!"

Rufus wanted to laugh. The rush of amusement went through him painfully, as it had done at the sight of the absurd couple in the graveyard the night before. He hardly had strength for it, and clutched the chair more tightly as a quick, firm tread crunched over the gravel outside.

The back door swung open to admit a broad-shouldered figure in overalls, wiping his hands on a cloth. Dark hair was tumbling into his eyes. He knocked it back, leaving an oily smear across his brow, and announced, seemingly oblivious to Rufus, "Blasted thing. I give up with her. Is the kettle boiled yet, Mrs Nettles?"

Maybe the sunbeams were passing through Rufus. He felt like eggshells, like a piece of paper half-consumed by fire and ready to crumble to ash. He made a last effort. "Good morning. I'm looking for the Reverend Archibald Thorne. The Royal Museum sent me to investigate the church."

"You're... Oh!" The tall man focussed on Rufus. He coloured deeply. "The Reverend Thorne, eh? Take a seat and I'll see if I can find him."

He strode out of the room. His voice faded off up the stairs, calling on Mrs Nettles again. Rufus sat down obediently. The dog took up a watchful post beside him. He'd clearly stumbled into the Reverend's servants' kitchen, where the handsome man-of-all-work took advantage of his master's absence to tinker with motorbikes, while Mrs Nettles the housekeeper kept him supplied with tea. A nice little world within a world. Like everything else in Droyton Parva, untouched by the conflict that had swept the rest of the planet away on a river of lava and fire. Distractedly Rufus stroked Pippin's head, and she whined uneasily and pushed her nose against his knee, as if trying to keep him awake.

Footsteps on the stairs again, this time measured and calm. A strange, suspended half-minute passed by, the house or the sunlight seeming to hold its breath, and then the man-of-all-work appeared in the doorway. He brought a faint tang of diesel in on the air with him, but his hands and face were clean, his hair brushed neatly back. The overalls were gone, replaced by a grey waistcoat, black shirt and trousers. His only adornment was the band at his throat. "I have to beg your pardon. I was fixing my, er... trying to fix the generator."

The man in his overalls had looked about thirty years old. He'd put on a decade along with his clerical garb. How had he reached such an age without realising he was a terrible liar? Rufus scrambled up and offered his hand. "That's quite all right. My name's Denby—Dr Rufus Denby."

"Marvellous. You must be my mole."

"Pardon me?"

"The gentleman I asked my cousin Caroline to send." The Reverend returned Rufus's handclasp with a knuckle-popping grip that matched his vigorous frame. "I say, did you motor down? I'm rather keen on—that is, if you've brought a car, you're welcome to garage her here."

"No. I'm afraid I came down by train."

"Really? Have they got the Thursday services running again? They stopped a lot of the weekday ones during the fighting, you know, as if that would help. Stop Hitler from invading until the weekend, anyway."

Rufus hadn't known it was Thursday. There was too much light in the kitchen, or too little. For the first time he noticed the blackout curtains hanging at the big sash windows. It had been the same in London, many houses still saddened and blinded, as if their tenants had forgotten or were still lost in dazed disbelief that the bombing had stopped. "I got here yesterday," he said, and then added—because Thorne was nodding encouragement, and seemed to expect more—"I went down last night to take a look at the church. It's certainly worthy of some research."

"You think so? Ah, if you were there yesterday evening, perhaps you can help me with something. Mrs Hill from the village went to see about the flowers, and she came back in a terrible state. She said a tramp had broken in and was sound asleep on the choir-loft bench. I'm sure I don't mind, but I suppose I'll have to investigate, or she'll never supply us with her hideous chrysanths again. I wonder if you saw anything? She said he was a skinny chap, with fairish hair and a..." He paused, smile fading, looking at his visitor with more attention. Pippin had retreated a little way under the table. Another blush, mortification this time, spread over his handsome, strongly marked features. "And a dog. Oh. Good heavens."

"An understandable mistake. For the record, I didn't break in."

"No. No, of course not. I never lock the church. You never know when someone—a lost traveller, for instance—might need shelter." He examined Rufus more closely, in dawning dismay. "But you don't mean to say you spent the *night* there?"

"I'm afraid I did. The inn was full."

"What—the Maidens'? Mrs Trigg is lucky if she manages to lure more than two guests a month into her damp little... But here I am, about to speak ill of my neighbour, as if I hadn't already made a bad enough impression. Why didn't you come here?"

"I did. I rang your bell on my way down."

"And found the house locked up and empty." Thorne bumped the heel of his hand off his brow. "I'd given Mrs Nettles the day off because I'd been called to a diocesan meeting in Ashfield. I didn't get back until late, and then I had—well, a lady parishioner of mine was unwell, and..."

And you chased her through the churchyard in the moonlight, because I recognise you, now that I see you in your uniform. It was air the room was lacking, not light. "Please don't give it a moment's thought. I was comfortable enough in the church. You'll have to excuse me, Reverend Thorne—it's very warm in here, and I think I'd better talk to you some other time."

"Ah. Yes, it's all or nothing with this stove, I'm afraid. But here's Mrs Nettles, and the kettle's just boiling. Won't you stay for some tea?"

Rufus would have given a month's pay for some a few minutes ago. Now the offer made his stomach lurch. How could he shoulder aside this nice man and his housekeeper—a small, sweet-faced woman now beaming a welcome from the doorway—and make his escape? He had to try for a polite withdrawal first. "I'm terribly sorry. I have to leave now. I..."

"Why, you're soaked in sweat, man. Mrs Nettles, come and help me with his coat. I believe he's ill."

They converged on him, kindly hands outstretched. Too much for Pippin, who had cringed further and further under the table as her master's tensions rose: she launched herself, with the force of an uncoiling spring, at Mrs Nettles. Rufus made a hopeless grab for her. The air around him had filled with drifting sparks and his strength was draining out onto the old slate flags. His grip closed on nothing. He dropped to one knee, knocking the chair aside. "I'm sorry!"

"Quite all right." Thorne had seized the dog in mid-leap. He stilled her with gentle, absolute force, one fist tightening on her scruff. She broke into a peal of yelping snarls that had more of grief than rage in them, as if she too had once led a mannerly, decent life and couldn't quite believe what had become of her. "We startled her, that's all. Stop. Stay."

"She's not really mine. She went for someone in London as well, a..." Rufus tried and failed to push to his feet. "I think it might be something to do with women."

"I think it's because the poor beast is half-starved." He gestured to the housekeeper, who had jumped back at the dog's attack but was now approaching once more, expression cautious but determined. "I'm sure Mrs Nettles can help her get over her prejudice. Will you take her to the scullery?"

"Yes, Reverend. There's some nice scraps in there for you, girlie. Come on, now. You come with me."

The string was still hanging around Pippin's neck. Thorne handed her carefully over to the housekeeper. She cast one heartrending look back at Rufus but submitted, shivering, tail tucked between her legs.

Rufus couldn't fathom these people at all. First they offered tea and civilities to someone who looked like a tramp, then they took his savage dog and led her off to be fed. He had to get up and say thank you.

The effort was a mistake. For a second he was afraid that the vicar would hoist him up by the scruff of his neck as well, but instead the big hand closed on his arm. The world began to fade.

"Dr Denby? I think you'd better sit still, old fellow. I say, Maria, never mind the dog—run and fetch Winborn, fast. Denby? Denby?"

Chapter Five

"You know, Archie, you really are the most dreadful Philistine. What's the point of subscribing to the *Archaeology Review* if you never read it?"

Cool air was drifting over Rufus's face. The new voice should have interested him, as well as the source of the breeze. But the horrible effort of keeping upright and awake had been removed, and for now the inside of his eyelids was enough. He drifted with the air, which smelled of golden roses. He'd grown so accustomed to having his collar drawn back, measuring fingers pressed to his throat and his wrist, that these things no longer alarmed him. Not enough to force him to the surface, at any rate, back into the world of action and pain.

"I do read it. What makes you think I don't?"

"If you did, you'd know who'd just fainted clean away in your kitchen. Have a look at the last issue. The main article, I think it was—mysterious tombs on an island south of Crete."

Papers rustled. Light came and went, human shadows in a shady room. A sound of pages turning, then: "Good heavens. *That* Dr Denby?"

"I'd say so, yes."

"But why on earth would Caroline send him down here? I only asked for one of her very smallest moles."

"Well, you seem to have landed a big one. I don't think he has anything infectious. A touch of fever, though I'd say that's due to exhaustion and malnutrition."

"How does the Royal Museum's star archaeologist end up in Droyton Parva, in a worse state than his poor dog?"

"I'll leave you to ask him that yourself when he wakes up. I read in *The Times* that there was some sort of fuss out on the island, one of their team going crazy from sunstroke and attacking one of the others." A hard, dry hand interrupted the air's caress on Rufus's brow. "If he's dangerous, no doubt you'll handle him. I have to go and see Drusilla Hazelgrove now. Hicks tells me she broke the latch on her window last night, and her feet were covered with grass stains and mud. Still, she seems to have come back of her own accord. I don't suppose you know anything about that, do you?"

"Me? Er... no. I'm glad she got home."

A sigh, brief and impatient. "I know you try to shield her, Archie. But the Hickses can't look after her forever. She's getting worse, and the money old Gorringe left is running out."

"I'm aware of that, Winborn. Just do what you can for her, and get Hicks to mend the damn window."

"All right. I'll drop over this evening to check on your guest."

"Do, and stay to dinner. Mrs Nettles has got a shoulder of mutton."

"Another one? I swear, that woman's dealings with the butcher don't bear examination."

"That woman, as you call her, is a genius. Besides, what the eye doesn't see, the heart doesn't grieve over."

A low chuckle. "Is that the Church of England line these days?"

"These days, yes. You'll have to share your mutton stew with old Lady Birch and the farmhands—Farmer Challen can't feed them all. Oh, and Maria and my brat, or course."

"You're generous with your ill-gotten gains, I'll grant you that. Until tonight, then. Keep your mole cool, and make sure he drinks plenty."

"Maria's got some cordial ready for him when he wakes up."

A door closed softly. The sound restored a broken connection inside Rufus's head. His world was more than a soundtrack. He was more than a ghost, released from his flesh and left to merge painlessly with the walls of this house, his hearing the only sense left to him. Words like *tonight*, like *evening* and *dinner* forced the passage of time back upon him, and with it came the sense of changed place. Not the hot kitchen, not the slates or the rug whose foot-worn pile had formed his last memory. He was lying on a cushioned surface. Someone had put a cold cloth on his brow.

He opened his eyes. The Reverend Thorne was sitting on an upright chair in front of the sofa, elbows on his knees, expression thoughtful. His gaze met Rufus's quietly, as if they were continuing a conversation they'd begun long ago, in a time before bloodshed or gunfire. Beside him—on her own upright chair, as if drawn into position for the purpose—a small girl was watching him too. She had jet-black hair, pulled so tightly into pigtails that they stuck out at right angles over her ears, lending a touch of comedy to a face otherwise utterly solemn.

Rufus jolted upright. "Sorry," he rasped, pulling the cloth off his face. "I'm sorry. What happened? Sorry."

"I rather think Winborn wanted you to leave that where it was. Elspeth, go and pour our visitor a glass of cordial."

The child slipped obediently to the floor. She clambered onto a stool by the table and began to pour the contents of a jug half as big as she was into a glass. Ice clattered and splashed. Thorne picked up the cloth and passed it back. His gaze was steady and kind. "You don't have to apologise, you know. You haven't done anything wrong."

"But... where am I?"

"Still in the Droyton rectory. You came to see me about the church. Then you became unwell, but Winborn assures me you don't have cholera, Black Death or anything else that would force me to evacuate the village."

"Winborn?"

"Our village doctor. You fainted, so I called him here, and between us we carried you through to the library, where it's cooler. I hope you don't mind."

"Mind? God, no." Rufus rubbed at his forehead. His throat was aridly dry. The child returned, clutching the glass in both hands. She extended it to him, small face grim with concentration. "Thank you," he managed. He began to drink. The sweet tang of elderflower—summer's heart distilled—shot to the back of his throat, filling his sinuses. Tears blinded him. He just stopped short of swallowing an ice-cube whole: sat forward, coughing. "Thank you. That's... very good."

"I'll tell Mrs Nettles you enjoyed it. Now you have to eat one of her scones."

"I couldn't. I'm afraid I'm not hungry."

"In Winborn's opinion, being hungry is your main problem. I do understand that it isn't always nice to eat alone. Elspeth, bring the covered tray, and three small plates, please."

The girl did his bidding at once. She was like a scaled-up mechanical doll, and Rufus watched in fascination while she hitched herself back onto her seat and handed round the plates. The scones were golden-brown beneath their muslin cover, each one sliced in half and well buttered. Gravely she handed one to Thorne, then to Rufus, and took a third for herself.

She and Thorne began to eat, and Rufus followed suit on social reflex. Once he started—discovering that the scones were fragrant, packed with moist, fat sultanas and still warm from the oven—he became afraid that he would never stop. The girl handed him a second without being asked, and when he was launched into that, turned to Thorne and asked, "Why didn't he die, Archibald?"

Thorne winced. "Because he's fine. He's young. Not everybody dies young, and please don't call me Archibald."

"He'll probably go mad, then."

"Elspeth, have you finished your scone? Don't you have your chores to do for Mrs Nettles?"

"Yes, Archibald."

"Go and do them, then."

She pattered away. Rufus watched, surreptitiously wiping butter off his chin. "She's very... er, sweet. Is she yours?"

"Who?"

"The little girl. Elspeth."

"God forbid. She isn't even Elspeth, only Mrs Nettles couldn't abide the outrageous heathen name she arrived with, so she gave her a new label."

Rufus wondered what the heathen name had been, and whether it had suited the eldritch little creature who'd just left the room. He shook his head. He had no business enquiring into Thorne's family arrangements. "After all, I couldn't even keep control of my dog."

"I'm sorry?"

"Nothing. It made sense inside my head."

"Your dog's fine. She's had a meal and a nap. Shall I fetch her for you?"

"Has she been all right? She hasn't bitten anyone?"

"The beast isn't vicious, Dr Denby. She's very nervous, though, and she thought Mrs Nettles meant to harm you when she came to take your coat. Stay there, please—I'll only be a moment."

In the quiet room, Rufus made an effort to orient himself. This was the front of the house. Like many older buildings whose occupants expected to grow their own food, it faced north, leaving the gardens, vegetable patch and orchard to the sunny south. Three walls were lined with books—a wonderful library, even at the barest glance, well-worn spines giving promise of subjects wildly above and beyond the ecclesiastical.

Everything seemed faded, washed by the waters of time until only the best, toughest fibres remained. The wall facing the sofa opened into a clean-swept fireplace, hooded in copper and framed in cracked blue tiles. There was a painting above it, too dark to make out. Through the casement windows, he could see the rose arbour, the iron gate, the track he'd followed in order to come here and pass out on the kitchen rug.

He groaned at the memory. He'd made an utter fool of himself. Had the Reverend taken his feet or his shoulders, when he and his friend the doctor had carted him through here like a sack of potatoes? Sometimes during his blackouts he screamed, flailed, shouted obscenities. Had he done any of that, in front of the vicar and his neat little pinafored housekeeper?

Maybe he could escape without having to find out. He tried to untangle his legs from the blanket that had been tucked around them, but that brought up the question of who had unlaced and removed his dusty boots, and before he could solve either problem, Thorne was back in the room again, the housekeeper at his side.

She was holding his dog by a new leather collar. Pippin was wide-eyed but calm. Her fur was curling oddly in patches. Mrs Nettles glanced up at the Reverend, who nodded as if in permission. "Begging your pardon, sir, but I took the carbolic to some bits of her. I hope you don't mind. And..."

Another glance at Thorne, who cleared his throat. "Go ahead, Mrs Nettles. I, er—I find it's best to let her speak her mind on some occasions, Dr Denby, especially where I share her concerns. I hope you'll take it in good part."

Bewildered, Rufus looked from one to the other. "I'm sure I shall. Please, Mrs Nettles."

"Well, it's my opinion that a gentleman who has an animal—a dog, for instance—and he can't keep that animal fed, and free from vermin and suchlike... Perhaps that gentleman's circumstances of life dictate that he oughtn't try to keep such a creature. In which case he could leave it here, if he so wished. Just to make sure it was safe."

Elspeth had smelled faintly of carbolic, too. Was this how Thorne had ended up with a houseful of farmhands, old ladies and children who didn't belong to him? "Thank you," he said awkwardly. "But the dog isn't mine. That is—I wouldn't let an animal get into that condition, no. I only found her yesterday, on a bombsite."

"A bombsite!" Mrs Nettles echoed, as if that cleared up the matter entirely. "There, Reverend. I said he didn't look the sort to neglect an animal."

"I shouldn't have taken her away. She was starving, though, and I..." He chuckled, and Thorne put a hand briefly on his shoulder, as if he'd heard the dangerous edge to the sound. "I thought I couldn't make things worse for her."

"Well, Mrs Nettles is right. If you want to leave her here, we'll feed her up a bit, then I'm sure we can find her a home on one of the farms."

It was a good offer. Already the gaps between the dog's ribs seemed less deep. Some of the patches he'd taken for scabs had just been accumulations of dirt and matted fur. "Sorry, Pippin," he said wearily. "That might be for the best."

She tugged herself free. Rufus hadn't succeeded in getting his feet out of the blanket, but he swung them to the floor, ready to restrain another outburst. The dog emitted a low, anxious whine, and leaned against his knees as she had in the rubble.

"Pippin," Mrs Nettles echoed doubtfully. "That's a nice name for a..."

"Sweet, plump little spaniel," the vicar supplied. "This one looks like she has some Doberman in her. And a dash of wolf. But she does seem to be yours."

"Yes. I'd better keep her with me, if that's all right."

"At any rate, she can stay for her dinner. As will you, I hope, although we've got rather a full house tonight."

Rufus nodded, stroking Pippin's head. "Old Lady Birch and the Challen farmhands. And your... Elspeth. I could hear you talking to your friend the doctor, though I couldn't quite seem to wake up and tell you. Thank you for the invitation, and for everything you've done for me. I've already taken up much too much of your time, so—"

"Well, the blessed cheek of it!"

Rufus blinked. But Mrs Nettles was staring out of the window, not at him. She seized a duster from the sideboard and scuttled off, slamming the door behind her. Her voice carried back from the hallway. "Fingerprints! All over my clean glass!"

"Oh, dear," Thorne remarked, putting his hands behind his back and looking for the first time a little like Rufus's preconception of a vicar. He strolled over to the window. "A dispatch from behind enemy lines."

Finally Rufus disentangled himself. He pushed upright, and when the marvellous books stopped dancing and blurring, made his cautious way to join him. Thorne caught his elbow, as if he too could feel the sway of the room. Mrs Nettles had taken up position in the porch. Through the blue and amber frames, an odd little drama was taking place. She was planted squarely, hands on her hips. In front of her, a grubby child was darting from side to side like a boxer looking for a way past his opponent's guard. He was clutching what looked like a note.

Thorne leaned a little way out of the window. "Jebediah Trigg!" he bellowed, making the boy spring a foot into the air as if electrified. "Save yourself some time and deliver that directly."

The boy tried to tug his forelock, recoil and step forward at the same time. "Yes, your Reverence! Beggin' your pardon, your Reverence, but... what?"

"Wretched brat," Thorne breathed. "Wish he'd just be rude to me and have done, but his mother insists on polished manners, from everyone but herself." He raised his voice again. "Bring the note here."

"At once, your Reverence! Only no, your Reverence, because my ma said on pain of a slapping I were to give it direct into the professor's hand."

"Oh, I see." Thorne let go of Rufus, leaving a warm patch where his grip had been. "Luckily for you, I have the professor's hand here, together with the rest of him. Denby, would you like to collect your mail?"

Cautiously Rufus leaned out. Jebediah, po-faced and stuffed tight into his school uniform, came bustling across the lawn. He raked Rufus with a glance. "Is that him? Your Reverence?"

"This, child, is Dr Rufus Denby, a very famous archaeologist from London, as I'd guess your ma just found out. Judge not the outer man, lest ye be judged by thy falling socks and protruding shirt tails, Jebediah."

The boy held out the note, attempting at the same time to tuck his shirt into his short trousers. "Thank you, Professor. And begging your leave, Professor, but Ma says you'll be welcome at the chapel on Sunday, as Hosea Evans is a-preaching."

He backed away, not turning until he'd regained the safety of the path. "Hosea Evans," Rufus said wonderingly, opening the envelope he'd been given. "I never dreamed of having the honour. Who on earth is he?"

"Our local hellfire preacher. The Triggs are Dissenters, so nothing to do with me." Thorne dug in his pocket, leaned out of the window again and gave a piercing whistle. "Here! You had quite a trot of it. Go round the back for some of Mrs Nettles' cordial." The housekeeper threw him a look of anguished reproof, but jerked her thumb to tell the child that he should do as he was told. Thorne turned back to Rufus, smiling. "I'd have given him tuppence, but his ma hates me so much she'd have probably sent it back wrapped in a tract. I take it you didn't get the red-carpet treatment on your first visit to the Maidens'."

"I was barely allowed on the carpet at all."

"Sent you away with a flea in your ear, did she?"

"She was more concerned by the fleas in the dog's."

Thorne rubbed his hands in unclerical satisfaction. "She must have blown a gasket when she found out who you are."

"I'm not sure how she did. The deputy director said she'd write, but it's too soon for a letter to have reached her."

"Maybe Winborn put the word out. He's the soul of discretion normally, but he'd have wanted to scotch the tramp rumour. May I see the note?" He lifted it gently out of Rufus's grasp. "*Mrs Trigg pays her compliments to the professor, and assures him she intended no offence in their unfortunate rencontre*—rencontre! She's been at her French novels again—*yesterday afternoon. If the professor will do Mrs Trigg the honour of returning to her establishment...* et cetera, et cetera. I've never heard the old devil so contrite. Humbling herself into the very dust for you."

Rufus took the note back. "Nobody should have to do that. She was frightened by the dog, that's all."

"Trust me—if Pippin had arrived with a bonnet on and a letter of recommendation from some proper person in Bayswater, she'd have her own room by now. And chilly, damp little cells they are, too." He looked Rufus over, the inspection warm but somehow impersonal, easy to endure. "Dr Winborn said you may have been unwell for some time. If you'd rather stay here, we have plenty of space."

"Oh, I couldn't possibly."

"You mustn't think too much of the offer—waifs and strays pass through here all the time."

"But I'm not a waif or a stray." Rufus straightened his shoulders, hoping the action would support his claim. "I'm not a professor, either—just a common PhD. It's a kind offer, Reverend Thorne, but I'd better go back to the Maidens' and show Mrs Trigg there's no hard feelings." He smiled. "Goodness. No wonder she doesn't care for you, if you give free bed and board to perfectly good paying guests."

Thorne's eyes widened. "Do you think that's it? You know, it never occurred to me. I suppose I have been taking business from her."

"Well, it's a good thing—very good—for people who can't afford her rooms. But I can. The museum specifically instructed me to stay there."

"Who—Caroline?"

"Well, not *instructed* as such. But she did suggest it, and I can't intrude on you here any longer." Rufus noticed that his jacket had been neatly folded over the back of one chair, his hat balanced on top. His satchel was waiting for him on the table. "I've made a tremendous nuisance of myself. I wish I could thank you—Dr Winborn, too—for all you've done, but... I'm rather short of resources just now."

"So it would seem. Are those all the things you arrived with?"

"What, my..."

"Your satchel. And the clothes you're standing up in."

"I'm afraid so." That sounded pitiful, sad enough to warrant a lie. "I've come down in advance of my luggage, that's all. My trunk ought to get here tomorrow."

"I see. I tell you what—just wait here for one minute. Help yourself to cordial and scones."

Rufus could wait, but he couldn't eat. Left to himself, he watched the door for a moment, grateful for the renewed energy of the food he'd already had, unable to take anything more. He found his boots beneath the table, checked that their soles were clean and quickly put them on. He shrugged into his jacket, fastened his reassuring satchel strap across his chest once more. He'd never have had a Sam Browne belt, he suddenly recalled, if his regiment hadn't been sent to the Front hopelessly underequipped and partway kitted out in uniforms dating from before the '39 Battledress introduction. He'd had a Browne holster too, designed to fit the belt and to carry his Webley revolver. They'd cut the belt and strap off him in the field hospital near Fort Roche. What had happened to the gun?

By the time Thorne returned, he was standing at attention, blank and serene. Thorne absorbed the changes at one glance. "Here," he said, setting down a small holdall on the table, not approaching nearer. "Mrs Trigg and her kind judge respectability by suitcases. That ought to help you out a little."

"What's inside it?"

"Just a change of clothes."

"Yours?"

"No. You'd have to roll the trousers up, and we want to add to your dignity, not detract. There's a shirt and a few things for overnight—until your luggage arrives. Don't worry, there's no sad history behind them."

In so many houses, there was. A beloved son, a father or a brother, the only earthly traces left of him a wardrobe full of civilian clothes, hanging like man-shaped echoes. Rufus took the holdall. "I don't know how to thank you."

"Come back for dinner tonight. The table is a free-for-all, but we'll get some quiet afterwards, and you can tell me what you think about my church."

Rufus had almost forgotten. He grabbed the lifeline of his duty. He'd been sent here to do a job. "Of course. I have a great deal to say to you already, especially about your wall paintings. It's a fascinating place."

"You'll come, then."

A neat trap. Rufus tipped an eyebrow at Thorne in acknowledgement. He was to receive the bounty of the house like any other waif, whether he liked it or not. All he could do was surrender with grace. "I'd be delighted."

"Excellent. Bring the dog. You can tell me then why I asked Caroline for a junior and got Arthur Evans instead."

Rufus shuddered. "Don't mention Evans."

"You can explain about that after dinner as well. By the way, I only got a quick look at the article in the *Review*. Did they spell your Denby right, or is it with I-G-H at the end?"

"No, with a Y—like the china."

Again, that assessing, painless look. Thorne held the door so that Rufus could step past him into the hall. "Yes. Good stuff, that—hard to break. Not impossible, though."

In the porch, Rufus stopped. The blue and gold light was falling in a patchwork, and even in winter must give an effect of barley fields beneath a sunny sky. The dog circled his ankles. Rufus touched her collar, hefted his own bag. "Why have you done all this?"

"I'm the vicar. I'm meant to show hospitality to strangers. Don't want you running off to join the Dissenters, do I?"

Rufus shook his head. Whatever was motivating this strange, kind man, he was fairly certain it wasn't religion. "Would you really mind if I did?"

"Heavens, no. They dance and speak in tongues and generally seem to have a good time." Thorne pulled a rueful face. "A better one than I could show them, anyway. It's been a pleasure to meet you, Dr Denby. I'll see you tonight."

"Yes. Er... that generator of yours, the one you were trying to fix when I arrived? She sounds like a Norton to me. War Department 16-H, 490cc. I can have a look at her sometime, if you like. I'm quite good with bikes."

Chapter Six

Mrs Trigg was hovering on the kerb outside the Maidens' to greet him. She'd have been in the middle of the road, except that Jebediah was hanging onto her skirt from behind, holding her clear of passing traffic. "Professor!" she cried, as soon as he came into sight. "Such a pleasure, Professor Denby! Come in, come in!"

Rufus decided not to correct her regarding his title, not until they were indoors at least. *Professor* sounded more impressive shouted down the high street, and everyone deserved a second chance. Taking his own with good grace, he presented himself in front of her: respectable suitcase, well-washed dog in handsome collar and all. "Good afternoon, Mrs Trigg."

"Good afternoon, dear Professor! I'm so pleased you got my note, and I must say, it's just like the nicer sort of London gentleman not to take a poor woman up on a mistake. A war widow, you understand, who has to keep an eye on the tone of her establishment...?"

"I understand. I'm afraid I still have my dog, though. I'd prefer to keep her in my room with me, and if that's against the rules of the house—"

"Rules? Oh! No. That's just to stop the blessed farmers bringing their sheepdogs and terriers indoors when they come for a pint. It doesn't apply to a..." She clasped her hands and tipped her head to one side, and Pippin looked back at her, as if challenging her to find something good to say. "...an attractive companion animal like this. Come along, come along. Your room's all ready for you—the best we have, Professor, looking over the courtyard on the inside, so you won't be bothered by these dratted newfangled cars."

He followed her through the hall and up the narrow stairs. This house smelled of damp too, and it wasn't ameliorated here by roses and baking scones. God alone knew how old the place was, and he was afraid that Mrs Trigg might be offended by the question, as coming from an archaeologist. She was bustling ahead of him, floral skirt flicking. "It's just up here, Professor. Not like what you're used to, I'm sure, but the best a widow lady can provide."

That was the second mention of the widow. There were so many of them in this altered world that he hadn't noticed the first. He wasn't alone in having undergone certain changes since their last meeting, was he? The skirt was new, the hair piled up in an elaborate bun. A scent of *Evening In Paris*—familiar to Rufus from city bars and coffee shops, supplied as gifts by handsome American soldiers to a female population long deprived of such delights—drifted back to him on the air. He shook himself. Probably she was just trying to make up for her faux pas earlier. If not, Rufus couldn't think of a worse tree for the poor woman to have chosen to bark up, but still it was his duty to be nice.

He could just about manage that. He smiled at her, squeezing past her in the tiny upstairs corridor. "Thank you. What a lovely room." Pippin gaped at the lie. The courtyard looked as though it had never seen sunlight, and the sound of the occasional passing car would have been preferable to the dank silence rising up from it. But in fact it was all Rufus wanted at that point: four walls, a door he could close behind him, if only Mrs Trigg would stop hovering anxiously and go. "This is fine. What's the tariff, please?"

"Five shillings a night, or a pound and fifteen paid weekly." She sounded as proud of her weekly rate as if it hadn't simply been her daily one multiplied by seven. "Although some guests prefer to settle in advance. For their convenience on departure, you understand."

"Yes, I understand." Rufus got out his wallet. "I probably will be staying for the week, but I don't know for sure just now, so can I pay you now for tonight and tomorrow?"

"Certainly, certainly."

"Here you are. It's good of you to stretch a point about the dog."

"Oh! My pleasure." She dropped the coins into her pinafore pocket with a zeal that suggested she didn't normally get her up-front fee, or at least not in cash. "That includes your breakfast, of course, Professor. No nasty hidden extras here."

There had better not be. Rufus was almost cleaned out. "Well, if you don't mind, I'll settle in."

"Of course! I'll leave you alone. Dinner's at seven, if you'd like it. That's, er...."

"Extra. Yes. No, thank you—I'm dining out tonight."

"At the rectory?" She didn't wait for his response, but sidled a little further into the room, eyes wide, mouth tightly pursed. "Don't take this the wrong way, Professor, but if I were you, I'd mind what I was doing with the Reverend. I'm sure he's a good man, but that household... Irregular. Highly irregular goings-on."

"I'll bear it in mind, Mrs Trigg. By the way, I'm Dr Denby."

"I'm sorry, sir?"

"Not a professor. Just doctor."

Her face lengthened, as if she might have put on her *Evening In Paris* in vain. "And is that... a very different thing?"

"Yes. A professor has tenure at a university, and maybe a department of his own. Doctor is just an academic title."

"Oh, dear. Well, never mind. You might meet with some silly snobbery around this village, but everybody's equal here. No third parties in the room, please, and no food what's not been bought on the premises."

She flicked the edge of her pinafore at invisible dust motes on the bedstead, flashed Rufus what was probably meant to be a winning smile, and disappeared. Alone, he subsided onto the edge of the shabby chair by the window and pressed his fingers to his mouth to keep back laughter, at least until she was out of earshot. *No snobbery here. No, we're Liberty Hall, we are, Professor.* The sounds he was making seemed to disturb Pippin, so he pulled himself together and stroked her head until she settled beside him. Was the Trigg brand of snobbery—ingrained, natural as breathing—worse than his sister Rosemary's, acquired by marriage and fear?

He could hardly remember what she'd wanted to see him about. Oh, yes—Charles, who'd died with Rufus on the muddy plain outside Fort Roche.

But that was wrong. Only one of them had died. He sat back, counting the beats of his living heart. They'd picked up an echo. A broken gutter above his window was dripping onto the sill, rhythmic and remorseless. *Bang, bang, bang...*

A floorboard creaked in the corridor, breaking the chain-reaction of recall. He listened, intrigued. Pippin had cocked her head and raised one ear. She wasn't growling. Her expression was one of affronted surprise, and when the door gave the tiniest shift in its frame, she glanced up at Rufus as if in a plea for him to deal with this absurd situation before she had to do it herself.

He got up very quietly and walked across the room. He jerked the door open, and Jebediah Trigg fell inside ear-first. "I wasn't!"

he shrieked, before Rufus could ask. "I didn't, only she made me. I never!"

Rufus helped him up. "Right. You weren't listening at my door, but if you had been, it's because your mum makes you keep an eye—or an ear—on the guests, especially single ones who arrive without much luggage."

"Yes, only she never. I never!"

"I get the general idea. Jebediah, do you think you can stand there for two minutes while I write a note? Or do I have to set my dog on you?"

The boy stood as if cast in bronze while Rufus tore a sheet from his notebook and began to write, leaning on the window sill. He would have loved to sit at the rectory table that night and listen to Archibald Thorne as he entertained his guests. He'd have a word for everyone, Rufus was sure, from the old lady to the farmhands to the strange little girl who wasn't his. He'd have set everybody at ease. Rufus would have liked to have seen the doctor too, to thank him and put a face to that dry, pleasant voice. But it was no use. There were things inside his memories of Charles and the Fort Roche mud that made him unfit for human company. Something in the drip of water from a pipe—or the click of falling pebbles in a tomb, or the threat from a foolish old man to line up the damn natives against the wall and shoot them, bang, bang, bang—that drained out the life and strength from him, leaving him an empty vessel.

Ready to be filled by a screaming lunatic. Rufus had missed his dose of Veronal the night before. He folded the note and handed it to Jebediah. "Can you take this to Reverend Thorne? It's just my apology for not coming to dinner tonight, to save you reading it. I understand that tuppence is the going rate for messages."

"Tuppence ha'penny."

"Payable after delivery. And I don't wish to be disturbed any further tonight, so we'll settle up at breakfast. Agreed?" The boy nodded reluctantly. "Good. And would you ask your mother to send me up some sandwiches on a tray at dinner time, if that's not too much trouble?"

Jebediah scuttled off. Rufus decided he rather liked him. All his badness was displayed on the surface for anyone to see, and he was so incompetent in his villainy that he couldn't pose a threat. That was refreshing, after six years at war. Briefly distracted, Rufus lifted the suitcase Thorne had given him onto the bed and opened it.

The clothes inside were neatly folded, and smelled faintly of lavender. He took out a white cotton shirt, crisply pressed. Underneath it was a waistcoat and trousers in moss-green tweed. The fabric was light, the waistcoat's back a subtly iridescent silk. It was a pre-war outfit, a gentleman's turn-out for a summer afternoon, tea on the lawn and maybe a spot of croquet or cricket. There was a suppressed Edwardian gaiety to the cut of the jacket. Rufus took the things out carefully. He hung them in the little wardrobe on the theft-proof coathangers welded to the rail, then turned back to the case. Reverend Thorne had also provided a dressing gown of fine grey wool, and a pair of striped pyjamas.

Rufus couldn't put any of these things on his soiled body. He'd slept rough for one night, but that wasn't the problem, not that kind of ordinary dirt. Trapped in his armpits and the creases of his groin he could smell the chemical tang of a panicked beast, the odour his flesh produced in the grip of his blackouts. Left to his own devices—without this gift from the rectory, all the nice clean things—he would have lain down as he was on the bed. Now, because of the striped pyjamas and the fresh lavender scent, he took out the washbag and shaving kit from his satchel, hung the dressing gown over his arm and went in search of the bathroom.

It was tiny, equipped with a small shower-bath and a feeble supply of hot water. Rufus barely noticed these discomforts, stripping down and crouching in the tub. He liked to stay a long way away from his body if he could, its various needs and treacheries exhausting him. It hadn't always been that way. He'd allowed Henry to awaken nerve endings from his scalp to the tips of his toes.

Quickly he scrubbed himself clean, dried off on the balding towel provided. Everything in the suitcase had looked as if it would fit him perfectly, but the dressing gown was a little long in the arm. He rolled the sleeves back, wondering if it was Thorne's own. The thought gave him an odd comfort as he made his way back to his room.

Pippin looked up and banged her tail tranquilly off the skirting board as he came in. He cleared the bed and sat down. Nothing wrong with closing his eyes until dinnertime, especially if he took his medications now. He'd be alert enough to wake up when his sandwiches arrived, and after that he could drop into dreamless barbiturate sleep.

Mrs Trigg had taken very seriously the usual landlady's policy of single beds for single guests. Rufus wouldn't be luring any third parties in here to join him. He bumped his elbow off the wall as he stretched out on the candlewick bedspread. He swallowed his pills with a mouthful of water from the glass on the bedside table, and wondered if one day a cure for loneliness might be found inside a little brown bottle with a screw-cap lid.

The bed creaked, mattress dipping perilously. "Pippin, no," he said, but the dog only looked at him from her perch at his side. "Mrs Trigg will have your hide and mine." She flopped down beside him. He made a half-hearted effort to push her away, but she laid her head on his ribs, and while he tried to think of ways to persuade her to get down—stern discipline, perhaps, or a sock enticingly thrown—watched him with unfathomable eyes.

***

In the rectory garden, someone was pruning the roses. Already a clear path had appeared between the gate and the front door. The shape of the pergola was emerging, sunshine finding mossy timber and the damp stones of the path. Before Rufus had time to wonder if he'd preferred it the way it was before—the thicket of briars guarding the enchanted castle—a slender figure straightened up to greet him, pruning shears in hand. "Good morning! You must be our visiting archaeologist."

She was perfect. She met Rufus's preconception of a vicar's wife head-on. "Yes. You must be Mrs Thorne."

"Mrs... Oh, Archie's wife? No. I'm Alice Winborn. I think you met my uncle yesterday."

"The doctor?" Rufus returned her handshake. Her fair skin was freckled in the shadow of her sun-hat, everything about her wholesome and fresh. "I didn't meet him exactly. I wasn't well, and he helped look after me. I'm hoping to do better today."

She smiled, a shy glimmer. "We were all sorry you couldn't come to dinner last night. How are you feeling now?"

"Much better, thank you." Rufus wasn't insensitive to female beauty. Sometimes he felt it all the more deeply for his absolute lack of physical response. "You seem to have your work cut out for you here."

"Haven't I just? I'm a landscape gardener by trade. There wasn't much call for that during the war, so I became a Land Girl. Now the boys are back in their fields again, we're not wanted there either, so... here I am, visiting my uncle and pruning the vicar's roses." She tucked a strand of hair behind her ear and blushed. "Sorry. I always run on too much when I meet someone new."

"Not at all." Rufus knew a nervous talker when he heard one. "I go the opposite way and say too little, then people think I'm unfriendly."

"Do they? I don't think I'd have made that mistake about you." She coloured more deeply. "This must be the dog you found on the bombsite." She took off one leather glove and let Pippin sniff her hand. "Poor old girl. But you'll be all right now, won't you? I hope Mrs Trigg didn't make you sleep in the yard."

"No. She let us both indoors eventually."

Alice broke into laughter. "Archie told us the story. How could she have mistaken you for a gentleman of the road? You look so nice, and it's lovely to see someone dressed the way we used to dress before..." She cut herself off and looked at the ground, sighing. "There I go again. I seem to have forgotten how to be demure."

"Reverend Thorne loaned me these clothes," Rufus said gently. "I wasn't very tidy when I arrived—I left London in rather a hurry. So perhaps Mrs Trigg's mistake was forgivable, and as for being demure, I'm not sure how women who've worked on farms and in factories for six years are supposed to... well, I don't know. Go home and return to their embroidery."

"Heavens, Dr Denby! Please let Archie and my uncle take care of you. You may be one of the few men left in the world who still makes sense." She was smiling properly now, nerves forgotten. "Archie's very keen to start boring you to tears about his church. He's out in his shed, if you'd like to go straight round, working on his... I think we're meant to say his generator. Or next Sunday's sermon. I can't quite remember which."

"Thank you." Rufus picked up Pippin's lead and retreated. A narrow track led through the dandelion-scattered grass around the side of the house. Ivy ramped abundantly here over tumbledown outbuildings, and abandoned flowerbeds lay placidly under their easy new harvest of weeds. The vegetable plots were still clear, runner beans scrambling up their pole frames, potato leaves turning a rich summer green. The orchard beyond them was being cared for too, drooping branches propped. Rufus halted for a moment as the breeze brought him a wave of apple-blossom scent, and a brief confetti shower of pink-white petals. "What a beautiful place," he said absently, to the dog, or to whatever spirit of the orchard had just engulfed him.

Between the first of the apple trees and the mossy garden wall there was a big wooden shed, double doors standing open. Sounds of metallic hammering came from within, then a clatter and a volley of swearing. Pippin began to dance on her lead, and Rufus unclipped it from her collar, trying not to laugh. "Go on ahead, girl. Give him some warning."

She disappeared between the doors. By the time Rufus entered, the Reverend Thorne had had time to get to his feet and dust down his overalls. "Ah, Denby," he cried, coming forward to shake hands. "There you are. Hope you didn't overhear that—just a few vocal exercises, you know. For Sunday. How are you feeling this morning?"

"Fine. I just called in to say sorry again about yesterday, and to let you know I'm on my way down to start work on the church." He surveyed the shed's interior, the shafts of sunlight picking out the shape of a magnificent Norton motorcycle propped up on a rack in the corner. "Unless I could help you out here a bit first."

Thorne beamed. He looked ready for a track race at Brands Hatch, not Sunday morning service, his dog-collar incongruous in the open neck of his overalls. His sleeves were rolled back to display the rich veins and musculature of a hardworking man. His tanned clasp of his spanner was capable and firm. "Would you really? It's not very churchy of me, but I'd love to get the old thing going. There's another set of overalls on the bench. Do put them on, because..." He paused, shading his eyes to look at Rufus properly. "Well. I believe Mrs Nettles would say that you scrub up very nicely."

"Thank you." Rufus had slept well. He'd got dressed awkwardly in the new things, which fitted him perfectly and almost gave him a sense of time regained, as if he could really embody Alice's vision of the past. He gestured to Pippin to sit, and went and shook out the oil-stained overalls. "Do you keep a suit of clothes ready for all your visitors?"

"No, and I'd better give you the history of that one, to set your mind at ease. The previous rector here was rather a racy chap, it seems. Sharp dresser, and none too careful about relationships with his female parishioners. In fact he had a child with one of them, and when the scandal broke, he left the place and shipped out to Tuscany rather than face the music."

"Good Lord." Rufus glanced down at the suit which had managed to see so much action in such a sleepy village, and carefully buttoned up his overalls. "Did he ever come back?"

"No, although Mrs Nettles keeps all his things fresh and laundered, just in case."

"Was it Mrs Nettles who..."

"Oh! Heavens, no. She's very loyal to anyone she keeps house for, though, rector or vicar. She keeps me fresh and laundered now, too."

Rufus absorbed this, running a diagnostic gaze over the Norton. She was a beauty, and although they'd been produced in their thousands for the war effort, had been lovingly maintained.

Her cylinder case was set at a slightly odd angle. He dropped to his hands and knees to have a better look, then stretched out on his back beneath the rack. "I meant to ask you about that, actually—the rector-or-vicar part. The house is a rectory, and the previous incumbent was a rector, but..."

"But I'm just a vicar. Yes. It happens a lot in old country parishes like this. Matthew Gorringe was a wealthy fellow, and as rector, he had the right to tithes from all the land in the parish. He had this house built, and it was quite the show place in his day. But he managed to run through his funds. The house went to rack and ruin, and when the war came, the parish couldn't afford to support him in his living anymore."

"So when you came to take his place..."

"It was on a vicar's terms. The church is financed from outside now, and I receive my pay just like any other farmhand. I'm rather like a hermit crab who's crawled into an enormous shell and doesn't know what to do with all the space."

"You fill it with stray children, dogs and archaeologists."

Thorne broke into laughter, a rich and uninhibited sound. "I suppose I do. I can't afford repairs, but at least I can share the place while we all wait for it to fall down."

"Pass me that screwdriver, would you? What happened to her—the lady parishioner, I mean?"

"Who had the rector's baby? Ah, that's not my story to tell. Although you look like the sort of chap who can keep a secret, too."

Rufus moved a section of casing out of the way so he could squint at Thorne. He'd encountered a playground bullying technique which began that way—forgivable in schoolboys, but not in vicars. He'd come across it in army barracks, too. *You seem a decent fellow, so do keep your mouth shut about whatever heinous act I'm about to commit.* "That depends on what it is."

"Very wise. Would you mind much if I smoked?"

"Not at all. Just stay back from the engine. Oh—was that the secret?"

"I'm afraid so. Mrs Nettles, you know. Doesn't like it in the house."

You're not in the house. You're in your own garden shed. Rufus forgot to say the words aloud. The high-voltage cable that carried the spark from the ignition to the carburettor had become dislodged and was discharging to the casing. A scent of good tobacco reached him through the fuel. Thorne was guiltily lighting up, glancing over his shoulder. "I can see she's in charge of the place," Rufus said past the screwdriver in his mouth. "Hardly seems tyrannical."

"She's not. But my lungs aren't quite what they should be, and she worries." A fit of coughing racked him. "With reason, it seems. Oh, dear—excuse me for a moment."

Rufus listened with concern to the sounds coming from outside. Then, unexpectedly, his efforts with the cable bore fruit and the Norton burst into snarling life. He scrambled out from underneath and squeezed the throttle on the handle bar. The engine responded, filling the shed with blue exhaust fumes but settling into a rhythm. What she needed now was to be in motion, setting a charge on a battery almost dead from long disuse. He undid the straps holding her onto the rack and rolled her down. Without thinking, he swung one leg over her saddle, found his balance and rode her out into the yard, Pippin trotting behind.

Thorne emerged from behind a tree, pale and wiping his eyes. "Bloody hell," he shouted over the engine's roar. "What did you do to her?"

"Disconnected cable. Jigged it back into place."

"And where did a mild-mannered archaeologist learn to do that?"

Rufus let the revs drop to an idle. Out here in the sunny garden, with a vicar smiling down on him and the dog romping happily around, it didn't seem too hard to say. "I was with the British Response Force in northern France, the motorcycle corps. We learned how to fix the bikes as and when they broke down."

Thorne's expression shadowed. "The BRF? That unit got caught behind the Maginot Line before the Battle of France, didn't they?"

"How does a mild-mannered vicar know that?" Rufus gave the bike a cheerful rev. "She could use a good long run, next time you get the chance."

"I can't believe she's working. Why don't we take her out now?"

"Now? I couldn't. I really have to get down to the church and start work."

"We'll both go. If we take the bike, I can show you the scenic route there." Thorne began shrugging out of his overalls. "Come on. It's the least you deserve for fixing her."

His excitement was catching. Rufus hesitated for a moment more, then pushed down the kickstand and dismounted. "Maybe I should keep these on. Don't want to get the Rector's suit dirty."

"You can have another one if you do. And Mrs Nettles says she'll wash the things you travelled down from London in, because—and I quote—if you wait for that old bat at the Maidens' to offer, you'll go dirty to your own funeral."

"But I wouldn't expect Mrs Nettles to launder my things. Not Mrs Trigg, either."

"Well, don't worry about it, old fellow. It's just until your trunk arrives."

"There isn't any trunk. I didn't pack anything. I just... I just came down."

Thorne set his overalls aside on a wooden bench outside the shed. He stood very still, watching Rufus. The questions in his eyes remained unspoken, and after a moment he came and stood behind him. He took gentle hold of the shoulders of Rufus's overalls and tugged them down. "Come on," he said. "It's going to be a nice hot afternoon—a good day for a ride."

Rufus swallowed hard. Admitting to his blind flight from London had set a tremor back in his hands. "I don't think I'd better drive."

"All right. You take pillion."

"What about the dog?"

"She can stay here, and Mrs Nettles will... Ah, Maria!" Thorne helped Rufus step out of the overalls and raised his hand to the housekeeper, who'd emerged into the garden at the sound of the Norton's purr. "Look what Denby did."

"Fixed that dirty old bike of yours, by the look of it, Reverend. About time, if I may say so." She smiled broadly and patted her knees for Pippin to come to her, and the dog bounded off across the lawn, all trace of yesterday's terrors vanished. "Morning, Dr Denby. Go on, the pair of you, and take that noisy thing out of my orchard."

Thorne got onto the bike. He rolled her off the kickstand and sat propping her. He gave the seat behind him an inviting pat. "Coming, Denby?"

Rufus moved as if hypnotised. He climbed on board behind Thorne. Not knowing what to do with his hands, he held on to the rear edge of the seat and tried to maintain an inch or so of space between his crotch and the vicar's backside. Thorne shot him an amused glance over his shoulder, but didn't argue the arrangement, and began to bump the bike slowly along the green track towards a gate Rufus hadn't noticed before, a wide five-bar that opened onto the lane.

The gate had two guardians. Alice Winborn was leaning on the top of it, smilingly watching their approach. Beside her was a sandy-haired, spare-boned man in his sixties. There was just enough resemblance between the two for Rufus to guess who he was, and the voice confirmed it, pitched to carry over the rumble of the bike. "Archie! What on earth are you up to now?"

"Going for a ride," Thorne shouted back amiably, stopping by the gate. "Denby fixed my engine. Denby, this is my friend, Paul Winborn. You met him yesterday, but not in the best of circumstances."

"Pleased to meet you, Dr Winborn," Rufus called. Manners prompted him to dismount and shake hands, but he had a feeling that something might happen to prevent him from getting back on, and now he was in motion, Thorne's handsome bulk in front of him and the engine purring underneath, he wanted to stay. "I'm sorry I made such a fool of myself."

"Not at all, not at all. It's good to see you back on... on your feet."

Rufus repressed a grin. *On the back of the Reverend's bike* wouldn't have had the same ring at all. Winborn's brow was furrowed. "Is that thing safe?" he asked Thorne, keeping one hand on the chain that bound the gate shut.

"I'm not sure. Only way to find out is to take her for a spin."

"Don't you think you should take off your dog-collar first?"

"Don't you think I'd look even more disreputable if I did?"

Winborn laughed. "Maybe, at that. Look, Alice and I were hoping you would come over to lunch today. Dr Denby too, of course. We'd like to hear about his plans for the church."

"Poor chap's barely had a chance to see it yet. That's where we're off to now."

"On the motorbike? It's a ten-minute walk from here, and—"

"Uncle Paul," Alice interrupted suddenly. She was blushing, as if this mild tussle had embarrassed her. "Stop making such a fuss. Archie and Dr Denby can come to lunch anytime."

She reached past him to lift the chain, but Winborn didn't shift his grip. "Winborn," Archie remonstrated, laughing in his turn. "Open the gate."

"In all seriousness, Archie—I don't think tearing around the neighbourhood on this stinking machine of yours is in keeping with—"

"Open the damn gate!"

Everyone jumped. Rufus stared in surprise at Thorne's broad shoulders. He wouldn't have guessed he could produce such a roar, not at so slight a provocation. "It's all right," he said, too softly for Alice and Winborn to hear, not sure why he thought Thorne needed the reassurance. The doctor, a little pale, was undoing the chain. "He's doing it. We can go."

"You'd better hang on, then."

The bike snarled and jolted. Rufus grabbed at Thorne's waist on reflex. Winborn retreated from the gateway, pulling Alice after him. Sunlight and shade flickered across Rufus's vision as Thorne revved out into the lane. Once clear of the gateway and Winborn's astonished gaze, he relaxed and eased off the accelerator. "Sorry, Denby. My temper got away from me."

"What was that all about?"

"Oh, Winborn. He's a good fellow, one of the best. But I've known him since I was a boy, and he still thinks I am one. Trouble is, he's probably right—about tearing around the lanes in my dog-collar, I mean. I'll have to apologise to him later, and to poor Alice." He spared Rufus a quick glance over his shoulder. "And you."

"Why me?"

"I'm sorry you saw that."

"No need. I don't like a closed gate myself. Er... this isn't the way to the church."

"No. We'll go through the village and take the ridgeway road. I want to show you something. Besides..." He steered the bike between two deep, sun-baked ruts. "...if we're going to do this, we may as well scandalise the whole of Droyton while we're about it."

Rufus had no objections. Thorne reached the end of the lane and turned left onto the main road. Once out on the tarmac, Rufus didn't need to hang on, and he sat upright and kept a straight face while the vicar sailed down the high street. A scrum of little boys left off punching one another in the schoolyard and rushed to squeeze their faces through the railings. Thorne laughed and waved at them, and they set up a ragged cheer. Mrs Trigg emerged from the Maidens' dark interior and stood as if paralysed on her doorstep, mouth hanging open. Now it was Rufus's turn to wave. He did it as solemnly as possible, a bare lift of one hand, but even that was enough to increase her horrified gape, and he drew a breath of relief when Thorne had carried both of them out of her sight.

Out of the village and onto the flank of the hill that rose to the west. The road narrowed to a single track between huge banks of flowering hawthorn, white and festive pink. The scent of the blossoms—strange always, sweetness underlain by primitive musk—wrapped itself around the tang of petrol and summer chalk-country dust, making Rufus's head spin. The front of the bike rose up to meet the first part of the climb, engine growling. She was long enough to take a pillion but hadn't been designed to carry the second rider securely. The seat of his trousers began to lose traction on the smooth leather. "All right back there?" Thorne yelled cheerfully. "Do put your arms around me, old fellow, or you're going to fall off."

He made it sound so natural. And it *was*, between one normal man and another. Simple and natural, like sharing a shower room or a rugby tackle, or any of the other friendly man-to-man activities that had made Rufus wish himself blind over the years, or conveniently numb from the waist down. Fiercely he imagined his way into the skin of a normal, natural man. He took hold of Thorne's waist, lightly at first, then grabbing hard to save himself as the bike surged forward.

All the way around. He clenched a grip on his own wrist. There was nothing erotic about Thorne's back, decently clad in clerical black as it was. The trouble was that it was warm and strong. It made Rufus want to lean his brow on it and close his eyes. He resisted the melting impulse. The roadside hawthorns were thinning out, admitting glimpses of the river in the distance, and then, as the road swung round to follow the crest connecting two hills, the village they'd left behind them, nothing more than a crossroads with a scatter of red tile rooftops interspersed by slate.

They reached the ridge, and warm wind blew up from the valley, striking the Norton like a big flat hand. Thorne corrected her, his laughter vibrating back through Rufus's ribs. "There! What do you think of the view?"

"Incredible." Rufus had to catch his breath against the bouncing gale. On the far side of the ridge, the chalk hills stretched out into hazy forever, only a glitter of streams and distant church spires giving a sense of scale. "Can you stop for a moment? I'd like to see."

"Just a little further. Hang on."

Thorne revved the bike hard. Rufus had made a good fix to her cable: she flew up the last hundred yards of the slope, dipping alarmingly to the left as Thorne negotiated the curve. Rufus gasped, but momentum and his white-knuckled grasp held him in position, and then they were coasting to a halt in a broad patch of turf by the side of the road.

Rufus dismounted as soon as the bike had stopped. He tried not to let the movement look like a recoil, but could barely contain himself. His pulse was racing, his armpits damp. He couldn't get away fast enough from a contact he so painfully wanted to prolong, terrified that Thorne would notice his reactions. He strode to the edge of the escarpment, pushed his hands into his pockets and stood still.

The wind dried the sweat on his brow. The world opened out before him like the palm of God's hand. Breeze-borne scents of gorse and turf helixed up at him from infinite space. He could see for miles, clear to the turquoise shimmer of the Channel to the south. Thorne killed the Norton's engine. In the reverberant hush that followed, Rufus could follow his footsteps on the white chalk gravel as he came to stand by his side.

"I've often wondered if this was what the old man meant, when he talked about broad sunlit uplands."

"Churchill?" Rufus was relieved that his voice was steady. "I think he meant a hypothetical place, an ideal of freedom and peace. But this would do very well."

They stood side by side, watching the circles of a kestrel in the bright air below. Thorne was as frank and fearless as Rufus was chained. How quickly that friendly touch would change—shoulder to shoulder, a guiding pat to Rufus's wrist to direct his attention— if he knew the truth! Rufus had gone through it over and over again. *Not this time*, he vowed. He watched the hawk, a russet-backed arrow against the green. The hillsides stretched out beneath a sky made indigo in contrast with the chalk, green flanks patterned like butterfly wings by the passage of clouds. *Broad sunlit uplands... A land worth fighting for.* His throat tightened on a hard knot of pain. *This time I want a friend. No matter how kind and handsome he is, I won't betray him or myself.*

"Denby, are you all right?"

"Yes, of course. Why?"

"I don't quite know. You're like a coiled spring somehow, even when you're only standing looking at the view. If there's anything you'd like to talk to me about, you know, I am the local vicar, despite the motorbike. I don't need to say I'd treat anything you told me as confidential."

Don't crack me open. Not when I've just made my vow. "Thank you," he replied, sounding cold and standoffish to himself, unable to help it. "I'm not a religious person, I'm afraid."

"Oh, nor am I."

Rufus couldn't have heard that right. He blinked up at Thorne, who was still watching the kestrel, his face unreadable. The wind must have mangled his words. "I appreciate your kindness, really. And I'm certain my behaviour yesterday must have left you wondering if I'm in need of help, but I'm not. I'm prone to certain... attacks, that's all. I have medication for them, and yesterday I missed a dose. I'm quite well now."

"Good." Thorne nodded. "That's good, because in a moment I'm going to put you back on the bike and drag you all the way down into the valley again. Can you see the church?"

Rufus shaded his eyes. Beyond the rooftops of Droyton and the long verdant stripe of Pilgrim Lane, the river curved round with the grace of a sheltering arm. Right in the centre of the meadow bounded by the water to the west, he could just make out the old stone tiles of the roof beneath which he'd passed such a strange night. Unexpected laughter rose up and tried to escape him. "Drusilla isn't a cat."

"I... beg your pardon?"

"I'm sorry. Oh, dear. My memory works strangely these days, and it sometimes takes me a while to string things together. I can see the church down there, and it made me think about... Well. Let me show you." He'd transferred Thorne's letter to his cousin from his satchel to the pocket of his trousers, reluctant to be parted from it, as if it served as a passport or papers of entry in this new world. "Deputy Director Taylor gave me your letter, so I'd have your address. You mention a Drusilla here in the last paragraph, and I thought she must be an animal of some kind, for the gamekeeper to be bringing her home in a hessian sack."

"Ah. Yes, I see how the confusion could arise."

"She's a person, isn't she? I didn't mean to overhear your conversation with the doctor, but... Drusilla Hazelgrove. She'd broken the latch on her window and let herself out."

Thorne sighed. "Yes. Stark naked, and as usual she headed for the river. I saw her belting off down Pilgrim Lane just after I got home from Ashfield, and I ran after her. When you said you'd spent the night in the church, I was afraid you might have seen something, and... it looks as if you did."

"The dog woke me up. I went outside, and there you both were."

"God, I was still in my full-black and dog-collar, wasn't I? Chasing a naked woman through the churchyard.... Heaven only knows what you must have thought."

"I thought I was dreaming, to tell you the truth. Why didn't you tell Dr Winborn?"

"He thinks the poor woman belongs in an asylum. And he's probably right, but I can't bring myself to hasten the process. I caught her eventually, and I managed to get her back home without anyone else seeing her, so... Well, I didn't take into account her muddy feet and the broken window latch."

Rufus drew a breath to ask more. Another echo had come to him from his half-awake stasis on the couch. *The money old Gorringe left is running out...* Then he remembered Thorne's gentle deflection earlier, concerning a story that wasn't his to tell. Rufus had no doubt that, if he'd been able to confess his own secrets, Thorne would have kept them as sacredly as any Roman priest. "I'm pleased you got her back," he said quietly. "Yes, I can see the church. It's on a mound in the middle of the flood plain."

Thorne gave him a pleased sideways glance. "Thought you might notice that. Curious, isn't it?"

"Very. Has the river ever burst its banks since you've been here?"

"No, and not in the memory of the oldest people in the village. I've made a point of asking, because..."

"Because it's significant. Very. The mound must be an island when the flood plain's full, like a small-scale Glastonbury Tor in the water meadows."

"Exactly. I say, if you can do long-distance archaeology like that, I can't wait to see what you'll make of it all close-up. Did you see the murals I mentioned in my letter?"

"Yes. My initial thought was that they were some kind of medieval remnant, but... parts of the church are much older than that, aren't they?"

"I think so. I don't have any proof, though, so when the diocese ordered the restoration, I wanted to get someone here to take a look at the place before they turn it into a neo-Gothic monstrosity. I thought Caroline would maybe send me down an apprentice, if you have those in museums. Not Rufus Denby."

Rufus looked down at his boots. They were beginning to acquire a pall of chalk. Thorne's were deeply marked with it. On Sabros the dust had been ochre, and just as penetrating.

"Someone did go crazy on the Mediterranean dig and attack one of their colleagues. It was me."

"Winborn wouldn't have spoken like that if he'd known you could hear."

"He didn't say anything bad. It's the truth, and it explains why you got me instead of the apprentice."

"And... *was* it sunstroke?" Thorne shifted a little. Rufus thought he was edging away, then realised he was only getting enough distance to give him a wry, amused look. "Because it's pretty warm up here, isn't it? Maybe we should get you under cover."

Chapter Seven

The inside of the church was cool. By the time Thorne had driven them back from the ridge and through the long green tunnel of trees that led to the river and the mound from the opposite direction, Rufus had almost become used to his proximity. He'd asked nothing further about Sabros or the story of Rufus's arrival, as if it didn't matter to him that his visiting archaeologist was prone to outbreaks of madness.

Maybe it didn't. Rufus stood in the aisle, deliberately taking up the same spot where he'd first noticed the murals. That was important in many archaeological investigations, a trick overlooked by specialists anxious to open up the ground—to get a view of the site as its builders might have seen it, to occupy the space from which its most important features would be seen. Time was a factor, too. Sunrise, sunset, solstice and equinox, midsummer noon when light would fall to illuminate the key to some long-buried mystery...

For himself, it helped create a barricade, safe walls in his mind. Twenty four hours ago he'd stood here, unaware that any such man as Archibald Thorne existed, beyond the bare detail of his name. His kindness and his humour and his warm strong spine: those things had been unknown, wrapped up among the secrets of the universe. Rufus didn't think it would take him much more than a couple of days to assess the church and write a report for Thorne to present to his superiors in the diocese. He'd like to get a photographer up from Brighton or Lewes to record the murals, to back up the sketches he planned to produce on his own. Three days, then, or possibly four. Four sets of twenty four hours, sealed compartments which need have no ongoing connection with the rest of his life. Thorne, with his tumbledown, beautiful home, his motorbike, his powerful grip—he would recede, reabsorbed into the continuum, and just as he would cease to have impact on Rufus's world, Rufus would be forgotten in this one as soon as he was gone.

Relieved, lonely, he looked around. Maybe the obliteration had already begun. He couldn't see Thorne anywhere, although they'd entered the church together, leaving the bike on the track outside. He was alone with the red-painted figure and her upward gesture, eternally seeking her counterpart in the choir loft above.

Something hit the floor in the north aisle and exploded into a cloud of white dust. Another followed immediately in its wake. Chunks of dislodged plaster... Rufus dodged around the back of a pew and broke into a run, just in time to hear Thorne yell his name. A stepladder was swaying perilously beside the timber scaffold propping the roof. Rufus grabbed the ladder long enough to steady it. Thorne was perched at the top, struggling to wedge a beam back into place. "Help," he gasped, then lost breath for more as the timber jolted in his grasp, sending another hailstorm of plaster pattering to the floor.

Rufus scrambled up the ladder's other side. He grabbed the beam and joined in Thorne's efforts to hoist it back onto the rafter. "Bloody hell. What happened?"

"Saw it was sagging. Thought I could—"

The beam snapped. The ladder buckled and crashed down sideways. Rufus made a cat-leap for safety: saw open sky through a new hole in the roof, the old stone tiles—deadly missiles in an avalanche like this—beginning their slide. The stone arch in the vaulting overhead cracked too, one block of masonry then the next jolting out of their places. He jumped over the fallen ladder, grabbed Thorne from his startled heap on the floor and half-hoisted, half-tackled him out of the way.

They hit the wall in a tangle. Thorne turned Rufus round and dropped to his knees with him, shielding him from the explosion of thunder and dust.

When it was over—new light touching the ancient space, the first of the swallows diving through to investigate—they helped each other stand. Thorne's expression of dismay was comical, and Rufus bit his lip. The poor vicar had just torn a hole in the north aisle of his church. To hide his face and help repress the gale of laughter gusting about inside him, Rufus began to dust him down. "Are you all right?"

"Yes," Thorne replied distractedly. He shrugged out of his jacket, wadded it up and began to use it on Rufus in his turn, brushing fragments of plaster out of his hair. Suddenly he looked up. "My God, the report in *The Times* was right. You *are* insane."

"I... I'm sorry?"

"Well, let's face it. Sane people jump *away* from piles of falling rubble, not right into the middle of them."

Laughter left Rufus in a bark. He sounded like Pippin at her worst, and he seized Thorne's jacket to stifle the outburst. Thorne broke out too, rich and deep. He held Rufus awkwardly by the shoulders, and they propped one another, making the church's broken roof resound. A bout of coughing reduced Thorne to breathless silence, and he straightened up, wiping his eyes. "It's all very well, Denby. But what am I going to do now?"

"It's your stone tiles. They're original, and very fine, but they're weighing down the structure of the church. It's the first thing I meant to tell you in my report."

"Better late than never, I suppose." Thorne let him go, slung the jacket over the back of the nearest pew and rolled up his shirt sleeves. "Goodness me, I'm going to have to try and clear some of this up. How am I meant to hold my Sunday services in here?"

"I'd advise you not to, or at least to cordon off this whole aisle before you do."

"Will the rest come down, do you think?"

"In time, unless the restoration work can give you a roof of slate or terracotta instead of your Horsham stone."

"Ah, they *are* Horsham. I thought so. They really have to go?"

He was crestfallen beneath his layer of dust. "To preserve as much as we can of the fabric of the building, yes," Rufus said. "But you don't have to lose them. The floor tiles in the main aisle are Victorian at the earliest. I could recommend that the whole central section be re-laid using the Horshams."

"Ah, could you? That would look splendid."

"Yes, I think it would. You'll have plenty, and you could sell the rest of them off to help fund the restoration, if you can bear to part with them." Rufus guided him a step or two further out of the danger zone. Fragments of plaster were still dislodging themselves and dropping into the rubble, their tapping sounds magnified by echoes—*bang, bang, bang,* more than enough on any other day to bring down whatever hellish storm of memory his brain was holding back. Today they didn't matter. He had too much to think about, and Thorne's presence was like warm wings. "You've put in a lot of work here, haven't you? On your own, I mean."

"Doing more damn harm than good, from the look of things. Yes, I tried to make a start—shoring up that south wall, and taking the plaster off the murals once I'd noticed them. Do you think I've damaged those too?"

"I don't think so. They're not medieval, and whatever pigment they're made of seems deeply imprinted into the stone, not an overlay." Rufus paused. It was touching and strange that this vicar—who'd come here so recently, and only in the capacity, as he'd put it himself, of a paid farmhand—should worry so much about a church in his temporary care. "I want to have a better look at them. Let's tidy up a bit here first, though—see if we can wedge another beam into place to support the rest of the south-aisle roof."

"You don't have to do that."

"I know. Famous archaeologist and all that. If you'd any idea how useless I've felt lately... Come on. Let's pick up some rocks."

They worked for the best part of an hour, clearing enough space to move, piling the fallen masonry carefully against the wall. Hard labour on a May afternoon: they spoke little, sweat dampening dusty brows, making the blocks slip in blistering palms. Thorne dispensed with his waistcoat, and Rufus strove not to notice the shift of muscles over his ribcage as he bent and straightened. The ladder had almost been reduced to matchwood, so they rigged a low scaffold out of a couple of pews and the remaining unbroken timbers. This time Rufus clambered up to try and fix the beam. Thorne passed it up to him with a powerful heft, and all he had to do was seize the end and guide it across the exposed top of the wall.

The south side of the church was part of the medieval construction, a flint outer layer with an infill of rubble behind it. Rufus glanced at the infill to make sure he'd laid the timber on a section firm enough to hold it. Automatically he discarded the shapes of the flints and small broken stones in the gap. He was trained to sort random patterns from the work of human hands. There was seldom anything there to be seen.

Almost never. On one occasion in ten thousand...

He reached into the rubble. Nothing but two curves, probably happenstance, a couple of rounded flints. No. Flint held in its blue-brown core the warmth of a silicate stone. This little object was cold. Heavy, too, when he tried to ease it out of its bed in the wall. "Thorne," he called, reaching back blindly. "Pass me up something I can use as a wedge. A broken end from the beam, anything."

"Are you all right?"

"Fine. I just need... Yes, that'll do." He took the piece of wood Thorne handed up to him, jammed it as firmly as he could behind the object without touching it. If it was embedded, he couldn't risk moving it, but if it had dropped into the rubble from above when the rafter fell... "I think we've found something. Look."

He extracted the solid little shape with fingertip care and cradled it in his palm. He couldn't take his eyes off it: misjudged his jump down onto the pew and was grateful for Thorne's steadying catch. "Bronze," he managed, stepping down to ground level. "A figurine—late Neolithic in style, to judge from her exaggerated feminine attributes. But that's impossible—all the representational ritual objects from that time were made of stone."

"And what is she doing in my church?" Thorne leaned over Rufus's hand to examine her. "Goodness. Those are extraordinary... attributes, aren't they?"

Rufus nodded, his reserve concerning flesh-and-blood female anatomy burning off in the excitement of discovery. "Huge, heavy breasts, like the Venus of Willendorf. But this lower portion is more like the Venus of Laussel, this big pubic triangle... Beautiful. Look at it!"

"Really, Doctor. I'm not sure that I ought."

"Don't be absurd, man. There's a twenty-year-old Lithuanian girl called Gimbutas developing a theory about the symbolism of that—the womb, the ancient sign for water..." Belatedly Rufus realised Thorne was teasing him, and shook his head, smiling. "I don't know what she's doing in your church. She's bronze, which either means she's some amazing link between the Stone and Bronze Ages, indicating a hitherto unsuspected continuity of belief, or—more likely—she's a medieval fake, placed here for heaven only knows what reason in the fourteenth century ready to fall out onto our heads today."

"May I see her?"

Rufus subsided onto the edge of a pew. Thorne sat beside him, and took the statue into a careful grasp. "What an extraordinary thing. She is a beauty, isn't she?" He ran a fingertip along the line between her shoulder and hip. "She looks as if she's asleep."

"Yes. More like the figurine they found at Hal-Saflieni in Malta than the Venuses."

"According to Drusilla, they shouldn't be called Venuses at all."

"It's a good point. Whatever they represent, it's something far older than any Roman concept of an alluring goddess of love. Misleading nomenclature." Rufus had presented a paper on the subject before hostilities had broken out. It took a moment for Thorne's phrasing to catch up with him. Drusilla Hazelgrove... Perhaps she wasn't crazy all the time. Maybe, like Rufus, she had her spells of clarity, and the handsome vicar, with his friendly disregard of social and personal barricades, had befriended her too. Maybe he did it with everyone. "Whatever she is, she's an unexpected find. Possibly important. I should take her back to London, or write and tell Taylor you need more than an apprentice down here."

"Well, you could do that." Thorne handed the figurine back. She seemed to curl herself comfortably into Rufus's palm. Her face was finely worked and peaceful. "Does it have to be straight away?"

"Probably, yes. Timely reporting and recording is part of good curation."

"Oh, I see."

"The thing is, I've never really *found* anything before."

"What? Dr Denby, golden boy of the Naxos and Peloponnese expeditions?"

"Ah, you've been catching up with your copies of the *Archaeology Review*."

"Well, Winborn's right. I do buy them out of curiosity then let them gather dust. You've made some of the most important discoveries of the last ten or so years."

"I've led teams to discoveries, yes. It'll sound odd, but I've never actually taken anything significant out of the ground myself. Not... laid my own hand on something."

Thorne leaned forward and rested his elbows on his knees. It was his characteristic pose when he wanted to think, or to catch the tenor of someone else's thoughts with a sidelong glance. "I suggest you keep her. Just for a while, until you've had time to think about what she might mean." He picked up his jacket and produced a large white handkerchief from the pocket. "Here, you can wrap her in this."

"It's highly unethical." Then again, so had been throttling a senior professor. The Royal Museum was probably ready to melt its golden boy down for scrap. He folded the little sculpture up— goddess as she was of fertility, motherhood, a deep and dreaming communion older than time—in the handkerchief, and carefully tucked her inside his borrowed waistcoat. "All right. If anyone ever asks, you never saw Rufus Denby steal an artefact from an unexcavated site. Let's go and take a look at your murals."

"Mm. At least those are too big for you to stick into your pocket and take home."

Rufus refused to laugh at him. He preceded him back into the nave. It felt important to resist Thorne's playfulness, the occasional push of gentle teasing, as if neither he nor Rufus were the grimly serious souls their backgrounds seemed to dictate. They were dangerous, those bright sorties, capable of undermining Rufus's frail walls. "Do you know anything about your rood screen?"

"Not much, except that it is medieval, and the archdeacon wants it removed. He's told the bishop he doesn't think it's appropriate for a congregation to sit and look at while they're contemplating the ultimate fate of their souls. That's partly why I was over at Ashfield when you arrived—to put in a good word for it."

"Do you think it's appropriate?"

"What, all those leaves and flowers? I can think of worse ultimate fates, can't you?"

"Hundreds. I've often wondered if that's what happens to us. That we go back to the earth, I mean, and if we have any kind of immortality, it's that kind of return. With the summer, just lifting up out of the soil." Rufus stopped in the patch of sunlight in front of the altar. His own earthly fate kept leading him to this place. A stray vision touched him—the life of a normal man, who one day might hope—assume the right, almost—to stand here with a chosen companion. "I probably shouldn't share such thoughts with a vicar."

"Probably I shouldn't love the screen." Thorne shook himself, as if to dismiss the question of the afterlife. "Have you seen the choir-loft mural?"

"Yes. I slept up there. The first thing I noticed was the male figure—how he's reaching down towards the female."

"But not touching."

"No. More as if each one wants to show or understand something about the other's world."

"Why didn't the artist just paint them on the same wall? On the level, I mean, rather than cramping one of them up in the rood loft?"

"I don't know. The first thing that comes to mind is a matter of perspective. Not an artist's perspective but the way we have to get into a certain place to see something." Rufus tipped his head back a little, closing his eyes in the light. "I'm not making a lot of sense. I do have other thoughts about the meaning, but they're much too old to fit a Christian site. If you don't mind my saying so, Reverend, you seem to have some very unchristian problems here. Pre-Christian ones, anyway."

"Indeed. And I don't understand, because surely even the very oldest parts of the building can't pre-date Anglo-Saxon times, can they?"

"It seems very unlikely."

"And I'm afraid that people like the archdeacon will come in here mob-handed with a restoration team and strip out everything pre-Christian and unseemly and paint over the rest. That's why I've been trying to find out as much as I can about it on my own."

Rufus opened his eyes. He took a step away from Thorne and the sunlight so that he could think clearly. "Here's what I propose we do. I'll carry out an assessment to try and identify and date the various building phases. If I find something old enough to be rare, that works in our favour. Meanwhile, you carry on uncovering your murals. I'll arrange for them to be professionally photographed, and I'll pull whatever strings I still have left to get our findings published in the next *Review*. I'd defy your archdeacon to come rushing in here with his whitewash after that."

"Good heavens." Thorne turned to him, eyes kindling with interest. "I believe that I'd defy him too, Denby."

"Rufus, please. Everyone who's called me Denby for the past five years has been shouting at me."

"In that case, call me Archie. And I accept your proposal, on condition that tonight you really do join us for dinner."

"I'd be pleased to. Meanwhile, I need some tools. Just some basic things. Is there a hardware shop in the village?"

"No, but the blacksmith sells most things from his yard at the top of Pilgrim Lane. I can run you up there if you like."

"It's all right. I'll pass it on my way back to the Maidens'."

They left the church together, swallows carving the air inches above their heads, distinctive alarm cries bouncing off the walls of the porch. Rufus followed the flight path of one swooping pair across the flood plain and over the trees to the north. They spiralled upward, melting into the distance. "That's the hill where we stopped, isn't it? Where you showed me the view of the church."

"That's right. George Mount, it's called."

"George as in George and the dragon, or..."

"Sadly not. The Prince Regent. He honoured the village with his presence back in the 1820s sometime. Probably brought one of his mistresses from Brighton for a cup of tea, and a loyal public decided to name our tallest hill after him."

"Does it have an older name? I think I can see..." Rufus shielded his eyes. "Yes. Are those Iron Age hillfort markings at the top?"

Thorne came to stand close by his shoulder. "I don't know. I've never noticed them before."

"They're very faint. Just dints in the outline of the crest on either side. Still, I'm not sure how I missed them while we were up there."

"Well, that's one curious thing I *have* noticed over the years. You can't see the top of the mount while you're climbing it, and the whole crest only really appears between the hills on either side of it when you're right here on the church steps."

"Just as the church is only visible from a particular spot up there."

"Good heavens. You'll think I'm an idiot, but that never occurred to me—the reverse, I mean. Like our two painted figures inside, each showing the other a specialised point of view."

Rufus didn't think the vicar was an idiot at all. How long would it have taken him to make that connection himself? He'd used to be good at it, at reading not only the proposed site of a dig but the whole of the landscape surrounding it. Nothing existed in isolation. He'd found one temple in Greece because a double-crested mountain had cast a horn-shaped shadow over the shattered remains at dawn.

He couldn't answer. The easy pleasure of Thorne's company, the sense of living in the moment that had sustained him since the roof-fall, all drained away like water spilled on Sabros sand. The little goddess weighed heavily in his pocket. He knew he shouldn't take her off the site, but nor could he abandon her, his only tangible evidence of what he could do. What he once had been. He couldn't even address his new friend by his given name. "Thorne," he said dryly, the word like prickling dust in his mouth, "I need to go back to the inn."

"Are you all right?"

"Yes. It's these damn pills—they make me want to sleep at inconvenient times."

"I understand. Has Mrs Trigg given you a decent room?"

"Her best, she tells me—looking onto the courtyard."

To his surprise, Thorne shuddered. "I'm sure she thinks it's grand. Something about that yard always strikes me as rather grim, though. Come on, old fellow—hop on the bike and I'll give you a ride back. You can pick up your dog on the way."

Chapter Eight

At half past seven that night, Rufus presented himself at the rectory door. He'd made himself as tidy as his resources would permit. His dog, who now followed him freely without a lead, sat down at his feet to wait for a response to the bell.

The door swung open, apparently of its own accord. Rufus hesitated, but Pippin nosed her way inside, and a moment later he found her face-to-face with the Reverend's strange small house-guest, tail waving slowly from side to side. His neighbour in London had had children, he suddenly recalled. The fat, spoiled mongrel had been fond of them. He slammed the lid down on the memory fast enough to greet Thorne's appearance in the hallway with an answering smile. "Good evening. I hope I'm not late."

"Not at all. When Mrs Nettles makes one of her scurrilous deals with the butcher, the second night is always broth—ready when we are. Come in, come in."

Elspeth looked him over critically as he wiped his boots. "He isn't dead," she observed to Thorne flatly. "When he didn't come last night, I thought he might be dead. He may still be insane."

Thorne scooped her up and set her on his hip. "Sorry," he said to Rufus, pulling a face. "She's a bit obsessed with madness and death at the moment. Be quiet, changeling. Come through into the library—everyone's here."

The library was a different space at night. The windows were still open to admit the evening air, but otherwise Rufus struggled to recognise the room where he'd floated to surface the day before. It seemed to be full of people. Dr Winborn and his niece were in occupation of the sofa, Mrs Nettles in an armchair by the fire. She had set aside her apron and was smartly turned out in a black velvet dress with lace collar, beaming benignly, a sherry glass in her hand. Opposite her, in the other best seat in the house, the tiniest, most fragile old lady Rufus had ever seen was sitting bolt upright. Thorne set Elspeth down and the child scampered over to her, used her footstool as a step and joined her in stiff-backed perusal of the room. Pippin trotted after her, and completed the peculiar triad by settling alertly beside the arm of the chair.

In the window seat, two well-scrubbed lads in their late teens were perching nervously under the baleful gaze of an old man in gaiters and tweeds. "Dr Denby," Mrs Nettles cried, her rich Sussex accent still in place, everything else about her transformed from housekeeper to easy-mannered hostess. "We're so glad you could come."

Rufus repressed a nervous impulse to bolt straight back out through the door. Thorne was at his shoulder, a reassuring warmth. "Good evening. Thank you for inviting me."

"You know some of us, don't you? Dr Winborn and Alice on the sofa there, and Reverend Thorne and Elspeth, of course. This is Lady Birch from Birch Hall, and over there is Farmer Challen with Toby and Giles, his two best boys from the farm."

Challen glowered at the compliment, which he clearly felt to be undeserved. Toby and Giles fared no better, bobbing heads and grabbing at fringes too short to be tugged. Rufus nodded as politely as he could in response, hampered by sudden bewilderment: Toby was a strapping, everyday farmhand, but Giles—despite the haircut, britches and lounging legs-apart slouch—was clearly and obviously a girl.

If a joke was being played, everyone was carrying it off with straight-faced aplomb. Before Rufus could formulate a question, Alice gave her uncle a none-too-gentle push to open up a space on the sofa between them. "Come and sit here, Dr Denby. You got past us both this morning, but I'm afraid there's no escape for you now."

Winborn looked as though he'd have let Rufus escape without question, but made the best of it, getting to his feet and holding out a hand. "Denby. It's a pleasure. Of course we went through all Archie's magazines once we found out who you were. We hope you won't be afraid to talk shop, if you don't mind such uninformed customers."

"I'll be happy to, but—"

"Oh, Uncle Paul, do give the man a chance. Archie, doesn't Dr Denby get a sherry?"

"He's beginning to look as if he needs one." Thorne cast a sympathetic glance at Rufus, but could hardly leap in and rescue him from a radiantly pretty girl whose one objective seemed to be to make him welcome. "We don't keep much of a cellar, Rufus. Will Rector Gorringe's pre-war Amontillado be all right for you?"

"Yes, thanks. Lovely." Rufus subsided onto the sofa between Alice and Winborn. Something in his situation seemed to disturb the dog: she set up her hackles and began to whine. "Are you sure you don't want me to take her down to the kitchen, Thorne? She's better, but..."

"She's fine," Mrs Nettles interrupted comfortably. "I'll answer for it there's no more fleas on that dog than any natural creature ought to have. She won't be any trouble, either. Will you, miss?"

Pippin settled, as if having someone believe in her was enough. Thorne poured Rufus a glass from the decanter on the table and brought it over, then scanned the room to make sure that everyone else was provided for. "Lady Birch, you could manage another, couldn't you?"

"If I must, Reverend Thorne. If I must."

"Just a small one. Well, here we are, all assembled. Maria, is it time, do you think?"

"Yes, Reverend, if you don't mind."

"Excellent. Excuse me for a short while, everyone."

Rufus watched him leave, his tall frame vigorous with purpose. Mrs Nettles turned in her chair, smiling. "It's one of his butcher nights," she said by way of explanation, "though I wish he'd think of something else to call them. If I get something particularly good from Reg Varley, who I won't deny owes me a favour or two, the Reverend invites everybody around to eat it. And he says it's a shame for us all to be sharing one shoulder of mutton and nothing else, so he brings us all together and tells us to forget about whatever we do in the outside world. To forget about our so-called *places*. That's what he says, Dr Denby—*I* would never presume."

"I see. And has he gone to—"

"Yes, to the kitchen, to finish off the broth with his own hands. He won't let me stir to help, not once I've got my good frock on. He's a man in a thousand, you know, Miss Winborn."

Rufus was beginning to get that impression. He wasn't sure why Mrs Nettles' last observation had made Alice shrink back in her seat. "Did he start doing this during the war? To help out with the rationing?"

"Oh, he wasn't here during the war, Dr Denby. He—"

"So, Denby, tell us about the Sabros excavation. Is it true that you were hoping to find the Minotaur's labyrinth?"

Rufus turned to Winborn, startled. "Er—no. I'm not sure how that rumour began. There are some legends connecting Crete and Sabros, but all we found was a system of tombs, robbed and desecrated. Until I left, anyway—my colleague Professor Hargreaves has made some far more significant discoveries since." He was surprised at the steadiness of his own voice. There was something about Paul Winborn that demanded firm, prompt replies. His grey eyes weren't cold, but a challenge stood in them, as if he had a duty to bar the way. Rufus couldn't blame him. "I know you've heard about my illness out there. I want to assure you that I'm quite well again now."

"Uncle *Paul.*"

Rufus glanced at Alice. She was sitting on the edge of the sofa, clasping her brow in both hands. "It's all right, Miss Winborn."

"It isn't all right. Dr Denby's led dozens of excavations, Paul. Why pick that one?"

Winborn had the grace to look uncomfortable. "I didn't mean anything by it. And I didn't ask Denby to—"

"What else is he going to say, when you ask him about Sabros and he knows you know what happened there?"

She was very striking when she was cross. Her fair English colouring gained depth and fire. "Please don't concern yourself," Rufus said gently. He glanced up to encompass the room. Mrs Nettles was staring in horror, Challen and the farmhands gawping. He'd better get this over with now, in front of everyone. "Dr Winborn wants to be certain that I'm not a danger to his family and his friends. He has every right. I'm a stranger here."

"And we owe better hospitality than that to strangers." Winborn sat forward. "I should take our vicar's example. Forgive me, Denby."

"There's nothing to forgive." He and Winborn had already shaken hands. Each being who he was, there was no other contact they could make now to signal renewed friendliness, and an awkward silence descended, broken only when the library door swung wide. "Come along, everyone," Thorne said, swirling a tea towel like a matador's cape in front of him. He'd rolled up his shirtsleeves and was flushed with his exertions in the kitchen. "Dinner, such as it is, is prepared."

He drew Rufus to one side in the hallway. "How are you feeling now? Did you get some sleep?"

"Thank you, yes. I didn't think I would. But I put our sleeping goddess on the table by my bed, and she seemed to give me the right idea." He shook his head. "I'm aware that I'd be sounding like a lunatic, if..."

"If your reputation as one hadn't already preceded you."

"Something like that, yes. It's quite liberating."

"Well, I'm glad she helped. What do you think of my social experiment?"

"Your... Oh, your butcher nights?"

"Yes. They do need a more elegant name. But I thought that if I kept at it—bringing in the doctor, the housekeeper, Lady Birch, the farm boys, and mixing them all together—I might be able to pull down some of the ridiculous class barricades we have in this village. I thought all that kind of thing was going to be swept away after the war. Do you think it's working?"

"Mrs Nettles seems in her element. I'm not so sure about the farm boys." Rufus stole a look at Thorne, but his face was serious and open. "As experiments go, it seems a good one. But... you know, you don't need an excuse for being generous and sharing what you have with your neighbours."

Thorne blushed, as if he'd been caught in an act of wrongdoing. "Never mind. Will you do me a favour and take

Alice down to dinner? Winborn's dragged her here on a longer visit than usual, and she's out of her mind with boredom."

"Not sure I'll be able to help her with that."

"A handsome archaeologist from London? You'll be a gift from heaven to her."

"Well, I'll do my best, but…"

"Don't worry about making conversation. She'll do it gladly, with just the smallest input from you. And she's the sweetest, most tactful creature you could imagine—you'll be all right."

That was nice. Rufus had no objection to talking to Alice Winborn. His problem was the heat building underneath his collar because Thorne had called him handsome. Pippin had trotted out into the hallway, and he bent down over her to hide the response. "Doesn't Alice like visiting her uncle?"

"It isn't that. She was going to be married when the war broke out, though, and… Well. The young man didn't return. So her life is in pieces, like so many other lives, and Winborn thinks that coming here will help her put it back together."

"Poor Alice. Of course I'll talk to her, not that I imagine I'll be the least assistance."

"Oh, you'd be surprised. You strike me as a rather sweet and tactful creature yourself."

This time Rufus had to hide his face entirely. He crouched beside Pippin and pretended to examine one of her bald spots. "Mrs Nettles is very kind, but this beast isn't presentable yet. Are you sure you don't mind her in the dining room?"

"Not at all. Elspeth has taken to her, and she'll give the child a chance to sneak away her supper under the table without upsetting Maria."

"Doesn't she like to eat?" Now seemed a good time to ask about the changeling's other morbid preoccupations, but a stir in the library heralded the arrival of Lady Birch, dangling precariously off Farmer Challen's arm. Alice followed after her. Rufus wasn't aware of offering his arm to her, but she took it as if doing so was the graceful and obvious thing. Thorne beamed gallantly at Mrs Nettles, who bobbed him a curtsey and tucked her hand into his elbow. Elspeth had Pippin for a partner, which left Winborn and the farmhands to make their way as best they could. With a last puzzled glance over his shoulder at Giles, Rufus let Alice guide him off down the hall.

The rectory dining room must once have been magnificent. Dark oak panels lined the walls, and a vast rococo chandelier dominated the space above the table. "Lovely, isn't it?" Alice said, noticing the direction of his gaze. "Rector Gorringe had it fitted out with wires so it would run by electricity. That looked awful, so Archie disconnected it and set it back to the way it was. Of course the old pulley's broken, and it can't be lowered to put candles in it anymore, but..."

The chandelier could symbolise the whole of the house that Rufus had seen so far: too elegant for a utilitarian post-war world, too costly to be restored to its own. Candles were dancing in silver candlesticks the length of the walnut table, providing the room's only light. "It's beautiful. Reverend Thorne must have his hands full keeping this place up."

"He does. He'd be the first to admit he'd rather be out tinkering with his bike, but he spends every spare moment he has at work in here or in the church. He's a good man," Alice added fervently, as if Rufus had denied it. "He doesn't always need reasons for the good things he does. He just thinks it's better to do them."

It was clear that she thought so too. She would be a perfect helpmeet to any man, and she was obviously fond of Thorne. Rufus held back a little so that she could go ahead of him and take a seat beside Thorne's at the head of the table. Winborn was stationed there too, as if waiting. When Farmer Challen approached, he politely blocked him, pulling out the chair for his niece. To Rufus's surprise, she ignored him, choosing a place of her own three seats down. Lady Birch let go of Challen's arm and ducked under Winborn's, and settled in the place of honour as if it had been her royal due. Rufus took the vacant place between the old lady and Alice. Farmer Challen had been routed to the table's other side along with Toby, and after a frowning hesitation, Winborn recovered his genial demeanour and went to sit beside his niece.

Thorne entered the room last of all, ushering Giles ahead of him. He'd recruited the young farmhand to help him, and Rufus watched in amusement as the tweed-clad little figure set the tureen down and began to ladle out the broth with neat-handed grace. Alice seemed the last person likely to fail to notice the small hands, the lack of Adam's apple in the open neck of Giles's shirt, but she and the others looked tranquilly on until everyone had been served. Thorne followed Giles around the table, pouring each guest a generous glass of straw-coloured wine from a hand-labelled bottle. A savoury scent of good meat and apples filled the room.

When at last he returned to his place between Lady Birch and Mrs Nettles, Thorne tapped his knife off his glass to draw everyone's attention, and Rufus realised with a shock that he was going to say grace. Why this should have struck him as odd, coming from the vicar at a rectory dinner, he couldn't have said, except that he struggled to reconcile the motorbike mechanic with the man of God. He looked down at his napkin, crisp white linen with the former rector's monogram stitched into it. "Bless everybody gathered here tonight," Thorne said quietly. "Let's thank the spirit of the sheep which gave us these two meals, and the spirit of the orchard in Mrs Nettles' apple wine, which I should warn our newcomer is deadly strong. Let's thank Mrs Nettles for the broth, and for God's sake let's eat it before it gets cold."

A ripple of laughter passed through the room. Thorne raised his glass in a brief toast, his gaze locking to Rufus's for one unreadable moment. Then he sat down and scooped up Elspeth, who'd been waiting by his chair. He set her on his knee and placed a small bowl and a glass of water in front of her before commencing his own meal. Pippin took up a discreet position on his other side, out of Mrs Nettles' line of sight.

"Would you like a bun, Dr Denby?"

Alice was holding out a basket to him. She was radiant in the candlelight. Surely there could be few sights more pleasant than a kind-faced woman offering bread. Men like Rufus had been known to overcome their proclivities and lead normal lives. She'd manoeuvred twice to sit beside him: the least he could do was be civil to her in return. "Thank you. Yes." After that brilliant conversational sortie, his mouth dried. He took the basket in his turn and offered it to Lady Birch, who was serenely ignoring him. "Good evening. I hope you're quite well tonight?"

"I need to die, dear. But of course, with things as they are, I can't."

Rufus wondered if he'd misheard her. She wasn't cracking open her crusty bun with the air of a sick woman. "Er... I'm sorry to hear that."

"Never mind me, dear. I'm not really here, or I shouldn't be." She plunged her spoon enthusiastically into her broth. "Talk to lovely Alice. She's stuck between you and her uncle, and Winborn's a boring old fart."

Rufus almost spat out a mouthful of wine. Winborn was on the edge of hearing range, and Alice well within it. "It's all right, Dr Denby," she said, touching him lightly on the arm. "Lady

Birch and Paul are old friends. She can't forgive him for doctoring her, that's all."

"Being doctored's a good thing, isn't it?"

"You'd think so." She lowered her voice so Rufus had to lean closer to hear her. He caught a trace of perfume—not *Evening In Paris* but something older and fresher, maybe just the scent of her garden work clinging to her. "For the last year or so she's had the delusion that she ought to be dead. And Paul keeps giving her vitamins and tonics, so they've fallen out."

"Ah. I see." Rufus didn't, but compared to the high strangeness of Giles and little Elspeth, this eccentricity seemed mild. "Has Dr Winborn lived here long?"

"Yes, all his life. He used to be the doctor at Ashfield College, where Archie studied theology. Archie wasn't well after his parents died, and my uncle took care of him, gave him a room as a lodger. They've been fast friends ever since. Archie met his wife in Uncle Paul's house, actually."

Her last words hit Rufus an unexpected side-swipe. "His wife?"

"Yes. She was called Celia, and she was lodging with Paul too while she did her nursing training. She died of TB just before the war. Archie had a parish over near Brighton back then, and when this one fell vacant because Rector Gorringe abandoned his post, Paul made interest with the Droyton parish council to bring Archie over here, where he'd be among his friends."

"Of course. He must have been devastated—Reverend Thorne, I mean."

"Oh, I'm sure he's asked you to call him Archie. For a vicar, he's really not keen on his title."

It was an odd evasion. Alice didn't look the type to dodge a straightforward question, so Rufus let it go. After that she asked about his work on the Naxos dig, and Thorne turned out to have been right: she expanded on his replies with such lively intelligence that conversation between them became effortless. One by one the others around the table tuned in to listen. Thorne was beaming in pleasure at this small social success, and if Rufus was collecting the odd glower from Winborn, he could cope with that. Maybe in another world he'd have told the doctor how little he had to worry about when it came to designs on his niece, but just for now it was pleasant to have her attention. She'd downed her first glass of wine rather fast and was bright-eyed and flushed. Rufus began to talk as he hadn't done since before Henry left him. The dragging, limping time began to fly, and Elspeth fed the bulk of her supper to Pippin beneath the table unchastised.

***

It was late by the time the gathering broke up. Farmer Challen and the farmhands had left an hour or so before, a dawn start ahead of them. Alice and Dr Winborn said their goodnights in the library, and Winborn led her away, leaning a little unsteadily on his arm. Rufus had seldom seen a woman who looked less likely to overindulge, but she'd gone through three glasses of the powerful wine at the table and brought a fourth through with her afterwards, refusing Mrs Nettles' offer of coffee.

Well, everyone had their secrets. Elspeth, who apparently had no bedtime, was whispering hers to Pippin on the hearthside rug. Old Lady Birch, settled in her armchair throne, watched the dog and the little girl benignly. Thorne had followed Winborn and Alice through to see them out, and in the firelit hush, Rufus could almost hear what the unearthly child was whispering. *Andrasta, Andrasta, Andrasta*, over and over again in a kind of litany. *Andrasta...*

Thorne let himself back into the room, breaking the spell. "There," he said, coming to join Rufus by the window, where intoxicating scents of summer night were stirring the curtains, joining with the pitchy tang of woodsmoke from the hearth. "That didn't go too badly, did it?"

"Your social experiment? From my own selfish point of view, I'd say it went very well."

"You were excellent company. It's a special art, to be able to speak about technical things without talking down to people or bewildering them. You must have done some teaching as well as digging in your time."

"Yes, I... I did." *Digging and teaching at the same time, leaping in and out of trenches to expound on myths and methods, and kindle in other breasts the excitement in my own...* "I used to enjoy that part."

"Even old Challen looked as though he might be off to excavate something on his farm. I expect you to teach me all about my church as we work on it, of course."

"I will. I'd best be going, if we're to make a full day of it tomorrow. Does Lady Birch live far from here? I'll see her home, if you like."

"That's kind of you, but she generally stays over with us on my butcher nights. You do know you'd be very welcome to do the same?"

Involuntarily Rufus glanced around the room. Everything was shabby, clean and warm. The ceiling was high, the space generous. The spines of the marvellous book collection gleamed intriguingly in the shifting shadows from the fire. He thought about his sterile box at the inn, and almost surrendered. Like Alice, he dodged the question. "Did the Reverend Gorringe leave all those books behind, or..."

"No. They're mine, I'm afraid—the one thing I seem to have collected over the years. You'll have noticed that we didn't retire into the drawing room after dinner? There is one, but it's derelict. It seemed more sensible to look after the places where we cook, eat and keep ourselves warm."

"And read?"

"Ah, yes. The library is an enormous indulgence of mine. But since the room doubles up as our drawing room and parlour, I don't feel too guilty about it. You can come here and read any time, or work if you want. Feel free to borrow, too. My overdue fines are very reasonable."

The man's sweetness passed like a blade through Rufus's heart. He turned away, not trusting himself to respond. Once he'd mastered his voice, he went to crouch beside Pippin on the hearthrug. "Come along, old girl. Time to go home."

Elspeth scrambled onto her knees. She'd been curled up so tightly by the hearth that she'd almost become invisible, in her matronly little black dress and absurd pigtails. She threw her arms around Pippin's neck in a sudden passion of distress. "Don't make her die and go away!"

Rufus laid cautious hold of Pippin's collar. She'd stayed still beneath this assault, but he wasn't sure enough of her temperament to leave her unrestrained with an upset child. "She's not going to die, Elspeth. She survived a whole war in London, trotting around on her own. She's going to live for a very long time."

"She was telling me her secret name."

"Is that what you two were whispering about?" Rufus was shy of children, but for the most part he liked them, and had looked forward to becoming an uncle to his sister's boy. "Is it something you can tell me?"

"No, or she'll lose all her powers. I may only tell a true seeker, in bounds of the circle, properly prepared."

"Good grief, Elspeth." Thorne strode over, plucked the child off the rug and held her, putting a gentle hand over her mouth. "Hush. What will Dr Denby think?"

Rufus smiled and frowned, examining the pallid little face. "I don't know what to think. Why does she talk like that?"

"She's been reading something off my shelves, I should imagine. I don't always police her the way I should. Elspeth, if I take my hand away, can you try to speak like a natural child?"

She nodded, and Thorne lowered his hand. "But Pippin," she remonstrated at once, as if the problem should have been obvious. "Pippin."

Rufus gave Thorne a questioning glance. "I think the Reverend already has a full house of people and creatures to look after. Doesn't he?"

"Probably," Thorne agreed. "This is the first time I've seen her take a fancy to any living thing, though. Isn't it, hobgoblin?"

"Maybe we should leave it up to the dog," Rufus suggested. "Pippin, come here."

She heaved herself off the hearthrug and came to stand between them, tail waving. Mrs Nettles had taken her down to the kitchen after supper and apparently fed her until she could contain no more. A house like this was made for dogs and children. "What do you think?" Rufus asked her. "Would you rather stay here, or come back and eat your dinners in Mrs Trigg's cold scullery?"

She went to sit on Thorne's feet. Elspeth gave an eerie crow of pleasure and wriggled until he put her down. "So much for canine fidelity," he observed, then looked suddenly at Rufus. "Maybe she goes where she's most needed. Can't I persuade her master to stay too?"

Rufus had run out of reasons why not. What the devil was he reading in Thorne's warm gaze? He'd learned to analyse eye-contact carefully. His dignity, safety and freedom might depend on an accurate guess. The other man's, too.

Thorne had been married. Only recently widowed, and probably still in mourning, though his cheerful, bluff exterior efficiently concealed his grief. He was a little naive, that was all, and didn't realise the charm and potency of his own stare. "No," Rufus said, and because he'd run out of reasons, didn't try to offer one. "Thank you, but you can't. I should go now. Good night, Reverend Thorne."

"*Please* call me Archie."

"Archie, then. Good night."

Chapter Nine

When Rufus let himself back into his room at the Maidens', the little goddess figurine was gone. He stood for a while in the sliver of moonlight that made its way into the courtyard. The bedside table where he'd left the statue was bare apart from the expensive travelling alarm clock he'd bought for Henry and quietly reclaimed when Henry had turned out to possess a much nicer one already, a gift from another man. The rest of the room was quite undisturbed.

Maybe he'd put the statue somewhere else and forgotten about her. The vast dark gap in his memory sometimes stretched out tentacles to consumer smaller incidents, like where he'd left his satchel or his hat. He took off his jacket, hung it neatly on the back of the door, checked its pockets and those of his waistcoat, and began a systematic search of the room.

It didn't take long. He sat down on the bed, missing Pippin's presence, the weight of her scrawny frame against his knee. He felt sick, his supper turning to acid in his gut. He didn't want to raise the alarm or go running out into the Droyton streets to find a policeman. He didn't want to turf Jebediah Trigg out of bed, pick him up by the ankles and see what fell out of his pockets. The child's ambitions ran to shillings and lemonade, not stolen bloody antiquities. The only fault here lay with Rufus himself, from the moment when he'd thrown aside a lifetime of training and ethics and stolen an artefact from a site.

A deep passivity took hold of him, weighting his limbs. He kicked off his shoes and lay down. He'd been told time and again that he was a survivor. He'd read the article in *The Times*. *Dr Denby, survivor of the Battle of France...* He'd been allowed to see the notes from his debriefing. *Captain Denby, who with a handful of others survived the assault on Fort Roche...* He had never consciously sought to outlive his comrades, or even his enemies. Whatever currents of chance had borne him this far, they were running out, leaving him to sink in deep waters. Every mistake he made carried him further from shore. Taking the goddess figurine simply because he liked her—allowing himself to linger in Thorne's house because he liked that, liked *him*... These were the actions of a light-hearted man, a stranger who had never been to war.

An indefinable time later, a throaty roar snagged at the edge of his hearing. It died almost as soon as he'd registered it, and he wondered if he'd fallen asleep and begun to dream of his motorcycling vicar. He rubbed his brow. A deep blue night had fallen, his sliver of moonlight migrating around to glimmer on the ceiling over his bed. Maybe the dream would continue, if he could close his eyes again and dive...

Footsteps rang out briefly in the yard, then merged to scraping scuffles, so distinctive a sound of a big man struggling to be quiet that Rufus uncurled from the bed and went to the window, pulse quickening with surmise. Yes, there was Thorne— *Archie*, Rufus corrected himself, something like laughter struggling under his lungs—down on the cobbles below, poised in the act of aiming a pebble at the glass.

Rufus pushed the sash up as soundlessly as he could. Archie froze. "Rufus!" he whispered hoarsely. "You're awake."

"Can I help you, Reverend?"

"Please. There's nobody else I can trust."

"What do you need me to do?"

"It's a little hard to explain from here."

Rufus drew the window back down. He pushed his feet into his boots and laced them tight, not wanting to take the time but aware that falling down Mrs Trigg's stairs would complicate matters just now. He let himself out into the corridor. Every floorboard and stair tried to creak as he made his way to the front door. His landlady wasn't one to encourage nocturnal adventures: it was barricaded on the inside with a mortice lock, two bolts and a chain. Remembering dank air blowing through the house from the scullery where he'd been sent to feed his dog, he padded through the shadows and into the kitchen. Yes, there was a back door, less ferociously guarded. Heavier than he'd expected, too— as soon as he'd pulled back the Yale and stepped outside, it swung closed as if glad to be rid of him, clicking smugly shut.

There went his chances of a discreet return. It didn't matter. Nothing did, by comparison with Archie's summons. *There's nobody else I can trust...* He set off down the lane at the side of the inn, and almost ran into Archie, emerging from the yard. "Here I am."

Archie steadied him. "That was fast!"

"I was still dressed."

"That's more than can be said for poor Drusilla Hazelgrove. She's on the run again. If I tell Winborn, he really will have her hauled off to the funny farm this time."

"Where is she now?"

"On the crags on the far side of the river. The gamekeeper came banging on my door to tell me she was out. I tried to catch up with her on the bike, but she went tearing off through the fields. She got across the river at the ford, and I could just see her in the distance, starting to climb."

"Come on, then. Did I hear your bike a few minutes ago?"

"Yes. I left it at the top of the lane so as not to wake up the whole village. This way."

He set off at a run. Rufus darted after him, across the moonlit main street with its darkened shop windows and tightly curtained house-fronts, round the corner and into the leafy hush of Pilgrim Lane. By the time they reached the Norton, propped on its kickstand under an oak, Archie was winded, breath rasping and catching in his lungs. He seemed too lean and fit a man to be breathless after such a short run. Rufus didn't get another moment to worry about it: Archie grabbed the bike, jumped astride and brought her roaring into the middle of the lane. He patted the seat behind him. "Come on!"

This time Rufus didn't hesitate to wrap his arms round him and hang on. The acceleration would have knocked him straight off the back otherwise. Thorne was a fearless and skilful rider when he had a mission to fulfil. The blacksmith's house whipped by, then the orchard and the rectory gardens. Rufus dipped his head, allowed himself to rest his brow on one satin-clad shoulder. Archie must have thrown on his shirt and waistcoat from the evening before. Beneath it he was bony and warm, his shoulder blade like the root of a wing against Rufus's cheek. He half-expected the Norton to take flight. In moonlit flashes, he saw the dried mud of the track narrow down between green verges, the stripe of turf down the centre spreading out to meet them. They passed the turn-off for the church. Trees sprang up around them as the lane began to peter out. Archie revved the bike as hard as he could over a thickening tangle of undergrowth and rocks, then jerked her to a stop before her front wheel could sink into mud. "This is as far as I can get her. We'll have to go on by foot."

"All right. Where's the ford?"

"Half a mile through the woods here. Then we'll have to double back along the far bank, and... Oh, no."

His gaze had fixed on a distant point through the trees. Reluctantly letting go of him, Rufus dismounted. He shielded his eyes against the disorienting ripple of moonlight through the oak leaves overhead and focussed on the cliffs that rose beyond the river, where a female figure had just broached the skyline. All he could make out was pale skin and a cloud of dark hair. "Is that her?"

"God, I hope so. I can't cope with more than one."

"Are those rocks safe? They look hollowed out underneath, where the river's eroding them."

"They are. We don't have time to go round by the ford."

Rufus put out a hand and helped him scramble off the bike. "What are we waiting for, then?"

They set off full pelt through the trees. Archie's long stride bore him ahead of Rufus for the first minute, but then his breathing began to hitch and catch again and they drew level. Even so, he was a formidable runner, unhesitatingly choosing the best gap between rocks and through brambles, leaping exposed roots with a steeplechaser's grace. Rufus had to give it his all to keep up with him. Where had a vicar learned such good cross-country skills? Together they broke through the willows that lined the riverbank and emerged onto the shore, water-tumbled rocks sliding out from under their feet. "Drusilla," Archie called to the woman poised on the cliffs above them. "It's just me—Reverend Thorne. You know I'm not going to hurt you."

She didn't seem concerned. She was planted solidly, feet hip-width apart, arms raised above her head in two passionate arcs. By an odd trick of perspective, from where Rufus stood she'd caught the half moon in her embrace. Her head was tipped back. Over the wash of the river a low rich chanting reached him. He heard something about the beauty of the green earth, the stars, the mystery of the waters, and then the breeze bore her voice away. "What is she doing?"

"I don't know, but she's early this month. Usually she waits for the full moon. She's like this for three nights, and then she's practically catatonic again." Archie bent over, propped his hands on his knees and coughed painfully. "We've got to get her down from there. Drusilla? Step back, for God's sake, just a little. You're standing on a hollow ledge."

"Will I scare her if I swim over?"

"I doubt she'll notice. You can't, though—not on your own. The current's too strong."

Yes. Rufus could see it, just as he'd learned to read other hazards in the landscape. Memories flashed up at him of the woods outside Fort Roche, of trying to assess the terrain in front of him for the safety of the men under his command. But he hadn't made it to the woods, had he? As he'd told the brigadier back in London, a stray chunk of shrapnel had taken him out of action before the real battle had begun. He couldn't trust any vision that arose from that amnesiac swamp. Only the river was important: the water with its current like an eel or a concealed muscle, curving around beneath the cliffs, slowing to an eddy between an outcrop of rocks. He bent down and tugged his bootlaces undone, stepping out of Archie's restraining reach. "I have to try."

"Then I'm trying with you."

"No. You told me yourself your lungs are bad. Stay here and—"

"Priest!"

The woman's voice sliced through their tussle. Both looked up. "Priest," she called again, plaintively this time. Her arms fell to her sides. "Why can't I draw her down on me? Have you forbidden it?"

"Drusilla—I've told you before, I'm just a vicar. And I don't forbid anything except standing about on crumbling bloody rocks. *Please* come down."

For a moment, Rufus thought Archie had persuaded her. The tensions dissolved from her body, leaving it middle-aged, ordinary. Then an attitude of crushing despair overcame her. She closed her eyes, took two blind steps forward and dropped.

She hit the water like a stone and vanished. Archie cried out in shock. He darted to the river's edge and, before Rufus could draw a breath to stop him, leapt in.

Rufus crushed his instinct to follow. That would just put three people at the mercy of the eel-muscle current. He kicked off his boots and ran downstream, stumbling on the rounded stones. The outcrop was further away than he'd thought. By the time he reached the point on the bank where the waters slowed, he was gasping, the soles of his feet bruised and raw. The surface heaved and fragmented and Archie was there, Drusilla clutched in one arm, swimming valiantly with the other. Rufus had perhaps ten seconds to put himself in their way. The riverbank rose up here into a little mud cliff. That would do. He grabbed a breath, charged up the bank as hard as he could to gain momentum, raised his arms and dived.

The water consumed him in one cold bite. Even on this May night, it shocked the air from his lungs, turned his guts and marrow into copper fire. His first few swimming strokes were convulsive, barely voluntary. Silvery reeds and bubbles swept across his field of vision. He found a rhythm—strong thrust of shoulders and arms, legs propelling him on. He met the current with all his strength: used it, once he was out in midstream, to swing round towards the outcrop. He scrabbled for purchase, found a grip on one jagged crest and hung on. "Archie! Over here!"

The river delivered both of them to him, so hard that he almost lost them a heartbeat later. Archie sailed first into his outstretched arm. He shouted in fear and relief and clutched him tight, denying the water its prize. Not this man, no, not this living miracle of flesh and bone. Archie broke into half-drowned laughter and hung on. "Can you... Can you grab Drusilla for a second?"

Rufus got an arm around her waist. She was clay-cold, her face an unconscious blank behind streaming hair. He swung round so that his back was to the rock, the current pinning him into place. That way he didn't have to relinquish his hold on Archie's shirt. "What are you doing?"

"Taking my belt off. Hang on a minute, then I'll want yours too." He pulled the glimmering strip of leather out of the water. "Let me get this round her wrist. Right, I've got her. Can you give me yours?"

The idea was a good one. Rufus saw it, and quickly slipped his belt free of its loops. "Here," he said, thrusting the buckle end at Archie. "Hang on to that, and pay her out as far as you can on yours. I'll let you go as far as I can too, and the current ought to carry you both..."

"Yes, over there into the shallows. But I'll stay here and be the anchor, not you."

"No. Why?"

"The truth is, I'm a little done in, old fellow. She'll need help out of the water."

"So will you."

"I know. But you'll think of something." Before Rufus could protest again, Archie had fought his way upstream. The force of the river pressed them briefly together against the rock, sending a hot shudder through Rufus in spite of his fear. He tried to keep his grip on the outcrop, but Archie dislodged him, half-lifting him out into the stream. "I've got you," he gasped. "Get her to shore, Rufus. Please!"

The current pulled Drusilla under. Rufus dived to save her: hauled her up by the belt wrapped round her wrist, got her into a tow-hold and rolled onto his back, keeping her face clear of the water. His die was cast now. Silently damning the vicar and his heroics, he clung to the anchoring line till the river's grip slackened around him, then let go the belt and sculled strongly for the bank with his free arm. The stony bed surged up to meet his efforts, painfully nudging his spine. He flipped over, got a precarious foothold and hoisted the woman by her armpits, relieved when she began to fight. "That's it. Get your feet under you. Just a few steps more."

He deposited her on the bank. She was shivering violently, and he stripped out of his shirt and wrapped it round her, not sure why he was making the gesture but anxious to shelter her in any way he could. Then he whipped round and scanned the roiling surface for Archie.

The outcrop was empty. Sick fear tightened Rufus's throat. He ran back to the water's edge, ploughed in thigh-deep and looked around again. This time he caught a darkness more vivid and solid than the moonless troughs between waves: Archie, surfacing briefly, hair gleaming like an otter's pelt. He'd almost made it to the place where the current eased but was plainly exhausted, losing his fight.

Rufus seized the overhanging alder branch above his head. He got both hands around it, bore it down with his whole weight. "Archie," he yelled, the next time the dark head broke surface. "Here!"

For a second he thought he'd missed. The branch was long, but forked at the end into twigs that would scarcely offer a handhold. Archie's arm shot out of the water: flailed among the leaves then found purchase. As soon as he was convincingly attached, Rufus let go the branch and plunged out to meet him. He took a fistful of his shirt, slung an arm around him. "Come on. Hold on to me."

Archie nodded. Spasms of coughing were tearing at him. Between them they tackled the last effort of escape, floundering up through mud and treacherously rolling stones to the bank. "God almighty," the vicar declared, dropping to his hands and knees. "Bloody Drusilla! Thought I was done for that time." He glanced up at Rufus, still struggling for breath. "Thank you."

"My pleasure." Rufus tried to keep a beaming smile off his face. He felt extraordinary. The river hadn't borne away either of the two lives that had fallen into his hands tonight. Elation rose inside him, golden paper lanterns. He clapped Archie on the back and stumbled over to Drusilla, who was hunched up, intoning strange fractured syllables to herself. "Can you walk?" he asked her gently. "Archie, can you? I've got to get you both somewhere warm."

"Absolutely. I'll be right as rain in a minute."

He was trying to get up. Rufus went to help him, but came to a halt a couple of feet away. Something in his movements—head down, stoically pushing his body into gear before he had strength for it—made a final puzzle piece click into place. The restless activity, the readiness to run, swim, tackle each situation head-on... Rufus crouched in front of him. "You were there, weren't you?"

Archie wiped water out of his eyes. "Where?"

"During the war. You saw action. Were you a soldier?"

"Not exactly. I was an army chaplain, but... the roles seemed to merge. Is that important just now?"

It was important to Rufus. A barricade had formed between him and everyone who hadn't seen what lay beyond the green fields and broad sunlit uplands of ransomed England. He'd waited for it to appear between him and this vicar, who had surely waited out the war in his sheltered rectory. "No," he lied easily, the lanterns of elation still rising and glowing in his chest. "What are we going to do with Drusilla?"

"She has a cottage a mile or so from here. Thank God we won't have to go through the village. A vicar on a motorbike is one thing, but a vicar with a naked woman riding pillion..."

Rufus helped him clamber to his feet. He'd almost forgotten that he was half-naked himself, and he didn't recoil in time from Archie's sudden focus on his shoulder, the side of his neck. "Don't look at that."

"I'm sorry. I don't mean to. Are those shrapnel wounds?"

"Are they..." Rufus's throat closed and he had to try again. "Are they important just now?"

"Yes. My God, this must have almost killed you." Archie put out a hand, extended a finger as if to trace the scarring into Rufus's hairline, the place where his scalp would never be smooth again. "Close range?"

"Couldn't have been much closer. Archie, please. Drusilla's cold."

Chapter Ten

Firelight flickered brightly through the cottage bedroom. Drusilla, curled up in her narrow iron-frame bed beneath a pile of quilts and blankets, had stopped shivering at last. Rufus put a cautious hand to her shoulder. "I think she'll be all right. She's warming through."

"Good." Archie glanced up from feeding kindling into the fire. "What about you?"

"I'm fine. Trotting alongside your bike warmed me up, not to mention scaling the trellis and the balcony to get up here. Is that how she's been coming and going?"

"Yes. I'm surprised she hasn't broken her neck. Just as well Hicks hadn't got round to replacing that window catch for tonight, but I'll have to make sure he does it tomorrow."

"At least you remembered to wash off her feet this time. She might get away with it, if she hasn't caught her death of cold." Rufus pushed tangled hair off the woman's face. He looked around the cobwebbed, low-ceilinged room. "Poor creature. I didn't mean to eavesdrop on you and Dr Winborn, but... is she living this way because Reverend Gorringe's money is running out?"

Archie sighed. "It ran out months ago. She's living this way because at least up here she's quiet and safe, and I can't afford anything better."

"Oh." Rufus drew the quilt up. He and Archie were both wrapped in blankets, their soaked clothes steaming on an airing frame by the fire. Their nakedness beneath didn't matter, because—for tonight, at any rate—Rufus was an ordinary man, who'd reclaimed his friend's life from the river. He crossed the room and sat down in an armchair opposite Archie's. "You're paying for her?"

"I didn't mean to. She was part of the chaos I inherited from Gorringe. Elspeth, too."

"How does Elspeth fit into it?"

Archie sighed. "It really isn't my story to tell. But I've made you part of it by involving you, so..." He sat forward in his chair. Rufus noticed that his bare feet were bony and shapely, his shins lean. "Maria tells me that Drusilla just blew in out of the night, a couple of weeks before hostilities began. She could barely speak or remember her name. She was all dressed in black and her hair was down around her waist, and a few superstitious idiots here took to calling her a witch and a harbinger of war. You can probably guess the ringleader."

Rufus made a face. "My landlady?"

"The very one. So Gorringe—thinking to be kind to her, I suppose—found a cottage for her outside the village, to keep her out of the way. It wasn't all charity, though. His visits there were suspiciously frequent, and when he did his flit and I arrived to replace him, poor Drusilla was crazier than ever, and heavily pregnant."

"Ah. Elspeth?"

"That's right, although Drusilla named her Andrasta, for some unknowable reason."

"That's the word she was saying down on the riverbank." Rufus made an effort of recall: the rectory dinner seemed like weeks ago, not hours. "I think Elspeth was saying it to my dog, too."

"Yes. Perhaps they were exchanging secret names."

"Does anyone know where Drusilla came from, or how she ended up here?"

"Not a bit of it. I hired a nurse for her and tried to hush things up, but the scandal was endless. I don't know if Gorringe's attentions had driven her off the edge, or being called a witch and a whore by the good chapel folk of Droyton, but her behaviour got stranger and stranger. She developed a delusion that poor old Lady Birch was her mother, and every full moon she'd be found on some hillside or right in the middle of the open fields, not a stitch on her back, chanting and dancing."

"Could it be true? About Lady Birch, I mean?"

"Well, it would explain a lot, but Lady Birch is a spinster who's lived here under the scrutinising gaze of her neighbours most of her life. All this went on for nearly three years, and of course the child was terribly neglected. Finally Winborn decided Drusilla ought to be committed, and Mrs Nettles insisted on taking the little girl in at the rectory."

"That was good of her."

"Well, it was meant to be. But Elspeth had a tremendous mind of her own even then, and she made such a fuss that Winborn in his wisdom told her Drusilla had died."

"What? Why?"

"He thought it would be easier for her. I was in France by then, or I wouldn't have let it happen."

Rufus reached for the clothes on the rail. Even after all he'd seen and done, news of cruelty offered to an infant or a dumb beast made his throat burn with tears of stupid rage. He was making great steps in his pose as an ordinary man, however: he turned over Archie's underpants without a flicker. "Poor kid. Didn't anyone tell her the truth?"

"Mrs Nettles wanted to, but Elspeth got desperately ill after that, and she and Winborn only just saved her. When she came out of her fever, she'd accepted the story. Drusilla was very sick too, and there was every chance that she'd die in the asylum, or at best be locked up forever, so..."

"It was kinder to leave things as they were."

"I think so. I don't know. The sad thing is that Drusilla did come back, but she seemed to have forgotten she'd ever had a child. She certainly wasn't capable of looking after one. When I came home I had her brought here, for the Hickses to look after her, and Elspeth stayed with me and Maria."

"That's a sad story. Still, the little girl seems happy enough, if..."

"A little unhinged? And obsessed with madness and death, which is hardly surprising. Gorringe must have felt some compunction for his part in the matter, because although he didn't leave a penny for Mrs Nettles' wages or the upkeep of the rectory, he set aside a small fund for Drusilla."

"But that's run out."

"Yes, and what I can provide is inadequate. Hicks is just a handyman, and his wife a housekeeper and nurse of sorts. I'm afraid Drusilla will get hauled off to a looney bin again, even though she's harmless, and..." He glanced around the room. "I suppose this is better than that."

"Much better. And at least with you, the little girl is safe."

"I hope so. I don't know." Archie got up, just barely catching his blanket in time as it fell. He hitched it round his hips and went over to the window. "It's a dangerous world, but sometimes it feels damn small and stifling. Do you think Drusilla would be all right if I opened this?"

"Yes, I think so." Rufus didn't mean to admire the shift of muscles around Archie's spine as he raised the sash, but maybe even that was permissible, if he could tame his gaze to that of an artist or a sculptor. Being ordinary didn't have to mean that he was blind. "Sometimes the world seems small to me too, after... after being away."

"Yes!" Archie brought his palm down on the window sill, hard enough to make Drusilla twitch in her sleep. "That's it. And I've tried so bloody hard not to let it be that way. This place, the village, the rectory, the hills—they're everything I thought we were fighting for. Why does it feel so suffocating now?"

He was struggling for breath. Rufus pushed out of the armchair and went to stand beside him. Drusilla's cottage was set into a fold of the hills behind the rectory, no other houses visible. The breeze was bringing apple-blossom scents from the orchard. "I think," he said softly, "that sometimes people find themselves where they ought to be, even when it's the last place in the world they imagined."

"I'm a vicar, Rufus. You can't tell me I found my natural home on the Western Front."

"You're telling *me* that. All I can see is someone who came home and spent every waking hour after that working, patching his house and his church together, helping every waif and stray within reach. Somebody who really, really liked our gallop through the woods tonight, and the ducking afterwards. Even if we did nearly drown."

Archie began to laugh. His deep-seated cough flared again, and he rested his elbows on the window sill and lowered his head in frustration. "Damn. The really wicked thing is... I'd kill for a ciggie just now. Or even my pipe. I started smoking one when I came back. Thought it might help squeeze me back into my skin, if you know what I mean. Into my dog-collar."

"The respectable vicar?"

"That's it. A little bit eccentric, maybe. Was I convincing?"

"Sometimes. Sometimes not even close. Did you enjoy your war *very* much?"

"It seems such an appalling thing to say. Everything was very... direct. I tried to see to the spiritual needs of the wounded men in my unit, but when the field hospital outside Luxembourg came under attack, I grabbed one of their guns and helped defend it. I didn't even think. I was good at it—far better at that than persuading dying men that God had intended their pain." He straightened up, looking out to the moon-gilded flank of the hill. "The officers were scandalised at first, but as time dragged on and we lost more and more men, they stopped complaining. I learned how to ride a despatch bike and took messages back and forth behind the lines, wearing my collar and black coat. I think I confused the German snipers, because they never took a shot at me. I was active all the time, every waking hour of every day, until..."

He tailed off into racking coughs. Rufus listened attentively, and this time laid a hand over the place where the painful wheezing sounded most directly: left lung, under the broad and handsomely sprung ribcage. He did it fearlessly, thoughtlessly, and Archie stayed still for it. Leaned into it a little, as if the touch comforted or pleased him.

You wouldn't, if you knew what I am. For once Rufus pushed the thought away. "Until something happened to your lungs. If this was the last war, I'd say gas. But..."

"But this time around, everyone obeyed the Geneva rules on that stuff, even while they developed the A-bomb and dropped that instead. My unit blew up an unsuspected stockpile of chlorine on the Franco-German border at Esmar. Nobody knows to this day if it was German or Allied. It might have been a spectacular own goal. I didn't get too much of it, and Winborn says I'll be fine, if I stay away from the fags and my pipe and just about every other pleasure that makes life worth living, but...."

"That was you out of the fight."

"Yes. They shipped me home a year last January. They were very decent, the officers who'd taken such a dim view of me at first—they knew I loved that Norton, so they sent her back with me on the same boat."

Rufus chuckled. "Your warhorse."

"Yes. You know, I've never spoken to anyone about any of this. Not even to Winborn, beyond the medical necessities. Why is it so easy to tell you?"

Rufus let his hand fall. *Perhaps you sense I'd never judge you. That I love the idea of the warrior priest—and not just the idea of him, either. The flawed, kind, noble reality is starting to knock me off my feet.* He leaned into the window frame himself, far enough that Archie couldn't see his face. "It's a beautiful night."

Archie shuffled his elbows a couple of inches forward. The skin of his forearm brushed across Rufus's, a swift electrical flicker. He gave Rufus a sideways look that told him the gambit of distraction had worked—for now. "Very."

A rustle of bedclothes made them both turn, hitching at their blankets. Drusilla was sitting bolt upright, staring at them with wide eyes. "Where am I?"

"You're at home," Archie replied. He glanced at Rufus in wonder. "She hasn't spoken properly in months. Drusilla, can you understand me?"

"Yes," she said rustily. Her damp hair was tumbling over her breasts, the concealment imperfect. She seemed unselfconscious, her gaze fixed on the moon. "You're Reverend Thorne. I don't know the other gentleman, though."

"He's a friend of mine, Rufus Denby. You went on one of your... expeditions. You fell in the river, and he helped rescue you. Do you remember?"

"A little. And you doing the same, Thorne, many times before." She reached out a hand. "Please come here."

She was a majestic sight, even rumpled and tangled from her ordeal. Rufus watched in amusement while Archie went to her, keeping his eyes front and centre like the gentleman he was. He sat down gingerly on the edge of the bed. When he tried to pull up the bedclothes, she gently put his hand aside. Then she reached suddenly upwards, and Rufus wondered if, from her perspective, the moon was once again framed between her arms. *"I who am the beauty of the green Earth,"* she whispered, *"and the white moon among the stars, and..."*

Her voice faded out. She gave a lost cry of frustration, and let her arms fall. "It's all right," Archie said, tucking the quilt around her. "What were you doing?"

"It looked to me as if she was trying to bless you."

Archie glanced up at Rufus, who had come to stand at the end of the bed. "Oh. Well, she mustn't do that."

"Why not?"

"It's my job. To bless her, I mean. They have to receive their experience of God through me." He stopped, thoughtful, smoothing the bedlinen. "Apparently. It's one of the things I've never quite been able to understand. Drusilla?" She had buried her face against her knees, and made no response. "Drusilla, don't slip away from us again. There's something you might like to know about. Dr Denby here found something exciting in the church—a figurine, a little sleeping goddess. You can see her, if you just stay calm."

She unfolded like a strange dark flower. "You *found* her?"

Rufus went cold. But it wasn't the time to tell her he'd taken the treasure away and unforgivably lost it. "We found something of great interest, yes. Whether it's ancient or some kind of reproduction, we don't yet—"

"Ancient!" She cut him off eagerly, nodding. "And always new. *I who am the beauty of the green Earth, and the white moon among the stars, and the mystery of the waters, and the desire in the heart of man, I call upon thy soul...*"

"Oh, Drusilla," Archie groaned, when she stopped to draw breath. "Please try not to do this. It doesn't bother me, but Dr Winborn doesn't understand, and... I'm doing everything I can to keep you here."

"Winborn?" She gave a haughty snort. "A little man."

"Big enough to cause you problems, if he decides he has to commit you again. Lie back now and try to get some sleep. Rufus and I have to be going—Mrs Hicks will be up shortly to give you your breakfast. God, your hair's still quite wet, isn't it?"

"Don't be concerned, Thorne. I will tell Mrs Hicks that I tried to wash it myself."

Archie sat back, eyebrows rising. "What a good idea! Carry on with that kind of thinking, and we might get away with this yet."

She offered him a faint smile, then laid a hand on his wrist. "Andrasta?"

"You... You remember her?"

"Yes. I never forgot. But things were best as they were, when I was allowed to return."

"She's fine. Mrs Nettles is taking good care of her. We'll get her to school once she's a bit more settled, and..." He paused, giving Rufus an enquiring glance. "I'm not sure, but I think she may have a new dog."

Rufus pulled his blanket more closely around him. He felt oddly bereft, but this was for the best. Dogs, children, archaeological treasures, stout-hearted warrior priests... He wasn't fit for any of them. Better to let them go of his own accord than wait until they were stolen or stripped away. "Yes," he said firmly. "She definitely has a new dog."

"Your kindness is unbounded, and the cost of it is seen." Drusilla rubbed her eyes and looked suddenly, wearily sane. "What on earth was I doing? The moon isn't full yet at all."

"No," Archie said kindly. "Not yet."

"I must have thought that a half moon was better than none."

***

Between them, Rufus and Archie rolled the motorbike back along the dawn-hushed lanes. A beautiful day lay ahead, flaring its promise to the zenith already in wings of green and gold. It was half past five in the morning. If anyone was awake in Droyton Parva, it could only be Farmer Challen, Toby, and the inexplicable girl who dressed in britches and called herself Giles. Birds were calling from the dew-laden hedges. Archie's hand closed over Rufus's on the Norton's handlebar, and because they were so close to the rectory now—because Archie most probably hadn't even noticed—Rufus didn't pull away.

He felt curiously empty and at peace. He didn't mind the cling and scratch of his still-damp clothes. Even his guilt over the lost goddess had fallen into abeyance. When Archie drew the bike to a halt outside the rectory gate, he stood still, swaying a little with exhaustion.

"I think I might have said to you before, in the fairytales Elspeth makes me read to her, three is a magical number."

Rufus nodded, not concerned about the oddness of this statement. "In mythology, too. And from there into archaeology. A three-headed dog at the entrance to Hades. Triple spirals outside the Newgrange passage graves, and triple-goddess figures everywhere—Ireland, Greece, even up at Hadrian's Wall in the north."

"That's nice, but I was aiming lower. You're a mess, Dr Denby. I was hoping you might accept my offer of a bed and facilities, and... well. This is the third time I've asked."

It was. Probably there would never be a fourth. Nevertheless Rufus shook his head, smiling. "I can't. House rule of Mrs Trigg's—be there for breakfast, or she won't set a place for you next day."

"From what I hear about breakfast at the Maidens', that might not be a bad thing. Mrs Nettles makes drop scones on Saturday mornings."

"Is it Saturday? For God's sake—I've been here for three days, and I haven't done a stroke of significant work on the church. I'll go and catch a couple of hours' sleep, and I'll make a start this afternoon."

"You'll be lucky if your landlady lets you back in. Come here for a second—you still have some reeds in your hair."

Rufus leaned towards him. The scarring had left his scalp painfully sensitive in the places where it wasn't numb, and he held still with an effort while Archie tidied him up. "Am I fit for Mrs Trigg?"

"Well, you looked like a tramp the first time she saw you..."

"And now I'm a drowned rat."

They both began to laugh, hushing one another in the birdsong quiet. No more sacred peace could have prevailed in any church than that which the summer night had left behind, caught and held tenderly beneath the oaks in Pilgrim Lane. First sunlight was turning the new leaves to translucent coins. "I'll join you in the church later," Archie said at last, "if that's all right."

"Please. I'll need all the help I can get, and you can go on uncovering the murals. Will you want to conduct services there tomorrow?"

"Services? Er... yes, of course. One, anyway. Sunday afternoons are for tea on the lawn in Droyton Parva."

"It doesn't sound too awful."

"Part of what you fought to preserve, isn't it? The green and pleasant land."

"What *we* did." Rufus thought about those Sunday afternoons, and how his vicar might have spent them before the lamps had begun to go out for the second time across Europe. "Archie, I... don't know if I should mention this. Alice—Miss Winborn—she said that you'd been married. That you'd lost your wife before the war. I'm sorry."

"Oh." Archie's brow creased. He picked another half-dried reed strand out of Rufus's hair. "Yes. Celia was a great loss. She was a good woman. I was lucky to have had such a companion."

It was how you might speak of the death of a good friend, not a spouse. Rufus didn't get time to reflect on the strangeness of this: Archie suddenly took him by the shoulders, smiling. "You've saved my life twice now, you know. According to the rule of three in Elspeth's bedtime stories, the third time ought to be spectacular."

"Perhaps..." Rufus's mouth went dry and he had to start again. "Perhaps next time you'll save mine."

Chapter Eleven

Ten minutes later, he stood on the pavement outside the Maidens' Dance. It wasn't yet six o'clock, according to the clock above the strikingly ugly redbrick building just down the road. He wondered if that was the Dissenting chapel where Mrs Trigg and her friends went to listen to their fire-breathing preacher, to dance and speak in tongues. The street was quiet, almost deserted. A van was parked outside the baker's shop. The postman trundled by on his pushbike, nodding and calling out a casual greeting as if Rufus had lived there for years.

He considered going round the back, the way he'd left the night before. Mrs Trigg employed an oppressed teenage girl, shy to the point of speechlessness, in the kitchen and bar. Rufus didn't know her hours, but he might be lucky. Maybe she'd recognise a fellow sufferer, and would help him keep his nocturnal venture a secret.

Then, Rufus was a paying guest. Creeping round the back like a guilty cat held no appeal at all. He'd saved the vicar's life last night—and, yes, once before that, if you counted the roof-fall in the church. He climbed the three well-scrubbed steps to the front door, and gave the bell a jangling ring.

After a brief delay, a figure appeared behind the glass. Rufus straightened his face: his landlady was an early-morning sight to challenge the manners of the best-behaved guest. Whatever promise Rufus had shown, whatever had prompted the hairdo and the *Evening In Paris*, he'd clearly been demoted. She was clad from throat to ankles in a purple dressing gown, ferociously buttoned. Her head was majestic with curlers. She opened the door, revealing lime-green carpet slippers.

Well, he was no fashion plate himself. Rufus nodded as pleasantly as he could. "Morning, Mrs Trigg."

"Morning?!" She sounded as though she'd have liked to dispute it, to make the dancing May sun drop back below the horizon and come back when it was sober. "May I ask if you know what time it is?"

He ducked out for another glance at the chapel clock. "Just after six. I'm sorry for disturbing you—I don't have a key for the outer door."

"No, sir! We don't *give* keys for the outer doors. I'm not that sort of establishment."

She was an establishment of some sort, though. She was pre-war England, unchanged by the convulsions that had transformed the rest of the globe. Rufus almost admired her, arbiter and guardian of rural morality as she was. "Nevertheless, I'd like one. My work might keep me out at awkward hours."

"Your work?" She turned a shade of puce to match her dressing gown, discretion failing her. "Your *work* was chasing that tramp Drusilla Hazelgrove around the countryside last night, from what I hear—not that I countenance gossip, I assure you, but am I to help it if Mrs Norrell has got up early, on account of Norrell, and come to have her cup of tea with me?"

"Norrell being..." Rufus tapped the heel of his hand off his brow. "Ah. The gamekeeper, of course."

"Norrell does his duty in telling about such goings-on. He and Susanna are chapel people, like myself. It's a scandal and a byword, the way Vicar Thorne carries on with that woman! If I was to think any guest of mine was going the same way..."

Rufus spread his hands. He let her take him in—rumpled hair, damp clothes, whatever proofs of a heinous night on some unimaginable tiles she chose to read. He let her take her time to weigh all that in the balance against his value as a guest. His reputation, magnified under the village lens to a kind of fame; the bed-and-breakfast tariff to be gleaned. He didn't care at all what the outcome would be. He didn't even have the welfare of a dog to worry about now. "I'm rather tired, Mrs Trigg. I'd like to come in." He straightened his shoulders: in for a penny, in for a pound. "I'll take my breakfast in my room—right away, please. You can send up my key for the outer door at the same time."

Her jaw dropped. For a moment he thought she'd pick him up bodily and sling him back into the street, to land at the feet of the milkman whistling his way down the pavement, crate in hand. Then—almost to his disappointment—she stepped aside.

***

Rufus knew he should speak to Archie about the missing figurine. His concealment was childish, a little kid pretending a thing hadn't happened because he hadn't told. But the day had kept all its promise. The afternoon was hot, the inside of the church deliciously cool. He had his work, soft breezes stealing over his skin from the open doors, swallows darting back and forth to their nests among the rafters. Best of all, he had Archie, perched at the top of a stepladder and singing wordless melodies to himself—bass, just a somehow-pleasant fraction off-key— while he chipped away at the plaster on the murals. Rufus couldn't analyse why the presence of this man had perfected the day for him, made him feel that his losses were restored. He couldn't bear the thought of disappointing or annoying him, even though his expression of dismay would have been so gentle and characteristic. *Good heavens, old fellow. Couldn't you have taken better care of her than that?*

No. Rufus had grown used to seizing good times when he could. He hefted the book in which he was making sketches and carried on about his task. The church was a fine medieval one. Already he'd gathered enough evidence to prove it unique, and a photographer was on his way from Lewes to record the rare piscina and font cover, the remains of the beautiful rood screen. Archie need not fear invasion by a neo-Gothic restoration team. Rufus would send his report and the photographs to Caroline at the museum, and she'd have sufficient weight with the Ecclesiastical Commissioners to get specialist workers sent here, sympathetic repairs carried out.

He paused to draw the western wall. That, and the south aisle where Archie was working, were the only parts of the building's fabric whose age he hesitated to guess. They were solid Horsham stone, not the flint-and-rubble construction he found elsewhere, and other than the murals bore no signs or style to betray their origins. Placing such large blocks of masonry—getting them here in the first place, in this chalk-and-flint country—must have posed enormous problems for craftsmen who'd pre-dated their medieval counterparts by centuries at least.

By millennia? Rufus set that possibility aside. Too exciting a discovery, for a disgraced archaeologist in an off-the-map village like Droyton. His drawing lacked scale. He leaned his back against a pillar and sketched in Archie on his stepladder, a stick man hard at work. Fleshed him out with a few strokes, smiling at the effect, then crossed the west end to get another perspective. Absently he noticed the sound his feet made on the flags, which had survived here despite the Victorian tiling in the main aisle. Every couple of strides, an alteration, as if he were dancing, not walking. Two normal beats and then a thump with the faintest reverb behind it...

"Archie?" he called out, repressing a grin when the vicar's sharp turn on the ladder almost brought him to grief again. "There isn't a crypt under here, is there?"

"A crypt? No. The water table's too high. You run into flooding about six feet down."

That explained the graveyard, set far back from the church in the hillside meadow to the north, although a few early burials had been made on the mound itself. Rufus walked back the way he'd come. Step, step, boom... The beginnings of flashback tugged at him, but today he could recognise them, put them aside in favour of the present. He was puzzled, though. A hollow space beneath the church would make the whole floor resound. A tunnel would produce one set of echoes, not this pattern.

Archie had uncovered the female figure on the east wall as far as the hips. A broad horizontal line was appearing halfway down her belly. Mentally Rufus completed the shape, drawing on the Bronze Age images from Crete and Malta, and the treasure he'd held in his own hand in this very church. A downward-pointing triangle, the symbol of water, the womb, the cauldron of rebirth...

But the ochre lady was reaching upwards. The world below was indicated by the male figure in the choir loft, perhaps quite literally her other half. Rufus laid his sketchpad down on the back of a pew, made his way along the north aisle and slipped through the door that led to the narrow staircase. He took the steep steps at a run. If the figure below had possessed eyes, she'd be rolling them at his stupidity. Her own gesture might be nebulous—sun, sky, the great beyond—but the male was pointing at the ground, perhaps at something earthly and specific. Rufus crouched in the corner of the choir loft, brushing away flakes of plaster with his sleeve. His heart lurched as the point of a second triangle appeared on the male figure's chest. Upright, this one, the sign for fire, and if you took the two and conjoined them they became the star of David, a symbol of union and harmony so ancient that they marked the deepest origins of human abstract thought, a Sanskrit of the soul. Nevertheless, that wasn't his interest now. One ochre index finger was tucked into the joint between two vast blocks. Rufus was willing to bet that marked the dead centre of the church on its east-west axis, and directly beneath that point on the floor below...

"Archie," he gasped, leaning over the choir-loft rail. "Can we move the altar?"

Archie stared up at him from the top of the ladder. "Move it? I don't think so. It's—"

"I don't mean any disrespect. I'm not a churchgoing man myself, but I'd never desecrate a sacred place I was working in. I know it's a lot to ask, but..."

"No. I mean I'm not sure we physically can. It's really heavy."

Rufus had only seen it covered by an altar cloth. "Isn't it just a table?"

"No, not at all. It's stone. Is that unusual?"

"Very, actually. The Reformation chucked most of them out along with the stained glass and statues. They were considered very pagan."

"How intriguing... Yes, of course we can take a crack at moving it, if that's what you want." He paused, chisel in hand. "This will seem a very odd question just now, Rufus, but—how old are you?"

The oddness bypassed Rufus entirely in his excitement. "I'm thirty five. Why?"

"When I first saw you I thought you were older—my age, maybe. Right now you look like a teenage kid. Is it because you're on the scent?"

Blood burned up beneath Rufus's skin. He felt young enough, in the warmth of Archie's regard, to put out green shoots like the oaks in Pilgrim Lane. "Perhaps," he got out at last.

"Then for God's sake, let's go and move the altar."

Easier said than done. Rufus felt the massive solidity of the thing as soon as he joined Archie in folding back the cloth, a chill beneath his fingers. No wonder the reformers of the sixteenth century had left this one alone. It was a monster, carved from a block of the same beautiful grey-green Horsham stone that worked so well for walls and so badly for roof tiles. He hesitated, reaching for the brass candlesticks, but Archie gave them a push in his direction. "Go ahead. When I was a kid, I thought I'd burst into flames if I came past the rail, let alone touched the altar itself. Take the cloth as well, if you don't mind, and just set them down over there."

"Are you sure it's all right?"

"You know, for all I'm the world's worst vicar in a lot of ways, I wouldn't let everyone do it. But you..." He smiled, lifting away the thin wooden board on top. "Some people profane everything they touch. I think you do the opposite." He turned his back to the altar before Rufus could even begin to formulate a response. "Let's try giving it a shove from this end first."

Rufus went to join him. He too set his spine against the block. They braced together and heaved. Nothing: a solidity of stone that seemed to deny the very possibility of movement, as if the block had been fused into bedrock. At a signal from Rufus they tried again, giving over their whole weight this time.

Archie grunted in surprise as his corner suddenly shifted. "Here we go."

"Yes. Keep it coming."

"I can't. It's jammed again. I tell you what—you come round to this edge and push as hard as you can."

"Why?"

"It seems to want to swing round here, rather than going straight across."

Rufus got into position beside him, cursing the circumstances that kept throwing him into physical proximity with this man. They were face to face, almost thigh to thigh, as Rufus got a grip on the corner of the block. Archie was beginning to smell of hard work on fresh linen, a summer's-day tang from rugby fields and rowing meets and all the other places where fit, forbidden male flesh tugged alluringly at Rufus's imagination. He channelled the frustrated need into a push that sent the altar jolting off on a diagonal, almost dumping Archie onto his backside. "Oh! Sorry."

"Quite all right." Archie regained his balance. "Did that help? What are you looking for?"

Not an untouched expanse of flagstone, clearly undisturbed for centuries. Embarrassment began to creep over Rufus. "I don't know. I thought the figure in the choir loft was trying to show us something."

"Maybe he is."

"Yes, but... in a spiritual sense, I think, not an X-marks-the-spot Boy's Own adventure."

"Don't abandon the adventure too soon. We're only halfway there, and I think this flag has a carved edge."

"Really? Where?" Rufus crouched to look at the spot Archie was indicating. His blood stirred with the pure, addictive joy of discovery. "Yes, so it has. Help me push again."

This time the block moved more easily. Archie was right. The final flagstone—smaller than the rest, dressed to about half the size—had a notch on its northwest corner, and the worn remains of a mason's mark.

No. Two interlocked triangles. Unthinkingly Rufus grabbed Archie's arm and pulled him down to kneel beside him. "Look!"

"Is that... My goodness." Archie leaned close, produced a handkerchief and brushed the little symbol clear of dust. "Did we find an ancient synagogue?"

"Well, good archaeologists don't discount any possibilities out of hand, but... I don't think so. The mural figures both have a triangle figure painted into their design."

"Really? I hadn't seen that."

"I've only just seen it myself. The woman—the goddess—hers is pointing down, the symbol for water. And the one on the figure in the loft is pointing up, for..."

"Fire? I've read about those signs. Tattwas, they're called. I have a wonderful book on that kind of thing in the library somewhere—by Mircea Eliade, I think. And here they are."

"Here they are, interjoined. It may be a coincidence. Medieval masons used all kinds of esoteric marks, some of them far from Christian."

"All right. Or it may mean that there's something very interesting underneath this flag."

Rufus sat back on his heels. He'd already done so much inadvertent damage to the archaeological investigation of this church. "Archie, I think we have to stop here. I don't want to, but there's so much more to this site than I'd imagined. We need to let the museum know about this, get some people down here who know what they're doing."

Archie chuckled. "You're charmingly modest. But I'm fairly sure Dr Denby of Naxos, Sabros and the Peloponnese knows a thing or two."

"Thank you. Medieval churches aren't my area, though, and..." *And I lost the little goddess. I lost her.* He couldn't say it. "And I have to document and report before I go any further. And the photographer should get some images of this stone in situ before we do anything with it at all."

"Or you could make another of your beautiful sketches."

Rufus had forgotten about his sketchbook. He'd left it open on top of the pew. "Oh. Yes, I put you in. Just for scale."

"I'm still flattered. Come on. You're top of your field, whatever's happened to you lately to make you think otherwise. You're not going to hurt this stone by lifting it and having a look."

"Well, it's not mortared in, so it's not as if I'd be disturbing..." He paused, shaking his head. "Reverend Thorne, I really shouldn't have to say *get thee behind me, Satan* to you in your own church."

A distant rumble interrupted Archie's response. Rufus straightened up, having to get away from the smiling mock-outrage that had lit up his new friend from within. "If that's the photographer on his way, his timing is excellent."

"Oh. Did he say he was coming by car?"

"No, but I suppose he'd need to, if he has a lot of equipment. Would you like it very much if he did?"

"I would," Archie admitted, pushing his fringe back and standing up. "That was another good thing about the hideous war we both went through—all the motors. I see one here a week if I'm lucky. What do you think he's got—a Wolseley?"

Rufus listened. He hadn't learned to love the staff cars, trucks and tanks that had roared around him all the time in Belgium and France, but he knew some of their voices. "Sounds like a Ford to me."

"Bet you two bob it's a Wolseley."

"Not sure which of us will go to hell first—you for making a bet in here, or..."

"You for taking me up on it? We're on, then." Archie clapped him on the shoulder. "Come on. Let's go and take a look."

A highly polished Wolseley Hornet was gleaming in the lane, her owner having decided not to risk her on the grass track down to the church. Rufus felt in his pockets, and hoped Archie could wait for his debt to be settled. He'd given his last spare shilling to the scared girl who served breakfasts, and was now living on his bed and board at the Maidens' and thin air. Two figures were making their way down the track—a stranger in his fifties, loaded down with tripod and camera gear, and, to Rufus's surprise, Alice Winborn, looking like a daisy in pale lemon sundress and white straw hat. Pippin had apparently hitched a ride, too. She caught sight of Rufus and rushed him at a gallop, recollected herself at the last instant and skidded into an obedient sit at his feet. "Hello, old girl," he said, rumpling her ears. "You look well today. Good afternoon, Miss Winborn."

She waved, smiling brightly beneath the shade of her hat. "Hello, Dr Denby. Hello, Archie. I was just taking Pippin out for a stroll—Elspeth loaned her to me—when Mr Phipps here overtook me in the lane. I told him the way to the church, and he was kind enough to give me a ride."

Archie and Rufus came down the steps to greet her. Rufus shook hands with the photographer and took some of his burden from him. Archie began to make introductions, and Alice slipped past them and ran into the church. "Dr Denby," she called from inside the porch. "*Do* come and tell me what you and Archie have been up to in here. I'm absolutely dying to know."

There was a strange edge to her voice. Desperation, if Rufus didn't know better... He recalled what he'd been told about her boredom, trapped in her uncle's house here at Droyton, and he gave Archie an enquiring glance. "Go ahead," Archie said. "Alice hasn't seen the murals yet. I'll help Mr Phipps get set up, then you can tell him what you need."

Rufus followed Alice into the church. At first he couldn't see her, then she emerged suddenly from behind a pillar, sunlight catching her drift of fair hair. The movement was at once playful and awkward, as if she'd thought about hiding from him then changed her mind. Altogether there was something *off* about her, an uncharacteristic lurch, as if she'd lost her way inside herself and was floundering...

He caught the scent of apple wine in the air, and was filled with pity. "Miss Winborn," he said, putting out an arm for her. "Would you allow me to show you around?"

She followed him quietly. Once anchored, she recovered her poise and her ability to hide what had perhaps been nothing more than one glass too many of Mrs Nettles' potent brew at lunch. Her grip on Rufus's arm was light and warm. She tipped her face to his attentively while he described to her the problems with the Horsham tiles, the vast span of time the building materials seemed to encompass, the murals and what they might mean. Their tour of the church brought them to the place where he and Archie had stood together, the best natural spot for viewing the strange ochre figure on the wall. They came to a halt. Rufus ran out of words, and she held his arm more tightly in the new silence. "It's strange, isn't it," she said, her voice edged with a tremor. "The tracks of your life can seem so certain. I thought mine would bring me here—not to this church, because David came from Brighton, and we were going to have our wedding at St Paul's, by the sea."

"Archie told me about your loss. I'm most terribly sorry."

"Thank you." She tried to shake off her mood, and a false brightness came over her, the same too-vivid smile he'd seen after dinner the night before. "But it isn't the same as if we'd been married, is it? Life has to go on, and I'm quite determined that mine will."

"That's good, but—"

"Oh, heavens. Who moved the altar?"

"Archie and I did. I wanted to examine the flags underneath. You're not offended, I hope?"

"Not at all, although it is shocking somehow, to see it pushed aside like that. Did you find anything?"

"I'm not sure yet. We—"

"Rufus! Grab that wretched hound of yours for me, would you, old chap?"

Archie's voice was rich with laughter. Pippin had seized an unattended tripod leg and was trotting proudly down the aisle with it. Rufus began to laugh too, although the poor photographer looked horrified. "Here, you bad girl," he called, patting his thighs. "Is that for me, then? Give it over. Give it here."

She set it down gently at his feet. He picked it up and examined it for teethmarks, but it seemed intact. "I'm sorry, Mr Phipps. She hasn't harmed it, though—here, let me bring it back."

He took it to the west end of the church, where Phipps was laying out the rest of his equipment on a pew. Archie was unfolding the other two legs of the tripod, his expression thoughtful, as if he too had caught the tang of alcohol on the air. It was wholly unfair, Rufus thought: neither of them would have batted an eyelid if the photographer or any other man had come here smelling a little of his lunchtime beer. "It's a pleasure to show Miss Winborn around," he said, unsure for whose benefit he was defending her. "She seems to have a great appreciation of historical sites like this."

"Yes. Alice is very concerned about their preservation. She was going to help me prepare an article for the local newspaper about this place, before Caroline sent you to save us."

Rufus nodded. Between them, they'd surely given Mr Phipps to understand that just because a slightly tipsy lady had waylaid him in the lane, she was a lady nonetheless, educated, refined, and...

"Oh, buggery and blast!"

A whiplash crack resounded from the nave. Archie and Rufus exchanged a glance, then ran to intercept poor Alice, staggering away from the altar with one piece of the broken flagstone clasped in either hand. "I dropped it," she said piteously. "I could see the interesting one. It had little marks on the edges. It looked as if it wanted to be picked up, and... and I did. But it was heavier than I thought. Oh, bugger!"

"It's all right." Rufus took the broken pieces from her. "Just a stone."

"No, it's not. And bloody Pippin's gone down the damn hole."

Rufus darted up the altar steps. Where the slab had been, a dark space now gaped, redolent with scents of earth and moss. He knelt at the edge of it. The flagstone had been no bigger than a manhole cover, the blackness it had concealed narrow and absolute. "Archie, do you have a torch?"

"No. I'll go and grab some candles from the vestry."

"Hold on," the photographer called. "I think I have a torch somewhere in my kit."

They arrived back beside Rufus at the same time. He could hear the dog scratching about below, and she barked in response to her name.

Why hadn't he jumped down after her? The drop couldn't be very far, and if she'd survived it without damage, so could he. The reluctance felt nothing like the horror that had seized him in the Sabros tomb. It was as if the very earth was saying *no* to him, a profound, flat-out rejection. The Sabrian word fit well for the sensation, though: *agapomenu*, forbidden...

Phipps put the torch into his hand. Rufus swallowed hard, gritted his teeth and overcame the crawling fear sufficiently to push his head and shoulders through the hole. Someone grabbed hold of his belt—Archie, from the press of bony knuckles against his spine. He concentrated on that, the solid grip from the world above, and shone the beam around.

Nothing but a hole. An excavation of the hard-packed earthen floor might reveal human remains, someone important enough to have earned burial within the church. More likely this was an aborted attempt at such an interment, called to a halt by flooding. Archie had said the water table was no more than six feet down. The floor and walls looked dry, though, clean and oddly smooth.

Pippin was scratching frantically at one corner, the only place where broken soil and stones could be seen. A slippage from above might have stopped the burial too, obliging the family of the dignitary concerned to let him rest his bones in the meadow like anyone else. "Pippin," Rufus said, and she stopped digging and looked back at him over her shoulder, less in fear than an invitation that he should join her in this game. "Stupid dog. Come here."

Obligingly she returned to the centre, sat on her haunches and tried to stretch up to sniff his hand. Rufus couldn't reach her. His grab for her scruff missed by inches. "Damn. I'm going to have to go down."

He sat back. He wasn't about to do this head-first. Climbing in at all was a ghastly prospect, but he didn't want Archie and Phipps to see his irrational dread. To his surprise, he found it reflected in their faces. "What's wrong with you two?"

Archie found his voice first. "I... don't know, exactly. But you can't go in there, can you? It's a horrible idea."

He was pale. So was the photographer. Before Rufus could begin to ask them why they shared his instinct of recoil, Alice shouldered her way between them. She was barefoot, her high-heeled summer sandals discarded in the aisle. "What on earth is the matter with all of you?" she demanded, crouching by the edge of the hole. "Somebody has to go and fetch that poor dog."

"I will," Rufus said. "I just need..."

"What? It's not very deep, is it? Just be ready to pull me back out."

He made a grab for her, but she wriggled like a ferret to avoid his grasp, pushed off fearlessly and dropped. Archie said something that sounded very much like *shit*. He seized the torch from Rufus and ducked his head into the hole. "Alice! What the devil are you doing?"

"Getting Pippin. It was my fault she went down. Come here, sweet pie—that's a good girl. I've got her. I'm going to lift her up to you, all right?"

Pippin's ragged ears appeared in the gap between the flags. Archie reached in for a handful of scruff, and Rufus caught her behind the forelegs. Between them they hoisted her out. "Right," Archie said. "You next, miss. Do you have any idea what your uncle is going to do to me when he hears about this?"

"Sod my uncle," she said distinctly. Her voice was calm, almost musical, as if something in the acoustics of the hole had helped her find her right timbre and pitch. "Do you know, I almost wish you would leave me down here. Put the altar back and forget all about me."

"Alice, you stop talking like that. Give me your hands."

She raised them tiredly. Archie took one wrist, Rufus the other, lifting her far enough to get her by the armpits. "It's a pity," she went on conversationally, as Phipps joined in with the effort of lifting her free, "that I don't have a scruff like Pippin's. Then you could have hauled me out by that. You think I'm drunk, I know, and the awful thing is that you're right. But I tried to go for a walk and sober up, only no-one would come with me but the dog." Shakily she began to dust herself down. "It's a sad thing, don't you think, when... when no-one will come with you but the dog?"

A harsh sob escaped her. The photographer was wide-eyed. Archie glared at him, and he backed up a pace or two. "Alice, let me take you home."

"I don't want to go home. I've told you, I just want to go for a bloody walk."

"I'll go with you." Rufus surprised himself with the offer. He felt horribly sorry for her. Liked her, too, for her fearless rescue of the dog, even if it had been fuelled by Mrs Nettles' homebrew. He wanted to get her away from the photographer's curious gaze. "That is, if you'd like that. And if you can spare me, Archie."

"Of course I can spare you. I'm supposed to be helping *you*, but..." Archie's eyebrows went up, as if a light was dawning. Then came a tiny flash of pain: unaccountable, swiftly hidden. "Of course. It's time I got cleared up for services tomorrow. Er... what shall I do about the altar?"

"I'll help you move it back now. I'll write to Caroline tonight about what we've found here. Perhaps Miss Winborn would show me the footpath up to George Mount."

She nodded, as if she'd been thrown a lifeline and was blindly groping for it. "Yes. That's where I was going."

"Good," Archie said, his poise recovered. "Mr Phipps and I will stay here until he's taken as many pictures as he needs. And then... I say, Phipps, old chap, would you let me take a look at your car?"

***

Alice set such a pace along the track that Rufus struggled to keep up with her. The mud was hard and dry this far up the flank of the hill, and she made rapid progress despite her heels. She wasn't much the worse for her plunge underground. Rufus could see how men would find her beautiful. Her dress fluttered around her. She was a perfect focus for a cloud-scudded, sunny afternoon. Eventually she seemed to wear herself out. She slowed up until Rufus could draw alongside her, and gave him a shamefaced smile. "I'm better now."

"That's good."

"I'm so mortified, though. What must you think of me?"

"Most people have reasons for acting the way they do."

Some of the tension left her. "You're a very different sort of man, Dr Denby."

"Rufus, please."

"All right. Alice, then. Miss Winborn makes me feel as though I'm in a Jane Austen novel. Not that they'd tolerate me there."

"I don't know. They tolerated Lydia, after a fashion."

She broke into reluctant laughter. He held out an arm, and this time when she took it, her touch was companionable. "I can't believe I broke the stone. Was that very dreadful?"

Not by contrast with removing and losing a priceless figurine. "Not at all. We have the pieces, and you found the cavern, which may turn out to be of the greatest interest."

"Do you think so? It's just a hole in the ground, as far as I could see. Nice, though, in a strange way. I really did wish I could stay."

"And yet Archie and I couldn't get away from it fast enough. Phipps, too."

"Well, maybe it's no-boys-allowed. You can all go off and be popes, priests, vicars and what-have-you, and we…" She paused, a small shiver vibrating through her. "We get the underworld."

"I don't think it can be that way anymore. Not now, when everyone's seen what women can do. Things might change from now on."

Her stride became easy beside him. Pippin came to trot at their heels. A group of ramblers appeared on the track ahead of them, heavily armed with blackthorn sticks and maps, and parted to let them through, smiling and offering cheerful observations on the beauty of the day. How would it have been, Rufus wondered, if he'd been here with Henry on his arm, or—the thought gave him a pang of longing—with Archie? Curious stares, downcast eyes. Probably no outright hostility, but how great a contrast to walking with Alice! He almost said it aloud to her as they passed. *We could almost be a normal couple.* Stranger things had happened.

They emerged from the treeline and onto the open hill. This was the route he and Archie had taken last night to get Drusilla Hazelgrove home, though it looked so different in sunlight that he barely recognised the track. There was the cottage, prosaic too when not silver-gilded by the moon, set back in as normal a country garden as anyone could wish. The gardener—Hicks, Rufus imagined—raised his cap in greeting, and then, as if everyone was making an effort at normality this afternoon, Drusilla herself appeared in the bedroom window and waved. She was startlingly clad in a frilled white nightgown, but at least she was dressed.

Rufus waved back. Alice did too, and after a moment the strange figure vanished from the window. "Goodness," Alice said. "That's the longest exchange I've had with Miss Hazelgrove since I started visiting here. Do you know her?"

"Not exactly. I've... had the chance to make her acquaintance."

"Poor woman. It's all right—I know her story, although Archie's done his best to stop the waggling tongues." She walked in silence for almost a minute, then added, as if by natural progression, "My uncle wants me to marry him. Archie, I mean. Please don't tell either of them I said so—Archie hasn't figured it out at all, and he'd be so embarrassed."

Rufus took this in. He fitted it for sense against Winborn's behaviour at Archie's butcher night, his unease and irritation. "How do you feel about that?"

"Well, for God's sake. Who wouldn't want to marry Archie? He's the dearest man alive, even if he does spend most of his time up to his elbows in engine oil. He doesn't have any money, but Uncle Paul will make that problem disappear, or so I've rather unsubtly been given to understand."

"I see." Rufus gave Alice a hand over the stile into the field, then watched in amusement as Pippin ploughed through the hedge to join them. "Actually, I don't. Why is your uncle concerned about who Archie marries?"

"I'm not sure. They're very old friends, you know. Archie's illness was more of a kind of... nervous breakdown, I suppose, and my uncle became very protective of him. My mother and I were staying with him at the time, and although I was just a girl, and not supposed to notice things, it almost seemed to me that he picked Celia out for Archie. Chose a wife for him."

"And now he wants to choose another?"

"That's right. Goodness, though—I'm not another Celia." She took off her cardigan, held it by the sleeves and let the wind blow it out behind her, as if yearning to take flight. "I just want..."

"What?"

"Some days, nothing. To be left alone with my gardening, or at the bottom of a hole. Other days..." She dropped the cardigan onto the turf and took a sudden step towards Rufus, so close that he could feel her warmth. The ramblers had disappeared and they were alone, out of sight of Drusilla's windows, with only Pippin and the blazing sun for witness. "Other days I think there should be more. You're very nice, aren't you? Very kind. You didn't want that photographer gawping at me, so you got me out."

"It wasn't just that. I—"

"It's all right. You're handsome, too, though I didn't think so when you first arrived. It was just that my David looked so different."

Rufus waited to see the light. This was it: a beautiful woman, with breeding, manners and education, everything any man could want, was silently asking him for a kiss. Even Henry had laughed at him for his lack of experience. *How can you know what you are if you've never tried a girl?*

Rufus knew. Alice, tired of waiting for a sluggish male world to catch up with her, leaned in. Her kiss miscarried at the last instant and landed on the corner of his mouth.

Rufus held her gently by the shoulders. She was trembling. "I'm sorry," she said after a moment. "Would you think me very rude if I went home now?"

"Not at all. May I walk you there?"

"I'd like you to, but I have to be alone. I have to think. Will I see you at church tomorrow?"

"Yes. I'll be there."

He picked up her cardigan, brushed it free of grass and helped her into it. She gave him a sweet, uncertain smile and retreated down the path, Pippin frolicking after her.

Rufus watched them go. Then he climbed up onto the fence by the stile and sat listening to the shimmer-song of larks in the heated air. The Mount's strange crown was invisible from this angle, all its mysteries departed. It was just a beautiful hill. Rufus closed his eyes and tipped his face up to the sun.

Chapter Twelve

Reverend Archie's Sunday morning service was the event of the week at Droyton Parva. Among a people who could no longer turn blindly to God for peace or the safety of their loved ones, in a church half a mile out of the village at the end of a long, bumpy lane, still he managed to draw in a good crowd. Even Mrs Trigg was there, helmeted in silk and artificial pansies, Jebediah at her side, so well scrubbed he almost shone. Rufus had had the dubious pleasure of walking her there himself, together with a dressmaker friend of hers, the scared girl who served breakfasts, and a handful of other household staff. Mrs Trigg had explained with great dignity that although her true spiritual path lay with the chapel—Mrs Pole's, too—they both felt obliged to appear in the enemy camp to set an example. The vicar, no matter how eccentric, must be honoured in his village, and any church was better than none.

Alice Winborn had a better explanation, whispered in Rufus's ear as he'd taken a place beside her in the pew. Mrs Trigg and her friend had to come to Archie's services because Preacher Evans didn't care for finery, and how else could they show off their new hats? Rufus had surprised himself—and the rest of the congregation settling down around them—with a loud bark of laughter. Alice had dissolved into silent, helpless giggles and was only just recovering now, pressing her handkerchief to her eyes.

The church too looked different in its Sunday best. The altar was back in place, clean white cloth ablaze with stained-glass sun and yellow roses from the rectory garden. The worst of the rubble from the roof-fall had been concealed under sacking, and a hand-lettered *no entry* sign in Archie's bold, elegant script was hanging from a rope across the top of the south aisle. To Rufus the church had felt more sacred before the arrival of the beaming, well-to-do butcher, the bored farmhands and the flock of ladies clearly determined not to let Mrs Trigg have it all her own way in the fashion department, but then he was used to places of worship that had stood vacant for centuries.

He sat still in his fourth-row pew, trying to see the place as others saw it. He hadn't attended a service himself in years, not since the days when he and Henry had still been trying to maintain their cover as respectable gentlemen in London. He couldn't imagine what a minister could have to say after the conflagration that had just passed. He could hardly sell the idea of a wholly benevolent God.

Archie emerged from the vestry without the air of a man with anything to sell at all. Rufus's restless thoughts ceased. He forgot about Alice, who was fanning herself with her hymn sheet, shooting him the occasional warm-eyed glance over the top of it. Forgot Winborn, clearly displeased by this arrangement and frowning at them both from across the aisle, forgot Mrs Nettles with Elspeth on her lap, exchanging *have-at-you, ma'am* looks with Mrs Trigg. He could only see Archie, tall and serious in his white surplice, making his way into the low pulpit like a workaday archangel and opening the Bible set out there.

He read from the Pentecost Acts, in preparation for Whitsun a few weeks ahead, and he made the words sound as though they had been written yesterday. Between each passage he paused, looking out across the congregation to see if his listeners were with him, if they followed and accepted the premise. He looked as if he'd welcome a dissenting voice, though none came: the babies stopped crying and the old men stopped rustling their paper bags of humbugs to listen to him. He seemed to be testing every word, tapping it to see if it rang true. When it was over, he flashed Rufus a tiny signal of comical relief, closed the book up and rested his palms on the desk.

"Right," he said quietly. "All those people suddenly able to understand one another's languages, eh? You'd think that would solve a lot, and people would use such a gift to fix things. *Lord, make me an instrument of your peace...* St Francis makes it sound rather easy, doesn't he? And if we just mean the peace of a sunny Droyton afternoon, I suppose it is. Or the kind of negative peace where we decide *not* to do something—not to throw a pitchfork at the butcher in a quarrel over the price of beef, for example." In the back pew, Farmer Challen harrumphed mightily, and a few snorts of laughter rang out. "And then there's the peace that's come to our nation, restored to us our broad sunlit uplands." Once more he met Rufus's eyes, unhurriedly this time, remembering a vision shared. "That was the hardest-won peace of all. It makes me think of the WH Auden poem. We were like that once—the people who *do not care to know where Poland draws her eastern bow, what violence is done, nor ask what doubtful act allows our freedom in this English house, our picnics in the sun.* It makes me think of peace with a sword, which is what we have now in our green island, a terrible sword like the Hiroshima bomb to hang over our heads."

He let the image take hold, in the drifting, golden-dust-mote hush of the church, spreading his hands in the effort to encompass it himself. Then he drew a deep breath and went on.

"And think about this—the other day I was with an old lady in Ashfield hospital, a lady at the end of her life. She told me she was worried about dying, because although she'd tried to make her final peace, she still hated her next-door neighbour, who'd stolen a string of fresh sausages out of her kitchen back in 1882." He shook his head. "I could hardly keep a straight face. But she made me realise that I harboured hatreds like those in my heart, as well. I can't forgive—I hope one day I will—the little brat in my grammar-school class who took the pencil box my grandfather had made me, the only thing I had to remember him by. So how am I, as your vicar, meant to stand among you and preach peace?"

Not a rhetorical question. Rufus, by now listening attentively, wished that somebody would stand up and tell him—that it was all right, that even if he didn't have the answers, no man could speak to them more plainly or with more humanity. That no minister could care for his flock more sincerely than by pulling the strays out of a river at midnight... It was on his lips to get up and say it when Archie found his voice again. "I told her what I'm telling you, what I've had to tell myself. If we wait around to have peace in our hearts, love and goodwill to all men, we'll never get anything done. The peace-on-Earth part will never happen. So I suggest that we do our best to mend breaches, forgive where we can, and beyond that—don't wait. Labour at it like any other task. Because it *is* a task, and it's hard. As Gerard Manley Hopkins said of his dove of peace, *He comes with work to do.*"

He fell silent. A long shadow had darkened the aisle. The church door was standing wide to the sunshine and the rustle of oaks from the lane. The back rows noticed the new arrival first, and then all heads began to turn. A gasp or two, a muttered exclamation... Mrs Trigg jerked round in her pew, mouth dropping open. No sound emerged from it: the thin wail was coming from Elspeth, struggling off Mrs Nettles' lap. She squeezed like a weasel past the barricade of knees, jumped into the aisle and ran.

Drusilla leaned down to catch her. She was dressed in deep blue velvet, her hair pinned up beneath a neat black hat. She lifted Elspeth into her arms and bent her head over her, then subsided with her into an empty pew. The child's sobs filled the church.

Archie made an assessing survey of his congregation. "That'll do for today. Look out for your chances of ordinary, hard-working peace, and you'll find they occur all the time. Please stand for the final hymn."

The organ wheezed out the introductory bars to *Eternal Spirit, Come*. In the loft, Archie's half dozen choirboys joined in, on key and off, each according to his gifts, the oldest of them cracking up and down into a startling newborn bass. Mrs Nettles and Alice led off among the pews, both of them clear and sweet, then Mrs Trigg unleashed her brass trumpet, and the rest faltered in gradually, Farmer Challen a saving grace towards the back with his fine baritone.

Towards the end of the final verse, Rufus got up. He'd been seated at the outer end of the pew, and could slip discreetly out of it into the north aisle. Sensing trouble rising like dust in the air, he made his way towards the door. Distractedly he noticed that Giles the farmhand was hiding under the wing of old Challen's voice, mouthing along to the words. The hymn ended as raggedly as it had begun, and a tense silence fell.

Archie marched through it boldly, striding up the main aisle with his surplice billowing behind him. He took up position by the door, just as if today was an ordinary Sunday with the usual collection of sinners under his church roof. He held out a hand towards Drusilla, who'd remained huddled up over her child. "Miss Hazelgrove," he said kindly. "It's good to see you looking so much better. You're very welcome here."

She struggled to her feet, Elspeth clinging to her like a leech. She pushed back the strands of hair that the child had tugged down. Her hat was smart and good of its kind, but to Rufus— coming to a halt at the other side of the door, instinctively bracketing her between himself and Archie—it looked like a disguise, a garland of daisies on a wolf. She let go of Elspeth with one hand, put it frankly and gratefully into Archie's. "Thank you, Thorne. Maria Nettles, are you here?" She scanned the crowd gathering in the aisle behind her: broke into a smile when Mrs Nettles emerged from its ranks. "Maria, thank you. Thank you for caring for my daughter."

Too much for poor Mrs Trigg. She was clinging to a pew end for support, her face brick red, huffing like the bellows of the organ. "*Thorne*?!" she got out at length, dragging Jebediah upright by his scruff as if it were his fault. "Maria?! Your *daughter*, madam, as you dare to claim here in this church, to the shame of any decent lady married in the eyes of God?"

Archie and Rufus exchanged a glance. "Mrs Trigg," Archie began, a dangerous rumble most unlike his everyday tone. "If you'll please recall where you are—"

"It's for your sake I do! *Thorne*, she calls you, as a man would, and a man who is your equal, at that. And you not five minutes done with your sermon! It's for your sake I call this Jezebel woman to account, for the temptations she's drawn you into, and the Reverend Gorringe before you!"

Rufus came to stand at Drusilla's other side. He had no idea what Archie meant to do, but whatever it was, he intended to help. Maybe they could sling Mrs Trigg into the font, or pick her up bodily and roll her downhill into the river, where the breathtaking grip of the water would soon cool her off...

Before either could draw a breath to speak, Mrs Nettles stepped into the breach. "Pardon me," she said, planting herself squarely between Mrs Trigg and Drusilla. "Pardon me, Reverend Thorne and Dr Denby, but gentlemen interfering at times like this only makes things more complicated." She wheeled round to face Mrs Trigg. "Hester, I have known you from school and up, just as my mother knew your mother, who was, if you'll excuse me for reminding you, no better than she should be, not but what I'm glad your old man married her in the nick of time, because he was a decent fella, even if a little bit tardy, and as randy as a rabbit in springtime, from the tales my ma told me."

The choirboys, who had made their way down from the loft and stood open-mouthed till now, as if frozen in mid-chorus, exploded into giggles. Mrs Trigg drew an outraged breath, but Mrs Nettles was just finding her stride. "We all have our skellingtons, Hester, and if the eyes of God isn't more merciful than the eyes of man when he looks into our closets, I call it a shame. I can't speak for Gorringe, but I'll tell you now that *my* vicar never laid hand on woman in a way that a Christian gentleman need blush for. And besides the point if he did!" she added, jerking up a hand to silence Mrs Trigg's next attempt to speak. "Drusilla Hazelgrove is under the protection of the Droyton rectory. If so be it she takes it into her head to run naked under the moon, let she who is without sin—or skellingtons—cast the first stone." She glanced over her shoulder. "Having said which, it's nice to see you as you are today, Miss Hazelgrove, in that lovely frock, and I'm sure we've never clapped eyes on such velvet as that from Ruth Pole's haberdashery." That was the death-blow to Mrs Trigg's lieutenant, who shrank back into the crowd. Mrs Nettles folded her arms. "Now, Reverend, was you and Dr Denby anxious to add a word?"

Archie glanced around the stunned little crowd, frozen in position in the aisles and pews of his church. His face was a picture. "No, Mrs Nettles," he replied, just before the silence began to set in stone. "I... believe you've covered the matter. I'll only say that I do regard Miss Hazelgrove as being under my guardianship. And, since neither she nor her daughter has ever harmed any one of you, I do ask that she be treated civilly. Kindly, if that can possibly be managed." He caught Rufus's eye, gave him the shadow of a wink. "Dr Denby? Anything from you?"

Rufus had nothing. At some point soon, he wanted to leave the church, walk into the woodlands, lie down and laugh until he wept, but for now he was as effectively paralysed as the rest of the congregation. He sensed that Mrs Trigg, though knocked back against the ropes with her ears ringing, was far from out of the fight, and he winced as she drew breath for a riposte.

But Drusilla cut across her, low and clear. "*I* have something to add." She set Elspeth carefully down, then laid a hand on Archie's arm—reached over and caught Rufus by the wrist. "These men are my friends. I mean no disgrace to either. But I know the goddess has been found, and I must see her. The goddess from the wall."

A stone lodged itself in Rufus's gut. "I'm sorry," he said hoarsely, hoping only she and Archie would hear. "I've been meaning to tell you. I took the statue back to the hotel, but..."

"Oh, she isn't with you," Drusilla interrupted him serenely. "She's with Jebediah. Don't be afraid, child—I understand how she calls. But she doesn't belong to you."

Mrs Trigg blanched with fear. "What do you mean, you madwoman?"

"Your boy. Poor boy. Always afraid, always hungry."

"Hungry? How dare you? Nobody in this village eats like my boy. Even when the rationing was on—"

"He wept because he had plenty while the other children went short, and they couldn't forgive him. There's a brotherhood in shared suffering. A lonely boy. So empty. So he takes what he can get."

Jebediah gave a strangled cry. Before Mrs Trigg could stop him, he shot down the aisle towards Drusilla. He slithered to a halt just out of arm's reach, pulled an object from the pocket of his shorts and dropped it at her feet. Then he ducked his head like a bull calf and charged for the door, dodging trousered legs and pushing skirts aside.

Rufus crouched by the little figurine. His hands were shaking. He picked her up, cradled her in one palm. She was undamaged, heavy and perfect and real. Tears of relief tried to burn into his eyes. Archie took hold of his shoulder, and he straightened up, unable to hide a broad grin. "Look. She's here."

"I can see that. Why didn't you tell me she was missing?"

"Because I was..." He looked at his landlady, who was trying to shrink back into the pew, out of the spotlight of attention. "I was so ashamed of losing her. Mrs Trigg, it's all right. I shouldn't have left her out in my room."

She gave a kind of dry squawk. She hadn't made anyone love her in Droyton Parva, and now her child had shown himself a common thief amid the people she'd looked down on for so long. "Jebediah," she rasped, although the boy was far out of earshot, probably on the run back to the village. She backed into the aisle, clutching her handbag to her chest like a shield. Archie reached out to try and stop her as she darted towards the door, but she shrank away and dodged him, plunging out into the daylight.

Archie, Rufus and Drusilla watched her go. The rest of the congregation began to file between them, buzzing with whispers and speculation. Mrs Nettles went out in dignified silence with Alice, who looked as if she'd have liked to be carrying her on her shoulders in a victory parade. Winborn, immediately behind them, seemed much less amused. He glared at Rufus in passing, as though he held him responsible for the chaos that had overtaken Archie's Sunday-morning service.

Which, in a way, he was. He waited until the last stragglers had gone, then turned to Drusilla. "How did you know? About Jebediah, I mean?"

She picked up Elspeth. The child had been falling asleep against her skirt, exhausted with emotion, and now buried her face against her mother's shoulder, pigtails drooping. "As soon as I knew the goddess was found," Drusilla said fervently, "my mind began to clear. Then I felt her calling me from here in the church. So I dressed in the things that women are meant to wear in these strange days, because I didn't wish to make a scandal, and I came here. For the goddess and my daughter. Though..." She looked up at Archie, frowning. "I seem to have caused trouble anyway."

"That's all right. Mrs Trigg's been throwing stones from her glass house for far too long anyway. I'll go and see her later, smooth things over if she'll let me." Archie paused, admiring the little figurine. "I think what Rufus and I would like to know is... how you managed to see through the very sturdy fabric of Jebediah's shorts."

"I didn't. But the closer I got to her, the clearer my mind became, until I could see everything, even things hidden from ordinary view. And I knew she was there, burrowed away by that poor boy, who just wants to *possess* things belonging to somebody else. Oh, he has a box under the floorboards of his room. Pocket watches, a silver cigar case. Let Mrs Trigg be told about it. Let the boy restore everything, quietly, just as he took them, and nobody need know."

Archie glanced at Rufus, wide-eyed. "I... I'll see to it. Drusilla, do you remember what's happened to you since you came to the village?"

"Yes. All of it. I've made the most tremendous nuisance of myself. I don't know how to thank you, Thorne—and you, Denby—for rescuing me."

Her habit of address *was* odd. Like an equal, as Mrs Trigg had said, or like a man... *No*, Rufus suddenly realised, looking at her and Archie caught in a column of sunlight. *Like priestess to priest.* "You can thank me," Archie was replying, "by getting better. Not just for your sake but for Elsp-... Er, for Andrasta."

Drusilla smiled faintly. "It is a strange name. But it was chosen for her, not by me. You've given her a home while I couldn't. May you be blessed for that, all your life long."

"It was no trouble. She eats less than Mrs Nettles' cat, and... Well. We're fond of her now, at the rectory. So I hope you won't mind if I say that we'd like her to stay with us, just until—"

"Ah, I neglected her!" Drusilla rocked the sleeping bundle in her arms. "What would have happened to her if you hadn't taken her in? You can't trust me with her. I understand."

"It's not exactly that. Mrs Nettles has rather rigid ideas about child-rearing, though, and it might be best if the girl had a few days to adjust. She's missed you very deeply, you see. I have an idea." He took Drusilla gently by the arm and guided her out onto the steps. "Sunday afternoons are always open-house at the rectory. We'll have some lunch, and tea on the lawn, and you can see how Andrasta's been living. Spend some time with her—that is, if you feel well enough."

"I do. I feel fine. The goddess is found."

Rufus came to a decision. It defied rationality, but so did many good things in Droyton Parva. He joined Archie and Drusilla on the steps, held out the figurine to her. "You should keep her. I have a feeling she rightly belongs to you."

To his horror, her eyes filled with tears. They spilled down her unaltered face, sudden as relieving rainfall after a drought. "You're kind," she said quietly. "But so very strange, to put such store in *things*. Don't you understand? Knowing she exists is enough."

"Then... what should I do with her?"

"Keep her. You're the famous Rufus Denby. You'll know what to do."

She detached herself from Archie. She shook his hand—upright, friendly and formal—then turned to Rufus and did the same. Mrs Nettles and Alice were waiting by the gate, in the dappling shade of the trees. Mrs Nettles waved and beckoned. "I will go to the rectory," Drusilla said. "Maria seems to wish it, and I wouldn't dare argue with someone who defended me so ably, and..." She stroked the child's hair, cast Archie a glance of woeful amusement. "And who makes pigtails like these. I thank you both."

She descended the steps, balancing the little girl easily. Archie and Rufus stayed where they were until she'd joined the other women. Mrs Nettles opened the gate, flashing a triumphant smile over her shoulder, and Alice blew a kiss—playful but stone-cold sober today—which could have been for Rufus, for both of them, or simply for the sweet breeze swaying the oaks. Between them, she and Mrs Nettles led Drusilla away.

Chapter Thirteen

"Bet you three bob I have her staying at the rectory by tonight."

Rufus's debts were mounting. "I still owe you two about the photographer's car. Besides, the odds are too long against me."

"Well, it's much more practical. I won't have to find the rent for the cottage anymore, and Elspeth—Andrasta—will be in heaven. Strange name for a child, isn't it?"

"I remember where I've heard it now. Andrasta was the goddess Queen Boadicea appealed to before her battle with the Romans. Aren't you concerned about the gossip?"

The wind caught Archie's surplice. Rufus wondered if he'd forgotten he was wearing it. They were making their way slowly down the turf track to the gate. Archie came to a halt by the gatepost, tipping his head back as if his lungs were tight and he needed air. "Do you know, I think I'm past caring? The only person who'd have made a fuss about it is Mrs Trigg, and she's been quenched for a while. It's an enormous house. It ought to be lived in."

Rufus was beginning to recognise his expression of subtle mischief. "Ah, I see. You think to have *two* new lodgers by the end of the day."

"Come on, Rufus. Join us. I have a kid, a dog, a warrior housekeeper and a part-time madwoman. I just need an archaeologist to complete my collection."

A surge of pleasure went through Rufus. It felt like champagne: hard to bottle up, intoxicating, dangerous. Bubbles rising in his chest and blood. The goddess was safe, a warm weight in the pocket of his waistcoat. He hitched himself up onto the drystone wall by the gate. "You don't understand. It's all the more imperative that I stay with Mrs Trigg now. Granted she's horrible, but if I walk out and stay with you, she'll be all the more disgraced."

"Her child stole your statue, Rufus."

"And is probably getting the life whaled out of him at this very minute. You heard what Drusilla said. He thieves because he feels empty. Can't you imagine that?"

Archie's attention settled unfathomably on him. "Yes. I can."

"And she's not my statue. First thing tomorrow, I write up my report as far as I can, and then I escort her to London in person, as I should have done in the first place."

"It seems to me that Drusilla wanted you to keep her."

"She's not a lucky charm or a rabbit's foot. She's a crucially significant artefact. If her antiquity can be proved... Do you know how few pre-Roman representations of deity we have in this country? There's the Grimes Graves figurine, but she's problematical, and the Ballachulish carving... Nothing like this."

"All right, Dr Denby. And... after you've done your archaeological duty..." Archie came to stand in front of him. He laid a hand on Rufus's knee, as if that were the natural and obvious thing to do, as if they'd been brothers or lifelong friends. "After that, will you come back to Droyton?"

"Yes, of course. I've hardly scratched the surface of the work I need to do in the church." Rufus was astonished at the calm in his voice. The cool of the stones under his backside, the scratch-caress of the lichen where his palm was resting on the wall, the warmth of Archie's hand—these things became vivid to him as symbols in a dream. "Your sermon was very good. I... couldn't help but notice that you never once mentioned God."

"Ah. That's right. I don't believe in him anymore."

"Isn't that something of an obstacle for a vicar?"

"You have no idea."

Rufus let go his grip on the top of the wall. Slowly, like a brother or a friend, he put his hand on top of Archie's. Strong bones, firm-sprung tendons: he wrapped his fingers round them and let his grip close. "Is it because of what happened to you in France? The things you saw?"

"Partly, but... Tell me, Rufus—do *you* believe?"

"Yes," he responded readily, surprising himself. He hadn't known. "Not necessarily in a church God, a Bible God, but—something. The hills and the trees, perhaps. The broad sunlit uplands. You."

"Me?"

"Yes. You're part of it, aren't you—all that splendour."

Archie swallowed hard. His lucid gaze had clouded, and Rufus could feel the leap of the pulse in his wrist. "And yet you saw worse things than I did. And unlike me, you don't talk about it."

"That's because I don't remember much."

"The parts you do remember—*would* you tell me someday?"

Yes. This man only. "Someday."

***

Archie's Sunday afternoons were as mixed and generous as his butcher nights. Half the congregation had made its way to his orchard and lawns, it seemed. Old Lady Birch was enthroned in a wicker armchair with an air of having been there for some time, at least as long as the foolish Christians had been tugging at God's coat-tails in the church. Alice had rolled an elderly gramophone out through the French doors of the dining room and was gingerly dancing a Lindy hop with Giles. Alice's pretty brow was rucked, as if she could sense something not *quite* conventional about her partner, but Giles was simply a picture of adoration and bliss.

Apple blossom drifted. Entering through the garden gate, Rufus felt as if he were taking his place in a painting: every detail rich and real, all seen through a transmuting lens of dream or magic. He and Archie had walked slowly back up Pilgrim Lane from the church, barely talking. Archie had hung up his surplice in the vestry, but wasn't quite back in his everyday skin. He'd stayed close by Rufus's side, his knuckles occasionally brushing the back of Rufus's hand. He looked without recognition at Winborn as the doctor came striding across the lawn, then blinked and pushed his fringe back from his brow. "What is it, Paul? Everything all right?"

"Yes, fine. Just a small business matter. A word with you alone?"

Winborn looked particularly sandy and annoyed today, as if he found the summer breeze abrasive. Archie went with him, casting a comical look of dismay over his shoulder at Rufus. Mrs Nettles appeared promptly to fill the gap at Rufus's side, holding out a glass of the elderflower cordial that had revived him on his first visit here. "Here, Dr Denby. Lunch is sandwiches on the sideboard indoors, so help yourself when you're ready."

"Thank you. I will. Er... that was quite a defence you made on Miss Hazelgrove's behalf."

"Quite a spectacle I made of myself, is more like it." She nodded serenely. "It seemed to me a shame that such a pleasant person should be kept from the society of her neighbours, just because she doesn't happen to meet Hester Trigg's views of moral decency. Doesn't it seem so to you?"

"Yes, it does." Rufus examined her curiously. "Have you lived here in Droyton all your life, Mrs Nettles?"

He wasn't sure why he'd asked. She smiled, though, as if the question had been a natural follow-on to their conversation. "All my life, and my parents and their parents before me. There's always been a Nettles in the parish register, just as there's always been a Trigg. There's an ancient enmity there. You'll have to excuse me, Doctor. Andrasta is upstairs helping Miss Hazelgrove choose a room to sleep in, now that we've got her safely here, and the Reverend will want me to make sure the bedlinen's fresh. You could dance with Miss Winborn, if you liked, or go and talk to old Lady Birch." Having safely disposed of him, she began to bustle off, then turned to look back, lips pursed. "Andrasta! What a name. And she's gone and taken her nice pigtails out, as well."

Rufus made his way across the lawn, trying to absorb yet another explosively-unfolding aspect of this strange place. *Ancient enmity!* Such dignity and conviction in the phrase, from a plump housekeeper in a flowered apron, as if her ancestors and Mrs Trigg's had once faced one another across a battlefield, swords in hand, pennants flying...

Alice caught his eye, and he wondered if he should take up the suggestion to go and cut in on Giles. Then a crushing sense of his own unfairness overwhelmed him. He remembered her kiss, and the wildly different sensation of Archie's hand on his knee— how one had been a mild pleasure, like sunshine or the brush of cool leaves against his face; how the other had made his heart race and burn. Did he really intend to use some poor woman as a passport to an ordinary life? Alice Winborn was worthy of wholehearted, whole-fleshed dedication, something he could no more give her than he could fly. He was ashamed. When she paused at the end of her next gyration, she was blushing deeply too.

A sadness passed between them, sudden and vast as a cloud shutting out the Maytime sun. Rufus turned away, relieved at the distraction of the dog he'd briefly owned bounding towards him through the vegetable beds. "Pippin, get out of there. Come here." She dashed to his side and began to sniff him over as if checking on the changes wrought on him by this house and its inhabitants. Her own were considerable, even since the day before. "Look at you. Scarcely a fleck of mange left on you at all. If we stay with Archie, will we all end up happy and fat?"

"That does seem to be the general effect of the house."

He looked up sharply. Drusilla was standing in front of him, holding Andrasta by the hand. She'd taken off her oddly unsuitable little hat, and her dark mane was down around her shoulders. The child was her reproduction in miniature, the corkscrew pigtails gone, pale face transformed by joy. "Hello, Miss Hazelgrove," he said awkwardly. "Andrasta seems pleased to have you here."

"She has a forgiving nature. I injured her greatly by my neglect."

"You were ill, not neglectful, as I understand it."

"Thank you for taking the benign view. The effect on my child was the same, however. I must speak with Lady Birch."

These ideas seemed in some way connected. The little girl stretched out her free hand to Rufus. "Mother," she said clearly, drawing her to a halt. "Dr Denby should come too."

"Ah. Yes, that might be for the best. Do you mind, Denby?"

"Not in the least, but..."

Drusilla nodded and set off, not waiting for him to finish. Andrasta followed, towing him along. "My mother isn't dead," she informed him placidly. "Not mad, neither."

"I can see that. So you can forget all about those things now, can't you, you odd little monkey?"

"Oh, no. One can never forget them *completely*. Lady Birch will die now."

She was so absurdly serious. Rufus snatched her up on impulse, wondering if he'd regret it. He hoisted her onto his shoulders, and to his relief she burst into hooting laughter. *"I am the soul of nature,"* she yelled, *"who gives life to the universe! Before my face, beloved of gods and of men, let thy innermost soul be enfolded in the rapture of the infinite!"*

Drusilla glanced back over her shoulder. "Really, child," she murmured, not as if displeased, and up ahead, in the leafy bower the apple trees formed around her wickerwork throne, Lady Birch stirred and sat up, opening her eyes wide. To Rufus's astonishment, Drusilla went down on her knees before her in the grass. "I'm here," she said, smiling up at the old lady. "Here, at last."

Lady Birch wriggled forward to the edge of her seat. "Is it really you?" She put out a frail hand and stroked Drusilla's face. "You came to me before, but your spirit wasn't within you. I didn't know you."

"No. The road here was long, and I was a stranger to myself. But I have been found, and so has the goddess, and this man here is guarding her. Denby, may she see?"

"What? Oh. Yes, of course." Rufus lifted Andrasta down and took the figurine from his pocket. "Can either of you tell me what she means to you? What you know about her?"

"It would take a lifetime I don't have," the old lady said wonderingly, running her hand over the little statue's curves. "And you wouldn't believe me. Your manhood condemns you to seek the truth through reason, though you're better equipped than most to make the attempt." Suddenly she looked up at him, eyes bright. "And Thorne will help you. Find you, when you become more lost than Drusilla was, and more of a stranger to yourself. I'm sorry such pain lies before you. How harsh it all seems! But my part's played out now, and I have to die."

She settled back in her chair. Drusilla took both her hands, and she nodded comfortably all around her, as if bidding farewell without grief to a world that had served its turn and owed her nothing. "From the earth to the earth," she declared, closing her eyes.

"From thee all things proceed, and to thee they must return." Drusilla lowered her head. The child began a weird, musical keening, and Pippin, out of nerves or sheer fellow-feeling, tipped back her head and joined in.

"For God's sake," Rufus breathed. "Lady Birch, you're not about to die. Dr Winborn's looking after you, and I know you don't like it, but..." He trailed to a halt. One of the traits he'd acquired during his military service was an absolute inability to kid himself concerning life and death. He leaned over Drusilla and cautiously pressed his fingertips to the old woman's throat. "Pippin, stop that. Elspeth—Andrasta—you, too. Go and fetch Dr Winborn, right now."

She stopped her chanting and looked at him serenely. "He can't do anything. But if you wish."

"I *do* wish. Scarper."

She trotted off, the dog at her heels. Rufus didn't know why he didn't just attach fairy wings to the pair of them and let them fly. He sat down unsteadily on the bench beside the old lady's chair. "Miss Hazelgrove, I'm terribly sorry. I'm afraid your friend may have been right."

Drusilla didn't move. A time passed, marked only by the fall and dance of apple blossom, and the slow approach of Alice,

Giles and the others among the Reverend's guests who'd become aware of the stillness in their midst.

Winborn broke their ranks apart. Archie was behind him, looking grim in a way Rufus hadn't yet seen, grey around the gills and sick. He caught Drusilla as Winborn jostled her aside, and helped her to her feet. "Paul, be careful."

"Why? Which one of the cast of helpless idiots you insist on gathering around you do you want me to watch out for now— Drusilla Hazelgrove, who should have been locked away months ago, or your new friend here, who sat and let an old lady die without lifting a hand to help her?"

"Oh, Paul," Alice remonstrated. "She's been talking about dying for months."

"Talking is one thing. Doing it's another."

He was right, Rufus realised with a cold shock. Why hadn't he tried to revive her? Her departure had been so peaceful, so absolute... "Sorry," he rasped, scrambling upright. "I should have done something. Can I help now?"

Winborn finished looking for a pulse in the fragile, blue-veined wrist. "No. She's gone, all right. Maybe if you'd come and got me right away, instead of sending this addle-pated changeling..."

Drusilla straightened on Archie's arm, jerking her head up suddenly. "What an enormous fool you are, Winborn," she said, her voice an exact replica of the old lady's, with all her own vigour and new sanity behind it. "As if this poor lost soldier could affect such events! We die when we find our true successor, and not a moment before. Kindly cease insulting my child and my friends, and make arrangements for the dignified disposal of Lady Birch's remains."

***

"She died in the right place," Archie said, lighting a cigarette and flashing Rufus a quick, edgy smile. "With the vicar at hand, I mean. Her doctor, too. I think she's even got her solicitor floating around somewhere amongst the mob who came back from the church. The coroner's arrived from Ashfield, and... and Mrs Nettles is a grand hand at the laying-out."

He waved away smoke. Rufus guessed that the fit of coughing was worth it, after what he'd been through in the last hour or so, and carefully patted his back as the convulsion seized him. "Are you all right?"

"Christ, I really shouldn't do this to myself. I wanted to say... I'm so sorry for the way Winborn spoke to you. I should've told him off."

Something deep inside Rufus which had noticed the omission and cared about it left off aching. He scanned the garden to make sure no-one had found Archie out in his secret smoker's refuge behind the Norton's shed. He'd followed him here wordlessly upon his hollow-eyed emergence from the house. "Don't be ridiculous. I can tell people off for myself if I have to. *Could* I have done more for her, though?"

"Not a thing. She had a weak heart, as Paul knew perfectly well. I don't know why he attacked you."

Rufus knew, or at least was beginning to pull together the threads of understanding. Nothing to do with Winborn's half-baked scheme to marry his niece to the vicar. He looked up at the sun-mellowed wall of the house, where Drusilla had found her place and where he'd have let Archie find one for him too, Mrs Trigg or no Mrs Trigg, by that evening. He'd forgotten the very possibility of a sense of *home*. But he was hurting these people—hurting Alice, hurting the one man whose wellbeing meant enough to break him out of the trance that had enclosed him for so long—by his efforts to remain. "It doesn't matter," he said, and because he'd come to his decision, reached boldly and in friendship alone to put an arm around Archie's shoulders. "I'd best be going now. Don't worry about anything, old fellow. All right?"

Archie stood very still. His breathing quickened. Then he jolted away as if burned, and Rufus knew that Winborn's work was done. "You don't have to leave."

"I do, as it happens. I have my report to write up, and... it's best."

"Let me walk you up the road. I've done everything I can for the old lady, and I just get under Mrs Nettles' feet at times like these."

"Come on, then. Better put your ciggie out, in case she's watching from the window."

Out in the lane, walking quietly at Archie's side—primly, tamely, a foot of empty space between them, none of the shoulder-jostling and hand-to-hand touches of their return from the church—Rufus allowed himself a vision. It never would have surfaced, except that he was sure that his proclivities had been laid on the table for discussion by Winborn, and they were like the devil, coming the more readily the more you feared him at the sound of his name. In the vision, Mrs Trigg wasn't on guard duty in or outside the Maidens'. The entrance hall was quite empty, no-one on the stairs. Archie said *let me see this room of yours*, and they went upstairs quietly, and no-one saw. Archie was weary after the upheavals of the day: took his shoes off and stretched out on the bed. Said *I know it's wrong, Rufus, but I want you. Come here.*

Blood surged in Rufus's groin, a tingling rush. His thigh muscles cramped in desire. The cut of his borrowed trousers wouldn't hide an erection. Horrified at himself, he turned off the track and leaned his elbows on the fence. "What's wrong?" Archie asked, coming to stand beside him. "Did you see something?"

"No. Er—that is, yes, I did. A bird." Bad choice, bad choice. He knew nothing about birds. He took a punt that Archie didn't either. "A lesser-spotted jackhammer, I think."

"A what? Do you perhaps mean woodpecker?"

Restrained laughter in Archie's voice. That was bad too, erotic and delightful. *Wood* was bad, and *pecker* was worse, and any minute the ground would open and swallow Rufus up. "Yes. That's what I meant."

"Interesting. I've never seen one of those around here."

Oh, for a cold drystone wall to lean on! As it was, the fence gaped open to the caressing summer breeze, and he was clasped and clustered in May blossom from knees to waist, its fishy, intriguing odours spiralling warmly around him. He'd forgotten who he was. Everything had gone underground with his memories of the battle of Fort Roche—his strength, his hopes, his youth, the very fact of his manhood, thirty five years old and still at powerful, unwanted sexual prime. Winborn hadn't done the trick after all. Archie was reaching for him in concern. Rufus had to warn him.

He tried to turn, and grazed his kneecap off stone. "Look," he said in desperation. "I think there's some kind of waymarker in here."

"Sure it's not a jackhammer?"

"Shut up. I'm an archaeologist, not a bird-spotter." Between them they cleared away enough of the hawthorn to expose an egg-shaped rock like a river boulder, unhewn except for a string of eroded letters. "Have you ever seen this before?"

Archie leaned in close, not helping Rufus one bit. "No. You have a gift for showing me parts of my parish I'd never have discovered on my own. Is that a milestone?"

"No, I don't think so. It says..." Rufus ran his fingers over the mossy indentations. "Pilgrim Lane. No—Pilgrim *Way*. That's odd—the change of name, I mean. Was the church ever a pilgrimage destination, do you know?"

"What—relics and suchlike? Here's a skull of St John as a young man, and..."

"Here's his skull when he was old?" Rufus released a breath, dared to laugh. Engaging his brains on an archaeological problem was cooling matters off down below. Any moment now he'd be able to stand up. "It's been painted white at some point, and the script looks seventeenth century or older."

"That's incredible. No, we don't have any relics in the church, skulls or other parts. I wonder when the track got demoted to a lane."

"*Way* does sound more ceremonial, doesn't it? Crowds of dusty-footed devotees on their way to Santiago, that kind of thing. As for my gift, I just seem to stumble over things, or have them fall out of the masonry when you knock bits of your church down."

"We make a good team, don't we? In our own way."

Rufus swallowed hard, dug his nails into his palms. He straightened and faced Archie squarely. "In our own way. But—"

"Rufus? Rufus, darling—is that you?"

The cry came like a bird's call through the fragrant air. Less like a jackhammer—distractedly Rufus wondered if Archie would ever let him live that one down—than a peacock, high-pitched and strange. No-one had ever called him *darling* except Henry in a temper, twisting the word into a bitter insult, and...

Rosemary. Rufus stumbled out of the hedgerow onto the verge. He'd almost forgotten his sister's existence, in the bubbling Droyton cauldron of people and event. Maybe he was hallucinating her now. The mad thought flashed past him that she'd come for Lady Birch's funeral: was dressed in black from head to toe, negotiating the ruts of the lane in precipitous heels.

The effect of her was almost comic. Then he saw the grief-scoured pallor of her face, and strode to meet her, holding out his hands. "Rosie! What are you doing here?"

She'd used to be so earthy. Now it was as if she'd been bound and gagged behind the elaborate wrought-iron of her new prejudices. She held his hands for a brief instant, then disengaged and began brushing invisible dust off her jacket, straightening her pillbox hat with its token veil. "Awful journey," she cried, "just awful, even in first class. Mannerless conductor... wouldn't hold the door for me... and then the so-called hotel, with the most *extraordinary* person in charge, speaking to me as if I were just anybody, telling me she wasn't paid to know your whereabouts at all hours—her very words!—but the chances were you were down this lane somewhere, *hobnobbing*—her word again—with the vicar. And I said that was *highly* unlikely, since no-one in our family had ever been given to *hobnobbing* of any kind, and..."

She ran out of steam. Tears were gently rolling down her face, making tracks in her powder. Rufus lifted the silly little half-veil and tried to brush them away, and Archie, who'd come up quietly behind him, produced another of his clean white handkerchiefs. "Good afternoon," he said, passing the handkerchief to her. "I'm Archie Thorne. I hope I can help."

Her eyes flew wide at the sight of Archie's dog-collar. "Oh. You *are* with the vicar." She looked at Rufus with new respect, as if he might be making decent friends at last. She drew herself up. "Good afternoon, Reverend. I'm Dr Denby's sister. Rosemary Spence, wife of Major Charles Spence of the British Response Force. That is, former wife." She blanched in fear that Thorne would think anything so unseemly as divorce might have touched her life. "That is, I'm his widow."

"I'm very sorry for your loss."

"Thank you. But that's not... I'm not in mourning because..."
She choked, sobbed, and at last gave up her reason for being here.
"My baby died."

"Oh, hell." Rufus turned away. That poor scrap, in his
cavernous cradle in Mayfair! His stomach lurched in pity. He'd
been overseas when the child had been born. He'd returned to
find Rosie newly widowed, newly a mother, holding the wailing
boy out to him as if he could change something, turn back time.
He hadn't known what to do.

Archie would have known. Ashamed of his selfish reaction,
Rufus looked back. Rosie was resting her brow on the broad,
black-clad shoulder, sobbing luxuriously. She'd come down by
train. Rufus imagined the journey for such a woman: sitting
upright in her compartment, lips clenched tight, inwardly
strangling rather than let a single tear disgrace her dignity. Archie
had taken ten seconds and a dozen or so words to crack her,
relieve her, end her arid drought. "Rosie, I'm so sorry," he said
awkwardly. "What terrible news. Why did the brigadier let you
come down alone?"

She got her head up, blew her nose copiously on Archie's
handkerchief, and looked for a moment like the girl Rufus had
known. "He doesn't know I'm here. He wouldn't have allowed
me. I've got to talk to you, Rufus."

"Of course. Come back to—"

"To the rectory, please," Archie interrupted gently. "Your
sister needs a rest, I think. A nice cup of tea, and..."

And the elderflower cordial, the apple wine, an invitation to a
butcher night, and sudden and subtle immersion in the whole
weltering world of life, love and death that swirled within the
rectory's shabby, beautiful walls. Rosie might survive it but Rufus
knew he would not, not again. He'd seize Archie's shoulder
behind the bike shed, or in the leather-fragrant library, and he'd

kiss him, and bring what was left of the world down around their ears.

Thank God their walk had brought them almost to the end of the lane. The rectory lay quarter of a mile behind them, and the Maidens' was just across the road. Rosie was swaying on her feet. "I think we'd better take her to the inn. She's dead-beat."

"Are you sure? I could run back and fetch the Norton, and..."

"What—pop her on the back?" The Rosie of his youth would have loved such a ride, but was hobbled today in a close-fitting skirt. "She'd have to sit sidesaddle."

"Ah. Yes, perhaps you're right."

"Will you bring her? I'll go ahead and smooth the way with Mrs Trigg."

"Of course. Come along, Mrs Spence. What a dreadful time you must have had! You'll be all right now."

Rufus set off at a run. He had to get clear of Archie's nimbus, the gentle gravity that drew all weary, sorrowful creatures to him for help and rest. It was just after lunchtime on a Sunday, and the Maidens' was less of a ghost ship than usual, a handful of tourists and locals making their way out of the dining room. Rufus dodged past them on the kerb and in the entrance hall, and found Mrs Trigg behind her usual desk, swiping viciously at dust motes on a lampshade with a feather duster.

She actually cringed at the sight of him. "Dr Denby!"

"Hello, Mrs Trigg. I was wondering, could I possibly—"

"Is it the police?"

"I'm sorry?"

"The police. You'll be wanting to bring them here. Because of Jebediah."

"Police? No, not at all. I just wanted..."

She dropped her feather duster like a knight surrendering his lance. "If I'd known," she rasped, "if I'd known for one second that the little brute was thieving..."

"Please don't concern yourself about it now. Though that does remind me—Miss Hazelgrove said he had some other things hidden under a board in his room, and if you were to give them back to their owners, there needn't be any more trouble."

The poor woman crossed herself with an unsteady hand. She'd aged ten years since Rufus had last seen her, and he guessed that her child's disgrace in the church had been in some ways the worst thing ever to befall her. "How does that witch know?"

"I don't think she's a witch—at least not in the sense that you ought to insult her with the word."

"I didn't mean no insult! I only meant—"

She was genuinely frightened. "Please, Mrs Trigg. There'll be no police, and Drusilla doesn't mean you any harm either. I just wanted to ask if you had a sitting room, somewhere private where I could speak to my sister, who's come down to visit me."

It wasn't Mrs Trigg's day. Her mouth dropped open. "A woman—a lady, that is—all in black? Your sister?"

Rufus fought depression. What had gone sour, in this tight-knit little English world, to produce the sharp-eyed doctors and landladies, the self-appointed guardians lying in wait to pounce on every human interaction and drag it down into the mire? A genocide had taken place. The H-bomb had dropped, nations had fallen, and still they squatted here like toads down holes, watching, waiting. Had the woman really thought poor Rosie was some kind of girlfriend, a tootsie on hire from London for the day? "Yes," he said tiredly. "My sister. She's in mourning for her child."

Mrs Trigg would have been ready to sell her own kid to the first bidder in the church that morning. Nonetheless a true horror touched her now. "Poor lady. I'll have the guests' parlour got ready. It looks on the courtyard, just like your room. I'll have some tea sent in."

"Thank you." Rufus hesitated. Mrs Trigg's wounds were mostly self-inflicted, but he still didn't like rubbing salt in them. "Reverend Thorne is bringing her over now."

She gave a kind of strangled groan and turned away. Rufus watched her go, then ran to help Rosemary up the steps.

She and Archie had picked Dr Winborn up, too. Winborn had one arm, Archie the other, and between them they steered her through the empty dining room and into the parlour. "Hello again, Denby," Winborn said brusquely, giving Rufus a politely savage look. "I gather this lady's your sister."

"Yes, she is. Rosemary Spence. Rosie, this is Paul Winborn, the village doctor here."

"Oh, Doctor," Rosemary gasped. "How fortunate that you happened along. I really don't feel well at all."

Winborn nodded soothingly. "Come and sit down. Reverend Thorne says you've had a long journey, and not much to eat. I'll take a quick glance at you, if I may."

Archie helped him deposit her in a stiff pink armchair, then retreated towards the window, drawing Rufus with him. He surveyed the airless, lightless room, its polished surfaces and dying aspidistra. "Good heavens," he said faintly. "Have you been spending your evenings in here?"

"You haven't really given me the chance." Rufus drew back a swathe of net curtain and looked out. "It's horrible, somehow, isn't it? Gives me the creeps."

"Me too, even more than Pippin's hole in the church. But why?"

"Something to do with this yard."

"Don't let Mrs T hear you. That's her pride and joy."

"I thought Jebediah was her pride and joy."

Archie's mouth quirked in brief mischief. "Not any more. Look, Rosemary is in good hands with Winborn, and she wants to talk to you. I'd better leave you to it."

"Don't go."

The plea came out with an urgency Rufus hadn't intended. Archie sobered. "Are you all right?"

"She wants to talk to me, yes. What about?"

Nothing good. The message passed silently between them. Archie raised his voice so Rosemary could hear. "Mrs Spence, may I order some tea for us all? I'd like to join you, if you don't mind."

"Please," Rosemary said weakly. "I couldn't speak in front of just anyone, you understand, but... a doctor, and a man of God..."

Winborn had been taking her pulse. "You'd like me to stay, too?"

"If you would. I haven't been well lately, and my nerves..."

He gave the faintest shrug. "As you wish."

Rufus felt suddenly sick. He sank down onto the overstuffed sofa, and didn't look at Archie as he came to sit beside him. "I've already asked for some tea. What have you come to say to me, Rosie? This isn't just about poor Charlie."

"No, it isn't, although... although..."

"Although it's often easier to start at the beginning." Archie leaned forward, quietly attentive. He might not be a man of God in the sense Rosie meant it, but for an atheist, Rufus couldn't help but think he made a bloody good vicar. "What happened to your little boy?"

"Nobody really knows. That's partly what's so hard. He was always small and weak, and one night he just... went to sleep. The brigadier was so disappointed." Rosie smoothed her hair and sat up a little, as if even now she found her connections a source of pride. "Brigadier Spence is my father-in-law, Dr Winborn. He

took me in—that is, invited me to share his home in Mayfair—
after I was widowed."

Winborn frowned. "And he was... *disappointed*, you say, by the
child's death, rather than—"

"Oh, he was grief-stricken too, of course. Everything was
proper. You couldn't imagine a better funeral than the one he
arranged. I'd have asked you, Rufus, only..."

Only he'd have shot me on sight. "It's all right. I understand."

"But Charlie was meant to be his heir, you see, since Charles
was gone. And I think he believed that if little Charlie had been a
bit stronger, or if he'd made a little more of an *effort*, I suppose—
or if I had..."

"Oh, Rosie. You were a good mother. Nobody could have
tried harder."

"Yes, but it wasn't enough, you see." She was crying again,
hopelessly now, not bothering to wipe the tears away. "I know the
brigadier's very fond of me in his way. But since the baby died,
I..."

She broke off as the door creaked open. Mrs Trigg crept in,
burdened by the weight of a wooden tray. She put Rufus in mind
of a strutting barnyard cockerel who'd fallen into the mud. She
avoided Archie's eyes as he took the tray from her. "Will that be
all, gentlemen?"

"Yes," Archie said. "Thank you. Look, Mrs Trigg, I'm sure Dr
Denby's already told you there's no need to—"

"Yes, Reverend," she interrupted him dismally. "You're very
kind. Very kind, I'm sure."

Rufus and Archie watched her go. "What a strange person,"
Rosie said, as soon as the door was closed. The interruption had
given her a chance to compose herself, and since her marriage
she'd taken a sickly pleasure in looking down on other women.

"She was rather rude to me when I arrived. Now she seems quite tame."

"Yes," Archie said absently. "I think she'd have preferred a stand-up fistfight to that scene this morning."

"I'm sorry?"

"Oh—nothing." Archie set the tray down, poured the tea and handed it round. "You were telling us about your father-in-law."

"Er... yes. He's a wonderful man, Vicar. Fought in the first war, and ever so many medals. He believes—and quite rightly too—that everyone should make an effort. That's how *this* war was won, he says."

"Interesting!" Archie stirred his tea. "Have you read *Dombey and Son*, Mrs Spence?"

"Well, I... I'm sure I did at school, but..."

Rufus had read it. He got to his feet, unable to contain the tingling rise of anger in his spine. "Rosie, are you telling me the brigadier's making you feel bad about losing Charlie? As if it was somehow your fault?"

"Oh, no. Of course he isn't." She set her cup down with an unsteady hand. When she spoke again, it was in the plain Sussex accent she and Rufus had learned at their parents' homely fireside, in their kindergarten school. "But you have to see it from his point of view. I'm living in his house. As long as I was his son's wife, the mother of his grandson, that was all right. With Charles *and* the baby gone, though—what am I now?"

Nobody. No relation, the last link severed. Spence wasn't a man to respect the bonds of a marriage he'd so violently opposed. If Rosie had possessed other attractions for the old goat, she'd either refused him or he'd lost interest: she had the air of a woman on the thinnest of ice. Rufus began to pace. "You don't have to live there. I don't have a place of my own just now—not much money, either—but that'll change. You can live with me. I'll help you."

Her mouth tightened. Maybe he wasn't much of a prospect even for a woman facing homelessness. "That's just it, Rufus. You can help me right now."

A new hardness had entered her tone. Peripherally Rufus saw Archie come onto the alert, an immobility of tension. "What can I do?"

"Do your new friends here know about Charles, and the horrible allegations against him?"

"Of course not." Rufus swallowed dryly, remembering how Archie had guarded Drusilla's story until they were both neck-deep in it. "That wasn't my secret to tell."

"If only it was a secret. That wretched corporal who came out of his coma at Farley Cross won't retract his lies." The Mayfair gloss was coming back again, the cut-glass vowels. "Reverend Thorne, Dr Winborn, I hate to speak of this, but I know I can rely on your discretion, and perhaps you can help my brother see things the right way. My husband died in battle for his country. He received the Victoria Cross for his heroic actions at Fort Roche. Now a deluded little NCO who was injured there claims that Charles committed certain acts—not just of cowardice, but *atrocities*, and against his own men."

She'd begun to tap her palm off one arm of her chair in her fervour. The rhythm of it struck Rufus as somehow vile, and he stopped at the end of his pacing line and sat down on the windowsill. *Not just cowardice, but atrocities. Bang, bang, bang...* "Nobody will listen to that poor corporal, Rosie. Not when senior officers are denying the story."

"But they *are* listening. Corporal Berry is well enough to appear before the board of investigators now, and as for the senior officers—there aren't any. There was only you."

Perhaps if Rufus repeated it often enough, the truth would stick home. Perhaps with Archie there to hear it... "Rosie, I'd do anything to change this. But I just... don't... remember."

"I know. I know. But I came here to tell you—not just about Charlie, but something exciting the brigadier's team of specialists have been doing at his hospital in Suffolk. It's a new place, Rufus, right beside the sea—oh, lovely, really, more like an hotel than an institution. They're helping shellshocked soldiers—men like you— to get back to normal. To get their memories back."

The room's atmosphere changed. Rufus had been staring at the carpet: now he lifted his head to find the source of the crackle in the air. Archie had set aside his attitude of benign listening along with his teacup. He was bolt upright, attentive. "Explain to me please, Mrs Spence," he said, and his growl was back too, the one he'd used on Winborn when the doctor had unwittingly crossed a line. "What's the nature of this... institution? What do you know about their methods?"

"Oh—very little, of course. The brigadier only said how effective it was. Something about electric-shock treatment, and lots of peace and quiet and fresh air. He said it might do Rufus so much good."

Rufus folded his arms. "Rosie," he said. "Did the brigadier send you here?"

"No! Didn't I tell you? I had to break the news about Charlie to you face to face, and he'd never have let me..." She trailed off with a sigh of impatience. Whatever had become of her in the Mayfair house, she hadn't yet grown a thick enough skin to persist in an outright lie. "Damn you. When Charlie died, he said I should come down and tell you about the hospital, because you'd never have listened to it coming from him. He said maybe Charlie's death would help soften you up."

"Ah, Rosie, have I been *hard* about this? I swear, if I'd had the least recall of anything that happened to me between Fort Roche and waking up in England—"

"Don't you see? This is your chance! Think about the disgrace—to me, to the brigadier, to..." She'd been about to add her son to the list of victims, and she paled as she remembered. But Rufus was a problem she could get her teeth into, something she could change. "Tell me that you'll try."

Archie got to his feet. He was an imposing figure, on the rare occasions when he wanted to impose. He was watching Rufus with an odd intensity. "So, Mrs Spence... your proposal is that your brother should—I don't know, accompany you back to London, perhaps, and place himself in the hands of your father-in-law, who'll then arrange for his admission to the hospital in Suffolk?"

In that moment, Rufus wanted to die. It sounded so sane, coming from Archie, so bloody reasonable, and why not? Sick men went to hospitals to get better. Archie had been his friend. Why would he not want Rufus to find a cure? Rosie had brightened. "Yes," she said, "essentially. But the brigadier is very generous, really. He wouldn't drag Rufus back to London—he'd send someone here to collect him."

"Over my dead body, Mrs Spence."

Winborn sat up sharply. "Archie, don't be a fool. This is an excellent chance for Dr Denby to—"

"Be quiet, both of you." Archie got up. He turned his back on Rufus, as if he was no longer part of the conversation. "Think about it. Here's this man—a soldier come back from the war. I was there for long enough myself to know that the actions he was involved in, the battles, were... incomprehensibly savage."

"I'm aware of that," Rosie managed feebly. "My husband died in one."

"You mustn't use your loss as a lever to influence your brother. I've had an interesting few days since he arrived. He's the quiet sort, isn't he? But I've seen him jump into a river to save a stranger, then into falling rubble to save me. And yet something so bad happened to him during the battle for Fort Roche that even *his* nerves wouldn't stand it. So he forgot."

To sit behind Archie's shielding right shoulder and hear himself discussed in the third person—as if he wasn't there—was a luxury Rufus couldn't permit himself. "Archie, don't," he said uncomfortably. "Rosie doesn't need to hear all this."

"I'm afraid she does, and so do you. Just imagine, Mrs Spence. Something so dreadful that even a battle-hardened soldier, the kind of man who jumps into rivers, had to wipe it out. And you want to force him to remember."

Rosie had her own kind of courage. She took the force of Archie's words full-on. "No," she said painfully. "I don't. But the brigadier says—"

"Your brother will remember in his own good time. To force him—to shock it out of him with electricity—strikes me as so barbaric I'm astounded you'd consider it even for a second. And, with all due respect, bugger the brigadier."

Winborn pushed upright. "Archie! That's enough."

Archie looked at him curiously. "Is it, Paul? I'm beginning to feel as if I never really got started."

A tap at the door broke their confrontation. Jebediah, still tearstained, put his head into the room. "Begging your pardon, Doctor," he said dolefully, "but Ma says to tell you Mrs Pole is in a 'pologetic fit."

Winborn sighed in exasperation. "I assume you mean apoplectic, you little ignoramus, though the other sort would be nice, and long overdue for calling me out night and day with her imaginary illnesses. I'm afraid you'll have to excuse me, Mrs Spence. Will you be all right?"

"Oh, can't you stay? I feel you understand me, whereas the Reverend and my brother—"

She was about to hang on to Winborn's coat-tails. Rufus had to end this. Something inside him was quietly falling apart with the relief and surprise of his new friend's defence, but he couldn't allow it. And although Rosie had stopped tapping the arm of her chair, the beat of it had stayed with him, growing louder. Soon he would have to get away. He took hold of Archie's arm. *"Bugger the brigadier,* Archie?"

He couldn't quite iron out the ripple of amusement from his tone. Even Rosie looked as if, in another world, she might have laughed. But Archie flushed up to the eyeballs. "Yes. I'm terribly sorry. Unforgivable way to speak to your sister."

"Obviously I can't allow it. I can't let you speak for me like this either, even though..." *Even though I love you for it.* "Winborn, you don't need to stay. My discussion with Mrs Spence is over. As soon as she's had something to eat, I'll see her back to her train."

Winborn surveyed him coldly. "Very well. Mrs Spence, it's been a pleasure to meet you, even in such difficult circumstances. Reverend Thorne will take care of you—won't you, Archie?"

"Yes. Yes, of course."

The door had barely closed behind him when Rosie broke once more into snuffling tears. "Over?" she echoed miserably. "You're putting me back on my train? You mean you won't even *consider* this, Rufus?"

"You can tell the brigadier I will, if that'll secure your position." He shook his head—that was the way you spoke to a harried lieutenant in a military strategy tent. "Rosie, are you sure you want to go back to him? Shall I ask Mrs Trigg to find you a room here overnight, and tomorrow we can..." He paused, trying to imagine a tomorrow through the splitting, furrowing pain in his head. "I'll go back with you if you like. Talk to him myself."

"No. I don't want to stay in this ghastly place. You think I don't care about Charlie, don't you?"

"What?"

"To let the brigadier use me like this. Because I know he has."

"That never crossed my mind. I know you're devastated, and I do want to help you, only..." He turned to Archie, a panicky nausea rising. "Archie, *will* you please look after her?"

"Of course. But what's wrong?"

"I don't feel well. It's nothing—probably Mrs Trigg's breakfast. I've just got to be quiet for a while."

"All right. I'll take care of your sister. Leave it all to me."

No. Too dangerous. "You don't need take her back to the rectory. If she wants to stay here, I'll pay for it somehow. I'll—"

"I'll damn well pay for myself!" Rosie jumped to her feet, clutching her handbag. "Kindly don't discuss me between you like a sack of potatoes, or that mutt you picked up in London. At least you seem to have got rid of that. Don't worry—I wouldn't stay in this benighted village if your precious Mrs Trigg was to pay *me*. I have a home in London. In Mayfair, and let me tell you, Rufus Denby, it didn't have to be as anyone's daughter-in-law."

"Christ. Let Archie see you to the station, then."

"I don't need him. I can walk, you know. I can..."

Time was up for Rufus. He felt the outbreak of clammy sweat on his brow, and recoiled from Archie's outstretched hand. "I have to go."

"Yes. You go on, old chap—you do look seedy. Nothing life-threatening, is it? Nothing like that turn you took the other day?"

"No, not like that at all."

"All right. I'll come back later to see how you are."

That wouldn't do. Not tonight. Now Rufus grabbed for the kindly offered grip, not caring who saw or heard. "No. If you care about me, Archie, don't come back. I just mean that I'll be asleep. Look after Rosie, and... just go home."

***

The bathroom was at the end of the corridor. The walls of his room were so thin that Rufus heard every step of every trudge-walk his fellow guests made in quest of ablutions, but at least once you got there you were private. He sat on the edge of the bath, clutching the sides. Slowly his nausea ebbed. In the white-ceramic silence, the tang of bleach making his eyes water, he was able to look calmly at his last half hour.

To lift out the heart from it, pure and still beating. Rosie had told him terrible things. When he thought of his nephew, wretched little scrap in that elaborate coffin of a cradle, his bones ached with sorrow. When he thought of the brigadier's hospital, with its gardens and smiling attendants and voltage-laden circuitry wired up and waiting, his guts lurched in a renewal of the sickness that had sent him stumbling out of Mrs Trigg's parlour, up the stairs and along the corridor to this strange refuge.

But he'd fled the scene too soon. He wasn't going to throw up or dissolve into a fugue. The heart of his last half hour was Archie, who'd listened carefully to Rosemary's modest proposal, and said *over my dead body*.

Rufus began to laugh. He pressed a handful of towel to his mouth: what kind of lunatic sat laughing alone in a bathroom in the middle of a Sunday afternoon? Archie had come—flatly, inimitably, in four words—to his defence.

Yes, Rufus had caved too early, scared of his body's reactions, anxious to hide them. He could still put things right. He could go back downstairs, catch up with Archie and Rosie, try and find some answer to her plight. He was her brother after all, and no matter what motives the brigadier had browbeaten into her, she'd come here because she'd lost her child. He could go with her to London, face the monster of Mayfair in person and tell him to leave both of them alone.

He got up, splashed water into his face and dried off. He ought to change his clothes. He still had a clean shirt of the rector's to wear, and he could put back on the suit he'd travelled down in, his city things, ready for battle. For the first time he wanted to fight for himself. Duty demanded that he fall in with the brigadier's plans, but Archie had defied them, and Archie wasn't a coward or a fool. Perhaps, despite everything, Rufus had a right to the shield of his amnesia.

Back in his room, he took off his waistcoat, hitched off his braces and let them dangle. He stood by the window, wondering just what it was about the courtyard that chilled the soul. The dimensions were odd, as if the buildings that had encroached on it over the years had done so reluctantly, holding back their skirts. In the centre was a kind of indentation, a sunken place where the cobbles stopped. Mrs Trigg had tried to plant flowers there, but they were languishing for want of light, or want of something, hanging wearily over the edges of their pots. The broken gutter was still dripping. *Bang, bang, bang...*

No. Rufus couldn't see any leak at all. Had he looked, the first time he heard it? No, and the weather had been so hot before and since his arrival that Mrs Nettles had bewailed the rectory rainbarrels running dry.

He fell back from the window. The noise was inside his head. Blindly he groped his way to the bed and sat down. The little goddess figurine was safe inside his pocket, but she couldn't help him with this. Drusilla had said that he, as a mere man, had to work through life's mysteries by way of reason. What was he supposed to do when reason failed?

The drawer to his bedside cabinet had a lock. He hadn't noticed it during his first three nights here, not supposing himself to possess anything worth stealing. Now he kept the bottle of Veronal locked away. He had no wish to poison Jebediah, despite the child's bad habits. He laid the goddess carefully in the drawer, took out the bottle and counted the pills he had left. Just as he'd thought—in the excitements and distractions, he'd missed at least one dose.

Then, why should an archaeologist need Veronal? A working man, befriended and occupied, making discoveries in his chosen field... He'd forgotten his drugs simply because he'd been too busy, too oddly *happy*, to remember that he was insane.

He remembered now. The thudding from the yard reminded him. Not water hitting wood but the remorseless discharge of a gun.

A pistol, an army-issue Browning. Rufus gasped, twisting around on the bed to find his enemy, the spectre that had followed him from Roche to Sabros to this peacetime village: that had found him out here, even over Archie's dead body. "Archie's alive," he pleaded to the stalking presence in his room, the bull-headed man from the labyrinth of mud. "Don't kill him. Stop shooting. For God's sake, put the gun down!"

The inn was daytime-empty, or he'd have been heard. He was on his knees by the bed, one hand raised to shield himself. He had no recall of falling there. He could fall much, much further, shout much louder, without recall or control.

The Veronal would stop him. The effect of it was like being darted in the arse by a big-game warden on the savannah. Even the rhino-Rufus, the armour-plated lunatic his flashbacks turned him into, could only gallop on a short distance after that.

Awkwardly he got to his feet, long enough to pour a glass of water from the dusty carafe on the chest of drawers. The doctor had said not to double up a dose if he missed one, but to hell with that. He might have missed three. And God knew something had to bring him down.

Chapter Fourteen

Somebody somewhere was crying. From cloud-fogged distances, Rufus moved towards the sound. Not a woman, though the terrified sobs were high-pitched. Maybe it was Charlie. Rufus drifted closer. Something dreadful would happen if no-one attended the baby. If Rufus could get there in time, maybe he could prevent it.

"Oh, dear God, Reverend. I'd never have called you, only..."

"It's all right. I'm glad you did."

The sobbing voice wailed on. Rufus strove to make sense of conflicting reports from his nerve-ends. There was carpet under his face. It stank—not wholly unpleasantly—of beer and smoke. Poor Archie, with his gas-racked lungs and his ciggies! But Brigadier Spence never touched the evil weed, and no breath of pollution would ever have disgraced the Mayfair living room, not while little Charlie—son and heir, dead son of a dead father—lay there in his coffin-cradle.

Yes. Charlie was dead. So Rufus couldn't have gone to London with Rosie and fallen asleep or passed out on the Axminster there. Relief flooded him, that he wasn't on such enemy ground as that.

The wailing was strained, and more than a touch theatrical. Rufus tried to lift his head, but someone was holding him down. It sounded like Jebediah Trigg, and probably had been genuine at first, but the lad wasn't one to quit just because the threat had passed. What was Jebediah doing here?

"Billy, I think you could ease off him a bit. He's trying to open his eyes. Er... Mrs Trigg, can't you take Jebediah out of here? I know he's scared, but he sounds like the air-raid warning."

"Mildred!" Mrs Trigg sounded as though she'd been doing some screaming of her own. Mildred was the scared girl who served breakfasts, Rufus recalled, pleased to have made a connection. "Mildred, take Jebediah away."

"Noooo! Mama!"

"Mildred, now!"

A door clicked. The child's protests faded as he was carted off. In the quiet that followed, Rufus had another go at his clues. A public-house carpet under his face. Jebediah and Mrs Trigg. That meant the Maidens', and, thank God, Archie somewhere nearby, because Mrs Trigg had said *Reverend*, and Rufus himself had heard his voice, the only source of hope or comfort in the world. He knew who Mildred was. Now he came to think of it, he knew Billy too. Billy was Mildred's hulking brother, so unlike her in size that rumours as to his parentage flew round the village, but sharing enough of her docile temper that Mrs Trigg could safely boss him around. Billy rolled beer barrels, unloaded vans. Apparently he sat on unruly guests too, immobilising them with his weight and an efficient half-nelson. Rufus seized another memory: on their way to church that morning, Mildred had confided in him with shy pride that Billy was training to be in the police.

Rufus thought he would do well. He was suffocating, though. He coughed, and the weight disappeared from his back. "I didn't mean to hurt him, Reverend," Billy declared, his voice a pale fragment of its usual boom. "Only he come at me out of nowhere."

"And the *noises* he was making!"

That was Mrs Trigg. She sounded shaken to the bone. Rufus had to find out what monster had caused all this trouble. He tensed his muscles—everything felt bruised, strained, as if he'd been running or fighting for his life—and heaved himself onto his hands and knees.

Mrs Trigg shrieked. Even husky Billy gave a cut-off yell. Somebody was made of stronger stuff, though: a warm arm closed round Rufus's waist, supporting and restraining at once. "Archie," he said, in utter relief. "You *are* here."

"That's right, old chap. Mrs Trigg sent for me. So you don't need to worry anymore."

"You don't ever seem destined to... get a full night's sleep in this village."

"Oh, no. That's quite all right—it's morning."

"Morning?" Rufus sank back onto his haunches and rubbed his gritty eyes. Grey light was pouring into the bar-room of the Maidens' Dance. "Did Rosemary catch her train?"

"Yes, yes. Sent her off with some sandwiches from the tearoom and told the guard to look in on her from time to time."

Rufus chuckled. He couldn't imagine Rosie munching sandwiches out of a paper bag. But Archie changed everybody. Keeping his head up was a blazing effort, like balancing a bucket of hot coals. He groaned and fell sideways and was caught.

"That's it. Let me help you. Mrs Trigg, I think I'd better take him back to the rectory. Do you mind?"

"Mind? No. For God's sake, take him away."

"He didn't mean any harm. He's not well, that's all—something to do with the war. Shellshock, perhaps."

But he *had* harmed somebody. Rufus had been drifting as the voices meshed back and forth across his head. Fiercely he clawed back—pushed himself off Archie's chest and looked around. Mrs Trigg was in the corner by the door, almost cowering. She looked unhurt, thank God, but Billy had a split lip and the beginnings of a shiner. "Christ, Billy. Did I do that?"

"That's all right, Dr Denby. I could tell as you wasn't yourself."

"What did I do? Did I say anything?"

"Well, you came down the stairs, and you was shouting about someone you had to stop. Your enemy." Billy was a nice lad: his bruised face softened into a smile. "No-one's your enemy here, sir. We'll be your friends, if you'll let us."

"Did I wake the whole house?"

"No, just them as sleeps down on this floor, Mrs Trigg and Mildred and myself. We thought you was a burglar, so I come in all ready to sort you out, but you got the drop on me." He rubbed his lip. "Powerful right hook you do have, for an academic gentleman. But it seemed that you was still asleep, in some strange way, and I managed to bring you down, and sat on you a bit, like, until we could get the Reverend up here on his bike. No hard feelings, I hope, sir?"

"Not from me. *You'd* be entitled to them." Rufus wanted to get up. To shake Billy's hand, to explain in some way that the raging beast he'd met on the stairs was exorcised, dead and gone. His legs were numb, though, and without the warm strength behind him, he'd have folded back helplessly onto the carpet. "Archie," he said despairingly. "I should've accepted it."

"Accepted what?"

"Your third invitation. The magic one." He shuddered. "But then I'd have been in *your* house when this happened, with Drusilla and the little girl."

"That's all right. I'd have dealt with you, just like Billy did. Anyway, it's passed now, hasn't it—this bad dream, or whatever it was?"

"For now, but..."

"And I'm not inviting you this time. I'm carting you back with me like a sack of old potatoes."

The image made Rufus laugh in spite of his lingering terror and remorse. "How, though? I'm not sure I can walk, let alone ride pillion."

"No need for either. Winborn has a car, though he's much too cheap to take it out of the garage and let me play with it. Emergencies only, he says, and apparently you qualify. He's on his way, and once we get you settled, he can have a good look at you."

Rufus didn't want Winborn anywhere near him. He couldn't explain the repulsion, and didn't dare voice it, in face of the rescue he was being offered. "Thank you. Mrs Trigg, I... I'm so sorry."

"It's all right, I'm sure," she quavered. "A terrible thing, is shellshock. I think I hear the doctor's car, Vicar. Shall I..."

"Yes, please. Go and bring him in."

She shot away, slamming the door behind her. "God almighty," Rufus whispered. "I've half frightened her to death."

"Pity you didn't do the other half," Billy said musingly, then broke into a cackle. "Sorry, Reverend."

"So you should be, young man. Rufus, is the door to your room unlocked?"

"I'm afraid I've no idea."

"Please go and have a look, Billy. If it is, pack up Dr Denby's things very carefully and bring them down."

"The goddess statue... I should..."

"Ah, yes. We have to take particular care of her. Where is she?"

"In my bedside cabinet, in a locked drawer. But I think I left it open. I'm useless, Archie," he burst out painfully. "I can't look after her. I can't even look after myself!"

"None of us can all the time. That's when our friends help us out."

"How can you be my friend? I've only known you for three days, and I've done nothing but foul things up."

"Rufus, hush. Here comes Winborn. We'll soon have you home."

Home. A dream, an idea that had worn itself out in the struggle of life in London with Henry. Trying to remember what home had once been, Rufus lost his grip on the present. Time and event began to pass strangely, aquatic creatures drifting past the windows of a diving bell. Billy was a sea lion, whiskered face shadowed with worry as he returned with Rufus's satchel and the suitcase Archie had loaned him. Winborn darted in and out of the darkness like a tench, hands chilly and hard. Rufus was on his feet, propped between him and Archie, and Mrs Trigg's hallway floated by, then the steps, then the dawn-lit street, cool and misty. Then the doctor's big black car: the belly of the whale, and although he tried to keep his head up, Archie was there in the back seat beside him, his shoulder warm and ready. Rufus closed his eyes.

***

A half-moon window, broad arch and deep sill. Beyond it, a noonday cobalt sky cut out in patterns of sun-shimmered oak leaves. Walls which must once have been white, mellowed by time to ivory, dove-grey in the play of shadow. A big square space that smelled of apples and good tobacco.

The room Rufus had been trying to avoid since before his arrival here. The scent of Archie's letter to his sister had started the runaway chain of associations. A house in the country, an orchard. Big attic rooms where the apples were stored, where a man lived who liked good things even if they weren't good for him. A man who didn't count the cost. A deep, breeze-blown serenity, cool air from an inched-open window stirring the cobwebs and worn velvet curtains. Bare boards with bright rag rugs on them, a glimmer of fire in the hearth, fresh iced water in a carafe on a table. A big double bed.

Rufus sat on the edge of it, as neat and upright as he could, feet flat on the floor. Veronal hangovers were horrible. They sent a creeping numbness through the veins, stole strength and will. They made even the simplest of actions heavy and complicated. He'd got as far as pushing back the sheets and patchwork counterpane. Any minute now he'd be able to stand up, take off the nightshirt someone had dressed him in, find his clothes and walk out.

Because if he didn't, this was the room that would break him. As long as he'd been contained within the bounds of shattered London, or cooped up in a cube at Mrs Trigg's, he'd been able to hold on. He'd borrowed the fractured ugliness of the city, the smallness of the hired room, and the pain and the sense of confinement had set hard inside him, a kind of scaffold.

A tentative tap on the door made him flinch. God, it was too late. Archie pushed the door wide. He was rangier, more absurdly handsome and in deeper clerical black than Rufus had ever seen him. "I came up to find out how you were, old fellow. What are you doing out of bed?"

Rufus held out a hand in desperation. "Don't come in. Please."

Archie froze. "What's wrong?"

"There's something I've got to tell you. Because I'm here in your house, and there's a child living here. I'm a homosexual."

Archie ducked back out. He glanced up and down the landing, then stepped inside, closing the door carefully behind him. "I'm sorry I left you alone for so long. I was making the arrangements for Lady Birch's funeral."

"Didn't you..." Rufus clenched his hands on the edge of the mattress. He couldn't say the words again. "Didn't you *hear* me?"

"Yes." Archie strode over to the bed, tugged the pillows straight. "I heard you. Best we talk about ordinary things while any doors are open, though. Winborn's been keeping an eye on you while I was out, and he's still in the house somewhere." He turned back the quilt and held it open. "Come on, now. Lie down."

"Archie, for God's sake..."

"You have to be careful. You must know how dangerous it is to speak out."

Rufus subsided onto the pillows. It was such an unmanning relief to rest his throbbing head, to stretch out his limbs in cool linen. He spread his palms in the ghost of a shrug. "Of course I bloody know."

"What has Elspeth got to do with it?"

"You're her guardian. Most people don't want men like me near their kids."

Archie sat down on the edge of the bed. An expression of weary distaste had suddenly put years on him. He poured a glass of water and handed it to Rufus. "Winborn says you have to drink plenty. You know, of all the lies that are spread about men like... men like you, that seems the vilest."

Rufus watched him. His heart was jolting raggedly. "What do you mean?"

"That because you find adult male bodies attractive—and precious few of those, I should imagine—you'd want to harm a child. A little girl, for God's sake. I just don't understand."

"I suppose the thinking is that if you're a... a pervert, the perversion is general." Deliberately Rufus kept his voice steady and low. Even in his current state, he couldn't hear Archie talk about adult male bodies without a marrow-deep frisson. "You're a wolf in the fold, a predator who'll go after anything."

Archie buried his face in his hands. "Dear God."

"I didn't mean to upset you. I didn't mean to *tell* you."

"It's all right." He sat up, resuming his usual smiling briskness of manner. This time it looked as though the effort hurt. "You know, I should have guessed. Chap as handsome as you are comes along, and doesn't talk about the wife and kids—and these days one doesn't like to ask, you know, what with..."

"What with the bombs and everything," Rufus supplied. "It was nice of you not to ask. I'm glad I got to know you a bit before you found out."

"It doesn't make any difference. You're a good fellow, Rufus, and when I think how you helped me with Drusilla..."

"Thank you. But it has to make a difference to some extent. It's why I was trying to stay out of your house, at least as..." He paused, chuckling ruefully over the choice of word. "...as an inmate. You have to let me pack up and go."

"That's just what I won't let you do." Archie turned to face him. His fringe had freed itself once more from its stern comb-back, falling across his brow in a sable cow-lick Rufus would have given the world to kiss aside. His face was pale and strained. "Listen to me. There's something I really want to—"

"Thorne?"

He and Rufus sprang apart. And that was the damnable thing of it, Rufus thought, lifting his chin as defiantly as he could to meet Winborn's stare: because Rufus had told his secret, because Archie *knew*, they'd never be able to sit together as careless, ordinary friends. A door would open, and Archie would jolt away.

"Dr Winborn," Rufus said, as calmly as he could—owing that calm to Archie, who'd had no practice at burying the pain, whereas Rufus was a seasoned hand at it, veteran of a hundred close calls. "Thank you for helping me this morning. I'm sorry to have thrown myself on your mercy again."

Winborn smiled thinly. "I usually treat warts and outbreaks of head lice. You're certainly a variation. Thorne, I'm afraid you're wanted downstairs. I have to go to Ashfield, and I wanted to check Dr Denby over before I leave."

"There's no need." Once more Rufus's skin was aching at the idea of Winborn's touch. Small hands, hard and dry... He found himself hoping the children of Droyton had a different doctor, to treat their measles and comfort their toothaches and whooping cough. "I'm much better now."

"That may be true, but this morning your pulse was high enough to trigger a stroke or a heart attack. And the drugs you take have side effects, so as long as you're here, I feel obliged to take care of you."

"Better let him do his worst," Archie said wryly. "It's quicker that way. I'll sit and chat to you if you like, while—"

"You'd really better go downstairs. A dozen or so of Lady Birch's relatives have just arrived by train, and they're milling about in the library now."

"Lady Birch's relatives? What on earth are they doing here?"

"There's been some kind of mix-up over the old lady's will, it seems. The solicitor's downstairs too, trying to explain, but it's Drusilla they're after."

"Drusilla... I don't understand."

"Nor do I, but they're calling her names, and Elspeth is hysterical and trying to stab them with cake forks."

"Oh, good God." Archie got up, straightening his dog-collar. "Excuse me, Rufus, while I go and break up the fight."

"Of course. Good luck."

The door closed behind him, and Rufus sat up, mustering what dignity he could in a borrowed nightshirt. He felt that he would need it. He didn't in the least doubt Winborn's tale of outraged relations in the library, but something was coming. This arid little man had something to say to him that Archie couldn't hear. Now Rufus came to think of it, he'd never told Winborn what medicines he took. Resignedly he pushed up one sleeve. "Where shall we start, Doctor? Blood pressure?"

"Er... yes. As good a place as any." Winborn set his leather bag down by the bed and extracted a cuff and bulb. He set about his task, hawklike face expressionless: pressure, pulse, and finally heart, having to steel himself to it, as if the skin of certain men could taint his stethoscope. "How are you feeling?"

"Much better. It was good of you and Reverend Thorne to come and help me. The medicine I take is meant to stop my nightmares, but sometimes all it does is prevent me waking up from them."

"Yes. Veronal will do that, especially in mild overdose." Winborn sighed and sat back. "Dr Denby, you'll have to forgive me. I took the liberty of making a telephone call to the Royal Museum while you were asleep. I learned the name of your immediate superior there, and she and I had a conversation."

"You spoke to Caroline Taylor?"

"Yes. She's Archie's cousin, as you know, and she was perhaps more forthcoming with me than she would have been with a stranger. At any rate she gave me a name and number for the doctor who took care of you at your London hospital upon your return from Sabros. I needed to know—because you'd landed in my lap, as it were—what medicines you'd been prescribed, and if..."

"If I was dangerous." Rufus wanted to help him out. He wanted this to be over as soon as possible. "I am. I've had enough of these blackouts to know that I'll attack the strongest male person I can find. I don't know why that is, but I don't intend to stay here and cause further trouble."

"You're leaving?"

"As soon as I'm strong enough to get to the station. Today, if I can."

"What about your work at the church?"

"It's proven more interesting than I'd thought, but Taylor will send someone else down to finish the investigation. She's a good woman. When I made Sabros too hot to hold me, she sent me here. It was make-work, to keep me occupied and out of mischief, but..." He hitched one shoulder, tried for a smile. "That doesn't appear to have worked. Does it?"

Winborn got to his feet. He paced the length of the room. Rufus guessed that it took a lot to make him nervous, but his brow was damp when he turned round again. "Do you plan to stay in touch with Archie?"

"I'd have liked to. One doesn't make so many friends—not at my age—that one cares to throw them away." He wedged a pillow behind his back. He could hardly get this encounter on a business footing, but he didn't have to take it lying down. "You'd prefer me not to, though. Maybe if you tell me why, we'll understand each other better."

"I doubt it. Caroline Taylor is a friend of yours, too, and very concerned about you. When I asked if she knew of anything that might be affecting your mental state now, she told me about someone called Henry."

Rufus could hardly believe it. Caroline, so discreet that she'd hardly dared open her mouth to condole with him about Henry's loss... "How much did she tell you, Dr Winborn?"

"Very little. Don't blame her—I'm afraid I put the case to her in a slanted light, and rather more urgently than it actually stands. I had to be sure of your proclivities in order to justify telling you something about Archie."

"Oh, God. I don't want to know his secrets."

"But you have to, Denby. I don't make a practice of turning a cold shoulder on strangers, or working to separate men who perhaps ought to be good friends. Listen to me, and then you can decide for yourself if your presence here—if your continued acquaintance—is good for him. No matter what I think personally of men of your persuasion, you seem decent enough in other ways. I'll leave it to you."

Rufus looked around the sunny room. For five minutes, with Archie by his bed, it had felt like an absolute refuge, a place set outside space and time. Here came the world. "All right," he said hoarsely. "I'm listening."

"Archie's parents died when he was quite young. He'd been very close to them, and the loss of them cast him adrift. He was my pupil at Ashfield at the time, and I endeavoured to supply their place as far as I could. But Archie isn't a man who can exist without love, Dr Denby, and I was just his teacher. He didn't love me."

"Someone, though."

"Yes. A boy named Richard Simms, a promising theology student too. They were barely eighteen. You think I'm an interfering old man, Denby, but in their case I didn't interfere soon enough. The dean caught them out one day, and the Simms boy couldn't withstand the disgrace. Before nightfall he'd destroyed himself."

"Christ. How?"

"He filled his pockets with stones and jumped off Ashfield bridge. The coroner ruled suicide while the balance of the mind was disturbed. They usually do, in cases like these, so there can be a decent burial."

Rufus sat up with an effort that nauseated him. He drew up his knees and wrapped his arms around them. "What happened to Archie?"

"The incident was covered up for the sake of the college. Archie was sick with shame and grief. I brought him to live with me. His parents had just died, but that had little to do with his illness. In fact he told me he was glad that they were gone, so they'd never have to find out what he was." Winborn pushed his chair back. He folded up his stethoscope and put it back into his bag. "You see, Dr Denby, I'm being as frank and fair with you as I can. I found Archie a wife. They were happy together, and I came to believe that poor Simms had been an aberration, a youthful folly. Now I see him with you, and I'm not so certain."

"He hasn't done anything," Rufus said quickly. "He didn't even know until today that I was—about me."

"You've told him?"

"He brought me to stay in his house. I had to. You've warned him off, and I understand why, but you don't need do or say anything further. Archie's only been kind to me. I know better than to read that as meaning anything more than it does."

Winborn looked taken aback, as if he'd been expecting a fight. "You really intend not to pursue him?"

"*Pursue*... My God, do you think I'd deliberately drag another man into my kind of life?"

"Then you'll have to forgive my intrusion. I did it for the good of my friend."

"You underestimate him." Rufus took a mouthful of water to combat the barbiturate-dryness in his throat. "With respect, you underestimate Alice, too. They'll both choose who they want in this life without interference from either of us."

Winborn bristled. "Kindly leave my niece's name out of this."

"As you wish."

Winborn sat back. He eyed Rufus coldly for a moment, then made a visible effort to recover his temper. "Homosexuality isn't a life-sentence, you know. If you dislike the choices it's forced on you—the exposure to danger, disease, disgrace—I might be able to offer you some advice. I was on one of the Civilian Medical Boards during conscription. I offered corrective guidance to dozens of potential recruits. Unless there's some kind of physical deformity—if the perversion is only mental—there's no reason why you shouldn't live a normal, healthy life. I helped Archie, all those years ago. Perhaps I could help you."

Rufus let go a breath. Deliberately he unclenched his hands. He wanted to put them around Winborn's throat and squeeze until his normal, healthy eyes popped out. "I'm grateful to you for bringing me here," he said tightly. "Just for now, though, you can *help* me by getting the bloody hell out of my room."

"Goodbye, Dr Denby. I'll have a prescription made up for a powerful sedative, and I'll leave it with Archie. If you really care about him, or the safety of the other people in this house, you'll take it."

Chapter Fifteen

"Well, old Lady Birch hasn't half set the cat among the pigeons."

The light in the room had changed. Now the trees beyond the half-moon window were weaving dusky shadows, and the air was full of evening scents from the river. Rufus blinked and turned his head on the pillow. "Have I been asleep?"

"I wasn't sure. I kept reading to you and talking to you anyway." Archie laid a book aside and sat forward in the armchair beside the bed. He smiled: a gentle glimmer in the half-light. "Country parsons don't necessarily expect their listeners to be awake."

"But I... Winborn was here. I think I was rude to him."

"I'm sure he had it coming. He's a dry old stick sometimes, and he forgets his bedside manner."

"He's concerned for you, that's all. And for everyone else here."

"Because of you, wild man? I'm certain Drusilla, Mrs Nettles and I can handle you between us."

"No. Not because of that."

Archie's expression darkened. "That's no business of his. You didn't need to tell him."

"I didn't. He's been in touch with your cousin at the museum. I did tell Caroline, a long time ago, because of..."

"Because of who *she* is?"

"Yes. I thought it was safe."

"It should have been. Caroline's lived her whole adult life with a devoted female friend. I can't believe she was so indiscreet."

"Don't blame her. Winborn put the thumbscrews on her, it seems, to find out about my illness. And of course she knew my... she knew Henry."

"Henry? Is that the name of your..."

He tailed off, his blush just visible. Rufus took pity. There were no kindly accurate words, and all the labels were cruel. "*My* devoted friend. Yes. Now tell me what's happened to Drusilla."

Archie got to his feet. He began to pace the room, a picture of nervous energy. "She's been transformed into the lady of the manor, that's what's happened. Lady Birch left her everything— house, land, rather a startling amount of money."

"Good Lord."

"The bush telegraph around here went into overdrive, and half a dozen hopeful relatives who hadn't been near the old girl for years suddenly turned up in the parlour."

"Doesn't there have to be probate or something?"

"Yes, but Lady Birch left everything wrapped up tight. Her solicitor was on hand, and he's spent the whole afternoon trying to calm things down. Poor Drusilla did get called some names, but she seems completely oblivious." Suddenly Archie left off pacing. He returned to the bedside and sat down carefully on the edge of the quilt. He took hold of Rufus's wrist, his grip warm and electric. "Never mind Drusilla. Tell me about Henry. Please."

Rufus swallowed. "The easiest part to tell you is that he's dead."

"Oh, God."

"It's all right. I'm all right about it. We were... Our friendship, our affair... It was over before that. The truth is, Archie, I never meant to get into this stupid war. I didn't know about the death camps then, and the Jews, and I—I thought I was a pacifist. I was going to declare as a conscientious objector."

"What—Captain Denby, the terror of the Western Front?"

"Yes. But back then I didn't believe in violence of any kind. I was an academic—I didn't see what any of it had to do with me. It did, of course. Yellow star, pink triangle..." He let his hand turn palm-up to meet Archie's grasp. Why not? His pitiful secret was out now, and Archie had a secret of his own, dropped into Rufus's lap by someone just as indiscreet as poor Caroline Taylor. Once, long ago, Archie too had kissed another man, held him and loved him. "It was to do with us all."

"What changed your mind?"

"I wish it was some good, noble reason. I told Henry what I meant to do. He was very young, very handsome, and I suppose I'd been... quite infatuated with him. He asked what I'd do if Germany invaded, if some big SS officer knocked down our front door with a gun in his hand."

"I've asked myself similar questions. What did you say?"

"I said that I'd die for him, of course. And he said he didn't want me to die. If it came to that, he expected me to pick up a gun, or a brick, or a poker from the fire, and fight for him instead. Then he walked out on me, and went to live with a wealthy Navy lieutenant he'd been seeing for weeks behind my back. And I decided he was right, so I enlisted."

"Oh, Rufus."

"It's all right, really. The ironic thing is that Henry was killed at home anyway, in one of the last raids. He'd gone back to our flat to get something, and the whole block was knocked down by a V2. I was at the Front. I didn't find out about it for weeks." Rufus couldn't have borne whatever sweet, shocked words Archie would have found for him: held up his free hand in a plea for mercy. "What do you think about it all, Reverend? Conscientious objection, and pacifism and all that?"

Archie cleared his throat. "Well, as a man of God, I'm supposed to be in favour of peace."

"Oh, we all are, aren't we? Even Oppenheimer and his damn bomb. We just have different ways of getting there."

"And it's not what you were asking, I know. I have thought about it a good deal. I was going to give a sermon on the subject at one time, but they'd lynch me from the nearest tree, all these peaceful villagers, if I got into the pulpit and preached in favour of objection now." Archie closed a tighter grasp on Rufus's hand, almost absently, as he tried to work through his thoughts. "It seems to me that the last choice left to a pacifist would be a negative one. You could have refused to enlist. You could have stayed in London, defended Henry with your flesh and bone in the last resort."

"That's what I intended, I suppose. To shield him from a bullet. And... they'd have stepped over my corpse and killed him anyway. I suppose he knew that."

"That's what I mean by the last choice—not to die for, but to die *with* your beloved. If you'd stayed in London, you might have died with Henry in the raid. Would it have done any good?"

Rufus extricated his hand. He sat up and hunched over, hiding his face. "I don't know," he said miserably. "It all seems like a damn poor game to me now."

"Well, don't frighten your dog."

He glanced down. Pippin was sitting by the side of the bed, staring at him anxiously. The door was slightly ajar, as if she'd nosed her way through it. "Does Mrs Nettles allow dogs in the bedrooms?"

"No, she does not."

"What about..." He broke off as the dog sprang up next to him, pushing her wet snout into his face. "What about on the beds?"

"Under no circumstances is a dog to get onto a bed in this house."

Mrs Nettles' household rules were made to be lovingly broken. Rufus stroked Pippin's ears, fending off the attack, and she slumped across his lap, tail thumping. The worst of his pain over Henry—the small, constant betrayals, the fear of exposure, the young man's shocking death—passed through him like a cresting wave. He subsided against the pillows. "I never thought I'd tell anyone about him."

"I'm glad you did." Archie scratched Pippin's ribs, making her twitch one hind leg in pleasure. "For what it's worth, I don't think you were wrong in the ideals you used to hold."

"Really? Weren't you something of a terror yourself, over there in France?"

Archie chuckled. "Christ on a motorbike, the privates used to call me. But... don't you think that to die for someone, or with someone, is ultimately the bravest choice a man can make?"

"The loneliest, too."

"Yes. My Church says Christ died for our sins—and we stepped over his corpse and kept on sinning anyway. We're supposed to emulate him. It's a deeply passive role, though, and those don't suit me very well."

Rufus closed his eyes. He needed to hide for a moment from his companion's intensity, the light that radiated from him when his heart and mind were fully engaged. What would it have been like, to have had such a friend while he was growing up? To have come home to such a man instead of poor strutting Henry, with his vanity and insatiable hunger for gifts and adulation...

Then, helplessly, in the darkness behind his lids, Rufus considered that word *passive*. Nothing to do with Archie's context, but Rufus had looked into medical texts to try and discover why he was as he was. He'd talked, carefully casual, to other men in the army: cheerful, worldly lads who'd taken a broad view of the pleasures to be had in foreign parts. A passive bugger. An active queer. A top, a bottom... He'd never understood how any of those words could describe his own case, but to hear Archie use one had sent an unwanted jolt of excitement through him. To avoid it, he opened his eyes, catching clumsily at Archie's last point. "Your Church says Christ died for our sins... I know you don't believe in God. Do you believe that?"

"Well, it all follows on rather, doesn't it? But setting aside belief—there's a question for me, personally, over whether I wanted him to." Archie got up again, the movement taut with restraint. He went to stand by the half-moon window. "Don't you think a man should carry his own damn sins? Don't you think he should be strong enough to commit them and bear them, and atone for them however he can—in this world, I mean, not a convenient purgatory?"

Archie meant his own sins with Richard. Rufus was certain of it, and didn't dare say, even though it might have cracked the ice on an ocean of held-back grief, released and redeemed it, just as his own grief over Henry had been lanced and made bearable. "A convenient purgatory?" he echoed wonderingly. "You don't sound much like a vicar now."

"I know, damn it." Archie pushed the pane wide. Rufus heard the rasp in his lungs again, and began to get out of bed, but Archie turned swiftly and came to restrain him, big hands commanding on his shoulders. "No. You have to stay there."

"I promised Winborn I'd try to leave."

"What the devil does he have to do with it?"

"He's your friend, Archie. I admit he's a sour-faced old sod, but he's got your best interests at heart."

"His idea of my best interests, maybe. I've never questioned that. Now I look back, though, I..."

This was a brink. Rufus held Archie's arms, letting his fingers clench on the black cotton of his shirt. But after a moment Archie let him go. "You've got to rest," he said gruffly. "And you're staying right here to do it."

"In that case you'd better give me the sedative he left."

"No. I'm not about to drug you like a troublesome beast. I won't let you harm anyone, and I won't let any harm come to you."

"How can you promise that?"

"Trust me." He straightened up. "I've got to go and check there aren't any disgruntled relatives of Lady Birch still hiding under the sideboards, and I'll fetch you some supper while I'm down there. Meanwhile, I was reading to you from this. You seemed to be enjoying it, in an unconscious sort of way."

Rufus took the leatherbound book he was holding out. "Oh. Thank you, but..."

"What, don't you care for your Trollope?"

Archie's face was quite straight, so Rufus smoothed out his own. "Never read him, really. Victorian melodramas, aren't they? Not much connection to the way we live now."

"Oh, *The Way We Live Now* is probably his finest. This one's the last in his Barsetshire series. I like it because it shows me the kind of country parson I shouldn't be, and the kind I once thought I could become. Give him a try."

Rufus had little choice. Archie closed the bedroom door gently behind him, and he was alone. He could cast himself adrift among his own thoughts and memories, or he could borrow those enshrined between the fragrant, well-worn covers of Archie's book, which must have a great deal going for it if it had become one of *his* favourites. Rufus stared at the door for a moment, allowing himself—it would have to be brief; he was bound by honour and commonsense to keep his promise to Winborn—the aching pleasure of being a guest in this good man's house. Of having a place beneath his wing. Rufus's eyes stung, and his vision sharpened on the title page as he opened the book.

Archie's tastes were old-fashioned. The first couple of chapters bore out Rufus's schoolboy distaste for the snug Victorian world called up in such detail. The snobbery, the merciless class distinctions, the ostracism of the brilliant, ascetic Reverend Crawley for no other reason than his poverty... Recalling his few days' experience of Droyton and Mrs Trigg, Rufus revised his opinion of the book's faded relevance to modern times.

Then he smiled. Josiah Crawley was Archie's ideal vicar. Oblivious to social rules and appearances, sharing his meagre resources with the destitute brickmakers of his parish. Teaching his daughter Greek and Hebrew without a thought for her gender, seeing only that she was human, and education was good for human beings. Loved to death and beyond by a woman who saw his imperfections and clung to the unimpeachable spirit beneath... If Archie had been there, Rufus would have told him he was glad that he didn't resemble too closely his ideal.

The willingness to share a last crust was there, and the sweet, noble impatience with social forms. But Crawley despised the material world, and Archie was in love with it. You only had to think about him standing in the sunshine on Pilgrim Way, turning his face up to the dance of the leaf-shadows, to realise that. Rufus read on, turning the pages more quickly as the story gently seized him. Crawley, accused of a petty theft he could no more have committed than he could have flown, began a mental disintegration whose stages Rufus knew all too well. Enter Mark Robarts with his clumsy efforts to help, and Rufus immediately recognised the other side of Archie's coin, the man he was afraid he'd become—the comfortable, sensual, hunting-shooting parson, too deeply lapped in wealth and comfort to remember his spiritual calling at all.

Not much resemblance there either. Rufus would tell him the moment he returned. He was the best of both worlds, a living soul who'd come through the war with his humanity intact, even if he'd left his faith behind in the mud. It was wicked that poor Crawley should have to suffer so. If Major Grantly pulled out of his engagement with Crawley's daughter, why, then, Grantly was a puling coward who deserved to be knocked down in the street, and Rufus would have liked to do the job. It was absurd that Mrs Robarts should have to smuggle jam and chicken to Crawley's ailing children because of their father's pride, and as for the Archdeacon, if he didn't recognise in Crawley a noble fellow-spirit in time to prevent the poor vicar's catastrophic disgrace...

Rufus turned the pages faster and faster in his growing anxiety for these figments of Trollope's long-extinct imagination. He lay down flat and read as he'd used to do in childhood, the book poised just off the tip of his nose, his toes clenched on the footboard as if he would otherwise float off into space. The Reverend Thorne's house held him like a hammock, like a chrysalis, like a deep embrace from strong male arms. Night came down, and at some point of shimmering non-darkness from the summer skies, a careful hand lifted the open book off his face.

***

He woke in the trenches, his enemy near him. This time the hallucination didn't eat him whole: the awareness was left to him, dim and distant, that his body remained in a beautiful place, guarded and cared for and safe. Utter misery seized him. No matter where he went, he would end up here. No matter who he reached for in friendship and love, the shadow would fall: a bull in a labyrinth, a faceless Minotaur, groaning and snorting in the dark, a demon with the power to take a firelit room and fill it with mud, blood and horror.

Rufus tore the bedclothes back and lurched onto his knees. He would kill the bastard this time, that was all. He flattened his hands to the mattress and let loose a long, raw howl of desolation. It was too bloody grim that every beauty he found, every safety and sweetness, could be ruined and torn down to shit. He burst into racking sobs.

The bedroom door flew open. Rufus seized his chance. He couldn't see, but that didn't matter—who else would dare find him here in the firelit trench but his enemy? "Charles," he roared, scrambling off the end of the bed and into the bullet-pocked hell of the earthworks behind Fort Roche. "Stop, damn you! I won't let you do it this time!"

He collided with flesh and bone. The devil of it was that he recognised Archie straight off, by scent and warmth and the well-restrained power that cushioned and held him even as it fended him off. "Rufus," Archie gasped in his ear, but it was no use. The logic of flashback ate both of them whole.

They crashed together onto the bedroom floor. Rufus made a grab for the gun at Charles's belt, but the coward had hidden it somewhere, ready for the atrocious scene that always followed on from this fight. "Give it to me," he grunted, rolling Charles over, and cried out as a huge strength lifted and rolled him in his turn, dumping him hard against the base of the wardrobe, whose scrolled and clawed feet Rufus couldn't account for here, unless the Minotaur had learned how to dance.

He lashed out wildly. The blow connected, sending a pang of exhilaration through him. He could taste his enemy's blood. Connections formed hotly in his mind: Charles was the enemy, the monster he'd been seeking through the mud-lined tunnels of his dreams since his return from the Front. Charles, his commanding officer. His brother-in-law, the sweet-natured boy he and Rosie had run with through childhood's meadows... "Charles, stop," he begged, aiming another knockout blow at the once-beloved face. "Stop. Please."

"I will if you will."

He couldn't. Wherever he travelled, no matter how far he ran, this dream would compel him to hunt down the nearest likeness of the beast, the greatest threat. He twisted out from under the beast's weight—so warm, this beast, smelling of love, not death—and struggled onto his feet. The beast stood too. "Rufus, stand down," the beast commanded, and this time it stopped his fist in mid-air. "You're looking for the strongest man? You've found him. I'm right here."

Chapter Sixteen

Rufus woke up. The mud and blood dried to thin, brittle shells on his skin and fell away. The trench burst wide open to dawn light. Archie was holding him, not Charles—Archie in rumpled dressing gown and brightly patterned pyjamas, staring at him in such a blaze of passion and pity that Rufus would have fallen in love with him right then, if he hadn't already dropped and dived and lost that battle somewhere among the Droyton lanes. "Archie," he whispered, lifting a shaking hand to caress the face he'd bruised. "Archie!"

"Yes. You have to stop this now."

Rufus couldn't. He slipped a hand around Archie's nape, pulled him down and kissed him—brief, hard, full on the mouth. Let him go immediately and stumbled back, almost thrusting him away. Easier to do that than be pushed, than to see shock gathering, rejection, distaste... But Archie only frowned. He touched his lip wonderingly, as if remembering. Then he shot out a hand and seized Rufus by the front of his nightshirt. "Come here."

"Archie..."

"Come here, man. For God's sake."

Rufus stumbled back to him. Archie didn't relinquish his grip: used it to haul him up and in, at the last instant catching him tenderly with his free hand, cupping his jaw. He dipped his head. A faint sound escaped him, a muffled sob of yearning. He closed his eyes and pressed his mouth to Rufus's in return.

Clumsy, awkward. He must have got at least one punch in—pain popped like a flashbulb on Rufus's lip, delicious and wild. Archie kissed like a man who'd been tied hand and foot while other people fucked and danced and loved all around him, inches away, untouchable. Christ, Rufus knew how that felt. He threw his arms around him, left off trying to keep his rising erection a secret. Archie groaned and pushed back at him, knocking him off-balance. They crashed against the wardrobe.

"Dear Archie. At least let me take you to bed."

"I can't. I... Oh, yes."

"Make sure the door's shut."

"It is."

"You'd better close the window. Pull the curtains too." Rufus clutched his shoulders. "Do the windows have shutters?"

"Er... yes, but—"

"Better close them."

"Rufus, this is my house. We're up on the attic floor. I won't shut us away in the dark."

"You have to. You don't understand. You could be jailed and disgraced for what you just did to me, let alone..." Rufus caught his breath. "Let alone what I'm about to do to you."

"Only the birds will see us. The moths and the bats flying home."

Rufus surrendered. When Archie pushed him towards the bed, he went. The Veronal was out of his system now, nothing to dull his reactions. He clambered onto the mattress, Archie following, and it was like being tackled by a bear. They thudded down among the bedclothes. Rufus writhed over onto his back. He opened his legs and Archie scrambled between them, hard cock pushing against his belly. What Rufus wouldn't give to hitch up the damn nightshirt, spread his thighs and let the man dry-fuck him now in the heat of the moment... Months since he'd had it like that, flat-out, teeth gritted, a thickset Greek sailor holding a pillow over his mouth to keep him quiet in his boarding-house room...

Not like that, not with Archie. Rufus would cope with it, but not the pure-hearted vicar who hadn't laid hand on a man in over twenty years. "Slow down."

"Tell me what to do."

"I am. Lie still. Catch your breath."

"But I want to..." Oh, the poor bastard couldn't even say it, was blushing brighter than the dawn rising over the hills. His fringe had tumbled over his brow, hot shivers racking his frame. "I want to *love* you. I don't know how."

"You've been doing that since we met. If you're asking how to have sex with me—you can't, not yet, not the way you're imagining. It's too soon."

"You can't know what I'm imagining."

"I think I can. Archie, listen—before you do anything at all—you have to know why the doctor's been trying to steer you away from this. Your whole life, your reputation here, Alice Winborn..."

"What on earth does Alice have to do with it?"

Rufus examined his face. Somehow, despite the doctor's unsubtle manoeuvring and the girl's mortification, Archie had no idea. How had Winborn managed to guide him into that first marriage? Poor bastard must have been sleepwalking, stunned with grief for Richard. Rufus kissed his damp brow, his parted lips. "Never mind. But even though I know you don't believe in him, you're meant to be a man of God."

Archie swallowed. "Looking at you," he said huskily, "I think I might have been wrong. About God, I mean. And believing."

Sunlight poured into the room. Rufus flinched as his irises tightened against it. Maybe Archie would think that had caused his tears. "Don't worry about any of it. Not now. Does this pyjama cord unfasten?"

"Yes, if I haven't got it knotted... What are you going to do?"

"Unfasten it. Pull your trousers down. Feel your cock against mine." The words hit Archie like blows. Rufus felt how he rocked beneath the impact. "It's all right. We can say things, do them. If God made us at all, he made us to love each other."

"I wish he'd made it a bit clearer. In the instructions, I mean—the Bible, and the Church, and..."

"I'm not sure that's God. I think it's just us."

"You damn beautiful heretic. What about *your* God?"

"Mine?"

"You told me about him. God of the hills and trees. The broad sunlit uplands."

"And you."

"Oh God, yes. And you."

Rufus unfastened the knot. "I don't think my God has a problem with it."

"The sunlight should burn up our skin."

"It doesn't, though, does it? Take off your dressing gown." Rufus helped him out of it, quickly unbuttoned his pyjama jacket and pushed that back too. For all Archie's mop of sable hair and the workaday tan of his hands, the wide shoulders were buttermilk pale. Rufus brushed moth-velvet kisses over them, found the hollow at the base of his throat where the fast pulse leapt. Gently bit at one collarbone, and Archie groaned and pushed with shuddering force between his thighs.

That would do. Ah, for now, for whatever snatch of time his own God allowed and Archie's would turn a blind eye to, maybe all the time they had—yes, that would do, and Rufus tugged the pyjama bottoms down over Archie's backside. Writhed and hitched his hips until the hot length of cock was tightly snugged against his own, and when push came to shove would meet nothing but kindred flesh. "Yes," Rufus said against his neck, into the fractured rhythm of his breathing. "Like that, yes. Again."

"But is it... is it enough?"

About to be more than. Rufus grabbed and cradled Archie's arse. Next time he thrust, Rufus heaved up to meet him, clutching him close at the bruising pitch of his effort. The dawn wind blew, rippling sun-faded curtains into the room like beating wings. "Again," he choked out, then jerked his head back against the pillow, squeezing his eyes shut, climaxing helplessly. Archie fell forward and buried his face against his shoulder. His cries—desperate, muffled even now for the sake of the world beyond the window—vibrated through Rufus's heart. The powerful spine strained once, twice, and one last time to deliver him. His seed came hard, a prolonged, hot spending, muscles turning to spasm-racked rock beneath Rufus's hands.

Rufus kept him close when he was done. Let the clasp of his thighs become an embrace, and wearily rocked him in it, just a little, back and forth. Now the shudders running through him were something else. Archie would never be a man to cry out loud. Rufus grabbed the quilt and pulled up as much of it as he could to shield him. "It's all right. You're all right."

A crushed-back sob. "I'm so sorry."

Rufus braced up. Despite everything, Archie's God might have won. He won all the time. "Sorry you did it?"

"No. No! Sorry I did it like that. I meant to be better."

You will be next time. Rufus didn't dare say it. Freshly fucked men, especially straight ones, didn't like to hear about next times, as if a fling could become a habit. A need. "You were perfect," he said truthfully. "Perfect for me."

"Maybe I'll be better next time. I was never much good, though, not even with..."

His voice cracked and faded. Rufus rolled him down into the tangle of bedclothes, keeping the shielding quilt in place. Would it be easier for him or worse, to know how closely Rufus understood? "Listen," he began, and gave the game away instantly: Archie looked up at him, eyes wide. "Oh. Winborn told you. The story about Richard."

Rufus would have loved to believe the whole tale a fiction. And he could do it, at a stretch—just Winborn's style, to keep a tragic boyfriend in Archie's closet, ready to tumble out on any new candidates. "Is that all it was? Just a story?"

"No. I wish it had been, more than anything." He flickered a shy smile that made Rufus's heart ache. "By the way, don't we have indiscreet friends?"

"They might as well carry bullhorns."

"Richard was real. And I'm sure the doctor didn't tell you any lies, but..." He stroked Rufus's face, tugged at the quilt until he too was shielded and warm. "It was so very long ago. I loved him. And I have mourned and done penance in every possible way I can think of almost every day since then, but it alters nothing. It doesn't alter me."

"What do you mean?" Rufus whispered. He knew what he wanted it to mean. Life couldn't be that sweet to him, though, or that paralysingly complicated for poor Archie. "About it... not altering you?"

"I cared for Richard very much more than I could ever bring myself to care about my wife, although I understood—as did she—what Winborn had tried to do for me, and she and I became good friends. I fulfilled my minimal conjugal duties, and thankfully she never wanted more. With Richard, it was like flying, or bursting into flames, or dying in the best way anyone could ever imagine, though I always..." He paused, shook his head. "I always flew, burst or died too damn soon. So what I mean by it not *altering* me is that I'm as much a homosexual as you, although I seem to have done my very lifelong best to avoid the fact."

"You had to. Even if you hadn't been a vicar—Christ, believe me, I know how it is. But you *were*."

"A godless one. Who warmed himself every night at the fire of his memories of another man."

"Oh, Archie. What was he like?"

"Beautiful. Dark eyes, slim as a whip. Smart as one, too, already asking questions our theology professors couldn't answer. We used to go down to the boathouse on Sunday afternoons when the college grounds were quiet, and... Can you bear to hear this?"

"I want to. Archie, forgive me. I want to in a way that's wrong, surely, or bad."

Archie's brow furrowed. But he couldn't stay puzzled for long, not pressed hip-to-thigh in their damp tangle of sheets. He pursed his lips, a spark of badly timed mischief kindling to shed light on this saddest of tales. "Oh. In a *sexy* way, Dr Denby?"

It wasn't a word Rufus used. Too new in the coining, too strange. And there was the Auden poem again, though not the part Reverend Thorne had quoted in church: *the sexy airs of summer, the bathing hours and the bare arms, the leisured drives through a land of farms, are good to a newcomer...* "I suppose so, God help me."

"Well, I'm telling you the sexy part. There's enough grief, old fellow, to make us both weep forever, so let's have the joy of it as well. We'd go to the boathouse on a Sunday afternoon, and close the landward doors and open the ones onto the river." Archie shifted a bit, and awkwardly laid his hand to Rufus's stirring cock. "That way we didn't even have to think about the world, you see. And we'd kiss until we were both frustrated and as erect as you're getting now, and we'd have a... bloody theological discussion about whether we'd go to hell, or just do time in purgatory. And how much difference it would make if we went the whole way, not that I'm sure either of us knew what we meant by that."

"Didn't you?"

"Go the whole... No, not as I understand it now. I've never done it to a man or had it done to me, although I've spent an absurd amount of time thinking about it."

"In your garden shed?"

"Yes, often. No wonder the damn bike gets such a hammering."

Laughter shook Rufus, but it was silent, driving still more blood downward. On blind, heated instinct he rolled onto his side, curling up. "Come and lie around my back. Are you getting hard too?"

"Yes. I didn't think it could happen again so fast."

"Depends how long you've waited. Let it go between my thighs. Don't push inside, because I don't mind a bit of hurt, but you would. Mind hurting me, I mean."

"I couldn't bear it."

"You won't. Just... Oh, yes. Into the crack of my backside." Hitching one leg up, Rufus spread himself, his hand damp and clumsy on his own skin. Just enough to make room. He lay very still, carefully regulating his breathing, while Archie obeyed. "Tell me the rest."

"About me and Richard?"

Such pain in the deep voice! "Now I'm hurting *you*."

"Not as much as twenty years of kindly, suffocating bloody silence. He *lived*, Rufus. He existed. He was real."

"I know. Tell me while you... Ah, yes." *Next time I'll let you carry that great big thrust all the way. Next time we'll find whatever people use for lubricant in this wilderness. As if we had next times.* "The boathouse. A sunny afternoon."

"It *was* sunny, that last time. It got too much, the kissing. I wanted to go on my knees and suck him—you know, take some of the pressure off. We'd both done that to each other before. But he was getting scared about it all even then, so we stripped off and jumped into the water."

"So nobody could see."

"So we didn't even have to see ourselves. It was deep there, just like the river here. The current carried us down to the bridge."

He filled his pockets with stones and jumped. Rufus closed his eyes against the pillow, let Archie lift and half-turn him like the perfect lover he would have been, in a world where beautiful boys didn't have to die. They began to move together, a deep, rocking grind. "What happened? At the bridge?"

"The current was strong. It held us both against one of the piers. He started doing to me... just what I'm doing to you now, and maybe we'd even have managed, with the water to help us. We were both so, so excited."

"Archie..."

"Yes." Archie wrapped one arm tight around him. He plunged his free hand down and took shy hold of his cock. "Am I doing it right?"

"Very right. Yes."

"I felt him, you know? I felt him all ready to go inside. But we were both yelling our heads off by that time. We'd forgotten everything. We just hung on to each other in the water and came and came."

Rufus flipped onto his belly. He spread his legs, shoved with all his strength against Archie's hand. This time the heat-flash burned up from his toes, went through him with slow, consuming power. He was grunting, making underwater movements too, only stopping world-ending shouts of his own by ramming his face into the pillow. Archie's shaft jolted and engaged by an inch despite all their caution—a natural homecoming, the best of conclusions—but they both were too far gone, as lost now as the half-drowned teenage boys had been. He burrowed into the pillow next to Rufus and went still.

***

"Tell me the rest."

"Ah, no, Rufus. Nobody wants to hear the rest."

"I do."

"All right. The dean of the college was walking his poodle and his self-righteous bitch of a wife across the bridge. Please excuse my language. The dog yapped, the wife screamed and fainted, and the dean made Richard and me walk back to the boathouse naked. We couldn't swim against the current, you see."

Rufus struggled over onto his back. He put out his arms, and Archie, glancing at him wide-eyed, as if this was the most surprising part of their encounter yet, laid his head on his shoulder. "Yes. I see."

"I think you really do."

"I see the river, and you and that poor lad walking back barefoot along the bank. He couldn't even touch you, could he?"

"No, not by then, although I tried to take his hand and help him over the rough bits. He was gone."

"What did he do?"

"Didn't Winborn tell you?"

"Yes. He wasn't going to let me know any of the good parts, was he? Only the terror and the pain."

"Mm. The cautionary tale, to make sure none of it ever happens again." Archie raised his head a little, surveyed the storm-racked mess of the bed. "So much for that. When we got back, Richard put his things on and went straight out through the boathouse front doors and disappeared. I wanted to go after him, but the dean wouldn't let me. That's the part I really can't forgive myself. He was such a little man, and yet..."

"How old were you, Archie? Eighteen?"

"Just barely. And stark naked in front of the dean of my college, and his bloody poodle. But still. If I'd got past him, knocked him down, run after Richard in time..."

He'd have found another way. It wasn't your responsibility. The comforting platitudes ran through Rufus's mind. He kept his mouth shut on them: Archie must have heard the lot, and none of them could absolve him. "There are things we have to live with," he said instead, throat gritty with all the forced-back yelling he had done. "I know sometimes people can't. I'm so glad you did."

Archie closed his eyes. Tensions dissolved in him, hot snakes whose dispersal Rufus could feel through his own skin. Somewhere in the far reaches of the house, a door banged, Mrs Nettles up and about to seize her day. Surely that was the signal for Archie to seize his. To remember who he was and recoil out of this bed of sin. He was too good a man to turn on Rufus for corrupting him, but good men before him had stood shivering in cold morning light, buttoning up their shirts and begging Rufus to forget.

Instead he wrapped an arm around Rufus's waist. He spread his hand over Rufus's ribs, pressing, caressing. Rufus swallowed. They were both done, weren't they? Men stroked each other before passion, not afterwards. Henry had hated the aftermath, the stickiness and mess. His flamboyance had rested on shaky foundations of shame. "Dear Archie," Rufus whispered, "I don't think I can again. Not so soon."

"Good God, no. Won't you rest with me for a little while?"

Rufus kissed his brow. "The daylight's caught up with us, old fellow. The house is astir. And don't you want to... go and wash?"

"Do you?"

"Oh, no."

"That's good." The arm tightened. "Don't worry. Maria doesn't bring me breakfast in bed, and she seldom sees me out of it before seven. We have an hour or so. I'm sure I'm meant to be up and about taking care of you, but I don't want to lose a moment of this—your scent, the feel of you in my arms. Of yours around me."

"Oh, God. Please stop."

"What's wrong?"

"You're killing me. And—and the *bedclothes*..."

"I'll say you had night-sweats. I'll strip the bed down and put the things through the laundry myself. She lives with a lonely bachelor, Rufus—she doesn't examine the sheets. Hold me harder, would you?"

Hard enough to make his vertebrae pop, to wring from him a groaning chuckle of relief. Despite everything Rufus thought for a moment that he would stiffen up again, roll on top and come for the sheer joy of sharing dawn light with a lover. But Archie hauled the quilt up, hooked one leg over his thighs, pressed a sleepy kiss to the side of his neck, and the faded chintz roses on the walls began to rustle and sway in the first breeze from his dreams.

Chapter Seventeen

"The trouble with me baring my soul to you about Richard," Archie said, taking up comfortable residence in an armchair by the fire, "is that now you have to tell me about Charles."

Rufus stared at the carpet. Of all the library's beauties, he thought this was almost the best, with its threadbare pattern of lilies. He set his mind to pick it out, to follow a woven path away from Archie's words. He didn't want to think. Archie and Mrs Nettles had between them helped him downstairs. She had brought him breakfast on a tray, and Archie had settled him on the sofa with tender force, tucking a blanket around him, lighting a fire in spite of the morning's warmth—for cheerfulness, he'd said, and to help keep sorrows at bay. The lily path doubled back on itself, so Rufus clutched at the book in his lap instead. "You were right about the Barsetshire novel. I've almost finished it. Was that one the last in the series?"

"It was."

"Do you have the others? I want to read them all."

Patiently Archie got up. He went to the shelf behind Rufus and took down five more calf-bound volumes. Leaning over the back of the sofa, he laid them one by one in Rufus's lap. "There you are. Now, before you start—Charles."

Rufus stared at him almost resentfully. By rights, Archie ought to have been shy with him this morning. Even the lovers who'd stuck around for breakfast had done so with nervous good-fellowship, spilling their tea and making small talk. Archie seemed just the same, except that his gaze rested longer on Rufus's when their eyes met, and somehow all his movements spoke of an awareness of his presence, a quiet grace that would neither force home nor deny their new standing. He was an insistent bastard, too.

"I think I've remembered something. Part of what happened at Fort Roche."

"Is that good?"

"I don't know." Rufus waited, holding his breath, rubbing at the gold leaf on *The Warden*'s spine, until Archie had resumed his seat. "The person I'm always looking for, the strongest man—I think it's him. Charles."

"And you didn't know that before."

"No. He was my brother-in-law, my oldest childhood friend. I thought I was looking for anyone *but* him."

"When you were having your nightmare, you said you were going to stop him this time. Can you remember what he'd done?"

"No." Rufus sat up, gathering the books against his chest and cradling them. "But... the thing is, if I can remember that much, don't you think I ought to be able to get the rest?"

"I'm certain you would, in time."

"But suppose there were ways of making me remember now?"

"You're talking about the brigadier's damn hospital."

"Perhaps. I'm starting to think I don't have the right not to go."

Archie pressed his knuckles to his mouth. "All right," he said after a moment, his voice measured, almost distant. "Try something for me now. Imagine yourself back there, back at Roche."

"I... don't think I want to. Not just now."

"The brigadier's doctors will make you do at least this much, before they come at you with drugs and electrodes. I don't imagine they'll leave you to choose a suitable occasion, either."

"Archie, why are you doing this?"

"Just try and remember. Try."

Miserably Rufus obeyed. He leaned forward, resting his brow on the top of the pile of books, as if by contact with that orderly Victorian world he could make his own new one make sense. He gathered his thoughts and pushed them along the well-worn track of his bad dreams. Deeper and deeper, as far as they would go, to the place where the tunnel in his mind became a labyrinth, and Charles the Minotaur. He understood his own imagery well enough. He was an archaeologist, and his first excavation after the war had been on Sabros, with all its connections to Crete and the kingdom of Minos. Sabros had placed a mask on his enemy's face, given him a structure for the containment of the beast. It was simple enough. He pushed harder, and his throat closed. "Archie," he choked out. "I can't breathe."

Archie sprang up and darted to his side. "I'm sorry," he said, lifting the books off Rufus's lap. "So very sorry. Here, lie back." He unfastened the neck of the fresh pyjamas he'd given Rufus in exchange for the rumpled, come-stained nightshirt. Glass clinked off glass, and the clean, hot smell of brandy sliced through the stench of mud and death. "Drink this." He cupped the back of Rufus's skull, helping him hold the glass to his lips. "Listen. I don't care who your enemy is or what he did. You're not going anywhere."

"But my sister..."

"I know you want to help her. But Rosemary cares about herself, not you. She'd destroy you without a second thought to protect her position." Archie eased him back against the cushions. "Besides, if Charles is your monster, you won't be remembering anything she could bear to hear."

"What if I'm wrong? What if it's not true? What about poor Corporal Berry, lying in hospital with nobody to believe him?"

"Rufus. You're going to fret yourself into another flashback, and it's my fault if you did. But I don't want to have to wrestle you again, and you've already given me a shiner."

Rufus examined the anxious face looking down at him. A blue-purple mark was just beginning to rise over one cheekbone. "Dear God. I have."

"It doesn't matter. All that matters is that you get some rest, and stop talking nonsense about leaving me."

"Well, if you insist on harbouring a dangerous lunatic..."

"I do insist on harbouring him. Move over a bit and let me sit down. I'll read to you."

"Don't you have pastoral duties to attend?"

"Not just now." Archie settled on the edge of the sofa, his hip wedged comfortably against Rufus's. "Don't worry, I'll find out soon enough if anyone needs to be christened, married or buried. Now, where were you with your Trollope?"

"John Eames has just gone off to find Eleanor Arabin so she can testify to poor Crawley's innocence. I'm warning you, Archie—if he doesn't get there in time, I may have to stop reading."

"Ah, have faith in the Victorian romance dynamic. Crawley has to be seen to be innocent, but Major Grantly has to keep his promise to Grace *before* he knows that."

"It's all rather tortuous, isn't it?"

"What would you do if I said the book ended there, or you never got to find out?"

Rufus pulled a face at him. He knew he should be on his feet, getting dressed, keeping his word to Winborn and leaving Droyton behind him in the dust. But the rectory felt so very much like paradise to him this morning, Archie an archangel under new orders, preventing him with a fiery sword from leaving. "I might have to show you what a violent lunatic can really do."

"That's the good fellow. Settle back, then, and listen."

Maybe Archie was the serpent, not the angel. An unlikely candidate for the role, in clean black clerical garb, but the top two buttons of his shirt were open, the dog collar nowhere in sight. And whatever happened later on today, or tomorrow, or in all the empty days and years to come, he had been Rufus's lover. His lover! A pulse of nameless emotion went through him, and he put out a hand.

Archie caught it blindly, not raising his eyes from the book. "Don't," he said, the edges of the word softened and made ragged by tears. "Dear Rufus, what a night we had!"

"We can't talk about it. I know. We can't... It can't happen again."

"Hush. Please just let me read."

He did it beautifully. Rufus hadn't been read to since earliest childhood, unless you counted Henry sarcastically going through the gossip columns at the breakfast table. Archie's voice effortlessly conjured Grantly, Robarts, poor beleaguered Crawley, the contrasts between the Archdeacon's fat-of-the-land existence and the parson's poverty. He'd been right to insist on Rufus's trust: the tale unspooled itself to all the conclusions justice and love could require. The good ended happily, the bad—and nobody was really dreadful—offstage, punished no further than their crimes had warranted.

Perfect, believable, wonderful. So far from any kind of real life that Rufus wanted to dig Trollope up and shake him. "Archie," he said restlessly, into the silence the story had left behind it. "You don't have to worry, you know. You're the best of both worlds—Robarts' *and* Crawley's. It is possible to enjoy the good things of this world with a pure heart."

"Is that how you think of me? Pure of heart?"

"I'd stake my life on it. If you think desiring other men corrupts you..."

"I don't. But look at me. I'm an atheist vicar. A—A queer one. I don't think I'm the best of any clerical world. To tell you the truth, I'm not sure I can go on in this one."

Rufus sat up. He was stiff from his exertions of the night before, his fight with Archie and all that had followed. "I've brought this on you. It's all the more reason I should go."

"You've brought nothing on me but companionship, and a pleasure I thought I'd never experience again. Listen—if I can't make my desires accord with my ministry here, maybe it's time I—"

"Archie, no." Rufus pressed silencing fingertips to his mouth. "You don't think about overturning your whole life because of someone you just met."

"Why not, if the someone makes my heart turn inside out every time I look at him? If all I can think about is touching him again, and having him touch me?"

"Oh, God. Where's Mrs Nettles this morning?"

"She's gone with Drusilla and Elspeth to look at the manor house. Their new home."

"It's really hers now?"

"The old lady's solicitor was with me this morning, before you got up. She tied it up for Drusilla so tightly that Carson won't even entertain a probate challenge from the relatives."

"I don't understand. They scarcely seemed to know each other, except at the very last when Lady Birch was dying here in your garden, and she said..."

"What did she say? I was in the house, being warned by Winborn of your homosexual proclivities."

"For all the good that did." He reached out, and this time Archie shifted yearningly to receive his embrace. "She said Drusilla had come to her before, but she hadn't been able to recognise her. Her spirit wasn't within her. Something like that."

"Makes about as much sense as anything else that goes on around here. Oh, Rufus. If you're asking if the house is empty, it is. Even your dog went out with the women."

Nevertheless, Rufus got up and closed the library door. There was no key in the lock, and he was willing to bet he'd find very few of them in the vicar's all-too-open house. He paused for a moment, fighting a tide of vertigo. Then he carefully lifted a chair from beside the table and wedged its back beneath the door handle. "There," he said. "What do you think?"

"I think you're not well enough. You shouldn't even be on your feet."

"I won't be. I'll be on the floor between yours."

A winded gasp escaped Archie. He looked ready to run for it, to take a leap through the open window and make his escape through the garden and down Pilgrim Way, or whichever other route he thought might take him to salvation. Then a deep blush suffused his features, and he said, "Close that casement, then. Draw the curtain a little way across—not so much that anyone would notice from the lane. The roses will hide the rest."

Rufus did as he'd been bidden. He was shaking by the time he came back to the sofa, racked by disbelief, excitement, sheer physical exhaustion. Archie saw it all: lunged gracefully upright and caught him. "Let me be the one on his knees this time."

"What?"

"Let me. I wasn't any good at the rest of it, but Richard used to say I... I..."

"Gave good head? Oh—an awful expression, but I heard the American troops use it, and it's nicer than some of the others."

"Hmm. Over-sexed, overpaid and over here, eh? Well, not in so many words, but yes. It was the one way I could force him past his scruples." Archie's grip on Rufus's shoulders became painful. "It was very wrong of me."

"Richard was just a boy, and so were you. Show me how a man does this for a man."

Archie eased him down onto the sofa, then knelt as if he would have fallen otherwise. Rufus spread his thighs for him, mortified at how hard he'd become just at the naming of this deed, the prospect. His hands were too unsteady to manage the cord of his pyjamas, but that didn't matter: Archie undid him precisely. "Look at you," he said in wonder. "I didn't get the chance to, while we were rolling around upstairs. You're so big."

"Not breaking any records, I shouldn't think."

"Not getting many complaints, either. Oh, Rufus. Can I really do this for you?"

"Don't make me beg you to." Rufus squirmed uncomfortably. "I don't understand how the rest of me can feel so exhausted, and yet..."

"And yet this beast still rages?"

"Mm. I think it'll be the last part of me to give up, with you around." Rufus tipped his head back a little, unable to bear the lambent gaze on his any longer. The half-drawn curtains had taken the glare out of the room, exposing its lines and shapes with subdued clarity. There was that strange painting on the far wall, the gloomy patina of age seeming to dissolve from it as Archie leaned in. The distraction was enough—just—to stop him from coming at the brush of warm lips over his tip. "Archie. Your painting—the one over the mantelpiece..."

Archie looked up, expression comical with disbelief. "Yes?"

"The hill in the background—it's George Mount, isn't it? The one with the Iron Age hillfort on top."

"I'm not sure. It's a grim old daub, that's all I know. But Maria showed signs of apoplexy when I proposed taking it down, so..."

"I think it must be that hill. I recognise the slopes to either side. It must've been painted from just outside the church, to get that view."

"Fascinating. Speaking of hills, you do know you're about to go over, don't you?"

"Hold me, then. Grip me round the base." Rufus demonstrated with his own grasp, then took Archie's hand and put it there in place. "It'll slow me up, and stop me pushing too far into your throat. Those aren't hillfort ruins on the top. There's something cut into the chalk, some kind of pattern."

"Rufus, you're a more experienced man than I am. Is it bad sexual etiquette for me to start without you?"

Rufus jolted with laughter. He could see the shape of Archie's straining cock in the crotch of his trousers. "Here, use this," he said, handing him the napkin left behind from his breakfast. "We can rinse it out and sneak it onto the washing line. One mark on those black trousers of yours, though..."

"And we're done for. I know."

He took the napkin, unbuttoned his fly, and Rufus forgot all about the painting and the pattern in the chalk. Archie was reaching into the front of his pants. He would suck Rufus to climax. They were safe and sealed up in this beautiful room, and nothing could touch or prevent them. Rufus spread his bare feet on the carpet. He had lilies underfoot, a strong and noble man between his thighs. He pushed his hips up, groaning, and felt Archie's answering sound as a vibration on the head of his shaft. The lovely mouth had engulfed him. He stared for a moment: the explicit movements of that dark head, shy at first then bolder, lips closing tight. His grip on the base of Rufus's cock still firm, holding back his first heaving effort to come...

Rufus couldn't look anymore. He tipped his head to lean on the back of the sofa, put an arm across his mouth so he could grunt and shout into the muffling wool of his dressing gown. He didn't get the second he normally counted on to warn his partner of imminent orgasm: but Archie never missed a beat, just let go his restraining clench and plunged to suck him down whole. Rufus braced his thighs, electric bursts of pleasure contracting every muscle. He came with a tearing sweetness he hadn't known his flesh could attain, a protracted wringing-out that left his cock flaccid, slipping out from between Archie's lips. "Are you there yet?" he gasped, leaning over him. "Archie?"

"Oh, almost... Almost..."

Rufus held him tight. He kissed his skull, shuddered in a backwash of sensation at the rhythmic pump of Archie's strong arm. Archie laid his brow on Rufus's knee: made a sound of absolute relief and release, and after long seconds when Rufus knew he was spilling helplessly into the napkin, into the enclosing tunnel of his own fist, fell forward into his arms. "Rufus. Oh, God..."

"Come here. Come up here to me." Rufus aided his blind scramble onto the sofa. His big rangy frame was a tough lift, but nevertheless Rufus hoisted him halfway into his lap. "I've got you."

"Yes." They clung together, shattered breathing subsiding. "You do have me, Rufus. Anything you want or need."

"Don't make promises, dear fellow."

"But I want to. I'll keep Winborn away from you. I'll stand up to him myself—it's long past time I did. You can stay here, and—"

"Archie, hush. Just sit beside me."

"Couldn't we wait a bit, and go again?"

"Are you making up for lost time, Reverend Thorne?"

Archie gazed down at him. His expression became utterly serious. "I would like," he said, "to lay you down and make up twenty years of lost time with you."

"Right." Rufus swallowed a pain in his throat. "And what time do you think it is now?"

"I've no idea."

"So I have to be careful for both of us. Half-drawn curtains and a chair wedged under the doorhandle won't save us if Mrs Nettles comes back. Go and sort it out."

"Oh, Rufus. This is what you've had to do, isn't it?"

"Yes. It's my world, and I know how to navigate it. Go on." He waited until Archie had thrown back the curtains, put the chair back in its place and left the door just as it had been, three innocent inches ajar. Then he caught his hand and drew him close. "Smooth your hair down. Where's that napkin?"

"Safe in my pocket."

"Well, it seems to have done the trick. You'll do. Now come and sit next to me, and we're just two gentlemen friends discussing a painting."

"Oh, bugger the bloody painting."

"*Archie.*"

"Yes." He thudded down onto the sofa, buried his face in his hands. "I'm so sorry."

Rufus listened carefully to the silence of the house, then briefly put an arm around him and pressed a kiss to his brow. "There's no need. There was a time when I wanted to shout it from the rooftops too, but this is a world that would destroy us both if it got half the chance. So we don't give it any free shows. Do you understand?"

"Yes. I hate it, but I understand."

"Good. What about me? Am I presentable?"

Archie sat up. "A little bit ruffled." Gently he rectified the damage, brushing Rufus's hair back from his brow, straightening the collar of the dressing gown. "Perfect," he said at length, with a stricken fervour that made Rufus want to forget all his hard-learned precautions and lie down for him in broad sunshine, right on the village green, if that was his pleasure. "All right. What about the damn painting?"

"Just look at it."

Archie obeyed, mechanically at first, and then with dawning interest. "It *is* George Mount, isn't it? How strange that I never saw."

"The half-light brought it out. Do you see the markings?"

"Yes, I do. They look like concentric rings cut into the chalk."

"How old is the painting? Do you know?"

"You'd have to ask Mrs Nettles. It actually belongs to her, as I found out when I tried to replace it with a nice modern watercolour. She had it from her grandmother, who'd had it from her mother before her—the usual tale, whenever I want to introduce innovations around here. That's why the place looks like it's falling down—my poverty, and her sentiment."

"She told me her family had a long history here."

"Yes, and all of it wrapped around the rectory. The male Nettleses were groundskeepers and butlers, and the women faithful housekeepers."

"Isn't Nettles her married name, though?"

"Ah, if she'd ever been married." Archie found an unconvincing smile. "It's not just the vicar who has secrets in

Droyton, you see. There was somebody once, I believe, and she keeps a portrait of a very dashing fellow in the housekeeper's room. But it didn't work out, and you know there's a practice—a benign one, I think—of turning a Miss into Missus, for women of a certain age in little places like this."

"So, always a Nettles at the rectory, and always a Trigg at the inn."

"That's right, and Maria wasn't joking about the ancient enmity. Those family lines go back around here to Henry the Eighth at least, and I suspect the Nettleses back then were ardent Catholics."

"And the Triggs stone-hurling Puritans. I can imagine that."

"I can, too. Trigg Roundheads to the Nettles Cavaliers."

"Always on opposing sides. Even now, the good Church-woman versus the Dissenter. What a place!"

"You know," Archie said thoughtfully, "Much as I'm certain both Maria and Hester Trigg are perfectly sincere in their beliefs, I sometimes feel their respective faiths are less important than..."

"Than what?"

"Well, than the fact of their opposition. I can't quite explain it, but when I think about them, I almost see them as heraldic beasts on either side of a shield."

Rufus nodded. The image came clearly to him, too. "Is there anything in the middle of the shield, do you think?"

"With one of them guarding it and the other always trying to tear it down? I don't know, but here's a wild idea for you—don't you think Drusilla would fit rather well between the two?"

"Yes, I do. She's a newcomer here, though."

"The funny thing is, so was Lady Birch, sixty years ago. The lady of the manor before her died intestate, and the hall stood empty for a year. Then—this is village legend, mind, so you may want your pinch of salt—an energetic young woman turned up out of nowhere, moved in and claimed the place as her own. We didn't have much by way of conveyancing laws back then, and somehow no-one cared to challenge her. The old house was called Birch Hall, and so Lady Birch she became, over time. There's an amazing power in names."

"There is. And now the place belongs to Drusilla Hazelgrove. I don't claim to understand, but the whole thing has its own peculiar beauty, doesn't it?"

"Yes," Archie said faintly, his attention fixing suddenly, yearningly tight on Rufus. "You do."

Oh, he would melt in the heat of that regard. He would forget himself, steal a kiss here and now with the curtains drawn back, the door open, ruin both of them in a single irrecoverable moment. "Don't," he said hopelessly. He didn't have the strength to run away now, but it would have to happen soon. "Listen. I have my own crackpot theory about names around here. Do you want to hear it?"

"I want to hear all your mad theories."

"Well, go and sit at your own end of the sofa like a good gentleman, and I'll tell you. It has to do with that painting, and a place called Caer Droea."

"Caer Droea... I've heard of that, haven't I?"

"I'd say so, to judge from your beautiful library. Droea is the old Welsh-language name for ancient Troy, or Troea. You can hear the connection between the words."

"Yes, I can. And the *Caer* part means fortress or castle."

"That's it. So we get the fortress or castle of Troy. But *droea* was often interpreted as if it was old-Welsh *troeau*, a plural form of *tro*."

"You've lost me."

"All right. Do you know what a Troy Town is?"

"Actually, I do. There used to be a beauty on the Downs near Brighton—my dad took me to visit it when I was no bigger than Elspeth is now. Huge turf walls. I ran around it for hours, completely intrigued by the idea of a maze you couldn't get lost in."

"Exactly." Having persuaded Archie out of arm's reach, Rufus had to resist the impulse to seize his shoulder in the pleasure of a shared idea. "So not a maze at all, but..."

"Oh. A labyrinth. Not a Troy fortress at all, but a *turning* one."

"That's it. A turning castle."

"A perfect description. The one near Brighton was high up on a hilltop, just where you'd expect an Iron Age hillfort or earthworks to be. Wait—I've got a book here somewhere." Archie levered upright and went to scan the shelves, running an eager, affectionate hand over well-worn spines. "This is it. *Mazes and Labyrinths*, by WH Matthews. Look."

The volume was a beautiful first edition. Rufus took it reverently, and Archie settled beside him, reaching to open the cover. "The illustrations are here. This one's from Visby in Sweden, and this one's carved on a rock here in England."

"Yes, up on the Derby moors. Three thousand years old at least."

"And this is a diagram, a kind of idealised schematic, I suppose, taken from all those real examples."

Rufus traced the printed lines with his finger, careful not to touch. His skin felt damp as hothouse grapes after his tussle with Archie. There it was—the pattern that had haunted him since the Sabros dig, the nested concentric circles looping back and forth, broken by the sudden incursion of two straight lines from the outside to the centre. The entrance and the exit, two separate concepts united, their opposition wiped away as if the difference between them were irrelevant, meaningless. "When we were excavating in Greece, my colleague Professor Hargreaves—the poor chap I attacked—he had hopes of finding something like this. The pattern's also called the Cretan key, although no labyrinth, and no maze, for that matter, has ever been found at Knossos. I'm beginning to wonder if we might have found one here."

"What, in Droyton?" Archie's eyebrows went up as his question hung in the air. "Oh. Wait. *Droyton.*"

Now Rufus did want to hug him. He held back, wondering if Archie could see the flying sparks that seemed to be filling the space between them. "Exactly. Droyton. Troy Town. And as if that wasn't good enough, it's Droyton Parva."

"*Little* Troy Town. Why would they bother adding that, unless there was a larger one somewhere, a Droyton Magna? I've often wondered about that. And there's no such place, as far as I'm aware."

"Unless we're looking at it." Rufus indicated the painting. He traced the shape of the hilltop in the air, the strange white markings that ringed its crest. "Droyton Magna—the great labyrinth. I have to get up there, Archie."

"As soon as you're well enough to hang onto the back of my bike. Which isn't today, so don't look at me like that. What on earth are they *for*, these labyrinths? Does anybody know?"

"Only speculation. Not for caging up the Minotaur, that's for sure—if he had the sense to keep going in the same direction, he'd stroll out in no time. It's a symbol, a concept, that's cropped up all over the world, across thousands of years. Simple and powerfully complex at the same time."

"There's one in the cathedral at Chartres, isn't there?"

"Yes, and that gives us a clue to a modern application—well, post-medieval modern, anyway. If you couldn't afford to make your pilgrimage to Santiago, or Fatima or wherever, you could gain the same benefit by ritually walking the labyrinth at Chartres. So I'd hazard a guess that it's all about making a journey— through life, or from one spiritual plane to another, or whatever you need. You see how the entrance and exit routes plunge up through the rings?"

Archie nodded, leaning close to examine the schematic on the page. "It should look abrupt. But it doesn't, somehow. I remember running between the turf banks, thinking I was about to find the way out, but then the route switched back on itself and I found I still had a long way to go."

"And later, when you'd decided you'd be in there for ages..."

"It delivered me quite suddenly, and I shot out into the light. Is that what it's about, do you think? Accepting that we never really know how long we've got left, or how far we'll have to journey on?"

"I believe that's part of it, certainly."

They both looked up at the creak of the front door. A moment later, Mrs Nettles and Drusilla appeared in the library doorway. "Ah," Mrs Nettles said, smiling benignly at the scene before her. "That's right, Dr Denby. You look better already. If you stay tucked up on the sofa there, we'll soon have you on the mend. And the Reverend has somebody to share his dreadful, dusty, boring old books with at last. He'll be happy about that."

"I am happy about it, Maria."

"And you both have some colour in your faces. That's a pleasant sight to see, though you have to watch out where you're going, Reverend—that bruise is coming up a treat, where you walked into the door."

"It's fine. Don't worry." Archie pressed a repressive foot against Rufus's. "How are things up at the manor house?"

"In a state, to put it frankly. I'm glad to say Miss Hazelgrove's consented to stay with us for a little while, until she can arrange to have some repairs made around the place."

"With your permission, Thorne, of course." Drusilla stepped forward, looking more regal than ever this morning, less like the lady of the manor than a Celtic warrior queen. "Please don't imagine your hospitality is taken for granted."

"I know it isn't. You're most welcome. How does my little monkey like her new quarters?"

"I'm sure she'd take pleasure in telling you herself. Andrasta?"

The child squeezed between Mrs Nettles' skirt and Drusilla's. She pattered over to the sofa, then to Rufus's surprise, veered away from Archie and came to stand in front of him. The two women had reached a compromise over her hair, which was plaited neatly down her back, and in no way lessened her resemblance to a strange mechanical doll. "What do I do?" Rufus asked, the question startled out of him. His experience of children was limited to peering anxiously at poor little Charlie in his cradle.

"Why, pick her up and sit her on your knee," Archie said gently. "That's what she wants."

Gingerly Rufus scooped her up. Her ribcage felt like a bird's beneath his hands. She broke into a beam of pleasure, then suddenly leaned against his chest as if they were old friends. "Goodness," he said, hoping the pang of tears at the back of his throat wouldn't touch his voice. "Hello, then, sweetheart. Are you going to live up in the big house soon, and..." He racked his brains for something a five-year-old girl might like to hear. "...and become a princess?"

"No," she replied, sounding a good deal like her mother—as if she appreciated the thought, but felt compelled to set the matter straight. "I *am* going to live there. But I'm going to become a *priestess*."

Mrs Nettles smiled. "A card, isn't she? We'll leave her with you for the moment, gentlemen, but mind you send her packing if she's a nuisance. We'll be in the kitchen, Miss Hazelgrove having kindly offered to help put up some of last year's apples for chutney."

A gracious inclination of the dark head. "Just so. Any such small returns for the friendship shown me are gladly made."

No sooner had Drusilla and Mrs Nettles turned away than the library door flew wide, this time beneath the impact of Rufus's dog, clearly in search of her new mistress. She gave a grunting bark of satisfaction at finding the child and Rufus in the same place, sat down hard at his feet and laid her ugly muzzle on his lap.

Archie got up and went to the window. Then he turned and watched Rufus in silence for some moments. "Well, that completes the set."

"I'm sorry?"

"You look very much at home there. You see, everybody loves you—children, dogs. The vicar."

"Oh, Archie." Rufus didn't know how to express the rush of pain, fear and joy such an innocent, impossible observation sent through him. There'd been a time when he'd viewed the kids and the dogs, the love of another human being, as a kind of birthright. He knew better now. He glanced at Elspeth, afraid of how much she might understand, but she seemed to be living in a kind of happy dream since her mother's return. Her eyes were closed and she was winding her fingers through Pippin's rough pelt. He lowered his voice, mindful of the still-open door. "Please listen. You have to be careful of everything you say, everything you do. Even how you look at me. It would kill me to see you learning the hard way."

Archie folded his arms. "Sorry," he said gruffly. "I'll do better, I promise."

"That's a good, rational chap. Now, apply those brains for me again. We have our crackpot theory on the whereabouts of Droyton Magna, the great labyrinth. As you said, *parva* implies a *magna*, and vice versa. So..."

"Where's the little labyrinth of Droyton Parva?"

"Precisely."

"I have precisely no idea. But it seems to me that all our mysteries round here begin and end in the church. Perhaps we should start there." He held a hand out to restrain Rufus's immediate response, which threatened to dislodge both Elspeth and the dog. "*Tomorrow.*"

Chapter Eighteen

Rufus had one duty to discharge before he could allow himself to dive with Archie into the tantalising mysteries of Droyton Parva church. He was mortified by the necessity, so he tackled it straight away, before his own shame or Archie's cunning could find a way to let him avoid the task. He breakfasted with his strange, ad-hoc rectory family—Elspeth, Drusilla, the dog on her own special cushion by the little girl's side, Archie and Mrs Nettles presiding contentedly over the meal—and then, disobeying Archie's instructions to sit in the garden and watch the apples grow, he waited until the vicar had departed about his pastoral rounds, got washed and dressed and set off for the Maidens' Dance.

Mrs Trigg was nowhere to be seen. Mildred, the frightened girl, had taken her place behind the reception desk, and seemed less oppressed than Rufus might have expected by the honour. In fact she looked subtly merry, a flush of interest on her thin face as she glanced around for incoming custom. "Morning, Mildred," Rufus greeted her, unable to stop an awkward blush of his own. The last time the girl had seen him, he'd been flat on his face on the bar-room carpet after a sincere attempt to kill her brother. "How are you today?"

She didn't appear to hold grudges. She lit up with a beaming smile at the sight of him. "Good morning, Dr Denby! I'm in *charge*."

"So I see. Is Mrs Trigg away?"

"No, sir." She checked behind her, then leaned across the desk to whisper. "She ain't showed her face downstairs since that set-down she got in the church, and that's the truth! She's poorly, she says. Ashamed, is more like it, and so she ought to be." Poor Mildred had been corked up hard for a very long time. Her words tumbled over one another in the pleasure of release. "Her with her nose in the air, always better nor anybody else! And that boy of hers no more than a common thief. He had a *watch* in his room, Mrs Ribble's gardener told me, and a necklace of Mrs Jessop's what's been missing for months, and her own maid dismissed at the time under suspicion! Locked in his room, is Master Jebediah, and madam-my-landlady so put about, I doubt when he'll see daylight again."

"Mildred..."

She restrained herself with an effort. "Eh, I'm sorry, Dr Denby. Rattling on like this, and never asking after you. Are you better today?"

"Much, thank you. I've come to say how sorry I am for frightening everyone, and I'd like to see your brother, if I could."

"Give it no thought, sir, give it no thought. You was poorly, like Reverend Thorne said, like lots of them that went to the war and had hard times. Seems to me your coming here has given this village a right shaking up in lots of ways, and none the worse for it. Billy's just through in the bar. He's in charge there, just as I am here, and when I asked madam for wage-and-a-half for us both— considering extra duties—she agreed to it, meek as a lamb. Wait here, sir, and I'll fetch him for you."

"Hold on just one moment, Mildred. I told Mrs Trigg I'd be staying for a week, and she's perhaps held my room for me when she could have let it to someone else."

"Bless you, sir, no. We're none so busy here at the Maidens' that she ever runs out of rooms. No-one would stay at this gloomy old hole of a place who had any choice in the matter, and that's *my* opinion."

Rufus thought it was probably a valid one. "Nevertheless, I had no choice when I first arrived, and she made me welcome after her fashion." He took out his wallet. "Here's enough to cover my stay up to this morning."

"Well, it's more than most gentlemen would have done, seeing as you've not been here the last two nights." She had the makings of a decent landlady herself, not waiting for Rufus to offer twice before running the money nimbly into the cash register. "You'll be staying at the rectory now, no doubt. Good, good. The vicar'll look after you, like he does all our waifs and strays around here. Oh—not meaning any offence to you, sir."

"No offence taken," Rufus assured her, fighting laughter. "Listen, though, Mildred—I'm in no place to lecture you, and I don't mean to. But when very proud, strict people like Mrs Trigg get a fall, especially in front of all their neighbours and friends... Well, it can hit them very hard. I know she hasn't given you and your brother an easy life. But Billy will be off soon to be a policeman, and you won't be stuck here all your life either, I'm sure. Can you try to be a little bit kind to her, now she's down?"

"Oh, Dr Denby. If you only knew..."

"That's just it—I don't, so I've no right to speak to you like this. I'm asking it as a favour to me, not to Mrs Trigg. She might really be feeling ill, after all this disgrace. Will you just go up and ask her if she'd like a cup of tea, something like that? And check on Jebediah, as well. She mustn't lock the poor lad up forever because of this."

Mildred thrust out her lower lip. "Well—since it's you who's asking, sir, and you a famous professor who might be said to know the rights of things..."

It wasn't the time to make light of his qualifications. "Thank you, Mildred."

"I'll send Billy through to you. And I'll go up and see after the dragon straight after, since you wish it."

Rufus hardly knew if he'd done the right thing in appealing to her better nature. She was a different girl in the wake of her tyrant's overthrow, a lilt in her step as she vanished through the door into the bar. He didn't have time to think about it before Billy appeared, if possible even happier than his sister under the new conditions. He would make an excellent policeman if he could hold onto his gift for not taking personally attacks from villains and madmen: strode across the hallway, big hand held out to clasp Rufus's. "Well, Doctor! You're looking better today."

"I wish I could say the same to you. That cut on your lip's my work, isn't it?"

"It's nothing. You was having a nightmare, and didn't rightly know your friends."

"Can I still consider you my friend?" Rufus had to steady his voice. He'd left two fine men bruised and bloody in this village now. "I've come to apologise. And—although I'm afraid of adding insult to injury—to ask if you'd accept the price of a round of drinks from me, to treat your friends and show there's no hard feelings."

Billy's brow creased. He was a sweet-natured man, honour and kindness knit into him from the bones of his native earth. "I couldn't allow that, sir. You did no harm, and me and my friends'll raise a glass to your health without being paid for it."

"All right. Thank you, then. I'd better be on my way—I've got a lot of work to do at the church."

"Ah, that's grand. We'll all be waiting to hear about the things you find in there. Perhaps when you're done, you'll give us a talk in the village hall or some such? I'm sure folks'd love to listen."

"I will do that, yes." Rufus shook hands with him again, and turned away. He had to get out into the air. He was recovering fast, but weariness still tugged at his limbs, and there was only so much contact he could bear with strangers—even the best of them—without longing to hide himself once more in Archie's embrace. Thoughts of the rectory, of Archie opening the garden gate to welcome him—the images pulled at him like cool water on a blazing day. He opened the street door and stood breathing deeply, tucking his wallet away. God, just as well poor Billy hadn't accepted his gift. He wasn't sure he had enough left now for the train fare back to London, and he had to talk to Archie about paying for his keep...

"You should have let me come with you, you know."

He whipped round. There was the man himself, leaning in the shade of the shop-awning next door, looking pleasant and fresh as new daylight. "Oh. Did you follow me?"

"Not at all, old fellow, but in a town this size, I didn't have to look far."

Rufus went to join him. So much had changed between them that he had to give conscious thought to their casual meeting, and he could sense Archie's effort to do the same. "I'm much better today. You don't have to worry about me."

"It can't have been easy to go back there."

"Well—no. But I had to settle up for my board, and I wanted to see Billy and make matters right with him."

"Both missions safely accomplished?"

"Yes, I think so." Rufus checked that greengrocer was out of earshot, stacking cauliflowers on his outdoor shelves. "There's a minor revolution going on. Mrs Trigg's taken to her bed after Sunday's debacle, and Mildred's seized the reins."

"Good for her. That old devil bullied the life out of her. Still, if I know my Rufus, you gently reproved her and advised her to be gracious in victory."

"Good Lord. I can't decide if it's awkward to be so well known, or..." He paused, throat tightening. "...or lovely. Since I'm working through my errands, I have to tackle you next. I'd like to stay and investigate the church and the hilltop, Winborn or no Winborn, and—"

"You're about to ask me about rent."

"Apparently my skull is made of glass today."

"Before you worry about any of that, don't you think..." Archie put a hand on his shoulder and indicated the tailor's shop over the road. "Don't you think Dawkins has some nice shirts in the window? I'm not saying you don't suit the rector's turn-of-the-century style, but if you're staying—and Winborn has *absolutely* no say in whether you do or not—you might like to buy some new things."

"Oh. Yes, maybe I will. Not today, though. It's time I got to work."

"You don't have a shilling left in the world, do you, Dr Denby?"

Rufus went still. Archie's gaze on him was penetrating and kind. Too much for Rufus to bear: he growled out, "Walk with me, will you?", and set off back towards the shelter and shade of Pilgrim Way.

Archie kept pace with him. He let Rufus stamp the worst of his chagrin out into the dust, then said, conversationally, "I thought you might have come to me last night. I rather unsubtly left my door open."

"Hush, Archie. Even the rose bushes have ears in places like this." But there were long, generous gaps between the houses on this part of the lane, and after a moment he said, "I thought of it. You've omitted to give me a map of your ramshackle maze of a house, though, and I didn't dare blunder about in search of you."

"I realised that after a while, and went in search of *you*."

"In that case you'll know I left my door open, too."

"Yes, but I arrived too late. You were sleeping like a fallen angel—flat on your stomach, no nightshirt. I couldn't have borne to wake you." He drew an unsteady breath. "Which isn't to say I didn't go back to my room and do unspeakable things on my own."

A wave of warmth passed through Rufus despite his embarrassment. "I'd like to know what a Church of England vicar considers unspeakable."

"And he might tell you—if you tell him how a famous doctor of archaeology comes to be flat broke."

"Oh, God."

"Put your hand through my arm. This is an old-fashioned place—gentlemen stroll like that all the time. Besides, you're an invalid." Courteously he held out one elbow, and waited until Rufus had shyly accepted the offered support. "I have a feeling, and forgive me if I'm wrong, that Henry may have something to do with the story."

No point in denial, not with a transparent skull. And Rufus didn't even want to keep the miserable business a secret anymore. "Henry decided he didn't love me. But he *had* grown rather fond of my income, and not having to work, and the flat in Piccadilly and all the rest of it. So he decided he'd keep the money, if not the man."

Archie's arm tightened. "Blackmail?"

"Yes. He was very young, you see. And he could act the part of injured innocence very well. You must think me utterly pathetic."

They were passing the door of the rectory. Archie turned suddenly, lifted the rickety gate and drew Rufus into the green, fragrant tangle of the pergola. He was getting better at this: made sure they were deeply enmeshed among the yellow roses before pulling him into his arms. "Poor Rufus," he whispered. "What a little bastard."

"Only as much as I let him be!" Rufus gave up all resistance as a bad job, wrapped his arms around Archie and held on as tightly as he was being held. "I should have told him to tell and be damned. He'd never have let me go to jail. "

"Not while his goose had golden eggs to lay, no. But your job—your reputation..."

"I'd have let the job go hang, if that had been all. But my parents... There's not much love lost between us, but they live in a village a lot like this one, and they'd never have recovered from the disgrace." He sniffed involuntarily and gave a choked moan of disgust, but Archie had another of his clean linen handkerchiefs at the ready. He took it blindly. "The war solved my problem by blowing poor Henry to brick dust, but..."

"Heaven only knows how long it would have gone on for otherwise. Did he leave you anything at all?"

"Enough to scrape by on. He wasn't stupid. But I'd got myself into debt, furnishing the flat the way he liked it, taking him out, buying him things. I did love him, Archie. Even when he'd left, and I got the first blackmail note from him in the post, I still couldn't believe what he'd done."

"So you were cleaned out."

"Yes. When I got demobbed, I was going to use my first proper expedition pay-packet from the museum to settle my debts, but—"

"You were fired." Archie held his shoulders, tried to look into his face. "Wait, though. I know it's a pittance, but why on earth haven't you had your stipend through from Caroline for your work at the church?" After a long, painful moment—Rufus still couldn't quite bear to tell him—he clapped his hand to his brow. "Oh, no. *We* were meant to pay it, weren't we?"

"Not you personally."

"No, of course. The diocese. For heaven's sake, man, why didn't you say?"

"Could *you* have, in my place?"

"I think if it came down to a choice between Mrs Trigg's back room and the gutter, I might have swallowed my pride, yes."

"But I never had to make that choice." Rufus got his head up, met Archie's gaze with passionate fullness. "*You* found me."

"Well, thank God. Thank God."

"Yes, and unlike you I believe there's someone or something there to be thanked. But I've been racking my brains for some way to pay you for my bed and my keep, and—"

"Rufus, I won't hear of it. Truly, you insult me. I don't charge Drusilla for her board, and she's as rich as Croesus now."

"I'm sorry."

"Besides, if it worries you, the parish is really the debtor here. You've already excavated half the church out of the goodness of your heart."

Rufus chuckled reluctantly. "I'm not sure finding a hole beneath the altar counts."

"Not to mention the murals and the little goddess. Everything really is all right."

Rufus might have waited his whole life for someone to say that to him. He wondered if many supposedly responsible adults secretly harboured such a dream. When Archie said it, he believed. He rubbed his brow against the black-clad shoulder in its handsome waistcoat and shirt. "God help me, you're perfect. I have to go in and get my kit and my torches. I'd give anything to take you with me to bed right now."

"Can't we? I know you have a lot to do, but we could be quick."

"No. Never during the daytime, not with other people in the house. And if we do, it'll be anything but quick." Rufus failed to intercept Archie's hand in a downward plunge. Helplessly he strained against the squeezing, delicious pressure at his groin. "Damn you. I might have been sleeping like an angel last night, but I wasn't having angelic dreams, I can assure you."

"Tonight, then."

"Yes. If you can hold out until then, I promise. Anything you want."

***

Alice Winborn was sitting on a tombstone outside the church, looking rather like a graveyard angel herself. She was wearing a set of Land Girl dungarees, stout boots and a crisp white shirt. Giles from the farm was cross-legged on the grass at her feet, gazing up at her with undisguised adoration.

She rose quietly when Rufus and Archie approached. She was absolutely sober today, Rufus could tell. A strange new tension restrained her as she sought his eyes, and he remembered their parting on the flank of the hill: her daring, gallant kiss. Then her gaze expanded to include Archie—the hand Rufus had returned to the crook of his arm for the rest of their walk down the lane; the very air between them—and she smiled, in a perfect mix of comprehension, disappointment and relief. "Good afternoon, gentlemen. I went to the rectory, but Mrs Nettles said you were both on your way here to work in the church. I'd like to help you, if I can, and I hope to make less of a mess of it than I did the other day." She spread her hands. "I've even dressed the part."

"And very becomingly." Archie nodded genially to Giles. "You've had company while you waited, I see."

"Yes. Mr Giles was kind enough to sit and talk to me. You were on your way to check the woods were clear of traps, weren't you, Giles?"

The farmhand scrambled upright and began to back off into the shadows. Rufus was certain enough of Archie by now—of Alice, too—to be sure neither of them would deliberately prolong a hoax or a senseless joke. They were both quite simply, for whatever reasons, blind to Giles's gender, despite the delicate blush painting the poor kid's cheeks. Maybe Rufus would have been fooled too, if he hadn't come in from the outside. "Sorry to steal Alice away from you," he said, hoping to throw out a line of understanding, but he seemed to make things worse: Giles turned and fled, crashing into the undergrowth beyond the churchyard. "Oh, dear."

"Don't worry," Archie said, looking on sympathetically. "Poor lad has a bit of a crush, I'd say. I'm sure Alice is used to dealing with such things."

"Oh, yes, dear Archie. I'm constantly besieged by young lovers, of course." Gaily she seized Rufus's free hand. "Come along, the two of you. I bet you're wanting to get back into that fascinating hole under the altar. And it doesn't like men, so I'm willing to go first, like a canary down a mine."

She led the way down the turf track towards the church. Between her and Archie, Rufus had a sense of childhood days revived, the undemanding companionship of Charlie and Rosemary before the adult world had crashed in on them. If Alice's insight had failed her where Giles was concerned, she had certainly picked up a new signal between the vicar and his gentleman companion, and the knowledge had lifted a weight off her. Just for a moment Rufus wished he could stop time, hold this sunny instant here, the three of them in their strange balance. He followed her up the church steps, catching her smile like an infection. "You seem very bright today, Miss Winborn."

"*Alice*, for godsakes. If you knew how much I hate my family name... I was going to change it before the war, and that went wrong. And recently I've been having all kinds of stupid ideas about changing it again, mostly because my uncle regards an unmarried woman as an eyesore and an abomination. And, despite being a pinprick on the map, Droyton Parva does have *such* nice men!" She pushed the door open, smiling back over her shoulder. "But I've given them up."

"Men?" Rufus queried, laughing. Maybe Giles stood a chance after all.

"No, not yet. The stupid ideas. Oh, and trying to be demure, in case that isn't obvious. And I feel much, much better for..." She came to a sudden halt. Rufus grabbed Archie's arm to prevent them both from bumping into her. "Oh," she said flatly, her voice echoing weirdly in the dim-lit space. "Something awful's happened in here."

Chapter Nineteen

Archie stepped round in front of her. He was trying to shield Rufus, too—a luxury Rufus couldn't allow himself, though the gesture had touched him to the quick. He joined Archie at the top of the aisle, scanning the shadows. "What's wrong? I don't see anything out of place."

"Something is, though. Look at the altar."

The cloth and candles were undisturbed. The flowers from Archie's Sunday service were still fresh and glowing in their vase. In this place of careful symmetries, any line out of true caught the eye, and that was the problem with the altar. "You pushed it back into place, didn't you? To be ready for Sunday."

"The photographer chap and I did, yes. Someone's disturbed it again."

He and Rufus set off at a run. Alice remained frozen, clutching the back of the pew nearest the door. Rufus was puzzled: he'd have backed her for a headlong rush into the unknown any day. Then he heard the scuffling, scratching sounds beneath the church floor, and almost turned tail himself. "What the devil is that?"

"Sounds like an animal of some kind." Archie darted round behind the altar. "I wonder if your dog found her way back here? She was pretty keen on getting down the hole the other day."

"It's only been moved a little way." Dropping to his knees, Rufus pulled a torch out of his satchel. "Pippin? Is that you down there?"

He hardly expected an answer. To his cold shock, he got one, high-pitched and frantic. "No!"

"Bloody hell," Archie said grimly. "That sounds like a child. Here, help me push this all the way back."

Rufus set his shoulder against the great stone block. Alice, still pale with fear, appeared at his side, lending her strength to the effort. Archie pressed his back to the narrow end, and between them they heaved the altar off the mouth of the hole beneath it. "I know who that sounds like," Rufus said, scrambling for his torch again. "But..."

"But no mortal child who was already in such deep hot water as Jebediah Trigg would do anything to make matters worse." Archie knelt beside him. "And yet. Show your face this instant, young man."

The scuffling sounds increased. Soil and pebbles cascaded from the top of a new tunnel inside the cavity. Fearing a cave-in, Rufus got ready to jump, but Archie grabbed his sleeve. Something was emerging into the light of the torch—not a face, but a plump backside, clad in school-uniform shorts. Rufus would have laughed, but whatever stilling sense of horror had seized Alice in the doorway was now laying hold of him, too. "Jebediah," he managed, as the child squeezed all the way out and wriggled around. "What the hell are you doing down there?"

Jebediah held up an admonishing finger. "Bad to swear!"

"Er... all right. I'm sorry. What are you doing?"

"I been digging!"

That much was obvious. The child's pasty face was barely recognisable beneath its dirt. His hands looked like mole paws, gloved from wrist to fingertips in soil. Rufus tried the tactful approach. "You must have been after something very exciting, to work away like that all on your own. What were you looking for?"

Jebediah set his jaw. "Can't tell."

"Is that because you told someone else you wouldn't? You must have had help to move the altar and get down here."

"*Won't* tell."

"I tell you what," Archie interrupted pleasantly, taking the torch from Rufus and shining it straight into the boy's eyes. "You're so happy down here, digging away in the dark. Dr Denby and I can push the altar back and leave you to it. No-one would ever know where you'd gone."

"Archie," Rufus remonstrated, without much fervour. Poor Jebediah was the kind of kid who brought out the worst in everyone. "Nobody's going to leave you alone in the dark down there. Not if you tell us the truth, anyway."

Jebediah cracked. "She'n took all the things out my room, all my stuff! And she locked me away. But I got out the window, see? And Bobby Jakes says to me, that prof down from London's found treasure in the church. Old man Jakes were going past the door the other day and seen the altar all pulled aside. So he'll help me, he says, and we'll split what we find." An angry sob shook him. "I want to *find* something. I want my *stuff*."

"Yes, you've been quite a collector," Archie said, not unkindly. "Did you ever think about getting a paper round and buying some stuff of your own?"

Alice joined them at the brink of the hole. She still looked uneasy, but she extended a hand to Jebediah. "Ah, that's not as exciting, is it? Come here, you little tyke. I used to filch stuff all the time when I was his age. Got nabbed in Woolworth's once with my pockets full of lipsticks and Bakelite brooches. I didn't really want them—I just felt empty, and I wanted *something*."

"I bet Uncle Paul loved that."

"I didn't sit down for a week. So I do understand some of what's going on in your little pudding-basin head, Jebediah, though I never went in for larceny on the scale you have."

The child stuck out his tongue at her for this attempt at sympathy, and she hauled him none-too-gently up by the wrist, Rufus and Archie reaching in to help. "One thing beats me hollow," Archie said, once Jebediah was safe on the flagstones and struggling to his feet. "People round here keep their valuables locked up like the Crown jewels. How did you manage to nick old the squire's pocket watch? He's the biggest miser of them all."

"Easy. Magic key."

"You probably don't want to add insolence to your problems at this point, Jebediah. Or more fibs."

Jebediah bristled. There was honour among thieves, Rufus supposed. The child pulled a metal cylinder out of his pocket and thrust it up at Archie, the gesture as near to giving him the finger as he dared. "Opens anything, this does! Sent away for it from *Super Spy for Boys*. You squeeze the tube until it fits, you see, then swing the wards to the right—"

"Nonsense," Archie cut him off, not unkindly. Nevertheless he whipped the key out of Jebediah's fist and tucked it into his trouser pocket. "I'll take care of that, just in case. Right—come along with you. I'm going to have to see you home and try and explain the state of you."

Jebediah began to back away. "No!"

"We can say you fell in the mud if you like. You have to promise to stay away from here, though. How were you planning to get out on your own? Bobby Jakes is nowhere to be seen."

"Bobby Jakes is a halfwit! He's been an' wandered off. Catch me back here again, anyway. You and the prof can dig all you want—all you'll find is dead witches, my ma says. Piles an' piles of dead witches! Then she cries, my ma does, and she goes upstairs and shuts herself up in her room. So she don't care anymore if I'm down a hole or up a bloody tree!"

"Bad to swear, Jebediah. What does she mean about witches?"

"Can't tell. Won't tell. Damn, damn, bugger, hell, shit, shite, amen!" With that, the boy twisted away and fled towards the door as if he expected the devil to grab him by the shirt-tails. Archie pursued him for a few strides, then gave it up, signalling to Rufus and Alice that they should stop, too. "Best leave him alone. Chasing Drusilla is one thing—I can't be seen hounding small children through the lanes."

"Will he be all right?" Rufus asked, having to steady himself against the unsettling tug of the hole's dark maw. "He seemed half out of his mind."

"Yes, and Bobby Jakes is a sandwich short of a picnic, too. A big lad, though—our local poacher's son. I suppose he was the brawn of the operation. God help Droyton if those two have joined forces." He brushed dust off Alice's shirt, as absently as if she'd been a statue. "Don't worry—Jebediah will go to where the food is eventually, and I'll call round later on to make sure he's safe."

"What on earth was he babbling about, though, Archie?" Alice shivered, glancing around the church, which seemed huddled in darkness despite the golden afternoon light. "Dead witches?"

"Goodness knows. I do feel as if that hole—whatever it is— shouldn't be left open for one second longer than it has to be. Maybe we're all picking up on some kind of smell."

"It's more than that." She returned to the opening and crouched beside Rufus, who was playing the torch beam over the newly exposed dirt wall. "Whatever's down here doesn't want to be disturbed. However..."

"However," Rufus continued for her, throwing her a quick smile, "since Jebediah's already disturbed it, we might as well carry on. He must have been burrowing away here for hours. Look— he's been using a piece of antler bone, which is very Neolithic of him."

Archie leaned a hand on his shoulder and peered past him. "Is that what that is?"

"I think so, yes."

"Where would he have got such a thing?"

"I can only think he found it here. Which, if he did, adds greatly to the interest of the site. Tools like that were used to build the earth banks at Avebury and Stonehenge." Rufus checked his satchel. "I don't have anything much more sophisticated myself, but I do have a spare trowel. My feeling is that there'd be no harm in making a thorough examination of the walls and floor as far as we can see them. No further than that."

"Almost seems a shame, when Jebediah did so much work for us."

"Possibly all he did was destabilise the roof. I can't risk anyone in any kind of tunnel until the walls and ceiling have been propped." He flattened one hand to the flagstones and jumped down, careful not to land on the shard of antler bone. "I know it'll be a tremendous disruption, Archie, but I'd like to write my full report to Caroline tonight. I'll request a team to come down with scaffolding equipment and take the excavation from there. What do you think?"

"Anything that keeps the place out of the grasp of the archdeacon." Archie offered Alice a steadying hand while she too climbed down into the cavern. "You'd still be in charge, though, wouldn't you?"

"I doubt it, since I'm no longer formally employed by the museum. Anyway, you need an expert in church antiquities." Rufus looked away before he could see Archie's reaction. "I don't think it's very practical for all three of us to be down here without an easy exit. Could you fold one of the ladders right down and bring it over?"

"Good idea."

His long stride crunched away across the aisle. Once again Rufus heard the alternating tap and echo on the flags, and excitement rose in him despite the oppressive weight in the air, his old delight—lost in the sands of Sabros, he'd thought—in the connection of ideas. He turned to Alice, who was running her fingers across the arch of Jebediah's tunnel, her expression rapt. "Do you still feel afraid?"

"Oh, no. Not at all."

"That's odd. My skin is crawling."

"I wonder—if little Elspeth had decided to come here and start digging instead of Jebediah..."

"Would the guardian spirits be less upset? Superstitious nonsense, my excavation partner would have said."

"Was that the man you were working with on Sabros?"

"Professor Hargreaves, yes."

"Professor Hargreaves knew nothing. *Nothing.*"

Her voice was hushed with awe. Rufus didn't have time to look in her direction: Archie had reappeared at the edge of the pit, lowering the ladder into place. "Thanks. That's it—prop it against the side. The ground feels quite firm under this layer of earth, almost as if there might be another stone floor beneath. I suppose that if there *is* some kind of structure down here..."

"Rufus? Where's Alice?"

He whipped round. The space behind him was empty. He blinked, grabbed a torch and shone the beam into the passage Jebediah had created for himself. For all the boy's labour, it was barely three foot deep, and ended blindly in another mud wall. "She was just here. Alice!"

Archie sprang down to join him. "Is there another way out of here?"

"No, not unless she climbed out somehow on her own. But she was standing right here, looking into the tunnel."

"There's no way through there. How could she—"

A cry sliced through the morning. It came from the foundations and the sky at once, Rufus thought frantically, casting round to find the source. It sounded less like fear than astonishment, a wound of revelation ripping wide: peaked like music and stopped. "My God," Archie whispered. "That was her. Where is she?" And before Rufus could draw breath to answer, Archie strode into the impossibly short tunnel and vanished too.

Chapter Twenty

Not a tunnel but a turning. Rufus followed blindly, hands pressing outward against the walls, the tides of flashback heaving up around him. *Not this time*, he silently swore to the terrified animal inside him. Not this time, the mud and the blood and the desperate hunt for his enemy. Not a tunnel but a turning, a great gaping gap in the wall, three foot inside on the left. The place where Alice had gone, and Archie had gone after her.

Rufus liked Alice, but Archie was the heart of his whole world. He didn't know how it had happened, how six days could gouge out his empty core and place a treasure there instead—a rose, a blazing star. The reasons didn't matter. Rufus had to find him.

Somehow he'd kept hold of his torch. The air was dank but breathable. He made himself breathe it, made the beam cease its drunken leap from wall to roof to floor and shine steadily ahead. Not a tunnel but a turning, idea connecting fast to idea in his good archaeologist's mind. *Caer Droea*, the turning castle. Droyton Magna, the great carved coils on the hill. Droyton Parva...

Here. Here. He summoned the schematic against the red-flashing screen of his memory. Archie had said it himself: you were always either so much further than you thought from journey's end or so much nearer home. A sharp turn to the left that doubled you back on yourself... Yes, from here you would either plunge into the labyrinth's core, or...

He stumbled back out into the pit. Alice was already there, huddled against the far wall. Her hands were pressed hard to her mouth and she was breathing in tight gasps. "I saw him," she croaked. "I saw him."

"Archie?"

"No."

If not Archie, Rufus didn't care. "Climb the ladder and get out," he commanded, sounding for the first time since the battle of Roche like the efficient army captain he had been. "If I'm not back in five minutes, run to the village and fetch Billy from the Maidens'. Tell him to bring rope, twine, anything we can pay out. And torches, and any of his mates who can come. Do you hear me?"

She raised wide, vacant eyes to his. He waited until she nodded, then swung back round to face the second exit, hidden until now by the shadows and the overhanging brink. If the tunnels had been cut into like this, corrupted, the labyrinth would have lost integrity, the sacred internal order that brought lost travellers safely home. It would have become a maze. "Archie," he called, stepping into the dark. "Archie, stand still where you are. Don't go any further."

How could he have gone out of earshot this fast? But the mud walls were muffling, the darkness they enclosed impossibly thick, like oily fog, sucking the light out of the torch beam barely an arm's reach ahead. "Archie! Stay where you are. I'll find you."

No answering call came back out of the tunnel. Rufus forced down the panic reaction that would send him at hopeless full pelt round twist after turn, throwing away Archie's chances along with his own. With an effort of will he came to a halt, resting his brow on his knuckles, closing his eyes. He had to listen.

Just his own heartbeat, the frightened scrape of air in his lungs. No. Something more. He caught an inhalation and held it. Recent scenes flickered up at him like cine reel. Archie, breathless after a dash across the road. Pushing the window wide in Drusilla's cottage, because the world was small and stifling. Coughing and laughing at himself in mortification after lighting a forbidden cigarette. The rasp deep in his chest at these times, the warrior priest's unseen scar... Rufus could hear it, rhythmic but struggling, close at hand now. "Archie," he whispered, and his torch beam snapped off, as if he were allowed a certain ration of knowledge but no more. He took nine more steps on blind faith and fell over him.

He was curled up on the tunnel floor, like a winter bear who'd crawled into a den to sleep. A winter stillness was upon him. Rufus dropped to his knees beside him, seeking out movement: a throb in the throat, a lift of the strong ribcage. He found neither, and the rasping wheeze had stopped.

Rufus sat back on his heels. For nightmare seconds, he couldn't respond. The tunnel morphed into the Fort Roche trench around him, and the long shadow of the Minotaur, the enemy-beast, cut across his sanity. Then he hauled a drowning swimmer's breath. "Alice!" he bellowed, lifting Archie's head into his lap. "Alice, are you still here?"

She answered with a rapid thud of boot soles on the hard-packed earth, a wash of torchlight. She was swift and calm and everything Rufus needed at that moment: an extra pair of hands and a fiery determination to help. "What happened to him?" she demanded, crouching across from Rufus in the narrow space. "Is he breathing?"

"I don't know. We have to get him out of here. If I carry him by the shoulders, can you take his feet?"

"Yes. Quickly, before this little tunnel becomes a long one."

"Is that what happened to you?"

"I think so. I can't explain."

She bent to her task, and Rufus lurched up, getting a grip on Archie's armpits. Between them they carried him back to the pit. The distance was nothing in physical terms, but Rufus felt every step like the crawl-by of a nightmare. Perhaps that was how the labyrinth worked, expanding and contracting according to fear or desire... He set Archie carefully down, and once more probed for a pulse in his throat. It was there, but flickering and uncertain, and there was still no movement in his chest. "What's wrong with him?" he demanded of poor Alice, who was staring blankly into the middle-distance memory of her own encounter. "Why isn't he breathing?"

"He has trouble with his lungs. He was gassed."

"I know that, but—"

"Maybe he saw something that stopped him."

She was lost. She'd done what she could. She scrambled into the furthest corner of the pit and curled up, putting her hands over her eyes. There was no-one but Rufus to unwind the spell of the labyrinth. "Archie," he said passionately, and leaned over him. "I'll breathe for you, all right? Just hold on."

He'd learned to do this in the earliest days of his officer training. How bitterly useless it had seemed, to be taking the kiss of life into that arena of bullet-ridden death, as if he'd be rescuing drowned swimmers! The routine came back to him. A swift check of the airway. Cover the nose with one hand and hold the nostrils shut. Tip the head back a little. Breathe.

Archie still tasted of good tobacco and sun-warmed earth. Of the strawberry jam they'd shared at breakfast that morning. Grief flared through Rufus, terror of the loss he hadn't yet sustained, strong enough to close off his lungs and fulfil its own prophecy. Savagely he controlled it. He breathed, waited till Archie's solar plexus rose beneath his spread hand, sat up a little and waited until it fell. Pressed his warm mouth to the chilly one and breathed again. Again. Again.

Archie twitched, coughed, opened his eyes. His gaze found focus. "Rufus?"

"Thank God. Are you all right?"

"I think so." He tried to raise his head, taking in the dirt walls around him. "It is nice to see daylight again, though, my love. It is nice to see you."

Rufus lifted him into his arms. He couldn't see anything but the smiling face looking up at him, couldn't care for anything—clattering footsteps on the church floor, the swoop and shriek of frightened swallows, Alice's warning cry—but Archie reaching up to kiss him. He reached back.

Two shadows fell across the pit. Archie's fingers skimmed the scar tissue on Rufus's scalp, sought for purchase in the short crop at his nape. They kissed with shuddering urgency, each seeking the heat and proof of the other's life. "I thought you were dead," Rufus whispered when they drew apart.

"And I thought I'd lost you. That's what the tunnel told me—he's gone, there's no point in breathing anymore. So I stopped."

"Oh, Archie. What are we going to do?"

Something landed hard on the packed-earth floor beside him. The timing felt like an answer, but Giles was only there for Alice. "Miss Winborn! I was in the woods, and I heard you scream." Giles stumbled over to her, gave it all up and knelt outright at her feet. "I came running. I'll always come running when you need me. And I... I brought the doctor."

Alice pushed Giles aside. Her gesture wasn't rough, but it was absolute, her whole attention fixed on the stiff black silhouette at the edge of the hole. "Paul," she said warningly. "Don't."

"Don't what?" Winborn asked equably. His light-edged shape seemed to pick up and effortlessly swallow all the horrified attention settling upon him: Archie, pushing upright and throwing a protective arm in front of Rufus; his niece, like a guardian angel or Joan of Arc, striding over to block his view of them both. "Don't point out the bloody obvious—that this sick queer has spread his corruption just as I feared he would?"

"Winborn, shut up." Archie levered upright and stood shivering. "Don't you dare insult him."

"You can't insult that kind of man. They're already lost in their own degradation. Throw any word you like at them—it only describes what they are. The worse language you use, the more they enjoy—"

"I said shut *up*."

Archie wrenched out of Rufus's embrace. He scaled the ladder with frightening speed, and Rufus, who'd never seen his big frame wrought to the purposes of anger, scrambled after him as fast as he could. Vicar or no vicar, this was a man who'd braved German snipers with nothing more than his biker helmet and a dog collar to protect him. Winborn stood his ground, though his eyes widened in fear. Rufus caught Archie by the belt six inches shy of him. "Archie, for heaven's sake stop."

"No. Why should I?"

"Because he's right. I *don't* care what he calls me. I just can't bear for you to hear it."

Winborn broke into bitter laughter. "If you really gave a damn about Archie, you'd have left this village without laying a hand on him. You'd have left when you said you would. I thought you at least a man of your word, queer or—"

"Quiet!" Rufus surprised himself with the barked-out command, which frightened a pair of doves from their nest in the rafters. He didn't care what he was called, but he didn't have to stand around and hear himself called it twice. He wasn't a lost, sick queer anymore. He was a man with a place in the world, and Archie had called him *my love*. "You asked me some bloody impertinent questions, and I told you what was true at the time."

"You're not capable of truth. I told you why you had to leave Archie alone, and you preyed upon him anyway. Exploited his weakness, after all the years I've spent protecting him, providing him with—"

"With what?"

Winborn jerked round. Alice was standing by the edge of the pit, her arms wrapped desolately round herself. Tears were rolling down her face. "With a *wife*, my dear girl," Winborn said, his voice gentler, for the first time uncertain. "With companionship. A love he could celebrate in the eyes of God and society, not hidden away down back alleys. Don't you understand?"

"God and society? Those are the things you'd have sacrificed me for?"

"Sacrificed? Oh, Alice, what nonsense. Archie's a fine man, and he's always been your friend. You could have a good life here in Droyton."

The penny was only just now dropping for Archie. He glanced between Winborn and Alice. "My God. You meant me to *marry* her?"

"Yes, and impenetrably bloody thick you've been about it!"

"Why on earth would you tie her to someone like me?"

"I tied Celia there, didn't I? And you both thrived."

"Celia was a child doing what she was told. So was I, for that matter. I love Alice very much, but—"

"Shut up, both of you!" Alice ran a hand into her hair and tugged at it in grief and frustration. "I love you too, Archie, but don't... don't *discuss* me. Either of you. Ever again."

"I've been trying to help you," Winborn said with dignity. "I've had your best interests at heart all along."

"I know. That's why I've kept quiet. But *think* about it, Uncle Paul. I lost my David barely eighteen months ago. If we'd been married, I'd still be draped in black. I'd still have been mourning."

"Thank God you weren't married, then. You're young and beautiful. You—"

"How dare you say that? We were married in everything but name. I shared his bed when he was home on leave. When I heard he was gone, I prayed to God every day that he'd left a child in me."

"Alice!"

"I did. And when my monthlies came, I cursed God instead." A rough sob escaped her. "Nobody gave a damn, did they? I couldn't say, *my husband died*, so people would be kind to me and leave me alone. I wasn't a widow. I was just a bloody package, an inconvenience, something to be disposed of." She paused, caught her breath, gestured at her own fine long limbs, the cleanliness and vigour of her frame. "I was even starting to turn to drink. Me! And when Dr Denby came here—so quiet and kind, and not throwing himself at my head—I made a dreadful fool of myself and threw myself at his."

"No," Rufus protested. "Not a fool at all."

"But you're with Archie, aren't you? And he's with you, just as he should be." She swung back to Winborn. "Don't pull that face, as if you'd just sucked a lemon! You can't force people to love or not to love. I started to believe you, to believe I should stop loving David. That it was morbid of me, that I didn't have the right. And then, just now in the tunnel, I..." She swayed, and

Rufus let go his grip on Archie's belt and went to take her arm. She turned a tearstained face to him. "I saw *David* in the tunnel, Rufus. He was as real as you are. I don't want a new husband, or a new life. I want him. I'll only ever want him."

She broke away and set off down the aisle at an unsteady run. Her sobs resounded off the walls and roof, startling the doves again, until the whole church seemed to shudder with her grief. Winborn threw a glance of angry bewilderment at Rufus and Archie, then turned and ran after her. "Alice. Alice!"

They were gone. The woods and the sunshine took them with rustling, dappling completeness, just as they would much smaller and much greater disturbances in the lives of men. Their words hung in the air behind them. Rufus almost thought he could see them—Alice's drifting down with the feathers of the doves, Winborn's like a new sword of Damocles, gleaming and ready to fall. He turned in dismay to face his new lover, the perfect friend whose neck he'd exposed to the blade. "Oh, Archie."

"Yes. Poor Alice! I've been very obtuse."

"Not that, you idiot. I mean—yes, poor Alice. But what about you?"

"Me? Oh, now that Winborn knows the heinous truth?"

He was smiling. He had no idea. Rufus took him by the shoulders and lightly shook him. "This is serious. What are we going to do?"

"I don't know. But whatever it is, you'll be here to help me. Won't you?"

That really was the full extent of his concerns. Tears scalded up behind Rufus's eyes, making his nose prickle. "Yes," he said roughly. "Of course." He subsided against the broad chest, pressing tight so he could hear the thud of the living heart. "I thought you'd died."

"So did I." Archie held him tightly. "What is it down there, Rufus? Why did I get lost within five yards of the door, and why did Alice see what she did?"

"I don't know. I suppose there's a remote possibility of toxic gases, but in an area as geologically stable as this, it's unlikely. Maybe just the disorientation of being suddenly in the dark..."

"It is a labyrinth, then?"

"I think so. I've no idea how, or who built it, but..." He twisted his hands in the fabric of Archie's waistcoat. "...for now, I just want it closed off."

"Agreed. Come on, let's get the altar pushed back."

Reluctantly they disentangled. This was all wrong, Rufus knew. Archie had been exposed in front of his oldest friend, laid bare to Winborn's judgement and contempt. He should be keeping Rufus at strict arm's length, not retaining his hand until the very last moment, swiftly kissing its knuckles before letting go to seize the ladder. "Archie, hang on a second. Leave that there."

"What's wrong?"

"Where the bloody hell is Giles?"

"Oh. Yes, he was here, wasn't he? Rushing to Alice's rescue, poor chap. Did he leave when she did?"

"I didn't see him. I didn't even see him come out of the hole."

"Really? Oh, bugger." Archie seized the ladder and made ready to climb back down. "I'd better get after him. Heaven only knows what'll happen to *him* down there."

"You're going nowhere without me."

"I should argue. But that's too nice to hear. Come on, then."

Before Archie could begin his climb back into the pit, scraping sounds began once more beneath the flagstones. Rufus controlled a jolt of fear. The brooding, charged atmosphere in the church hadn't lightened. If anything it was worse, as if the tunnels still had terrible secrets to reveal. *Dead witches*, Jebediah had said.

Piles and piles of dead witches. What had put that idea into his tortured little head? Rufus laid a restraining hand on Archie's shoulder. "Hold on a second."

The scraping resolved into footsteps. After a moment, Giles emerged calmly from the passageway that doubled back beneath the brink of the hole, eyes wide and clear, face serene in the dusty light.

Jaw set square and firmly, a touch of stubble marking out its line. Adam's apple bobbing in the open neck of the shirt. "Don't come down, Reverend. I'm all right."

Archie extended a hand. "That's good. What possessed you to go off into the tunnel on your own?"

"I'm not sure. The same thing that possessed you, maybe. And Miss Winborn."

"Fair point. But come up here now, please. Quickly."

Giles accepted their assistance back up the ladder, and stood between them on the altar steps, swaying a little as if searching for a new centre of gravity. "Thank you. Reverend, this will seem disrespectful, but I don't intend it that way. Can you forgive me?"

Archie raised an eyebrow. "Well, intentions are important, Giles, but we have to think about the effects of..."

He fell silent. Giles was unbuttoning his shirt. Beneath it he was wearing an odd garment—not a vest but a kind of thick, elasticated bandage, now hanging slack across his chest. He undid the hook-and-eye fasteners, pulled the garment free and held it at arm's length. "There. That was so uncomfortable."

"It must have been, especially in this heat. Why on earth were you wearing it?"

"I had to. I had breasts, you see." He touched the smooth, flat place where they had been. "I was a Land Girl during the war. I wore trousers, drove a tractor, cut my hair. It was then that I realised I'd got into the wrong body by mistake."

"Giles, old fellow, it really *is* very hot. Would you like to sit down?"

Giles chuckled. "Old fellow! I like it when you say that. I used to like it whenever anybody said *he*, or *him*, or called me Giles instead of Gillian. So when I came to Farmer Challen's for a job, I just arrived with my binder on, and nobody looked at me twice. Except for Dr Denby."

"Dr Denby?" Archie glanced from Giles to Rufus in bemusement. "Wait. Are you trying to tell me that you were once a girl?"

"Until ten minutes ago, yes. I was a girl."

"That's impossible. We'd have noticed."

"I thought you would have. I wasn't a very convincing boy. But..."

Archie shook his head. "People see what they expect to see. Unless they're Dr Denby, apparently. Rufus, would *you* care to explain this?"

"I can't. Not this last part, anyway." Rufus shrugged. "I could see that Giles was female, yes."

"I knew that you saw," Giles said fervently. "I was so afraid, waiting for you to say something. Why didn't you?"

"Good heavens, why would I? You weren't doing any harm."

"Ah, are you one of those people who live in a glass house and have learned not to throw any stones? They're few and far between." Unexpectedly Giles stepped forward and took Rufus by the hand. "Oh, no. Not that, exactly. Not born in the wrong body, just—"

"That's really enough, Giles." Archie stepped between them, gently detaching Giles's grip. "I don't understand this, but it's nothing to do with Dr Denby, is it?"

"No, not at all. It was all to do with Alice. Which was stupid of me, because if she didn't care for me when I was a girl, why would she care for me now? She's still in love with David." Giles buttoned up his shirt, then paused and looked wonderingly at Rufus and Archie. "It really has happened, hasn't it? I'm just like you two. I'm a man." He laid one hand to the waistband of his trousers, then began to move it down.

"Giles, please. I've tried to be a lenient vicar, but do remember where you are."

"I'm sorry, Reverend." He smiled, lifted his head, clarity dawning in the new strong lines of his face. "I did love Alice. But I think she was more of a symbol than anything else, a combination of all the women I've yearned for. I don't know if I'll ever be able to make one of them yearn for me in return, but I suppose it'll be easier in this body." He turned suddenly to Rufus. "Don't you think so, Dr Denby?"

"Well, I... have met a few women who would have liked Gillian as she was, in her Land Girl gear. But this certainly widens your field."

"Yes. And now it's up to me—Giles or Gillian—to make the best of it."

Rufus and Archie watched him go. He had stuck the binder into one capacious pocket and was stepping out jauntily. The breeze blew the rags of a whistled melody back on the air. He began to unfasten the churchyard gate, then paused, took a few steps back, and cleared it in a flying, one-handed vault.

Archie rubbed at the back of his head in bemusement. "He does look different."

"You really couldn't see that he was a girl?"

"No. And you—you really could?"

"I thought it was some kind of village in-joke."

"No. I genuinely never knew." Archie returned his attention to the open pit. "What did you say the old translation of Caer Droea was? The turning castle?"

"Yes, but that's preposterous. Look, maybe he was just deluded, so convinced he was a woman that he managed to convince me."

"And then the delusion just... stopped?"

"I don't know." Rufus looked over his shoulder and shivered. Where was Winborn now? He'd had time to get back to the village. As a doctor, he'd probably thought it worthwhile to equip his household with a private telephone. How far would he go? A call to the local constabulary, a charge of public indecency... "We've got bigger problems, Archie."

Archie put an arm around him. He planted a fearless kiss to the torn-up scar tissue beneath the hair at Rufus's temple. "It must have hurt when this happened."

"I don't know. It's all a part of what I don't remember. Didn't you hear me?"

"I did." Archie cast one last glance after Giles, now a gleaming speck in the distance. "Yes, we have bigger problems. But surely we don't have any quite so strange."

Chapter Twenty One

That night, for the first time in many months, Rufus remembered a dream. There must have been others, of course, but only his nightmares had stayed with him since Fort Roche.

He was walking on a beach with Archie. The air was warm, and the lights of fishing boats floated and glimmered out at sea. Archie was dressed in a Sabrian djellaba, which suited him very well. *Yours looks good too*, he said, not needing to open his mouth for Rufus to hear him. They were barefoot, moving easily on moonlit sand.

The minister's nephew, handsome Zadi, was standing on top of a dune. He gestured, and Rufus and Archie were suddenly there beside him, looking down on the excavation. Someone—not Professor Hargreaves, some team with infinite resources and expertise—had opened up and restored the whole site. The sense of it came to Rufus in a flash. All those truncated little tombs, the passageways that crumbled to nothing—oh, not randomly placed graves at all. Pieces and scraps of a pattern so vast neither he nor Hargreaves had seen it. You'd need a plane to see it, the perspective of an eagle. *The later civilisations were using the old intact bits of a buried labyrinth*, he breathed, and Zadi turned and smiled. *The whole island's a labyrinth.*

The whole island, sayyid. Zadi gestured again, and the pattern rippled and changed. The dunes disappeared, replaced by the majestic sweep of the outer arm. Rufus grabbed at Archie for support, and Archie caught him, breaking into laughter. *Steady on, Dr Denby. A shame if you had a heart attack now.*

But look at it! All the walls are painted, just like that section I saw in the tomb. Dancers and butterflies and little axe-heads. The tunnels are roofed with beautiful corbelling, just like at Skara Brae. A place like this could last forever, if it wasn't deliberately destroyed.

No-one will destroy it, sayyid. Not while the people come here.

Zadi clapped his hands, and the walls became transparent. Among them, moving slowly amidst the butterflies, were dozens of men and women.

Men and women, and some others who flickered between one kind of flesh and the other, or hovered joyously in a space that was neither and both at once. Each one was naked or draped in the cool, gently drifting djellaba robe, each according to choice. Giles was there, and although he couldn't have Alice, who was peacefully walking down a tunnel of her own, hand-in-hand with her loved, lost David, every so often he would shimmer and morph into the shape Rufus had recognised as Gillian. Both aspects were smiling, their inner union and companionship sufficient. Men were walking with men, women with women. People in couples, threes, more, and people serenely alone. Even Henry was there, naked as day, clutching at the arm of a magnificent robe-clad gentleman old enough, rich enough and enough of a law unto himself to hush the poor lad's fears and cruel vanities forever. *Must be a bloody angel,* Archie said dryly, and Rufus looked up to laugh at him, and the scene began to dissolve.

He woke up in the rectory orchard. There was mud on his hands, but for once he wasn't alarmed. He had the feeling that he'd come downstairs, let himself into the garden, and maybe tripped over the hem of his pyjamas trousers, which were Archie's, and a little long for him in the leg. He should be grateful that he'd paused to put them on at all. He was otherwise naked. Perhaps the moonlight had called him, or the disjointed logic of the dream. It was fading already, all the more quickly when he tried to grasp at it, so he sat down on the bench where old Lady Birch had died, and looked up into the night sky instead.

The moon was almost full, drenching the starlight, but still he could make out enough of the Great Bear to hang his thoughts off, Arcturus and the Northern Crown lifting them up and away. His memories of the rest of that afternoon: making sure the pit was covered, persuading Archie for once to lock the church. Walking back with him down Pilgrim Way. Meeting Mrs Nettles in the rectory porch, her protective mettle roused, little short of barring the way to the kitchen where Alice Winborn had flown to find refuge, and was sound asleep in an armchair, and no help needed from you two or any other gentlemen at present, thank you, Reverend.

Sitting down in the library to write his report. Archie in the background, bringing tea, reading over sheet after sheet as he produced them. All the time waiting for a thumping fist on the door, but none had come.

None had come, and in the lamplight and the scent of the roses, he'd begun to believe none would. At quarter to twelve he'd gone to bed with Archie, leading him frankly by the hand up to the attic room, because he'd promised him anything, if he could only hold on until tonight. They'd stripped each other, tumbled together into the wonderful bed, and...

Archie's face had softened oddly, lust transforming in his eyes to a huge and loving comprehension. And Rufus, who for so long now had been soaked in a weariness so marrow-deep that he'd forgotten its existence, had fallen asleep in his arms.

Odd—there'd been no sign of Winborn in his dream, as if even the great turning-castle of Sabros couldn't find a place for such a man. Rufus counted the stars in the Crown. No sign of the dry little doctor there, either. Maybe he'd been wrong, to assign so much power to him. To all the watchful eyes he'd evaded over the years. When the honeysuckle rustled on the trellis by the house, and Archie called out softly, "Rufus, love?", he didn't try to hush him, because who was there to hear?

He got up and strode to him barefoot, not across clean white sand but the fragrant lawn. "Archie!"

They collided in the moon-shade of the orchard's oldest tree, whose lichen-wrapped trunk had tilted through almost forty five degrees. Archie pushed him gently back against it. "What are you doing here? Are you all right?"

"I'm fine. I had a dream—a good one—and I must have walked in my sleep again. But it looks as though I only came out here."

"Is that blood on your face?"

"I fell, I think. Look, my hands are grazed."

"Yes, I see." Archie turned them palms-up in the uncertain light, as if to read an uncertain future there. "Come indoors and I'll get out Maria's first-aid kit."

"Not yet. It's such a perfect night." The tree was like a tempting cradle: had pulled Archie just past his centre of gravity so that most of his weight was leaning against Rufus. Some previous rector had propped it with strong iron posts. Archie had said the fruit that it gave was the sweetest. For now it was only sending down wave after wave of blossom. "Are we allowed back in the kitchen now?"

"Yes, all clear. Maria announced before supper that Alice is going to be living with us now, too."

Rufus snorted with laughter. "This is ridiculous, Archie. Your whole situation here, your house, your life, they're..." He took handfuls of Archie's untucked shirt, tugging and caressing. "...ridiculous. And beautiful. What are those lines from your Auden poem, the ones that come after the sexy airs?"

"*Equal with colleagues in a ring, I sit on each calm evening, enchanted as the flowers?*"

"Yes. It feels like that. I wish it could last forever."

"Maybe it can. Stay with me, dear Rufus."

Oh, he wanted to. He could forget the rest of the poem and its message about the price of such hard-won peace. But here was Archie, all caution thrown to the petal-starred breeze, taking the tree's suggestive tilt and sway, kissing him, starting to shift his hips.

"Wait. Not here."

"Is it uncomfortable?"

"No, but we can't—not out in the open."

"No-one will come."

"Winborn doesn't give notice of his arrivals. And he'll be angrier still, if Alice has moved in here."

"Winborn's managed the extraordinary feat of making himself unwelcome in my home. You know that's not easy to do."

"Yes, I know, but—"

"I won't ever let him near you again."

"Archie, Archie, you won't be able to stop him, not if he turns up with a policeman... Not *here*."

"Where, then?"

"The back of the bike shed has good precedents."

"Oh, no. I'll take you back indoors, back to bed, rather than that. I understand the dangers—really I do—but there'll be no more sheds, no more back alleys, for either of us."

No. There would be trees beneath the moonlight, or the loving privacy of their locked, shared room. Throat tightening, Rufus gave in. He was more than half erect, and unfastening Archie's trousers, finding him warm-skinned and naked underneath, brought him all the way. "Why did you get dressed?"

"Habit, from night-alarms over Drusilla. I thought I'd maybe have to chase you naked through the fields."

The vision flashed through Rufus's head. "One day, I promise. Quick, get this knot out of my pyjama cord."

"What's the hurry?"

"You. You take away all my control from me. I'm going to—"

"Oh." Strong fingers, working deftly at the cord. A moment later releasing him, pulling his shaft clear. "Not without me, you don't."

Warm weight, shoving him hard and tight against the bark. The tree's own mute, electric life running up the length of his spine. He raised one leg, clutched Archie's backside and hauled him in. "That's it. Harder."

"I'll hurt you."

"You won't." His shoulders were aching in patches, as if he'd bruised himself somewhere without realising it, but the pain spread like hot handprints. "The sweetest apples fall here, Archie. The sweetest... Ah. Oh, *God*."

He came in a rushing whole-body spasm. Archie put an arm around his back and lifted him, clutching at the trunk for balance with his free hand. He drove his hips hard against Rufus's, grinding cock to cock, for five more shuddering strokes, then seized him, gasping, stopping him from falling with a quick, comprehensive catch. "Rufus! Are you all right?"

"Yes. God, I'm fine. I'm..." But Rufus couldn't find words to describe the state to which a come from Archie reduced him. Not even a reduction—a rebuild, more like, a miraculous redefinition of sex for him, so far from his lonely encounters with Henry and all the back-street strangers that he could hardly believe the act was the same. He let Archie lower him onto the grass at the foot of the tree, pulled him down to sit beside him. "I love you. Just give me a minute here, and then we'll go inside and... do what I promised. Cooking oil isn't too bad as a lubricant, if Mrs Nettles has any in her pantry."

"That's lovely, but..." Archie examined his face, his own shadowing with concern. "Do you know, I don't believe I'll take you up on it?"

"Why? What's wrong?"

"I believe that tonight I'll just take you back to bed." He caught his breath, laid one thumb to Rufus's lower lip and looked at him in absolute wonder. "I love you, too."

Chapter Twenty Two

There would be seven to the rectory breakfast that morning. Eight, if you counted the dog, and she seemed determined not to be left out of anyone's calculations, bouncing up and down the length of the hallway, barking and running in circles around Elspeth, who stood in the midst of the chaos, laughing as if she'd personally brought it about.

Rufus smiled too, making his way down the stairs. He turned back the sleeves of his clean white shirt. It was nice to get up in this house, to join with the flow of its life. He hoped he looked decent. Perhaps he could find work, here or in Ashfield. Nothing fancy, just the day-to-day of an ordinary man. Earn a salary and come home to Archie, who loved him.

He grabbed at the banister, a pulse of pure, disorienting joy passing through him. Archie had been right to order him back to bed. He felt strange, enervated. Maybe he hadn't yet fully recovered from his Veronal overdose, although he hadn't touched the pills for the last two nights. Anyway, his report was done, his papers ready and folded in their envelope for the morning post. Perhaps, if major archaeological work began here in Droyton, the museum would relent and let him head it up.

He was starting to think ahead, to have hopes again. Sharply he checked himself. He could only ever take one moment at a time. The river of life in Archie's house could swirl and hit rocks at any moment. An angry male voice was rising from the kitchen, louder than Pippin's barking, and probably its cause.

She didn't seem afraid. If a dog could laugh, Rufus thought she'd be doing so, her long tongue lolling in amusement at the scene. Not Winborn in the kitchen, then. Rufus firmly believed Archie's intentions to sling the doctor off the premises. He jogged down the last few stairs and found himself staring at Farmer Challen, whose bulk in the kitchen doorway almost eclipsed the light from the sunny garden beyond.

"Gone!" Challen declared, emphasising the word with a thump of his walking stick, as soon as he realised he had a new listener. "Gone, Professor! Left the pigs to find their own breakfast, and the cows to burst their udders in the fields, and gone!"

Rufus didn't have to ask. The question seemed inevitable, though, so he made a cautious approach along the corridor, catching a glimpse of Archie in the kitchen beyond, leaning wearily against the back of a chair. "Who's, um... gone, Farmer Challen?"

"That boy of mine, Professor! That slim-hipped lad I took in with no questions asked, though he looked like he couldn't lift a pitchfork, let alone a hay bale. Upped and left yesterday, out of the blue, or *into* it, I should say. Got into a motor car with some lipsticked madam from London or thereabouts, and a fine trollop *she* must have been, driving herself about for all to see—and *gone!*"

Rufus let the picture form. Handsome young Giles, strolling down the verge with his knapsack on his back. An elegant lady in an E-type, perhaps, catching sight of him, pulling in at a gateway and waiting, smiling seductively over her draped silken scarf. "I'm sorry to hear that. It must be a great inconvenience."

A choked howl of laughter came from the kitchen. Rufus saw a gleam of fair hair as Alice Winborn doubled up in the armchair by the fire. Farmer Challen began to swell like an outraged turkey, but before he could explode, she jumped to her feet and came running to the door. "I'm sorry, Farmer Challen. It was just my hay fever. I tell you what—can I come back with you now, and give the pigs their breakfast, and help those poor cows with their udders? I'm not as useless as you might think, you know. I was a Land Girl during the war."

So was Giles. Now it was Rufus who had to restrain a guffaw. Farmer Challen had dropped from wrath to red-faced gratification in one breath, and he didn't want to start him off again. Now he was banging his stick off the floor in sheer delight. "Well, that is *civil*," he announced, so loudly that Pippin began to bark again. "I call that *civil*, Miss Winborn! A lady like yourself! I take that kindly, ma'am, very kindly indeed!" He stuck out one tweed-clad elbow, and Alice put her hand through it, grave as a young bride on her way down the aisle. Challen switched her around, and together they made their way back through the kitchen towards the garden door, Alice pausing only to give Rufus one huge, absurd wink.

Rufus edged into the kitchen. Archie was pushing up off the chair, just barely holding on to sobriety. He looked at Rufus, tears of laughter still in his eyes. "Did you hear all that?"

"Yes. Giles has run off with some glamour-puss from London."

"Do you think she was pretty?"

"Knowing Giles's tastes, I'm sure she's a stunner."

"Well," Mrs Nettles said comfortably, turning to lift the kettle off the stove, "things turn out for the best in the end, don't they? Young Giles was far too nice a girl for that dirty old farm."

Archie's eyebrows shot up. "A girl, Mrs Nettles?"

"A boy, I mean, Reverend, of course. Tea for you, Dr Denby? Scrambled eggs?"

"That would be lovely."

"Off into the dining room with both of you, then. Miss Hazelgrove—the new Lady Birch, that is—will be down in a few moments, to capture that eerie wench of a child. Do you suppose it was ever baptised, Reverend Thorne?"

"If it ever was, I didn't do the job. I'll leave you to ask Drusilla."

"Ah. I don't think I will, though. There's more things in heaven and earth, isn't there? Who's to say which of them is sacred or profane?"

She swept away. Archie, in gentle imitation of Challen's courtly gesture, held out his elbow, and Rufus took it, heart still swelling with laughter and a happiness he wasn't sure he could contain. Pippin dashed around them, weaving one of her magical signs for infinity, then came to a sudden halt and sat down, hackles rising, ears flat.

She had placed herself right in the middle of the corridor, exactly halfway along. "What on earth is wrong with you?" Archie said, chuckling, then suddenly dropped Rufus's arm. He took a long stride and grabbed the dog's collar. "Winborn. How the devil do you dare come here?"

Rufus hadn't seen him arrive. He was a thin, spare shape in the blue-glazed porch. He would always be there, Rufus knew, in one shape or another—darkening doorways, peering through windows, soft-footed and watchful, seeing that morality was served and love kept to its proper, narrow course. Rufus had let himself forget. He restrained an impulse to take hold of Archie's collar, for much the same reasons as Archie's in grabbing the dog. "Don't, Archie. It's all right."

"It's damn well not. Get out of here, Winborn."

"Archie, please." Winborn took a nervous step forward, eliciting a snarl from Pippin. "Keep hold of her, will you? I'm not here about... about you and Denby, or any of that."

"What, then? Just to curdle the milk for our breakfast?"

"I remember a time when you'd have invited me to share it with you. I understand all the reasons why not, but—I have to talk to you."

"Talk, then."

"In private, for heaven's sake."

"There's nothing you can say to me that Rufus couldn't hear."

"For *his* sake, I should've said. Very well." Winborn compressed his lips, drew his shoulders back. "Billy from the Maidens' was assaulted last night. Brutally. He's in hospital in Brighton now."

"Billy Prescott?" Archie shook his head, then responded, with the rational illogic of shock, "That's not possible. I saw him just yesterday morning in the village."

"He'd worked until late in the cellars with a delivery. He was walking home through the lanes when it happened."

"Is he... Will he be all right?"

"He has a serious head wound. Nobody knows."

"Dear God. I'll go and see him. I'll..." Archie raised a pale face to Rufus, connections finally forming. "Rufus, whatever you're thinking—no. It can't be."

Rufus couldn't speak. Winborn replied for him. "Why can't it, Archie? Denby himself confessed his compulsion to attack the strongest man near him. He'd already singled Billy out."

"Be quiet. Rufus was here at the rectory."

"All evening, no doubt. This happened in the small hours of the morning."

Rufus had clenched his hands into fists. The grazed skin, which Archie had tenderly washed and witch-hazelled for him in the moonlit kitchen, stung and re-opened, beads of blood forming on his knuckles. "Archie," he said hoarsely. "Please don't say anything more."

Because here it came. Here was the moment when Archie would throw away everything. A kiss upon waking was one thing, the passionate gesture of one man to another who'd just breathed life back into his failing lungs. "Why not?" Archie demanded, his whole life there on the line, shining from his eyes. "This is nonsense, Winborn. He was with me the whole—"

Rufus pushed past him. "Let me go."

"No! This is your home now. You don't have to run away from anything."

"I'm not. I just feel sick." Rufus stopped at the foot of the stairs, a couple of feet away from Winborn, who creditably faked a flinch. "I'll be back in just a minute, and I'll go with you to the police. Don't listen to anything Archie says to defend me."

He took the stairs two at a time, snatching one hand away from Archie's restraining grasp as he went. A short dash across the landing, with its kindly shadows, faded carpet soft underfoot, and then two flights more, up to the attic room where he'd been granted such perfect refuge. He grabbed the door frame and stood still for a moment, forbidding his breathing to break into sobs or horrified retching. His bloodstained hands, the bruised ache in his back and shoulders... He could imagine how Billy would have tried to fend him off, letting him throw punch after punch until his knuckles were grazed. Billy would have dumped him down onto his back, tried to use his harmless honest weight to restrain him, good copper-in-the-making that he was. The beast inside of Rufus must be growing stronger, more vicious, to win a fight against such a man. What had it done—smashed Billy's skull open with a rock?

He stumbled across the room and threw up painfully into the washbasin. He'd been too occupied with writing his report to do more than touch the sandwiches Mrs Nettles had brought him for supper the night before, and cleaning up after himself was mercifully easy. He wiped the basin down with a flannel, dried it with a towel. Both these small amenities had appeared, fresh and clean, in his room every day, as if he'd been an honoured guest. Mrs Nettles, who didn't check her bachelor vicar's sheets but took benign care of everything else, had slipped invisibly up here on this very morning to set a vase of roses by the bed.

They were the yellow ones that grew in such profusion round the library window. Their scent had drawn Rufus here when the rectory had been no more to him than an address on a letterhead. The heavy heads were falling apart beneath the weight of their own generosity, scattering petals. Rufus sat down wearily on the bed. He brushed a few into his palm, and poured them between the leaves of the copy of *The Warden* which Archie had insisted on giving him, inscribing it to finish the argument. *My dear Rufus. With warmest affection and regards.* Not *love*, because Rufus had taught him the danger of that word in writing. Blowing the whole game out of the water after that with a large, undeniable X.

Unsteadily Rufus returned the kiss, brushing his lips to the paper. Then he closed the book up and put it into his satchel. He had, he thought, perhaps three minutes more before Winborn would become suspicious and force his hand. And how could the local constabulary—two rooms in a made-over barn, probably, staffed by a benevolent part-time sergeant in his sixties—contain the beast?

Rufus knew of a much better cage. He pulled his wallet out of the bag. He'd need enough for his train fare, and any few coins he had left over, he'd leave behind for...

The wallet rustled. Opening it, Rufus saw that its inner pocket had been filled with notes. For a nauseating instant he wondered if he'd robbed Billy Prescott as well as beating him. Then the amount, and the care with which the money had been folded into place, made sudden sense to him. This was his stipend from the parish, backdated to the day—almost the very hour—of his arrival. It was very like Archie's discretion not to have stung him by leaving more. Who else would have bothered to pussyfoot so around the rags of his pride?

Quickly Rufus set the notes out on the bed. He found a scrap of paper and his fountain pen in the satchel. *Dear Archie*, he wrote, struggling against a tremor to keep the words legible. *Please give the money to Billy's family.* A sweet breeze from the lunette window threatened to scatter the papers. He reached into the drawer of the bedside cabinet and blindly pulled out the heavy figure of the little sleeping goddess. *Send my report off, please, and give this to the excavation team when they arrive. Don't come looking for me. Winborn was right—I should have gone before.* He paused, long enough for a drop of ink to form at the tip of the fountain pen's nib and splash the paper like a black tear. How could he end, when the word *love* was forbidden, and at this moment of parting he had nothing but love to convey? *Warmest affection and regards*—no, his hand was in spasm around the pen, and he'd never get the words down. Instead he too risked all with single, unsteady X.

He placed the goddess on top of the papers, then stood up and looked around. He'd arrived with nothing but his satchel, and the clothes on his back. By chance these were his own today, laundered and ironed by Mrs Nettles. He tried to imprint on his vision the curve of the window's arch, the shifting lights on the ceiling. The way the curtains rippled in the breeze, a dance he'd watched, wide-eyed, ecstatic, while Archie had made him come.

Shivering, he fastened up his satchel. He threw the strap across his shoulder, feeling for the first time since his arrival here the Sam Browne grip of the leather, the battlefield clutch. These attic rooms, beautiful as they were, would once have been servants' quarters. Archie's modern ideas about equality couldn't fix all the old abuses at once, and Rufus was willing to bet that there would be a servants' staircase, too, so no civilised person would have to encounter anything so dreadful as a maid with a bucket of ash on her way down the main stairs. He slipped out into the corridor.

Not a moment too soon. Archie's voice had been a kind of background music for the last few minutes, resonantly ripping a living strip off Winborn down in the hall. Now it had stopped. Now there were footsteps on the stairs. Now the air burst behind him with anxious repetitions of his name. "Rufus? Rufus, are you all right?"

All the bedroom doors were standing open. Mrs Nettles liked to keep a well aired house. At the end of the corridor, only one door remained shut, edges dusty with disuse. Cobwebs stretched and tore as Rufus pushed it back, just far enough to let himself into the dark space beyond. Soundlessly he closed it behind him.

The stairs were made of limestone, polished over the years by hurrying, working feet. He wondered—clasping the rail for balance, eyes adjusting to the grey light from the single window halfway down the well—if his own flight would add the faintest extra gleam to their patina. He drew one deep breath, like a swimmer preparing to dive, and he ran.

The stairs emerged, as he'd expected, into the rectory kitchen. No, not even that much convenience for the maid with her bucket of ash—into the scullery, so cook, butler and housekeeper needn't be disturbed. Layers upon layers, wheel within wheel of society—as then, so now, the doctor and the vicar in the hall, the disgraced queer slipping out like a rat into the garden. Trollope's world, alive and well, barricades staked out for eternity in British soil. He lowered his head so he wouldn't have to look at the orchard where he and Archie had loved each other the night before.

Drusilla was sitting there, upright on old Lady Birch's bench. Did she see him? She gave no sign. Her long black hair was down, blowing in the breeze. Pippin and the little girl were playing at her feet. For an instant, Rufus hoped and feared that the dog would waylay him, come barking and jumping to ruin his escape. She did stop playfully tussling with Elspeth over a stick, but her gaze was as wide and unfathomable as Drusilla's, and she didn't stir.

***

The station was deserted at this hour, Droyton's commuters having been swept off at dawn. The 9:15 from London had just finished its end-of-the-line siding shunt to get the engine into place for the return journey. Rufus had chosen a good time for headlong, anonymous flight: the guard was checking the couplings, and didn't glance up as he climbed into the nearest compartment. He subsided wearily onto the bench seat, trying to catch his breath. It was done now. The doors would slam shut, the row of old carriages bump and shuffle like billiard balls, and he would be gone.

"Um. I say. Good morning."

Rufus jerked his head up. For a moment he thought he was seeing a ghost, or had flickered back in time to the departure of the troop trains from Victoria. A young man was sitting opposite him, pale and handsome, dressed in an army captain's uniform. "Good morning," Rufus offered cautiously in return. It didn't seem likely that Winborn had summoned military backup, but he couldn't be sure. Whatever the case, he would have to keep this conversation short, escape as soon as he could into an empty compartment. He didn't even have a dog now, against whose mangy fur he could bury the signs of loneliness and absolute surging misery. "Can I help you?"

"Well, that is... I don't know. Perhaps. I don't suppose you live here?"

"No. I've just been visiting."

"The thing is, I'm looking for someone. A lady I used to know. I heard she'd come down here, but it seems so very foolish to wander around the streets in the hope of spotting her, doesn't it?"

Rufus would have wandered with him. If time was in freeflow, perhaps he could start his encounter with Droyton again from the beginning, and wander until he saw Archie, and they would both remember. "There's really only one street, so your mission isn't hopeless. What was the lady called?"

"Winborn. Alice Winborn."

Rufus dropped his satchel on the carriage floor. His own sorrows fell into abeyance. "You're not... Your name's not David, is it?"

The young man leaned forward, going paler still. "As a matter of fact, it is—David Meredith. It's a little awkward. I've been in a POW camp, and it's taken me rather a long time to get home. I only arrived yesterday."

A little awkward. Rufus had met this type of young man before. They stood on battlefields, only frowning a little as enemy shells burst all around them. Returned home to find themselves lost and adrift, just the same shy, nice lads they'd been before, holding within themselves indescribable experience. Probably he'd sat in this carriage since the train had arrived, and would have allowed himself to be towed back to London in due course. Rufus stood up. He thrust out his hand to Meredith, who took it on reflex, automatically scrambling up too. "David Meredith!"

"Yes, that's right. Do I know you?"

"Not at all." Rufus wrung his hand. "Listen to me. Go into the village. Take the lane opposite the pub and walk for about a quarter of a mile. You'll see a big house on your right, with yellow roses outside. That's the rectory."

"Is Miss Winborn there?"

"If she isn't, carry on up the lane and take the right fork to a place called Challen Farm. Go in there and find her."

"But will she... I've been away for such a long time. And she's very beautiful. I was afraid that she'd found—"

"Captain Meredith. Promise me something. Do not leave this village without seeing Alice Winborn. Do you understand?"

"I... Yes, sir. That is, no. What I mean is that I won't. Leave, that is."

Rufus bit back laughter. He patted Meredith on the cheek, just stopped short of kissing him. "That's a good fellow. And if you need help, ask Archie."

"Archie?"

"The vicar. The Reverend Archibald Thorne."

Book Two
(Into the Sun)

Chapter One

Rufus had left his war medals behind. Archie discovered them an hour later, thrust into the back of a drawer. The sleeping goddess was on the bed, holding down a note and the money Archie had tried to give him. Archie read the note, and sat down on the quilt, the small black box in his hand.

It contained a Distinguished Service medal and a Victoria Cross. He'd slowly understood that Rufus had arrived here homeless, the contents of his worn leather satchel everything he owned. There were traces of sand in the box. Perhaps he'd taken it to Sabros with him, desperate souvenir of a war he'd been unable to remember or forget.

Had he laid down his burden here, his neck-breaking albatross? Archie offered up a plea to Rufus's god—the god of sky and trees—that it was so.

More likely he'd just forgotten. Archie looked around the room. The wardrobe doors were open, every drawer in the dresser and cabinets pulled out to full extent. He was ashamed to have ransacked his friend's privacy, but there had to be something, some trace or clue as to where he had gone.

"London," he said suddenly, getting up, spilling the medals to the floor. Winborn had appeared in the bedroom doorway, looking a decade older and shaken to the bone. "London," Archie repeated. "I'm an idiot. He'll have gone to find his sister and get himself clapped away in the brigadier's looney bin. The man Captain Meredith met on the train—it must have been him."

"Captain Meredith was in a state of high excitement, and couldn't describe the person who'd aided him at all. It could have been anyone."

A state of high excitement. From the room below, the bedroom where Alice had taken refuge the night before, two voices soared skyward. Scraps of words and laughter interrupted their music, and then they smoothed out into one long conjoined cry. "Archie," Winborn rasped, looking older still. "This is your house. A rectory, for heaven's sake. You should intervene."

Archie surveyed the familiar face, every line of which had become stitched into his childhood. "Intervene?" he echoed. "Do you know where Meredith's come from? The Japanese abandoned the camp, and he and the other men had to make their way through the jungle to the coast before they were picked up and brought home. They were starving before they set out. Two thirds of them died on the way."

"I'm aware of his suffering. Must we abandon all the proprieties, though, because—"

"Think what Alice has been through. What we all have, in one way or another. Can't you just let love be?"

"Not the kind that makes bestial noises in broad daylight. Not yours for Denby, if that's what you call it."

Archie controlled his temper with an effort. "You were a father to me," he said fiercely. "That's why I never questioned you. But I believe a time is coming—maybe now, in the wake of this terrible war—when we'll all start to question our fathers, our father *lands*. And then the proprieties are going to go out of the window in ways you can't even begin to imagine."

"Then I hope I don't live to see it. That's all." Winborn came to stand by the bed. "Whose are these medals?"

"They belong to Rufus. He left them behind."

"Why?"

"Haven't you noticed—in this past year, since it's all been over, some men can't stop talking about it, and others..."

"Others hide their honours and shut up." Winborn picked up the box and looked at its contents. An odd shiver ran through him. "Yes, I've noticed. These are some of the highest military decorations this country can bestow."

"That's right."

"Why did he leave here like a coward?"

"Because I'm quite sure he's thought up a punishment for himself that's worse than anything we could inflict on him here. That's why I have to go after him."

"No. You have to go to Brighton and see Billy Prescott. Now."

Archie exhaled unsteadily. "How bad is he?"

"Bad enough that he should see his spiritual advisor. Are you still capable of performing that role, Archie?"

"I can *perform* it, yes. It hasn't been real for years. But I don't suppose it has to be real for it to work, does it?"

"What are you saying?"

"That I don't believe. And right now, what I don't believe more than anything else is that Rufus did this to Billy."

"We don't have time to discuss it. Come along. I'll drive you there."

Mechanically Archie gathered up the money on the bed. Rufus's note was safe inside his waistcoat pocket, its three stiff lines redeemed by an ink-blotted kiss. From the room below, another cry soared up, this one just Alice's, explicit and wild with joy. "Well, what would you have me do?" Archie asked. "Send them to your house, to sit and hold hands on the sofa?"

"I wanted my niece to be married and respectable. I wanted the same for you."

"Of course I could have turned them out into the fields, to laugh and cry like that with no roof to shield them. Maybe in another world, that would be best, but..." Archie got up stiffly, muscles aching from holding Rufus against the trunk of the apple tree the night before. "Not in this one. In this world, love needs shelter. And as long as the rectory's standing, I'm going to provide it."

He followed Winborn down the stairs. He would do his duty to Billy, real or performed, to the best of his gifts. Afterwards, the direct line from Brighton would take him where he needed to go faster than the steam train from Droyton. Maybe he would even overhaul Rufus somewhere en route, catch him by his coat-tails at Victoria and prevent him from completing whatever devil's bargain he had in mind. Archie didn't believe he'd laid a hand on Billy Prescott the night before, but the truth was that he didn't care if he had—if he'd punched his way through the whole male population of the village in his efforts to find his enemy from the Fort Roche trench.

Half blind with anxiety, he almost walked into Mrs Trigg at the foot of the stairs. The encounter was so unexpected that he lurched back, grabbing the newel post. "Hester," he said, the name shocked out of him by the change in her appearance. "Good heavens, what's wrong? Are you ill?"

"No, Reverend." She was twisting her headscarf between her hands. "Maria Nettles and the new Lady Birch—that is, Miss Hazelgrove as was—brought me here. To speak to you."

They were stationed behind her in the hallway, one at each shoulder. They didn't look as if they'd frogmarched her so much as provided an escort. Archie couldn't have said why, but they formed an eccentrically pleasing triad, as if something broken had been put back together to find a purpose once more. "I'm in a bit of a hurry. Could it possibly wait?"

Drusilla laid a hand to Mrs Trigg's shoulder. "Don't be afraid," she said kindly. "Don't be afraid to speak and bear witness."

"Look, if this is about Jebediah... You really mustn't worry about it anymore. You've lost weight, and you don't look well at all."

"It isn't that!" Mrs Trigg grabbed at her long string of pearls and tugged them so hard that Archie got ready to catch flying beads. "Not that what's making me sick, Reverend. But I can't tell you. It's horrible—oh, horrible."

"Why are you here, then? Have you seen Billy?"

"Yes! That I have. Went down to the hospital with him in the ambulance, though he said I didn't have to bother. He's been a good lad to me, though uppish with it and needing kept down, same as his sister."

"Wait. He was talking to you?"

"Yes, yes. He couldn't at first, which is why Dr Winborn here telephoned for an ambulance, what with him bleeding so. But the driver said head wounds do, and before we'd passed Lewes he was sat up and demanding to be brought back home again. Only they wouldn't let him, and they kept him in overnight, and I stayed as long as I could then caught the first bus home, having the Maidens' to open, may the ground be accursed on which it stands. Oh, horrible!"

Archie tried to pull out a thread from this tangle. "Are you saying Billy's not in danger?"

"In danger? Oh, no. I left him eating his breakfast, right as ninepence, trying his nonsense on with the nurses, who didn't seem to mind it, hussies as they are these days. He thinks he knows who attacked him, on account of which, when I met Mrs Nettles and Miss Hazelgrove on the street, they deemed it important for me to come here straight away and tell you. So I came, not that the hospital gave me *my* breakfast, or so much as a cup of tea."

Archie restrained himself with a nerve-scraping effort. "Mrs Nettles will give you tea in a minute, and all the breakfast you can eat. Who attacked Billy?"

"That hulking lad of Poacher Jakes', the one my Jebediah's taken to running about with, to the increase of my shame. He was wearing a scarf round his face, but he couldn't even do that right, poor simpleton. Billy pulled it off and saw him clear as I'm seeing you."

"Not Dr Denby. Bobby Jakes."

"Bobby Jakes, Reverend. Billy feared it was Dr Denby, after the other night, but it was the Jakes lad who attacked him, no doubt in the world, and their cottage is empty this morning, not hide nor hair to be found. What none of us can understand is why."

"I don't understand either. But thank God Billy's all right. I'll have Constable Pennick in Ashfield begin to look into what's happened to Bobby and his father. Although," he said, quickly adjusting his priorities in this new light, "maybe you could do that for me, Winborn. I really have to..."

Silence met his trailed-off words. When he turned, only a gap remained in the hallway where Winborn had stood. "Looks as if the doctor's had to step out," Mrs Nettles observed, so sandily that the very air around her became abrasive, and realisation hit Archie like a truck.

Drusilla caught him in the doorway. She stopped him, and something comradely and strong in her grasp made him cease fighting. Had she too been through the turning-castle beneath the church and emerged transformed? No—this was simply her nature, which refused to be hidden forever or suborned. Just like Rufus's. Just like his own. "Don't," she said. "He's an old man."

"But why would he do such a thing? Did he... He *paid* the Jakes boy to hurt Billy?"

"Denby would never have left your side otherwise. Winborn calculated on his decency."

"I'll kill him, I swear, old man or—"

"Is he important to you now, Thorne?"

Archie stood gasping. He had to calm down, or the pain in his lungs would begin. He was surprised he hadn't already felt its clenching fist. "No."

"You should have checked Denby's feet."

"His what?"

"You always tended mine for cuts and bruises after you'd brought me home. You'd have seen that his were unmarked. He got his injuries by falling down the garden steps into the orchard."

"You saw him?"

"Yes. I was making my communion with the moon."

"Why didn't you fetch me?"

"He picked himself up, and you were already on your way. You felt obliged to interrupt me in *my* trysts, but I understand why. I saw no reason to disturb you in yours."

Archie's skin heated. He'd never before in his life been benignly teased for a romantic assignation. "Well, thank you, but... look, I have to go."

"Of course."

"If I leave now, I ought to catch the... Actually, hang the trains. I'll take the bike."

"A good idea. Be sure to pack your panniers—you may be gone for a while. And just stop by my room for a moment before you leave. I want to give you something."

Archie stepped back. He surveyed the hallway of his home, the strange confluence of so many lives. It was absurd for him to think that he could simply abandon his world here, his parish, his duty. But the man who had most steadfastly sold that world to him, insisted upon his observing its boundaries, had betrayed him to keep him trapped within it. And here were Drusilla and Maria, between them ferociously capable of dealing with any crisis that might arise in his absence. Even Elspeth and the dog had grasped the situation, and were waiting like a weird honour guard, one on either side of the open kitchen door.

Only Mrs Trigg seemed lost. She had slumped onto the bottom stair and was sitting with her face in her hands. Archie heard her whisper once more, to some judgemental deity only she could perceive, "Horrible. Oh, God, horrible."

He shook his head in bewilderment. "Maria, will you please look after Hester? Jebediah, too, if he turns up looking for her? And..." He glanced upstairs, where a reverberant silence had succeeded the cries of love. "Alice and the captain, too. Some endings are almost too happy to be borne."

"Of course, Reverend," Mrs Nettles said serenely. "Don't we always look after everyone? If you don't mind my taking the liberty of saying so, you should go and find your friend."

Chapter Two

What Drusilla had wanted to give him was a herb she called *wake-the-dead*. Sitting in afternoon sunlight in his cousin Caroline's office, Archie took the paper bag out of his pocket and sniffed at it cautiously. He jerked his head back, blinking. "Christ!"

Heels clicked on the polished wooden floor. "Good afternoon, Reverend," Caroline greeted him dryly, coming into the room. She closed the door behind her and sat down behind her desk. "Please tell me that smell isn't your tobacco. Didn't your doctor say you had to stop smoking?"

"I have," Archie said, surprising himself. He'd left his roll-up papers on his desk in the library the day before, and not thought about or missed them. "No, it's not tobacco. How are you, Caroline?"

"I'm very well. I've decided to take early retirement. Matilda and I have bought a small villa on Lesvos, and we intend to spend lots of time there."

A bold statement, but she could make them to him. She must have known that, despite his marriage and the blanket denial that had stifled them both since childhood. "That's good. Listen, could I possibly trouble you for some—"

"I asked for tea to be sent up as soon as I heard you were here. You came on your motorbike, didn't you? You must be parched."

"Thank you."

"And do take off that leather jacket. It's very hot."

Archie obeyed her reluctantly. He needed a drink after his four-hour ride, and he needed to speak to her, but further concessions to delay felt unbearable. "I'm sorry to interrupt your working day. It's about my... well, I think we agreed to call him a mole, didn't we?"

"The one I sent you? How long did it take you to find out that he was rather a good one?"

"Not long at all, but not because he told me. Dr Winborn recognised him."

"Ah. Winborn—he was your guardian, wasn't he? After Aunt Sybil and Uncle Joseph died, while you were at college. I didn't know he was living in Droyton."

"Well, he is, damn him." Archie clenched his fists in frustration at the sidetrack. "Rufus—Dr Denby, that is—we made friends, rather. You're aware of his war record, his troubles since he came home?"

"Only too vividly."

"That's why I thought you might help me. His blasted sister told him that her father-in-law—some kind of Colonel Blimp with a medical degree—has opened a hospital for shellshocked veterans, to help them recover their memories. Dr Denby had some... episodes of amnesia while he was with us in Droyton, and believes himself to blame for an incident which wasn't his fault. He's vanished, and I'm afraid he's gone to throw himself on the mercies of this hospital."

Caroline absorbed this without a change of expression. When her assistant arrived with a tray of tea things, she stood up calmly and took it from the girl, then set it down on her desk and waited until the door was closed again. "Oh, dear."

"Is that it, Caroline? Oh, dear?"

"Forgive me. Emotional outbursts have never really served me. In fact, given my position, my gender and my proclivities, I've learned rather hard to avoid them."

She had never mentioned her proclivities to Archie in her life. He'd only had Matilda and the cats to give him any hint that they existed. "I'm sorry."

"That's all right. The fact is that I'm rather fond of Dr Denby, and I thought the Droyton church would interest him, although it's far beneath his abilities."

"Be that as it may, he found some amazing things there. He's written you a full report—he was going to post it, but since I was coming here, I've brought it in person."

"Thank you." Caroline took the envelope from Archie's hand. "I'll give it my immediate attention. I hoped a good change of scene would be helpful to Denby, you see. And a good man."

"A good... I beg your pardon?"

"You heard me. I knew you wouldn't allow any strangers in the village to remain strange for long. Celia's been dead for eight years, Archie, and poor Richard Simms for more than twenty."

Archie sat forward in his chair. She circumvented any further action by coming to stand in front of him, holding out a cup of tea. When he just stared at her, she picked up his wrist and gently pushed the saucer into his hand. "I'm sorry," he managed eventually. "Are you saying that you... *aimed* Rufus Denby at me?"

She smiled. "What—aimed one handsome, clever, lonely homosexual man at another? Why on earth would I do something like that?"

"Oh, Caroline. My God."

"And it's not quite true. When Dr Denby came back from Sabros with his career in ruins, I aimed him at the church first of all. But you were a very close second."

She returned to her seat behind her desk. Archie got hold of his teacup and his wildly veering thoughts. "I wasn't even sure you knew about me."

"You knew about *me*, didn't you? Now, why is Dr Winborn being damned, and why is Brigadier Spence—a noted physician, though I only know him by reputation—Colonel Blimp with a medical degree?" She leaned her chin on her fist. "A stay in that kind of hospital might be just what Rufus needs."

"No. There's something else going on. Spence's son's been accused of cowardice on the battlefield, and threatened with... a posthumous court-martial, or whatever military types do to one another in these situations. According to Spence, Rufus was there when it happened. Rufus has forgotten, and Spence is determined to have it out of him by fair means or foul, and by foul I mean shock therapy. He isn't offering a rest-cure. I have to find him, Caroline, and I don't know where this new place is."

"I'm afraid I don't either. I'm sorry, Archie—you did get hip-deep with Denby and his problems in a short space of time, didn't you?"

"Isn't that what you intended?"

"Not at all. I just wanted you to have a friend."

"This is what friends do." Didn't she know? He examined her in the unforgiving light—lean, composed, lips firmly set. He had used to think her deficient somehow, empty. Now he understood that she'd learned to handle her fullness in her own way. Archie's hurt him like lava about to overflow. "I hoped you might be able to direct me to his sister, or the brigadier himself. That's all."

"No. Rufus only ever told me that they were living in Mayfair. I... Wait a moment." She picked up the receiver of the telephone on her desk, tapped her lip thoughtfully with a pen, then turned the dial. "Operator? Finchley 5632, please. The Murray Clinic, Dr Green's office. Thank you." She covered the receiver with her hand. "We wanted to help Rufus when he came back from Sabros, so the museum paid for him to stay in a private clinic at... Yes, thank you. I'll hold."

"Nice of the museum to do that. Next time it might consider paying his salary, too, or at least letting me know that the parish was supposed to."

She frowned. "Oh, goodness. I was going to write and tell you, but then Matilda caught flu."

"Is she better now?"

"Yes, much."

"That's good. But our mole is on the loose with very little more than his velvet coat on his back, and I've no idea where."

"That's what I'm trying to find out for you, Archie. How *was* my aim, by the way?"

Archie shook his head. No point in secrets now, he supposed. "Very good. Less of a mole than a missile."

She swallowed a laugh. "Ah, Dr Green. Caroline Taylor from the museum—we've spoken once or twice with regard to Rufus Denby. No, not at all as well as we could have hoped. Rather a relapse, I've just heard. The thing is, Dr Denby is brother-in-law to Brigadier Charles Spence, who you may have heard has opened up a new facility for shellshock cases, over in... Oh, the name was on the tip of my tongue just a minute ago... Yes, that was the place. I'm sorry, Doctor—this line's awful. I'm losing you, I'm afraid." She hung up, put her head on one side and looked at her cousin. "Where the devil is Colditch?"

"Somewhere on the Suffolk coast, I think. That was quite adroit of you, Caroline."

"Thank you. There was probably no need for the cloak-and-dagger, but I gather you don't want to advertise your approach."

"No, I don't. I've seen how far my friends would go to get him there. God only knows what his own would do to keep him."

"Do you want me to attempt a sly call of enquiry to the hospital itself?"

"Better not, Mata Hari. I can't think how you'd do it without alerting them." He rubbed his brow tiredly. "Rufus might not even be there."

"I think it's a safe bet. He has nowhere else to go in London, and if he's as broke as you say..." She tapped the pile of papers on her desk. "Find him, Archie. I lived a great deal on my own, watching my generation pair off around me. There's nothing wrong with such solitude if it's chosen, but mine wasn't. I don't believe I've ever told you how I met Matilda?"

"It hasn't been the kind of thing we've talked about."

"She'd been giving a speech in favour of conscientious objection for the Peace Pledge Union. She was a tremendous firecracker about it then, though she's not so certain now."

"She and Rufus would have a lot to talk about."

"So they shall. You'll come to one of our noisy little Bloomsbury dinners, and everyone will talk till dawn. Anyway, some reporters had been sent to the PPU, and very hostile they were, thugs from the gutter press. Paid to frighten Matilda and make a fool out of her, I imagine, and they'd cornered her in an alley behind the hall. So I rode my pushbike into them. By accident, of course."

Archie wanted to vault the desk and embrace her. "Of course."

"Goodness knows how many thugs you'd mow down on that Norton of yours to help Rufus. I can see that you're on your way to do it. Just don't make the mistake of equating your situation with mine."

"What do you mean?"

"Matilda and I don't exist, not in the eyes of the law. That's the only advantage women have reaped from millennia of amounting to nothing—zero plus zero equals zero. The same does not apply to men. You're hellishly visible."

"Rufus tried to teach me the same thing."

"Much good it's done either of you. Take heart, though, Archie. There is a great deal of satisfaction in having found one's own Matilda."

***

Archie left the museum armed with Drusilla's herbs in one pocket and, in the other, Caroline's letter of introduction to a formidably respectable landlady in Colchester, approximately halfway between London and his destination. She'd been at college with Caroline, and didn't normally accommodate single men, but would make exception for a vicar.

Feeling more than ever a wolf in black broadcloth, Archie recovered his Norton from the admiring group of porters who'd been taking care of her, and set off through the Bloomsbury streets. Although he'd left Maria and Drusilla far behind, he felt—breathed, in the dusty city air all around him, which ought to have made him cough but somehow now didn't—the presence of a new, vibrant network. Caroline was one of its nodes. So were the women of the rectory, and so had been Giles. The war had brought this web to life. Tractor drivers, steelworkers, fearless mothers of illegitimate children, stern bluestockings weaving their web from behind museum desks...

Dodging round the back of a bus, Archie wondered if the genie had come out of the bottle for men like him and Rufus, too. If laws would change, and one day Winborn and his kind would fulminate in vain. Archie had a kind of vision—insane, because even in a future of enfranchised women and queers, a vicar would still be a vicar—of walking down a golden beach with Rufus. Stupid to wear black broadcloth in such a place, or even the tweed-and-cotton uniform of the Englishman abroad. No, they'd both be dressed in long cool robes, barefoot, hand-in-hand...

He stopped two inches shy of rear-ending a black cab at a junction. Horns blared behind him. Unnerved, he veered off into the next quiet side road and let the Norton slow to a bumping halt beside a bombed-out building.

He didn't know London very well. He'd negotiated Piccadilly Circus a few minutes ago, the enduring, hopeful Eros—sober Anteros really, but embraced as the God of Love by a London population sorely in need of such guardianship—still hidden away in his wartime refuge. Rufus had said that he and Henry had shared a flat in a Piccadilly apartment block. It didn't seem likely that Archie had stumbled upon the very place.

And yet somehow he knew that he had. The feeling was so strong that he knocked his kickstand down, took off his helmet and goggles and dismounted. He stared up at the building's intact wall, flayed like a cadaver to show its intimate inside life. Wallpaper in chintz and flock, fireplaces gaping. Above the shadow of a mantelpiece on the top floor, a painting still dangling askew from its string. Archie looked about him, half-expecting to see Rufus somewhere nearby, flayed too by memories and the lack of them, drawn helplessly back to this bombsite.

No. Not now, though he might have come here first, making a stop on a dreadful pilgrimage. Archie clutched the Norton's handlebar for balance, shivering with the conviction that it had been so. If he'd got here a few hours earlier, he'd have found him amongst the rubble, just as Rufus had found his stray dog.

Even Pippin had been rescued. Colditch was a hundred and fifty miles away. That would be a brutal slog on the Norton, but Archie didn't intend to stop anywhere tonight. The bike had been modified to carry an illegal extra petrol canister on a rack at the rear, useful but all too likely to make a firebomb of her in a crash. There wouldn't be many all-night filling stations on the minor roads through the Suffolk salt marshes. All Archie had to do was stay upright and awake. Maybe that was why Drusilla had given him the herb. He had food in his saddlebags, a batch of Maria's door-stop sandwiches and a thermos of tea of near-warhead dimensions, refilled by the deputy director of the Royal Museum in that noble institute's kitchen.

He swung back onto the bike. He remembered how Rufus had clambered up behind him: the shy, strong clasp of warm arms around his waist. *Hang on, Rufus. I'm on my way. Hang on.*

Chapter Three

Seagulls hung motionless on the wind over Colditch Sands. Dune grasses, flattened in their growth to a monotonous offshore fretwork, lined the narrow road. The grasses and birds belonged to the same world as Droyton, but Archie was hard-pressed to believe it. Dunes and silhouettes of bombed-out buildings flickered like film transparencies behind his eyes. Droyton's great oaks and a bleak, flat expanse of grey sky. Scents of sunlight upon yellow roses—a fragrance he'd never noticed until Rufus had told him his whole house was soaked through with it—battled in his memory with the new tang of salt. At what point had the rectory become home to him? He'd lived in the tiny Brighton vicarage with Celia for thirteen years without once feeling this huge need to return. There was only one thing he wanted more.

The vibration of the bike had transferred itself into his bones. He was aching from wrist joints to testicles, but he couldn't stop now. At last, after nearly two hours of following this bleak coast from village to sleeping village, there were buildings in the distance, a collection of low modern blocks. With an eerie sensation that the Norton was moving on her own to carry him over this last stretch, he focussed on his destination.

The brigadier's architects seemed to have taken their inspiration from the Brutalist blocks going up in London to re-house a bombed-out population, or from the concrete cubes decaying on the beaches, last-ditch deterrents to a tank attack which had never come. White-painted breeze blocks and glass surrounded a vacant gravel courtyard on three sides. The windows had a blinded look. Archie realised, bumping to a halt on the driveway, that they were set too high up in the walls to be seen through from the outside, and too high to reach from within. His engine echoed strangely, the roar and clatter bouncing from surface to surface even after he'd switched off. The whole place was set uncomfortably on the coastal plain, with a look of shallow foundations and impermanence.

Forgetting his weariness, Archie got off the bike and made for the glassed-in entrance. He pushed one door wide, then the next, and came up sharp against a third, glass like the first two but shut fast by invisible locks. He stopped himself from banging his fists off the thick pane. There was an intercom buzzer: he tore off one glove and pushed that with his thumb instead, like a sane, quiet person, not at all a renegade motorbike vicar about to break every door and window in this place until his lover was restored to him. He had a story of sorts, and he drew a deep breath ready to deploy it as a white-coated figure appeared behind the glass.

Colonel Blimp with a medical degree. Archie kept hold of his breath. There was no reason why the chief medical director should be answering the door at this hour of the morning, but this was the man. Archie was sure of it. Hope rose up in him with choking force, and he exhaled, straightened his shoulders and pulled his jacket open far enough to show his dog collar. "Good morning," he said, as soon as the intercom buzzed. "I'm sorry to disturb you so early. My name is Archibald Thorne, and I'm searching for one of my parishioners, who left my village in... rather a state of spiritual crisis. I've reason to believe he might have admitted himself here."

The face behind the glass was expressionless as a slab of beef. Archie couldn't work out how such a mask was managing to exude fear and rage. The intercom buzzed again, and whatever unseen force was holding the glass door shut disappeared. "Electronic security," said the newcomer, as Archie let himself in and the door silently sealed itself behind him. "Operated from a keypad. The lack of traditional lock and key gives our residents a sense of freedom. Yes, Dr Denby is here."

Any sense of freedom was illusory. Every sound from the outside world had vanished, falling dead as it struck the glass. "May I see him?"

"A word with you first." His companion set off across the empty reception hall, its purpose defined only by the glinting white barricade of desk that ran its echoing length. "You surely haven't ridden up from London?"

Archie's capacity for small talk was minimal. "Yes," he grated. "Overnight. His journey must have been worse than mine."

"Oh, no. Not at all." There was a bare white room on the far side of a bare white corridor. Archie's companion looked like a falling marble pillar in his long white coat, something smugly massive pushed past its balance point. "Dr Denby didn't come here on his own. He went to my home in Mayfair, and his sister telephoned to me. I arranged for his transport by ambulance." He gestured to a chair. "I'm not aware that he had a parish, let alone a vicar, Reverend Thorne. Please sit down."

"He was working in my village. Everyone who comes there has a right to my time and resources, if they wish it, Brigadier..."

"Spence. That's right. And did Dr Denby wish it?"

The cold edge of insinuation barely snagged on Archie's mind. "He was deeply troubled about some episodes of violent behaviour he'd experienced. But he was getting better, and part of what I've come here to tell him—to tell you—is that he wasn't responsible for the attack upon a young man in Droyton the other day."

"Droyton?" Spence sat down heavily opposite him. His eyes were oddly glazed. "His sister mentioned that he'd gone there. But that's in the depths of Sussex, isn't it? You surely haven't travelled all this way to—"

"Yes, I have. Because this assault made him decide to commit himself, and..."

"Good heavens, Reverend. No-one is committed here. We're not an asylum."

"A hospital with locked doors, then, and he doesn't deserve to be in one. I think his violent outbreaks were caused by certain wartime experiences, which he's forgotten in order to save his sanity. I don't believe he ought to be forced to remember."

"I don't think we quite understand each other, Reverend Thorne."

Archie surveyed him. He'd met men like this during his own war. They were made for the trade, impossible to imagine on civvy street, their uniforms a better fit than their own human skin. "Maybe not," he said cautiously. "However, that's my message for Dr Denby. I'd very much like to deliver it myself."

"Dr Denby is a very courageous man."

I know. He left his Victoria Cross in my bedroom drawer. "I don't think there can be any doubt of that."

"How his wartime experiences may have affected him mentally, I'm not qualified to say. Forgive me if I tell you that I wouldn't be interested. This hospital is for wounded men, not hysterics and cowards."

"By hysterics and cowards, do you mean..."

"So-called neurasthenics, shellshock cases. This nation doesn't have the resources to nursemaid pitiful fools who should never have been let near a battlefield. This war was won by *men*, Reverend, and Dr Denby was one of them, as his injuries attest."

"His injuries? I know he was hit by shrapnel, but—"

"He allowed his hair to grow and hide the worst of the damage. Leaving fears and fancies aside, I'm certain that the cause of his nightmares and violent outbreaks is nothing more complex than pressure on his brain, and we can relieve that. I have a surgeon coming tomorrow, a specialist. And that is why Dr Denby is here."

Archie sat back. Since Rosemary's visit to Droyton, he'd never considered her motives as anything other than foolish at best, at worst malign and destructive. The brigadier had assumed Minotaur proportions for him, too. Perhaps Archie had misjudged him, picking up the infection of Rufus's fear. "Can he be... Is it that simple? Can he be cured?"

"I hope there's at least a chance, or Mr Wilson-Grey is coming here at great expense for nothing."

"But Rufus—Dr Denby—can't afford an expensive operation. Nor can I, although..." Possibilities flashed through Archie's mind: selling the bike, his collection of first-edition Trollopes. "I'll help if I can. If it'll help him."

"You do take your pastoral duties seriously. There's no need in this case, however. Dr Denby's medical bills will be covered by the new National Health Service legislation. Have you heard of that?"

"Bevan's scheme for free health care? Of course. I think it's marvellous. But—forgive me, Brigadier. I gathered from Rosemary that your first concern was to break Dr Denby's amnesia. I don't believe that can be good for him. That's why I came here—to dissuade him if I could, or dissuade you."

Spence straightened his tie. He was the perfect image of a military medical man, except for the sheen of sweat beneath his hairline, and that unfathomable glimmer in his eyes. "Rosemary sees things from her own point of view. It's not unnatural. We both want to preserve the memory of our boy."

The major had been Rosemary's husband, not her boy. The slip was an odd one. "I'm sorry for your loss," Archie said quietly. "But I don't believe you can sacrifice one man's sanity to spare the reputation of somebody who's passed far beyond such cares."

"His mother and I have not passed beyond them!" The brigadier caught himself, found a sickly smile. "That is, Rosemary and I have not. Still, I assure you, the only goal of Dr Denby's treatment is to relieve the pressure on his brain. If his memory returns as a consequence of that, so much the better for us all."

"May I see him, Brigadier?"

"This isn't a visiting hospital. And it's scarcely past nine in the morning."

"I can come back later."

"No, no. Come with me now, and satisfy yourself that he's here for his own good. After that, there'll be no access until after his surgery. Stay close to me, and please ensure that any locked doors are locked again behind you. Some very extreme cases are sent here."

Archie got up and followed the brigadier. The bare white corridor stretched out before him like a dream, making him wish to be back in the coiling tunnels beneath the Droyton church, where he'd lost his breath and Rufus had restored it to him. Despite his anxiety, he still didn't want a cigarette. A day and a half since his last... He ought to be ready to sell his soul to Satan for a drag. He let these thoughts distract him from the tight-closed doors they were passing, from the sounds that issued from behind some of them, grunts and roars and, briefly, a grown man's broken-hearted weeping. Dear God, if Rufus was locked away in one of these little cells...

He swallowed in relief as Spence led him into an open ward. A first glance showed him twenty or so beds arrayed along the walls. This was the seaward side, to judge by the chilly light, but the high windows were keeping their secrets. Only a handful of the beds were occupied. Spence sheered off at an urgent summons from a nurse, leaving Archie to find Rufus for himself.

Which should have been so easy. The one man of all others who'd entered Archie's world and turned it painfully, deliciously upside down: Archie could have picked him out among thousands, he'd thought, by scent alone if he had to.

But this place stank of Lysol, and Rufus, with his head shaved and his dapper suit replaced by hospital pyjamas, had blended with all the other bodies under blankets in the shifting sea-light. "Dear God," Archie whispered, finally seeing him. He swept up to his bedside like a hot wind. "I thought I'd lost you. It's all right. I'm here now."

Eyes like the clouds over Colditch Sands. The shorn head turned on the pillow. Archie could feel the effort of focus, as if a seagull's mewing had turned out to be a human voice, in need of response and attention. "Could you... pass me some water, please? My throat's dry."

"Of course." Archie perched on the edge of the mattress. The brigadier was in conclave now with another two white coats, and Archie couldn't have cared less anyway: leaned in and brushed the lightest kiss to the exposed brow. "Why didn't you tell me these scars were so bad? Here, let me sit you up a bit. Here's your water."

Rufus leaned back on the pillow Archie had pushed behind him. He held the glass awkwardly, like a man wearing thick sheepskin mitts, drank a mouthful or two then lost his grip.

Swiftly Archie reached in, wiped up the spillage with a napkin and held the glass to his lips again.

The clouded eyes watched him from a vast, lost distance. "That's enough. Thank you."

"Why can't you manage for yourself?"

"Not sure. Jolly annoying. Slipped me a mickey, I suppose—they always do, in here."

"You haven't been here before."

"Not this one, no. All the same, though, really, aren't they? I'm just hoping this one's..." He faded out, struggled to sit up a little further. "...a bit closer to home."

"You're not in a field hospital, Rufus. All that's over."

"Oh, I know it will be soon. With all the surrenders on the Eastern Front, things can't go on much longer. So you needn't look so worried." He put out a hand and briefly patted Archie's. "I say. You mustn't *cry* over it, old man."

"I'm not." Archie rubbed the napkin over his face. "All right, I am. Sorry. It's just that I've been looking for you all night, and... they cut off your hair."

"Do I look awful?"

"No. Like a fallen angel." Archie ran the lightest touch over his scalp, gingerly avoiding the scars. "An angel who fell on his head, though. They're going to make this feel better."

"That would be nice. Listen, though, Reverend. It's good of you to come and see me, but I'm not a believing man, not... not in that way. You should go and see Corporal Berry. His older brother was going to go into your line, he told me. Before he got called up."

Archie's turn to spill the water now. He placed the glass back on the bedside cabinet. "You don't know who I am, do you?"

"I'm sorry. Have you come to see me before? You'd think I'd remember a chaplain brave enough to come so close to the Front.

Especially one this handsome." Colour rose painfully into his face. "Forgive me. I *am* drugged."

"Oh, Rufus."

"Please don't tell anyone I talk that way."

"I won't." Archie fought back terror. "Listen. Do you remember a village, a church with strange tunnels underneath it? Do you remember..." He paused. Impossible to find words for what remained so lucidly clear in his own mind. "...being with me in the orchard at night?"

"No." The wan face became wistful. "Sounds lovely. I wish I could."

Archie had to pause before he could speak again. The sense of loss expanding within him was bigger, more eviscerating, than the pain he'd experienced on the first morning after Richard's suicide. A comforting graveside cliché: *the people we love are never truly gone as long as we remember them...* What kind of death-in-life would it be to have lost his place in this man's mind? "Don't worry," he said hoarsely. "Everything will be all right."

"What about this church, and the orchard?"

"They'll be waiting for you."

"I don't understand."

"It doesn't matter."

A faint, weary chuckle. "I must be worse off than I thought."

"What? Why?"

"Because you're holding my hand, Vicar. They generally only do that when we're about to snuff it."

Well, that was bitter truth. The rough semblance of training Archie had received for his front-line role had taught him to avoid physical touch, as prone to unstring the nerves and make lonely squaddies weep for home and their mum. He tightened his grip. "You're not about to snuff anything. You don't remember, Rufus, but I'm your friend. And as soon as you're better, I'm going to take you home."

Something in his conviction found its way to the lost man. He nodded, his brow smoothing. He lay back against the pillows, closing his eyes.

The brigadier was in consultation now with a doctor on the far side of the ward. Archie had been peripherally aware of him all the time. Not much that got said or done would go hidden in this merciless white space, but nevertheless he had been hovering, never allowing Rufus wholly out of his attention's grip. Suddenly he held up a peremptory finger to his companion, raising his head. "Quiet, please!"

Archie couldn't hear anything more than the background sounds of the ward. Then a faint tapping caught his ear. Some parts of this angular-mushroom building must still be under construction. Somewhere on the upper levels, someone was hammering a rafter or a wall. The brigadier pointed in the direction of the sound. "Didn't I give orders for that racket to be stopped?"

The young doctor nearest to him shifted uneasily. "Yes, sir, but it's difficult. The men said there's a storm coming, and that seaward section of the roof—"

"Roof be damned!" The hammering was louder now, settling into a rhythm. *Bang, bang, bang*, somehow meaning more than the sum of its parts as Rufus's hand went cold in Archie's, the fingers stiff and taut. "Send someone up there. It's unacceptable during rounds and consultations. They can carry on afterwards, when…"

Rufus tore his hand free and sat bolt upright in the bed. He ran both palms over his new short crop, fingertips brushing the ragged pattern of his scars as if his answers lay there. "The Minotaur," he choked out. "My enemy. I remember—"

The brigadier rounded on a passing nurse. "Restraint team for bed five."

"Five, sir? Dr Denby?"

"Are you deaf as well as disobedient, woman?"

The nurse shot away. Archie got up and went to stand at the end of Rufus's bed. "He doesn't need restraint. You've got him so doped up he can't remember yesterday, let alone hurt anyone." But orders went out fast in the brigadier's hospital: the ward door swung wide to admit four burly orderlies, one of them pushing a trolley. On instinct Archie stepped in front of that one, grunting as the metal impacted against his thighs. "Stop."

He might as well have been a stone in a stream. The flow simply parted around him. Two of the men made a dive for the bed. A third evaded Archie's grasp to push Rufus back and lean a meaty knee on his arm. The fourth—busy with a syringe, but still a fair, fine target—went down with a winded gasp as the vicar of Droyton landed a fist in his gut. "What the bloody hell are you doing?" Archie yelled, whipping round to find his next man and coming up sharp against the brigadier. "Rufus doesn't need this. Call them off!"

"You know as well as I do that Denby's nightmares lead to violence."

"He isn't having a nightmare. He's wide awake."

The brigadier's face was like stone. "It's time for you to leave, Reverend Thorne."

Archie twisted away from him. He caught one glimpse of Rufus between the orderlies' shoulders. His head was back, his eyes squeezed shut. He was fighting, but the stuffing was out of him, his movements weak and sluggish even before the third man scooped up the syringe from the floor and plunged the long needle home.

As soon as it was done, they fell away. They were dryly professional, Archie could give them that—returned to their positions around the trolley, the fourth having picked himself up without a trace of animosity. Archie darted to the bedside. He tucked Rufus's limp arm into the bedclothes, then wiped the unconscious face dry, savagely swallowing tears of his own. "Christ almighty. That was *not* necessary. Dr Denby has friends, Spence, and I'll tell them about his treatment here. I'll get him out, and..."

Spence was gone. He'd vanished between Rufus's last yell and the closing of his eyes, as if some bomb had been stopped in its countdown tick and he no longer needed to wait in fear of the blast. The nurse he'd sent to fetch the team reappeared at Archie's elbow. "Best not make a fuss, Reverend," she said quietly. "He's asleep now, and quite comfortable."

"What the devil did they give him?"

"A strong sedative." Together she and Archie eased Rufus back onto the pillows. "He has an important operation tomorrow, and it's best he be kept calm."

"I don't understand. Why is he amnesiac?"

"It's a common symptom with head injuries. That's what the brigadier hopes to treat."

"But these scars—bad as they are—they weren't troubling him when we met." Archie caught his breath as Rufus turned his head restlessly to one side. "What's this red mark? It looks like a burn."

"*Reverend.*" The nurse lowered her voice still further, looked furtively over her shoulder. "You attacked an orderly. Brigadier Spence doesn't normally overlook things like that. If I were you, I'd make good my escape."

"I don't give a damn about Spence."

"Yes, you do. This is a secure facility. If he bans you, you won't get back in." She smoothed the blanket. "Dr Denby will sleep for a good few hours now. You can wait in reception if you like, but I can't let you stay on the ward."

Chapter Four

She'd chosen the only argument that could influence him. If Archie got himself locked out of this airtight cube, Rufus would be truly on his own. Unsteadily he made his way back along the corridor and sat down in the empty waiting room.

Not a visiting hospital. The reception desk really did look like an unused prop. Perhaps it was manned for important patrons and guests, the brigadier picking out his most presentable and cooperative nurses for the job. Numbly Archie stared out across the gravel drive. Rufus had forgotten him. Archie had survived his loss of faith, but how hollow would the world turn out to be if the lights of recognition never returned to those eyes!

How empty the sky. He watched the pale horizon. Far out at sea, cumulus clouds were gathering, piling one on another like playful mountains. They were the only life in the whole bleak landscape. The perfect summer unfolding at Droyton had snapped back here into a blighted winter bud. It was hard to believe that the village still existed, with its moonlit orchard.

Desolation took hold of Archie like a granite fist. He clenched his own on the arm of the chair. He hadn't lied entirely when he'd said Dr Denby had friends, though they weren't the kind a sane and heterosexual doctor of archaeology might once have been able to summon. Rufus's army now consisted of a faithless vicar, a pinafored housekeeper and a person who in bygone times would no doubt have been seen as the village witch. A bluestockinged lesbian too, perhaps. Alice would certainly rush to the rescue, and if she came, Giles would surely follow, or Gillian, two for the price of one. Elspeth and the dog. Archie wasn't even sure that Mrs Trigg might not turn out for the occasion...

He was falling asleep. Worse than that, maybe—his neck was stiff, as if he'd already dropped off and started dreaming. He sat up with a jerk at the creak of rubber soles on white tiles, surreptitiously dabbed at the corner of his mouth. The nurse from the ward was standing before him, arms folded over her chest. She'd never get picked, Archie guessed, for the public-inspection days. The line of her mouth was too keenly aware. "I can't bring you tea," she said grimly, as if he'd demanded some. "It's not that kind of place. But the café in Colditch village ought to be open by now. It's about two miles from here."

"If I leave, will I get back in?"

"Nothing's certain in this world, Reverend, but if you buzz twice at the side door, His Nibs will think it's a delivery. There's a washroom down the hallway, if you want to make yourself presentable."

Wasn't he? Archie pushed stiffly upright, noting with embarrassment that his goggles were still on their leather strap around his neck, an incongruous match for the dog collar. A glance at his reflection in the sheet-glass of the doors told him that his hair was up in spikes from his scuffle with the orderly. His body chose that moment to remind him that he hadn't even pulled over for a pee since Ipswich, and he stifled a groan. "All right. Thank you." He looked at her. "Nurse, in your experience, do cases of sudden memory loss like Dr Denby's usually clear up?"

She shrugged. "There's lads in this hospital who can't remember what a knife and fork are for. Some can only remember one thing, like the bomb that knocked them silly in the first place, so they just stay stuck with that—screaming, mostly. Like I said, nothing's certain in this world."

"But Dr Denby had nothing wrong with his short-term memory. I think something's happened to him. Can't you tell me..."

"Buzz twice, Reverend. If you're lucky, somebody will come."

"All right. If he wakes up, let him know Billy Prescott is fine. It'll mean a lot to him if he remembers, and if he doesn't..." Archie shook his head. "Never mind. Please just let him know."

***

Two miles was too far. Archie drove the bike into a gap between the dunes, out of sight of the hospital in case evidence of his continued presence might in some way bring more harm to Rufus. He parked her there and set off along a track between yarrow and marram, scarcely knowing where he was going, drawn by the whisper of the sea.

The storm was shadowing the headlands now. Whitecaps stood out luridly against water of gun-metal blue. The wind hadn't yet blown up much surf, only a fretted cross-hatch pattern that made Archie's skin itch with impatience for the weather to break. He emerged through a notch in the dune-line and onto the beach. Shingle more than sand, a strip of mottled egg-shapes that ran off to vanishing point in both directions... Clumsily he made his way across the stones. Once he reached hard-packed sand, he took off his shoes and socks and rolled up the legs of his trousers. He walked into the water and stood dazedly, ankle deep, letting the breeze and the currents tug at him. There was no-one in sight all along the desolate strand. He could have been the last living soul in the world.

Without Rufus, he might as well be. Archie was old enough now to understand himself. Richard had been a boyhood passion, but if Rufus had forgotten him, Archie would be no more than a chalk scrawl on slate in the rain.

The wind was ruffling something high up on the seaward flank of the dunes. It was hard to work out scale in this landscape, and at first he thought a rook or a crow must have crashed onto the sand. The flicker of black feathers caught his eye persistently. He squinted against the glare still making its way beneath the storm clouds to the east, and gradually made out a human face.

The crumpled little figure didn't move as he approached. An air of defiance surrounded it despite the absurdity of its presence here, dressed from head to toe in smart mourning. Patent stiletto shoes, legs thrust out uncomfortably from the confines of a tight-fitting skirt. A jacket with tiny wasp waist, and, to top it all off, a pillbox hat, whose single black feather had been blown flat by the wind. "Rosemary," Archie said in wonder, drawing close. "What on earth are you doing here?"

She glared at him unfathomably. They had only met once, and he was out of his village context, possibly as much a black crow in the distance to her as she had been to him. "What business is that of yours?"

"Well—none, I suppose. But you must be freezing." He took off his leather coat and draped it around her shoulders. When she didn't move or protest, he sat down beside her and joined her in contemplation of the grey sea. "I think it's going to rain. I'm Archie Thorne from Droyton. Do you remember me?"

"Of course I remember you." She hitched her knees up as far as she could. Angrily, as if shamed by her need for warmth, she huddled into the coat. "I assume you know," she said icily, "being a vicar and all, that a woman mayn't marry her deceased husband's father."

"Er... I do know that, yes."

"And I suppose it's common knowledge, is it? I suppose I must be very stupid indeed."

"In fact, the changes in the Marriage Act after the Great War created some confusion. But allowing a widow to marry her brother-in-law made sense, in the wake of the conflict. Fathers-in-law are a trickier issue because the boundary between generations would be breached. Why are you asking me this?"

"I was nothing to him after my baby died. Nothing. He was getting ready to throw me out on the street."

"The brigadier?"

"Yes. And I didn't want to be nothing."

"Oh, Rosemary, you weren't. What about your brother?"

She gave a shiver. "Rufus scares me. Just... carrying on as he is, despite being queer and a disgrace."

"I'm certain he's never disgraced you. He's painfully discreet."

"Ah, but not because he's ashamed of himself. Just because he never wanted to get caught. He's not bothered about himself, not really. It isn't fair."

She was crying. "Why isn't it fair?" Archie probed gently. "Would you rather he was guilty and tormented?"

"No, no. He's my brother. But why can he just go on, loving whoever he thinks it's right to love—even that sick little monster, Henry—while I have no choice at all?"

Archie gave it thought. "That's not an easy question. I'd say that until now, it's been easier for a man—even a queer one and a disgrace—to make his independent way in the world than it has been for a woman. When it comes to love, though... why do you feel you have no choice?"

"I was married straight out of school, out of my father's house. I never worked a day in my life, and I never lived alone. When Charles died, all I had was... him. And he'd started eyeing up a wealthy widow, a private patient of his. I was in the way." She dug her long heels into the sand and visibly took the plunge into her own concept of disgrace. "But he's an old goat, so I gave him what he wanted. Do you understand?"

"Yes, I understand."

"Then I told him, if he didn't marry me, I'd make a fuss. I'd get drunk at his next bloody cocktail party, and tell all the fancy new doctors and specialists coming to his hospital that he'd made me his... his tart."

"Oh, Rosemary."

"And he was sort of laughing. He agreed, much easier than I'd thought, but he was sort of laughing at me, and he said that he'd take me to a register office. He must have known, mustn't he? About the law?"

"I'd say a man like the brigadier would have known, yes."

"So I went with him to this miserable little office in Clerkenwell. There was a man there who said he was the witness, and another who said he was the registrar, and the old goat might have been a bit more discreet, because I saw him paying both of them off afterwards. I suppose by then I was as deep in the dirt as he was. He didn't feel like he had to hide anything from me. He certainly hasn't hidden anything since."

She sounded bitter and sick. An ache of pity went through Archie's bones. "And you're living with him now as his wife?"

"Yes."

"You don't have to. You're not legally married."

"I know that. I looked it up at the library as soon as we got home."

"Then..."

"Why am I still doing it? I didn't know how to stop, and I don't care how pathetic that makes me. At least I had a roof over my head, and before I could start to worry about what the bloody Mayfair neighbours would think, he dragged me out here and put me into his hospital living quarters, up on the top floor where nobody would see me." She chuckled miserably. "He gives me use of his car, so I can't complain. I'm allowed to motor down to London and buy clothes, or whatever it is that fancy women are meant to do. I'm supposed to be there today. But I couldn't face the thought, so I came and sat here instead."

"Listen to me. Take his car and drive it to Droyton Parva. Go back to the rectory and tell Mrs Nettles I sent you. She'll give you a room, and you needn't be afraid of anything anymore."

"Aren't there a hundred people living there already?"

"If there are, an extra one won't hurt."

She raised her head. Archie couldn't read her expression. Slowly, fingers trembling, she removed her hat. Her hair came down in a sudden dark-blonde sheaf. Her resemblance to her brother wasn't striking, but Archie saw a little of it now, in the quietly determined set of her head and the storm-cloud grey of her eyes. "When he came to me," she said slowly, "he was crying."

"Rufus?"

"Yes. I was only at home by chance. I'd gone to collect the last of my baby's things, because I knew the brigadier had told the maid to throw them out while I was gone. I'd never seen him cry, not even when we were children."

Archie wanted to shake her. She had something to say about Rufus—something crucial, he was beginning to understand—and could only approach it via this tortured route. She'd been through hell, and the fact that it was of her own making didn't make Archie pity her less. He still wanted to kill her. "Tell me," he said, as patiently as he could. "What happened after that?"

"He sat and sobbed. He said he'd killed some young man down in Droyton, and he was a beast and he had to be stopped."

"Well, he didn't kill anyone. Somebody in Droyton— somebody else who thinks that men like us are a disgrace—set him up."

"Oh. And I still thought I could do something to please the brigadier, or I thought I should try, so I telephoned the hospital and told him. But do you know something? Bugger the brigadier."

Archie blinked. "I'm sorry?"

"You needn't look so shocked. That's what you said, back at Droyton, and you were right. Bugger him and his house and his rank and his lies." She hitched one leg up, awkward in her tight-fitting skirt, and tugged off a shoe, which she then pitched as far down the beach as she could. She had a pretty good bowling arm. Rufus had said that she and Charles had shared a passion for cricket before anything else. Then she glanced at him, wide-eyed. "Men like *us*, Reverend?"

"Yes," he said dryly. "Pardon my grammar. Men like we are, I should perhaps have said. Your brother is my... gentleman friend, my lover, however you'd like to put it."

He thought her jaw would hit the sand. But she looked less like a model of outraged decency than a small girl in a playground who'd found out a scandalous secret. The corners of her mouth twitched. "*No.*"

"Yes."

"But you're a..."

"A vicar, yes. And there is no way in which I can reconcile my nature with my station in life, so..." He tugged off his dog collar, which had mud splashes on it from his long journey. Immediately the wind began to tug at it. He let go, and it fluttered and rolled off down the beach, briefly touching Rosemary's shoe as if in benediction. He took a deep breath, deeper and more purely into the pit of his lungs than he'd ever experienced. "There it goes."

"It can't be that simple, surely."

"No, it won't be. Thank God I'm not a Catholic. Now, what happened to Rufus after he was brought here, Rosemary? I know there is something. I know you want to tell me."

She watched Archie's collar catch a wing of the gale and join the seagulls before it vanished against the restless sky. "A storm's coming."

"Yes, I know."

"I don't care. I don't care if I drown, or catch my death, and nobody else would care either."

"That isn't true. Your brother—"

"If he cares, he's stupid. I sold him."

Archie went cold. "What?"

"The brigadier wanted Charles's reputation cleared. That's why I came down to Droyton, and that's why I ran to telephone the hospital yesterday, when Rufus turned up at the house. Because Rufus held the key in his memory, and I didn't care any more than the brigadier did what it would do to him to get it out. I wanted to be a war hero's widow."

"I already knew that. I think Rufus did, too."

"What I didn't know was how the old goat planned to extract it. God, would I have done anything differently if I had? Can I confess this to you, Reverend, even if you're not a vicar anymore? Can you take it away?"

"You do need a Catholic for that," Archie said grimly. "All the rest of us can do is try and make it right, whatever it is. What the hell is it, Rosemary?"

"By the time Rufus got here, he was so distraught about this Billy person that he'd stopped talking. He was in what the brigadier calls a depressive fugue, and we don't have time for those here at Colditch. When men get into a state like that, we shock them out of it."

"Christ."

"I've seen it work sometimes, or I swear I wouldn't have let him... That's why they cut his hair, so they could attach the electrodes. I went into the chamber with him. I wanted him to know he wasn't alone, and the brigadier let me because I was keeping him quiet. They set up the equipment and gave him the first shock, just at the usual level, and Rufus sat up all of a sudden and said he remembered."

"That's good, isn't it? That's what you and the brigadier wanted."

"No. The brigadier wanted Rufus to remember good things about his son."

"And he didn't?"

"He and Charles were in the earthworks outside Fort Roche. Their units had joined forces there to try and shore up the Maginot Line. The fighting was bad but reinforcements were coming. There were Allied troops still trapped in the fort. Rufus wanted to go and save them, but Charles..." She looked at her feet, one nylon-clad, one still in its shoe. "The brigadier says there's no such thing as shellshock. Do you think that's true?"

"No," Archie said fervently. "I don't even think it's always about being shelled. Men can see too much. Their nerves can fail."

"My Charles was a major. You don't get to that rank if you're a coward, even if you are a brigadier's son."

"No, I'm certain of that." Archie took her hand, which she'd stretched out blindly between them. "What did Rufus say?"

"Charles must have... It must have been the things you said. He must have seen too much. His nerve must have failed."

"He wanted the unit to retreat?"

"Yes. And Rufus insisted, which he had no right to do. He was only a captain."

"But you know why he did it, Rosemary? You surely understand why."

"Yes, damn him. When Rufus insisted, Charles... Oh, God," she said hollowly, after a moment. "Are you going to make me tell you?"

"Not if you can't. Rufus will tell me some day."

"I only heard a little bit of it. When the brigadier realised what he was saying—that it matched exactly the story that stupid little corporal had been telling all along—he grabbed me and pushed me out into the corridor. After that they put Rufus into a secure room, and I wasn't allowed to see him anymore."

"But... when I got here, he was on a ward. They were rough with him when he had a flashback, but he wasn't locked up."

"The brigadier said to me that if I wanted to do something really useful, I could help keep Rufus here. He asked me if anyone was likely to come after him, and I said no, and then I remembered you. How you tore me into little pieces back at Droyton."

"Yes. I'm sorry."

"Oh, I understood. So I told the brigadier that you might come, and he asked how he would recognise you, and I said he'd have no trouble. He posted somebody to watch from a top-floor window, and this morning, along you came."

A vicar on a motorcycle, visible from three miles out along the long, straight road. Silently cursing his lack of subtlety, Archie squeezed her hand. "Are you telling me that he waited, and..."

"The nurse he'd posted came knocking on our apartment door. Then he gave orders for Rufus to be transferred out of his room and onto the ward, where he was just another wounded hero, getting help from Brigadier Spence in his marvellous new sodding hospital. So you see, I sold you as well as Rufus, really. Didn't I?"

Archie was out of excuses for her. Compassion was drying to a sour-milk taste in the back of his throat. "Never mind. Why all these lengths?"

"If you'd seen Rufus strapped down in one of those rooms, you'd have done something, wouldn't you? Made a fuss. Brought people here, tried to get him taken away."

I'd have set the hospital on fire. "Yes. I would."

"And it's vitally important that he keep Rufus here until Mr Wilson-Grey arrives tomorrow."

"The surgeon?"

"Yes. Do you know what a lobotomy is, Reverend Thorne?"

Archie jolted to his feet. He'd forgotten he was holding on to her. For a ludicrous moment he couldn't let go, and involuntarily dragged her with him almost a yard across the sand. She scrabbled to her knees and gawped up at him. "Yes, I know," he ground out. "Do *you*?"

"It'll help him. He'll be more comfortable."

"He'll have no connection between the frontal lobes of his brain and the rest of it." He snatched his hand away. "I know all about lobotomies. They're a well known cure—along with chemical castration—for being queer and a disgrace. Rosemary, how could you? He's your brother!"

"But the brigadier's not interested in curing Rufus that way. He just wants to—"

"To shut him up, yes. He'll be a childish shadow of himself at best—at worst, a vegetable. And no court in the land will listen to him if he tries to speak out about Fort Roche. Which is the point, I suppose." Archie's voice broke. Rufus, with his bright intelligence—his diffident smile, the shy joy that had dawned in his eyes on that first morning, waking in the attic bedroom by

Archie's side… "I won't allow it. This can't be legal. I'll call the police, and—"

"Rufus is being detained for his own safety. They won't help."

"Then *you* will." He lifted her to her feet. "You mean to, don't you? I can see it in your eyes. You're just not scared enough yet."

"I don't know what you're talking about."

"You're in an unhappy position, Rosemary. The brigadier will kill you if you help save your brother, and I'll kill you if you don't. Choose."

"You'd never hurt me." Something in his expression made her flinch and swallow. "All right. Yes, I decided to, as soon as I saw you there by the water."

"I know you're burning bridges. I'll help build you a new one."

"He's so damn proud of his electronic locks. Stupid of him— you can hide a key from an angry woman, but you can't always stop her looking over your shoulder. The combination for the secure wing is two-five-zero-five. He sometimes changes the others, but not that—it's Charles's birthday."

"Two-five-zero-five." Archie set the numbers into his heart, deeper than he'd ever laid any verse from of his Bible studies. "All right. Which is Rufus's room?"

"I don't know. No-one's allowed in that part of the hospital but the staff. If you're going to try anything, you'll have to wait till nightfall, and I… I asked the orderlies to leave a light on in his room overnight. That used to help when he had bad dreams as a child."

"So I'll be able to tell from the outside."

"If they listened to me. And the ward's on the second storey, with windows too high to get anyone out of."

"Leave all that to me. There's a side door for deliveries—is that on a combination, too?"

"No, they haven't finished work there yet. It's a temporary Yale. Even if you get past that, I don't know how you'll move him. He'll be heavily sedated, and the brigadier kept on with the ECT after he started talking, maybe to get him to stop." She wiped her eyes. "A little bit can help people. A lot of it makes them extremely..."

"Suggestible?"

"Yes. I'm surprised he didn't try it on me."

"He didn't really have to, did he?"

She choked miserably. "Oh, God."

Roughly he buttoned her into the coat. "I'm sorry. Look, all you have to do now is get away from here. Do you want to take off your other shoe, or do you want me to go and fetch the one you threw away?"

"Why?"

"Because you have to be able to walk to the car."

She toed off her remaining shoe and stood before him in her nylons. Something mutely stubborn in the way she lifted her chin reminded him so poignantly of Rufus that his heart clenched. "It's a nice gesture," he said faintly, "but won't you need them? At petrol stations, or..."

"I have others in the car. I only bought these because he likes his whores in high heels."

"God almighty. There's better days ahead for all of us, Rosemary, I swear." He surveyed her, noticing belatedly that she was in deepest mourning from head to toe, even the pins that had been holding her hair up finished with beads of jet. She hadn't been so steeped in black when he'd first met her in Droyton. He retrieved her hat and handed it back to her, shaking sand out of the veil. "Are you dressed like this for your baby, or..."

"Yes. But it's for Charles, too." She looked Archie in the face, her own tearstained but suddenly serene. "Don't you think it's time I mourned for my husband?"

Chapter Five

Two miles had been too far, but now Archie had to go further. Colditch village was too small to supply his needs, so he rode the weary Norton back across the marsh flats to Flincham, which had not only an army-surplus warehouse but a hardware store.

At the warehouse, he equipped himself with two insignia-stripped khaki jerseys, two woollen caps and a pair of dark, anonymous pea jackets. They were cheap, but still would have cleaned him out if he hadn't brought Rufus's wages away with him from Droyton. He was certain that his friend would approve of the outlay. Back at the bike, tucked away down a side street, he put one of the jackets on—he'd had a chilly ride of it over here in his shirtsleeves—and squeezed the other, the caps and the jerseys, into his saddlebags.

Without his collar, wrapped in his workaday coat, he'd looked just like the dozens of ordinary men about their business on the main street. The clerk in the hardware store hadn't batted an eyelid when he'd laid a torch and a pair of wire-cutters on the counter, together with a little metal plate for hanging a picture or mirror. He'd been almost sorry not to have to use the story he'd concocted en route, about his boss on the building site who'd locked himself out of the compound. But the sense of freedom was heady. Ever since his ordination, he'd been a man to whom eyes turned. Now all he'd had to do was pick up his goods, give the clerk a friendly nod and walk out. If he didn't look like a vicar anymore, apparently he didn't resemble a cat-burglar, either.

Which was very handy. He'd stopped at a newsagent's on the way back to the bike and bought the most recent edition of the *Nursing Times*, which he'd rolled up and stowed, along with the cutters and torch, in the panniers. They were now straining at their tough leather seams, but his supply run was complete. He refuelled the Norton's tank and her dangerous extra at the filling station on the outskirts of the town, and headed back the way he'd come.

This time he took a diagonal route through bumpy, potholed farm lanes instead of the straight coast road. He had to cross it on the approach to Colditch, but that was the work of a moment, no other traffic near him and well out of sight of the hospital itself. He was fairly satisfied that he'd made his journey there and back without drawing anyone's notice.

Because Archie had one shot. He knew it. Brigadier Spence was prepared to destroy Rufus in order to preserve whatever hellish secret he'd remembered about Charles. Between them, Spence and Winborn had closed a net which Archie would only get one chance at slicing through. Billy Prescott would declare the truth readily enough, but the lie had given Spence all he needed to hold Rufus captive until it was too late. Layers of naivety and sleepy acceptance were falling from Archie like outgrown skins. He couldn't count on his country's institutions to deliver justice, any more than he'd ever been able to ask their protection for himself and his kind. He'd gone underground to live his life, assumed the trappings of convention. Tried to make it up with kindness to those around him who'd fallen even further outside society's pale, but that had never been enough. He'd hidden, and Rufus had been taken from him. Now he had to fight.

He left the bike in the lee of a dune to the north of the hospital, rolling her as far as he could into a patch of gorse before switching her off. He snapped off a branch of the gorse and used it as a broom, sweeping away her tyre tracks all the way back to the road. Let Spence think he'd given up and gone, that Rufus was unprotected.

Making his way up into the crests of the dunes, he allowed himself to think for the first time about what that meant. Rufus on his own, strapped down in one of the cells Spence reserved for his extreme cases. Cut adrift even from the damaged memories left to him, frightened and burned and abandoned. "No," Archie whispered, frustration scalding up in him. He stopped himself short of broaching the horizon. How was he supposed to wait until nightfall?

Sharp hail stung in from the sea, a timely check to his impatience, as if perhaps down in Droyton, Drusilla had summoned the elements to warn him. He'd come this far. He crouched behind the wind-carved lip of the dune, drawing up the collar of his jacket. The loamy soil, and the fringe of stiff marram that grew above it, offered a shelter of sorts. He drew his knees to his chest for warmth, and the exertions of his last two days began to catch up with him. Despite his fears, he slept.

***

Just before dark, a delivery man knocked twice at the hospital's side door. This was a different matter to the glassed-in, spacious front: a flat layer of grey steel. It was late for deliveries, but Archie had had to wait until the night-shift crew had filed in from the bus and the day staff had made their departure. Even then, everything depended upon luck, on no further entries or exits. The odds were good, Archie faithlessly and shamelessly prayed. The brigadier's hospital wasn't the kind of place to encourage sly fag breaks out the back. "Buggering hell," said the delivery man, his woollen cap pulled down so far over his eyebrows that it was no wonder he had stumbled on his way out. "You want to get that step looked at, you know."

"Not my problem," said the porter who'd come to answer the door, picking the remains of a sandwich supper out of his teeth. With his other hand he hefted the rolled-up magazine Archie had solemnly handed him for signature. "This is what the Yanks call junk mail, you know. Not even anybody's name on it. No need for it to be courier-delivered, let alone signed for."

"Not my problem. Bloody awful night, isn't it?"

The porter glanced past his shoulder and offered a grunt of agreement. Hail was beginning to bounce off the unfinished tarmac of the yard. "Storm's been building all day. His Nibs'll be sorry he called off the work on the roof. Still..."

"Not your problem, eh?"

"Too bloody right, mate."

The steel door slammed. Archie glanced back once as he strode in the direction of the bike. The metal picture-plate he'd managed to wedge against the tooth of the Yale was still in place, one end protruding far enough to be grasped from the outside. It was bloody obvious, and would drop out the next time the door moved, but that wasn't to be helped. He climbed aboard the Norton, revved her and drove off with all the casual dispatch of his assumed role. If any of the brigadier's spies were on the watch, all they'd see was an anonymous figure riding away into the sleet.

A fine, filthy night to stage a rescue. Archie rounded the first corner and slowed up beside a tumbledown roadside barn. The farm it had belonged to was long abandoned, but it had a single saving grace: a lean-to shed with a corrugated roof, barely visible from the road. Gratefully Archie trundled the bike into its cobwebbed shelter, killed her engine and dismounted.

He'd always loved May evenings. Even in foul weather, the lingering light in the sky had gladdened him, bringing to mind open doors, the expansion of humdrum daily life into Churchill's broad sunlit uplands. Only once before had he wished the darkness down on such long days: sitting at the dining table in Winborn's house in the weeks after Richard's death, clenching his jaws against the tides of grief he'd been forbidden to express.

Then, and tonight. He secured the Norton on her kickstand and carefully leaned against her, staring out into the lingering cold light. This was a time—rain pattering on a shed roof, his tasks done, his hands idle—when he'd have loved a cigarette.

He still didn't want one. He almost missed missing them, which was absurd. If this went on, he'd have to find some other dissipated habit. If he wasn't a vicar anymore, he supposed he had a wider choice available.

All he wanted was Rufus. As bad habits went, that ought to be enough to serve him for a lifetime: lying with man as with woman, in blissful bloody depravity. He knew Rufus was right with his warnings, his hard-earned experience of a homosexual life. Archie really had no idea, having stepped into the closet Winborn had created for him and never emerged.

He would have to find out. He and Rufus would have to navigate a hostile world, day in, day out, for the rest of their lives.

He'd give anything to get the chance.

He couldn't see the hospital from here, but he folded his arms over his chest, lowered his head and prayed that the rain battering the corrugated iron over his head would spell out its message against the window of his lover's lonely room. *Patience and hope, and only a little time left for you to hang on now, dear Rufus. We just have to wait until dark.*

***

The brigadier's fence was made out of chicken wire. No doubt something sturdier would have followed, but for now it was designed to keep mischievous kids out of the construction works, not foil a determined attempt at a break-in. Archie had chosen his entry point with care, behind a pile of builders' rubble in the far corner of the yard. He planned to bring Rufus out the same way, with as little open ground to cover as possible.

His coat grew heavy as its fabric soaked up the rain. A gale had sprung up from the east as darkness fell. He worked as quickly as he could, snipping one hexagon of wire and then the next, while the wind did its best to tear the whole mesh out of his hands. He was glad that the motorcycle saddlebags were waterproof: he'd pressed one of them into service as a holdall, slung over his shoulder and packed tight with extra clothes. Pausing only to push back his wet fringe so he could see, he painstakingly cut enough room in the fence to squeeze through.

No windows overlooked this point. And Rosemary hadn't appealed to the orderlies in vain: he had counted, creeping the length of the fence where it bounded the windswept dunes, six dark panes from the building's south end before the seventh, faintly glowing from within. Six doors to count inside, once he got there. Holding his breath, Archie ducked through the gap and ran through the shadows of the yard.

His piece of metal was still wedged fast. He kept the breath held tight until he'd worked his fingers far enough behind the plate to push back the tongue of the Yale, then exhaled noisily in relief. The door was moving. One inch then two, and then he had a hand inside, his arm, his shoulder. He stepped into the lightless space beyond and eased the door shut behind him.

There was no sound but the dripping of his clothes onto lino. He'd gathered from his previous glimpse of the room that it was a kind of porter's lodge, and his gamble that it was only used in daytime had paid off. He unshipped his torch from his inner pocket and cautiously switched it on.

Only one interior door, directly opposite him. If the brigadier's security system began here, he was sunk. But as Rosie had said, this part of the building was the most recently constructed, and although a keypad gleamed on the wall by the frame, the handle gave easily to his touch.

For a moment it was just a relief to be out of the hail-whipped night. The corridor beyond the lodge was warm and silent, and Archie guessed that, like the empty reception, this part of the hospital was waiting in readiness for inspection. The carpet was thick, the walls freshly painted in soothing ivory. A few indoor plants, looking astonished at the lies they'd been asked to uphold, occupied elegant pots between nicely upholstered benches. This was where the brigadier's success stories would come and play chess and read their newspapers, while the rest of them—the basket cases, the unloved, the plain bloody awkward—screamed behind soundproofed walls, disturbing no-one. *I am going to close you down*, Archie thought distinctly, tucking his torch away. If he'd had a can of spray paint, he'd have scrawled the message on the ivory walls.

As it was, he didn't dare leave a wet footprint behind him. He unlaced his shoes, kicked out of them and tied them to the strap of his shoulder bag to keep both hands free. The corridor was empty. He padded along it in his socks. The door at the end swung open easily to his touch, and he found himself at the foot of a bright-lit stairwell which could only lead to the secure wing on the floor above.

He'd hoped to have timed his intrusion for after the last night-time round. He'd been close, but not damn close enough: a lock clicked above him, and brisk footsteps pattered on the steps. Archie glanced around in panic. No cover anywhere, except beneath the stairs themselves, open on two sides and painfully obvious to anyone coming up or down...

No choice. Feeling ridiculous, like a child about to lose a game of hide-and-seek, he ducked into the cramped space, pressing himself as far as he could against the wall. He recognised the orderly who appeared a moment later, carrying a tray full of empty medicine pots. If it came to a fight, Archie was almost sorry, having knocked this fellow down once before, but there was no help for it. Silently he got ready to spring.

At the foot of the stairs, just as his gaze must have turned upon Archie, the orderly looked upwards instead. A huge gust of wind had shaken the hospital. High in the roof space, a hollow rattle began, like falling plasterwork or masonry. The orderly shook his head uneasily, balanced his tray on one hand and let himself out into the corridor.

Well, that was one of Archie's cat-burgling nine lives gone. He unfolded from his crouch and took the stairs at a run before his luck could be tested again. Ahead of him was the kind of door the visiting dignitaries would probably never see: steel-plated, only a thickly glazed slot at eye level. A bedlam door, reeking of Victorian lunatic asylums, captivity and threat. Held shut by the numbers of a dead soldier's birthday, enshrined by his mad father in a combination lock. Gritting his teeth in the hope that Rosie had been right about the old man's obsession, Archie punched four figures into the keypad on the wall.

Behind the metal plate, a mechanism clicked. A deep electric buzz accompanied the sound, but that wasn't to be helped. Like Macbeth, Archie had reached a point of his journey where ploughing onwards made more sense than turning back, although he hoped there'd be less blood involved. He grabbed the door's metal handle and pulled it wide.

Yes, this was the place. He'd entered at the north, but that was no problem. He could see right to the end of the corridor, and all he had to do was count back from there, six featureless doors. "Rufus," he whispered, breaking into a run, coming to a halt by the seventh. He'd done it. He was in.

Six featureless *locked* doors. Archie stared stupidly at the rectangle of wood in front of him. He tried the handle, just on the off-chance that somebody in this hospital had been as dimwitted as himself and failed to turn the key.

Of course not. Archie fell back a step, then two, then suddenly folded up against the corridor wall. He hadn't eaten since Mrs Nettles' sandwiches had run out. He hadn't noticed his hunger or weariness, in the raw excitement of planning and executing his break-in here, his rescue mission. Between them, he and Rosie had covered everything—the fence, the porter's lodge, the entry codes, the timing.

Just not this one last bloody locked door. He banged the heel of his hand off his brow in frustration. As if the brigadier would leave his victims' rooms open, for their occupants to wander the corridors as they wished! An ache like tears began in the back of Archie's throat, and he fiercely forbade himself the reaction. He had to think.

He could try to kick the door in, though it looked like a tough customer, and the noise he made would inevitably raise the alarm. How the hell could he have been so stupid? His betrayal was total, worse even than Winborn's. Winborn didn't love Rufus, and might have been excused for buggering everything up at the very last minute like this.

Maybe knocking down the door was the best choice after all. Archie would at least have the satisfaction of going down in a vigorous fight. Rufus, if he was conscious, would have the comfort of knowing that someone had come here and fought for him at the last. Archie began to scramble upright, and winced at the prod of something sharp against his thigh.

He pulled a short metal tube out of his trouser pocket. It took him a moment to recognise the object, and he couldn't repress a hollow bark of laughter when he did: nothing more or less than Jebediah Trigg's magic key, confiscated in the Droyton church. Nonsense, Archie had called it, and nonsense it certainly was, a piece of trash designed to rob little lads of their hard-earned paper-round sixpences. What had Jebediah said it could do? Open any lock, if you just squeezed the tube until it fit, and swung the wards to the right angle...

Any damn thing was worth a try. He crouched in front of the seventh door. The wind howled again, and he'd have sworn he heard Drusilla's laughter in the gale. This was enough to make a cat laugh—a self-defrocked vicar on his knees in a looney bin, attempting to open a door with a magic key... The lock was quite a wide one, so he unscrewed the tube far enough to fit the hole, and eased the key in. He could feel by resistance that the lock clicked into place on the right. Very well, Jebediah—he would therefore spin the key's wards in that direction.

The wards engaged. Archie wrenched the key around, and the lock popped open, sweet as a nut.

Chapter Six

Someone had seen fit to strap Rufus down. Archie didn't break his stride or bat an eyelid, but still he inwardly vowed to track down whoever had tightened the thick leather bands that held the fine-made wrists to the bedframe, and splayed the poor bare feet wide apart like a helpless bird's to secure his ankles too. A strap round his chest to finish the job, as if being bound hand and foot wasn't enough.

Rufus lay oblivious to these indignities now, but his skin was raw around his restraints, as if he'd fought them until overcome by sedation. His shoulder felt bony and fragile underneath the thin hospital pyjamas. Archie shook it gently. "Rufus, old chap. Come on. Can you wake up?"

No change in the sleeping face, turned aside and vacant on the pillow. Archie set about unfastening the straps. They were only simple buckles, thank God, easy for any third party to undo, impossible for the man on the bed. He spared a moment to chafe Rufus's ankles and try to restore circulation to his blue-tinged feet. Never exactly a bruiser, he'd lost weight even since Archie's last proper look at him in Droyton. Carrying him out would be a damned awkward business, like a bag of flour over his shoulder, but if worst came to worst... "Rufus! Wake up. It's Archie. We're going home."

Nothing. Archie sat down on the edge of the bed to gather his strength. Before he did anything else, he had to get Rufus more warmly dressed. The storm was roaring outside now, fit to wake the...

To wake the dead. Archie clapped a hand to his coat pocket. Out of habit he'd transferred all the contents of his clerical jacket into this new one—his pen knife, wallet, box of matches. Drusilla's little bag of stinking herbs. He drew it out, blinking at the pungent release of scent into the room.

Well, he'd found a magic key in one pocket. He supposed anything was worth a try. He put a hand behind Rufus's neck, raised his head slightly and held the open packet under his nose.

No response. Archie felt stupid for trying. "Sorry," he murmured, settling him back on the pillow again. "We're still going, but I'll have to carry you. We've got to get you dressed first. Just hold on."

He leaned down to unfasten the motorbike's saddlebag, where he'd stowed the extra jacket and sweater. He should have thought about trousers, but that was too bad. And then there was the problem of shoes... "Oh, hell," he breathed, pulling out the garments. He'd be sure to plan his next jailbreak much more thoroughly than this. At least he could provide Rufus with socks, if he took his own off. He began to undo his laces.

Rufus jolted bolt upright on the bed. Archie catapulted off it in sheer fright. He fetched up hard against the wall: spun round, eyes wide, heart thumping. "My God. You're awake!"

"Of course I am." Rufus coughed, rubbed his eyes. "Where am I? Wait—I remember. I remember everything."

Archie hardly dared hope. "You do?"

"Everything, yes. I remember Fort Roche, everything that happened there. I remember... being lost in the dark inside my own head, and coming to Droyton, and..." He swung his legs off the bed, staring intensely at Archie. "And *you*. You, finding me. Bringing the light. Oh, my God. *Archie!*"

He sprang to his feet and dashed across the room. Archie grabbed him: caught him in his arms before he could realise his weakness and exhaustion, pulled him tight against his own strength. "I'm here. You remember me?"

"How could I forget?" His fists closed tight in Archie's jacket. He buried his face for one long moment, then jerked his head up. "What are you doing here? We have to get out."

"That's what I'm trying to organise." Archie couldn't keep a beaming smile off his face or out of his voice. The parts of his life that had vanished into Rufus's amnesia were being restored, their return almost painful, like blood into a cramped limb. "I've brought you some clothes. You have to get dressed, and then we're going out the way I came in, as fast as possible."

"You came to rescue me."

"To try. Hurry up, Rufus!"

He didn't need telling twice. He broke out of Archie's arms, grabbed the sweater and pulled it on over his pyjamas, then shrugged into the pea coat. His movements were swift and fierce, as if powered from some external source that had little to do with his own volition. "I *do* remember everything," he said, as Archie held the jacket for him and he shrugged into it. "My God—the fort, and Charles, and what he did. And Droyton, and the goddess, and the tunnels under the church, and..." He whipped round suddenly to face Archie. "Did you send off my report?"

"I put it into Caroline's hands."

"You've seen her? Did she say she'd look at it? Ah, I forgot to include my deductions concerning the murals. It's all quite obvious to me now—one figure's indicating Droyton Magna, the labyrinth at the top of the hill, and the other is pointing to the tunnels. As above, so below, as the witches say. Macrocosm and microcosm." He sought Archie's gaze, his own kindling up with unnatural fires. "It's all so *clear* to me. Damn!"

"Don't worry about it now. Good Lord, that's the last time I use any of Drusilla's potions on you."

"Her what? Listen, we have to find Corporal Berry. He's in hospital in Farley Cross, probably getting more doped up and fried than I was. Every word he said was the truth."

"We'll find him, I promise."

"Thank you. You came to *rescue* me!" He grabbed the front of Archie's jumper, pulled him down for a fierce kiss. Then he let go, suddenly all business. "The door to this wing is combination-locked. How are we going to get out?"

"Same way I got in. I know the code."

"How—"

"It's a long story, but you'll enjoy it when I tell you. For now, just put these socks on. They'll protect your feet a bit."

"Oof, Archie. How far have you travelled in these?"

"Don't be so bloody cheeky." Archie gave him a gentle shove on the chest to make him sit down, then knelt at his feet. "Here. Foot."

Rufus stiffened. "We don't have time."

"What?"

"I just heard the downstairs door opening. Rounds are over for tonight."

"So the jig's up," Archie said grimly. Through the clattering havoc of the storm, he began to hear footsteps. More than one pair, at a run. "Shit. You stay here. I won't let them near you."

He launched himself towards the door. He had no plan for this turn of events: only his absolute resolve to defend Rufus or die trying. He stepped out into the corridor. "Evening, gentlemen," he said pleasantly to the four stout figures pounding towards him—the brigadier's shock troops, he guessed, looking no less like thugs because they were in uniform. "I really wouldn't come any further."

The foremost orderly stopped short, as if Archie had pulled a gun on him. The impression didn't last long. "Out of my way," he grunted, signing to the men behind him to enter the room. "You think you're bloody clever, don't you? You left your wedge in the lock in the porter's room."

Archie winced. He had, too. He moved to block the doorway. "On the contrary, I think I'm a blithering idiot. But you're too late—Denby's gone."

"Bollocks. There's no way out from—"

The door swung wide. Before Archie could react, Rufus had ducked beneath his arm and darted to the far side of the corridor. "Oh, is that what you think?" he yelled, turning to face the astonished orderlies. His cropped hair was up in spikes, his eyes ablaze. In hospital pyjamas and oversized coat, he was still somehow a formidable sight. He seized the fire extinguisher behind him, cracked it out of its brackets and aimed its hose at the enemy. "What do you think about this, you bastards?"

He pulled the pin. Foam shot out of the nozzle, spraying a white arc across the corridor. The brigadier's men jerked back on reflex, and Archie seized the moment to whip the key from the lock. He grabbed Rufus, fire extinguisher and all, shoved him back into the room and slammed the door behind them. "Hold it shut!" he commanded, and while Rufus wedged his shoulder against the wood, locked up from the inside. "There. I can't believe this thing works."

"What is it?"

"Jebediah's magic key. Don't ask." He straightened up shakily, knocking foam off his jacket. The door reverberated under the first impact of a foot. "We've bought ourselves a minute at most. What now?"

"You think there's no way out too, don't you?"

Archie glanced at the room's narrow window, a long thin rectangle five foot off the ground. "It does seem that way."

"That's where you're bloody well wrong." Rufus gave the fire extinguisher another heft. "This place is built from shit and sawdust. Stand back and cover your eyes."

"What? You can't—"

But Rufus, woken from the dead, wasn't in any mood to hear what he couldn't do. He gave a kind of roar, took the extinguisher by its handle and swung it from ground level, like a shot-putter going for Olympic gold. The window shattered splendidly, a starburst of glass catching brief sparks and vanishing into the storm. He let the rebound fuel his next effort like a slingshot, this time slamming the extinguisher against the base of the frame. It buckled under the blow. Both ends tore out of the wall, bolts and screws flying.

Archie saw their chance. He got hold of the top edge of the frame, loosened now in its masonry. It was made from the new aluminium that was supposed to turn wood into a thing of the past, and it bent and curled back when he pulled. "Hit the brickwork there. That's it! Again."

The frame had been set in cement. Archie tore the metal strips away, and Rufus followed up with his battering ram, pulverising the mortar. The thudding at the door became more urgent, but neither paid it heed. The last of the frame fell away. Rufus dropped the extinguisher, suddenly exhausted, and Archie lifted it out of his hands and took over, slamming the base against the crumbling brickwork at top and bottom until there was room enough for a man to climb out. "Here," he gasped. He dumped the extinguisher and bent over, locking his hands. "Out you go. I'll give you a leg-up."

"No. Other way round, Archie. I'm lighter—I can climb over on my own."

Archie didn't like it. Their time was running out, though, choices diminishing as the lock began to bounce and disintegrate beneath the assault from outside. "Are you sure?"

"Yes! Hurry up, man."

"Are you strong enough?"

"For now. I don't think it's real, but just now I feel like Captain Marvel. Make the most of me."

Archie obeyed. He got a good grip on the lower edge of the gap and set his foot into Rufus's offered grip. Rufus gave him a hoist of unexpected power, and he scrambled out over the shattered brickwork. He hadn't thought to check if there was any kind of ledge outside, and found it gratefully as he swung his legs down. Immediately the wind tried to knock him off his fragile perch. "You now!" he ordered, reaching back in with both arms. "And for God's sake be careful. It's blowing like the devil out here."

"They're coming. You should jump while you can."

"Not without you." Archie took a fistful of Rufus's sweater for emphasis. "Never without you. Come on!"

The door flew open. Rufus made a catlike spring at the wall. Archie caught him by his jacket collar and the seat of his pyjamas and hauled him out into the night. No time to worry about the jump—their combined weight on the ledge snapped the slate beneath them, and they dropped into the dark.

***

Archie was first to get wind back into his lungs. He levered himself off the wet tarmac that had leapt up and dealt him such a blow, hoisting Rufus on reflex. "Can you walk?"

Rufus shook his head. "Can... run, though," he wheezed after a moment. He looked back fearfully at the window, which had sprouted four enraged, ugly heads. "We've got to run, Archie. Run!"

"This way, then."

"That's back towards the main building. If they come out the side door—"

"I meant to take you out that way. That's where I cut a hole in the fence. Our only chance, dear fellow."

"Then let's for God's sake grab it." Rufus suited action to words by catching hold of Archie's hand. He laced their fingers tight together and set off.

Exterior lights snapped on, dazzling them both, cutting the night into jagged shapes, the relentless white hexagons of the wire fence, the surreal pyramids of dunes beyond. The wind-driven rain became meteorites, each drop leaving a retina-trail. Rufus flew on, showing no signs of pain as they hit gravel underfoot. He veered toward the hole in the fence before Archie needed to point it out to him, pushed Archie ahead of him into the shelter of the pile of rubble. "Get through, quick. He's coming."

"Who is?"

"The bloody brigadier. And he's got a gun."

Archie had a heartbeat to glance back. He dragged aside the netting to let Rufus dive past him, and saw, like a nightmare from a shadow-puppet show, Spence's vast shape silhouetted by the light from the porter's open door. He was planted, feet straddled, hands in a practised and comfortable grip around a revolver. "Down," Archie gasped, dodging through the gap and throwing himself at Rufus. They hit the ground together as the first shot rang out. "Christ! You really pissed him off, didn't you?"

"You have no idea. He'll kill me before he lets me go."

"Let's not leave him any... choice, then." Archie's rugby tackle had carried them into the long grass and shadows of the first dune. "My bike's just down the road, a couple of hundred yards. Can you make it?"

"If he doesn't blow my head off, yes." Once more Rufus was on his feet and in motion first, his grip a longed-for pain around Archie's arm, pulling him upright. "Come on!"

He was faster than Archie on the flat. They sped along the sandy turf, following the line of the dunes for cover. The air above them snapped with gunfire three times more, and then the shining trail of the road became visible beyond the hospital walls. Rufus veered towards it, still towing Archie after him. "Are you all right?"

"Head still attached. Never better."

"I meant your lungs."

Archie hadn't given them thought. He should have been struggling by now, doubled up and disabled. As it was, every fresh intake of the wet night air seemed to flash fire and life into his limbs. "I'm fine. Isn't that the damnedest thing?"

"It's the turning castle."

"What?"

"Never mind. I can hear engines."

So could Archie. Headlights flared on the hospital driveway. He pointed to the gap in the hedgerow beyond the barn. "There, in the shed under those trees." He'd left his empty pannier on the floor of Rufus's cell, but had kept hold of the torch. Jerking it out of his inner pocket, he directed the beam at the bike, and he and Rufus covered the last few yards in a spray of mud. "Climb up behind me."

"Any chance they didn't see us duck in here?"

"Maybe, but I can't risk it. Going to have to ride like the devil—can you hang on?"

"Just try and shake me off."

The Norton roared to life. Archie rolled her off her kickstand, grinning at Rufus's passionate clasp of his waist. The closer the better: they would be one entity as far as the bike was concerned, one weight, one mass, and she would bear them round corners at whatever crazy angle the road required...

Starting with the peel-out from the barnyard. Archie gunned the engine hard. The headlamp beam leapt ahead, and he chased it, sending an arc of water and mud off to their left as they roared out onto the road. The vehicles from the hospital were in motion too, their lights flaring. Still out of immediate line of sight, and so they would remain for another ten seconds.

No more than that. Archie pressed the time to the limits, squeezed from it everything it could give. One brief rush along the flat, and then a swerve into a rutted lane. He didn't care where it took them. He knocked the headlight off and rode almost blind, taking it yard by yard as storm-washed moonlight revealed the route ahead. Another narrow road ahead—yes, perfect. He paused at the junction to check for oncoming traffic. Then he set off as fast as the Norton would go, doubling back towards the hospital and past it, hard and wild into the rainswept night.

Chapter Seven

Five miles beyond Kempsmead—nearly halfway to Farley Cross, a destination Archie had chosen despite the late hour, compelled by his companion's urgency—he sensed an alteration in the presence at his back. The electric tension that had held Rufus close to him dissolved. The change came so quickly that he barely had time to pull the Norton over to the verge. "Oh, God. Rufus?"

Drusilla's wake-the-dead fires could only burn so long. Poor Rufus was ashes, slumping forward in the saddle as Archie dismounted. He killed the engine, shoved the kickstand down and grabbed the worn-out body before it could fall.

They were on the edge of Borough Forest. The road was a quiet one, densely wooded on both sides, great beech trees in full leaf whose foliage perhaps had kept the ground dry near their trunks. Any shelter was better than none, so Archie hoisted Rufus bodily off the bike, lifted him clumsily, and stumbled with him into the whispering dark.

He set him down where one centuries-old giant had stretched out a branch like a sheltering arm. Last year's foliage was rustling-dry underfoot, the tough copper coins that took so long to decompose. Archie pulled off his jacket. The thick cloth hadn't quite soaked through, so he spread it out lining-uppermost, took

Rufus by the shoulders and eased him onto it. "There. Hold on just a few moments while I get the bike off the road."

By the time he returned, Rufus was sitting dazedly upright. His face transformed when he saw Archie, fearful shadows burning off in joy. "I didn't dream you."

"No." Archie dropped to his knees beside him. "But you did fall asleep on the bike."

"I'm sorry. Someone just switched all the lights off. How did you wake me up in the first place—in the hospital, I mean?"

"Drusilla gave me a herb. She wouldn't tell me anything about it, except that it was called wake-the-dead, and I'd know when to use it."

"I'm glad I didn't imagine the general weirdness of Droyton and its inhabitants."

"Oh, you've no idea." Archie put out an arm, and shivered in pleasure when Rufus crawled hungrily into his embrace. "The first thing you have to know is that Billy Preston's all right. It wasn't you who hurt him."

"What?"

"Little towns like Droyton aren't always weird in a good way. They breed up narrow, frightened minds. Winborn paid Poacher Jakes' thug of a son to attack poor Billy, and he set you up."

Rufus raised a pale, astonished face to seek the truth in Archie's. "Thank God. About Billy, anyway. Where is he?"

"Probably at home by now. Bobby didn't make much impression on his thick skull."

"Winborn, though—Christ. I'm sorry, Archie. Is he still in Droyton? How did you find me?" His fingers brushed the neck of Archie's sweater. "Oh. Where's your dog collar?"

"These are all good questions, and I will answer them." Archie traced the marks of weariness on his brow, measuring how much sand was left in his poor lover's glass, watching it flow. "But you need to sleep first of all. We can take some time here."

"Can't I have some more of Drusilla's herbs?"

"Not and stay sane, I'm afraid."

"All right. But I have to tell you... I want to tell someone who won't try to fry my brains for it..."

"About Fort Roche. The things you remembered."

"Yes. Oh, Archie, it seems terrible to talk about it. To destroy *your* peace of mind with such a story."

"You won't. And even if you did, isn't that part of my job from now on—to share your wars and your peace?"

Rufus subsided against him. They both stretched out on the leaf-litter, which gave off a scent of dry sunshine despite the ongoing downpour hissing like static in the branches overhead. "You have to rest, too," he said roughly. "I can't believe you came all this way on your bike."

"Not much of a knight in shining armour, am I?"

"Oh, you have no idea." Rufus put an arm around him, as if his presence was a bulwark against the past, the one place from which he could speak. "All right. Here it is. We lost the battle for the fort, no matter what the records say. That whole day was a shambles. My unit and Major Spence's got cut off in the earthworks defending the Maginot Line to the east. Reinforcements were on the way, and there were still some Allied soldiers..."

His voice rasped and faded. "I know a little of this," Archie said. "They were trapped in the fort, and you wanted to rescue them."

"Yes. We had no chance of a retreat, so why not? We'd have died doing something useful. How did you know?"

"Rosemary told me. Everything's up with her and old Spence, but don't worry—I've sent her to Droyton."

Rufus chuckled unsteadily. "Another refugee?"

"Mrs Nettles will take care of her. Go on if you can, old fellow."

"Well—it wasn't just blind heroism, trying to get back to the fort. It made sound strategic sense. We could've joined up with the soldiers there and tried to hold out until help arrived. But Charles... It was as if he'd found one last safe place in the mud there, and he wouldn't let anyone go."

"How many of you were there?"

"All that was left of his unit and mine. Me, Berry, a dozen or so others. They were frightened, but nobody was giving up. They all wanted to try for the fort." Rufus flattened his hand on Archie's chest in remembered frustration. "It was a chance."

"But Charles had holed up."

"Yes, and more literally than you think. He'd ordered the corporals to start digging into the earthworks, as if he could tunnel his way out, or hide. That seemed insane to me—we were coming under heavy fire from German tanks on the edge of the forest— so I told the lads to stop."

"Charles was their commander, wasn't he?"

"Mine, too, in that situation. He outranked me. Maybe it was my insubordination that drove him over the edge."

Too dreadful for Rufus, if so. Desolation lay beneath his words, the pit his amnesia had concealed. "No," Archie said, glad he was certain and could speak with conviction. "Charles had left his edge far behind by then."

"I don't know."

"You do, because when you think back, if you had your time again, you'd do the same thing."

"Yes! That's the damnable part of it all. Those poor boys... I ordered them to disregard Major Spence and make for the cover of the earthworks nearest the fort. I was too late. A shell hit us, close range, barely ten seconds afterwards."

"The one that gave you your scars."

"It must be, though I don't remember being hit. Just lying in the mud, deaf as a stone, and everything around me happening in slow motion."

"This is the worst of it, isn't it? Whatever happened then."

Rufus nodded, the movement small and fraught against Archie's shoulder. He had closed his eyes. "The other men were still alive. But they were like me—slow getting onto their feet, bleeding from shrapnel wounds. Charles must have been knocked clear, because he was all right. He was standing on the lip of the crater, looking down at them all, and he had his revolver in his hand. So I tried to find mine."

"Because you knew what he was going to do."

"He'd gone mad, Archie. I could see it on his face. He was scarcely human anymore, and he was roaring and groaning like a bull. It made me think of the Minotaur—the sun was setting behind him, and the light through all the smoke was giving him a kind of halo of horns."

"Bloody hell."

"I'd lost my gunbelt in the blast. I was crawling around, trying to find it, when I heard the first shot, but I was still so deaf that it sounded more like a pop. Harmless, like a champagne cork or something. But he'd shot Corporal Jenson in the head. And then—bang, bang, bang—he started to fire on the rest of them, one after the other. I was screaming and yelling at him to stop, but I could hardly hear myself. It felt like a dream."

The rain slowly lessened its bombardment, then ceased. A long silence passed beneath the trees. Rufus lay motionless in the deep hush, and then, as if by the consent of some spirit of place, went dryly on. "Only Corporal Berry was left. I found him in the mud, curled up and crying. So I lay on top of him, because I somehow thought Charles wouldn't kill me, and I could keep him safe. But I looked up, and Charles was standing over us. I was staring up the barrel of his gun. So I... I grabbed Berry's pistol out of his belt and I shot him. Hit him right between the eyes."

Archie fought an appalling urge to cheer like a kid at a football match. It would have been pure relief. There was too much horror here for exaltation. But at the last extreme, his gentle Rufus, out on the Front despite his conscience, had chosen to survive. "You lived," was all he could say. "Thank God."

A ragged laugh. "You don't believe in God, and I don't believe in war."

"It was his life or yours, Rufus. You know that."

"Is that all we ever come down to? His life or mine? That was why I was going to object—I couldn't see how to decide that. Couldn't see how we have the right." Rufus sat up, struggling away until he backed up against the root of the beech. "Charles wasn't the enemy. He wasn't even a bad man—he was a combat case, just like me. So who was I to choose which one of us deserved to live?"

"That wasn't the choice."

"What?"

"Your decision. It wasn't Major Spence or you. It was Spence or Corporal Berry. I'm terribly afraid you wouldn't have chosen as you did, otherwise."

Rufus stared at him. "I don't know," he whispered.

"I think I do. Anybody would have acted to save themselves in those circumstances. God or no God, war or no war, you've got a right to your life if somebody's trying to take it away. But I don't think that's why *you* did it."

"He was just a boy. They all were, and Berry was the last one alive. I... I do remember him, Archie. I used to help him spell his letters home to his mum."

Tears, at last. What deserts of sorrow had opened up in this good man's heart for the want of them? Archie crawled across to him. He didn't have his big pastoral handkerchief with him anymore, so he wiped the crumpling face with his bare hands. He opened up his arms and let Rufus fall into them, blind and choking. "Here we are," he said roughly against his ear, rocking him. "No more gods, no more war. I'm not a vicar, and you... you're not a soldier. Never again. There's just us, dear fellow— here we are."

Chapter Eight

At eight o'clock the following morning, Rufus walked into the Farley Cross hospital. Archie had stopped by a roadside stall catering to the early farm trade, and there acquired for him a mug of tea, a set of overalls and some gumboots, the only footwear available. In these he looked somehow more elegant than he had in the rector's Edwardian tweeds. His spine was straight, his head high. Archie stayed close by his shoulder as they made their way across the entrance hall, but didn't touch or attempt to deflect him. This was Rufus's mission, the journey he'd begun in the terror and mud of the Western Front. Archie was only there to see that no-one interfered with its conclusion.

Farley Cross was much less grim than the brigadier's manufactured hell in Colditch—a bright, ordinary redbrick bustling with visitors and everyday life—but something bad was going on. Shouts and sobs were echoing down a stairwell from the floor above. Rufus veered off his straight track for the main desk, pushed open the door at the foot of the stairs and began to climb them. His face was at once rapt and expressionless, as if at the end of a lifetime's sleepwalking, and Archie remembered the lesson of the labyrinth—that you could wander, but never truly be lost. The sounds increased, and they both began to run.

In the corridor, three exhausted-looking women were milling around, doing their best to block the progress of a wheeled stretcher surrounded by porters, nurses and white-coated doctors. The figure strapped down on the stretcher was barely visible beyond this human wall. One of the women was elderly, one little more than a girl. The third, stout and middle-aged, was struggling in the grip of an orderly. "You're not to take him," she wailed, lashing out with a string-mesh shopping bag full of grapes and oranges. "He's done nothing wrong. You said he could stay here until he got better, not get dragged off to some bloody asylum miles and miles away where we can't visit! Stop!"

Rufus darted into the crowd. The hospital staff fell back in surprise. They were used to the triad of women, Archie supposed, who had clearly been fighting their battle here for some time. Rufus was a strange face, and a pure one, grey eyes fixing on the boy on the stretcher. He stopped the stretcher by main force. "Lance Corporal Thomas Berry?"

The boy made a desperate effort to jolt up against his restraints. "Yes, sir!" His voice was barely more than a rasp, but then he cried out in recognition. "Captain Denby? Captain Denby!"

"Yes, Berry. I'm sorry it's taken me such a long time." Keeping one hand fixed on the trolley's rail, he turned to scan the small crowd. "My name is Rufus Denby, former captain with the British Response Force. I need to speak to the person in charge of this hospital, right now."

Silence fell. There Rufus stood with his brutally-cropped hair, his scars and his gumboots and ill-fitting pea coat. Every inch the commander, beyond question. One of the doctors stumbled forward, avoiding another swipe from the fruit-stuffed bag. "Er... that would be me, I suppose. Medically, anyway. If it's the admin side—"

"It isn't. Your name, sir?"

"Mackenzie." Rufus had made him forget his qualifications: he tried to draw himself up, and began again. "James Mackenzie, senior registrar. Might I ask what your business is here?"

"This boy—Thomas Berry—is not to be removed from this hospital, unless it's to the care of his mother and grandmother. And his younger sister Ruth, who's been feeding his prize pigeons for the last three years, and would dearly love to be relieved of her post."

The girl burst into sobs. Mackenzie ruffled up what was left of his sandy hair in bewilderment. He was young for his rank, like so many other men in this harrowed new world. "Nonsense," he said, with an effort at asperity. "Berry has been offered a free place at an excellent facility in Suffolk, the only one of its kind for the treatment of persistent neurasthenia. The call came through last night. He's to be transferred directly."

"He isn't neurasthenic. I will corroborate every detail of the testimony he's tried to give concerning the battle for Fort Roche. That's why I'm here."

"Well—for goodness' sake, Captain Denby, you can't just—"

Berry lurched up again. Mackenzie's restraints weren't as effective as the brigadier's, and the band across the boy's chest snapped and went flying. "Ma!" he yelled, pointing in triumph at Rufus. "It's him, my *captain*, the one what I told you about! The one what saved me when that major went berserk and shot my sergeant and all my mates at Roche." His face contorted. "Why didn't you come sooner, sir? I told them—all the brass that came and yammered at me round my bed to make me change my mind—that you knew the rights of it. Why didn't you come?"

"I had amnesia. I couldn't remember anything about it at all. I'm so very sorry."

Anger left the boy like sand from an upturned bag. One sincere word had tipped it out of him, even after all his sorrows. How many children like this had been packed off to the Front, Archie bitterly wondered—just as ill-fitted by nature for their violent trade as Rufus had been, just as trapped and despoiled?

"That's right," Berry rasped. He touched his own temple in the place where Rufus bore his scars, tenderly, as if he felt their pain for himself. "You was hit. Shrapnel in the head. Your face was all bloody, and you fainted clean away after you shot the major. Our BRF lads arrived just after—took the Hun tanks out, and got a line clear to the fort. I ran and got help for you then, sir. I was the only one left alive."

"Which explains—at last—how I got out of there. Thank you, Berry. Ah, but you mustn't upset yourself now, son—it's over, all over."

He tangled with the valiant, weeping mother in his attempt to catch Berry before he rolled off the stretcher—tried to transfer him into her arms, but Berry made a desperate grab for him and clung like a limpet. Rufus met Archie's eyes over the boy's skinny shoulder. Archie could read him with painful precision by now: mortified, longing to escape, determined with all the grim, white-faced honour within him not to recoil. Never to reinforce the miserable fiction that one man couldn't touch another, even at such an extreme. He winced and held still as Berry's hands clenched on his shoulders: stroked the lad's head, and gently eased him back down onto the pillow.

The girl and the old lady were there now as well, caressing, disentangling. Archie saw his opportunity and waded in. "Come on," he said, getting hold of Rufus's arm and towing him out of the melee. "Time for us to go home."

"I can't. I've got to give my formal report to Mackenzie, make sure no-one's got any reason or excuse to drag that poor lad off to Colditch."

"All right. But after that, we're finding a garage that can deliver the bike back to Droyton for me, and I'm treating you to a ride home on the train."

"I have to go to London first. I've got to correct the report I gave about Fort Roche, and maybe I have to..." He shivered, allowing Archie to draw him back towards the stairs. "Maybe I have to turn myself in. I killed a fellow officer."

"Don't be absurd. You stopped a monster."

"I know that, Archie, but I've got to set the record straight. The brigadier won't let any of this go until it's set in stone by the military investigators. If he doesn't come after me again, he'll certainly try to discredit Berry, and—"

The door to the stairwell burst open. Archie pulled Rufus out of the way just in time. A breathless young doctor ran into the corridor. He cast a puzzled glance at the scene around the stretcher, then shouldered his way to Mackenzie. "Dr Mackenzie, sir? I need a word with you."

"Can't it wait, Saunders? There's been a complication with the Berry case—as you can probably see—and I've got my hands full."

"It's to do with Berry, sir. There's been a telephone call from Colditch."

"I know that, Saunders! Brigadier Spence found a place there for Berry. That's why I've been trying—and so far, failing—to set up the transfer."

"Not that call. Another one, just five minutes ago. There was some kind of freak storm on the Suffolk coast last night, a gale that hit hurricane force in the small hours of the morning. It tore the whole roof off the hospital, opened it up like a..." Saunders waved his hands, searching for an image. "Like a tin of sardines."

"Good grief. Was anyone hurt?"

"None of the patients. But the brigadier insisted on going up into the loft space when the roof began to tear away. He dragged the foreman of the building crew up there with him, raging at him about shoddy construction. He tried to hold the edge of the roof down with his bare hands when the worst of the gale hit, according to this foreman, and... Well, there's a full-scale search underway, sir, but the brigadier hasn't been seen since."

***

"Like the Wicked Witch of the West," Rufus said musingly, gazing at the floor of the carriage. The compartment was empty other than the two of them, the Droyton train thumping its steady way across waterlogged meadows and farm country.

Archie set his newspaper aside. He hadn't been paying it much attention. He was sitting across from Rufus, their ankles intertwined. From time to time one of the gumboots would press shyly against his calf. "I beg your pardon?"

"In *The Wizard Of Oz*. The brigadier. I wonder if there was just a pair of shoes left behind."

He had returned his gaze to the world outside, and his expression was innocent. There was a new, subtle glimmer about him, though. Archie shook his head. "That's awful, Rufus."

"I know." He followed the track of a raindrop with one fingertip. "Isn't it strange? The whole time I've been away, I've thought about Droyton being just as it was when I left—drenched in sunshine, one perfect summer day after another. I had my perfect seven summer nights. But I suppose the storm must have hit them there as well."

"Mm. The paper says that rivers burst their banks all over Sussex, as well as down the east coast." Archie leaned to glance out of the window too. "I hope everyone's all right. I think of the place as somehow separate from the rest of the world, too. We do always seem to have beautiful summers."

"Do you think we can go back to it?"

Archie frowned in concern. Rufus had retained a bright lucidity since their departure from Farley Cross, his ease and confidence growing with every mile they put behind them, but his damage was still done, incontrovertibly written into the scars on his brow. "We're on our way. You don't have to worry anymore."

"Not like that. I mean... if you've been in a perfect place for a perfect time, can you return to that perfection? Or will it be different, like two photographic exposures of the same view?"

"I don't know." Archie gave it thought. Rain was still lashing the carriage windows, the grey sky turbulent. He shifted so that his knee pressed warmly against one of Rufus's. "All kinds of things will be different there once I formally resign."

"Are you sure that's what you want to do?"

"I have to. Droyton deserves better than a faithless vicar."

"I don't think they could have done much better than you, faithless or not."

Archie smiled. "Thank you. I have to be of some use somewhere outside of my parish, though. I've never had a chance to find out."

"Whatever it is, I'll help you. I'll be making a fresh start, too."

"Well, it's a big, wide world. But if any part of that perfection you remember in our little one was about you and me, and everything we did there, I'll make it perfect for you again, I swear. I'll take you up to your attic room, lay you down in the sunshine and—"

The train jolted violently. Brakes shrieked. The impact of sudden deceleration shot through the carriages as if they'd been billiard balls, catapulting Rufus, who'd been sitting with his back to the engine, neatly into Archie's lap. Archie gave a shout of startled laughter, and they clutched at one another as the train ground and shuddered to a halt. "So much for discretion," Rufus chuckled, when the danger had passed and Archie showed no signs of releasing him. He snatched a high-risk kiss. "Let me go, you idiot. Let's find out what's going on."

Archie took a moment to quell a nascent erection with thoughts of the brigadier's lobotomy doctor—*Wicked Witch of the West, indeed, and far may the twister have carried the old devil off!*—then got up, pulled his jacket straight and joined Rufus in the corridor. "We're closer to Droyton than I thought. That's the crest that hides the top of George Mount."

"Yes, I see. Can we go up there, now that I'm not a dangerous nutcase anymore? I'm dying to find out if it really is Droyton Magna."

"Just as soon as you're rested, fed, and dressed in something other than pyjamas and gumboots." Archie tugged down a window and leaned out. "Oh. I think I see why we've stopped."

Before Rufus could ask, a harried-looking guard thrust open the door between carriages. "You all right, gentlemen?" he called. "Any injuries this end?"

"Not as far as I know," Rufus said. "What's happened?"

"Line ahead of us is completely under water—from here right into Droyton, it looks like. River must have burst its banks. We can't go on, and we'll have to wait for an engine from Hassocks to tow the carriages back there. You'll have a long wait, I'm afraid, and the heating's broken down. We'll try and get some tea sent along from the guard's van."

He ducked back into the other carriage. Archie gave a low whistle. "The river hasn't flooded in living memory. If it's this bad out here, Droyton must be swamped."

"Can we walk from here?"

"Yes, if we go back along the tracks a bit and pick up the main road via the causeway from the north. We'll have a wet hike, and you're worn out. Sure you don't want to stay here and wait for your railway tea?"

Rufus was already reaching through the window to unfasten the carriage door from the outside. "Come on. Vicar or not, they'll be crying out for you." He glanced wryly at Archie, still resplendent in his workman's coat and sensible clerical shoes. "You'll have to roll your trousers up, I'm afraid. At least I'm suitably shod."

Chapter Nine

The village had been flooded out. Archie steadied Rufus over the last stile from the muddy fields. He stood on the roadside, shielding his eyes from the sun beginning to struggle through the clouds, trying to make sense of the landscape before him. The crossroads where Pilgrim Way and Station Road met the main street was a silent, four-armed lake, surface barely rippling. Near its centre, the Maidens' Dance stared grimly at its own image in four or five feet of water, the painted sign strangely eerie in reflection.

No signs of life at all. Archie reached out on instinct, drawing Rufus to his side. "My God. Where is everyone?"

"Where does everyone always go when there's trouble in this village?"

"Oh." Beyond the crossroads, he could just make out the lane that led to the rectory, an inch or so clear of the flood. The Way followed the edge of the river's ancient floodplain, and might have escaped the worst. "Good heavens. Poor Maria."

"Yes. We'd better go and bail her out—I hope not literally."

They set off into the thigh-deep water. There was no current, but the river had swept clouds of murky silt through the streets before receding, and Rufus kept a steadying hand on Archie's arm as they forged forward. "This is pretty different from my first view of Droyton," he said, as they came level with the station gates. "And my last. Archie, I'd almost forgotten—did a young army captain called David Meredith make his way to you a couple of days ago?"

"Ah. Yes, I'm glad to say he did."

"Please tell me he found Alice."

"Oh, yes."

"How did it go? Are they all right?"

"Let's just say that I doubt they noticed the flood. Careful here—there's a steep kerb down into the road. I don't know, old fellow—you don't seem terribly upset that I lost my destined bride."

Rufus snorted. "I'm sure Dr Winborn was upset enough for both of us."

"More than. None of his schemes panned out, did they? He vanished after Mrs Trigg came home with the news about Billy. I don't suppose the river swept him off for us, like the wind did with our brigadier."

"Too much to ask of Mother Nature, even at her kindliest. Or..." Rufus hesitated, negotiating the edge of a pothole. He shot Archie an odd glance. "Or of Drusilla."

"Drusilla?"

"I had the most vivid dreams about her, before you came riding to my rescue. I thought I heard her laughing in the gale."

"Well, it was a strange night." A prickling chill went down Archie's spine, but he was spared the need for further reply by the sudden apparition of Jebediah Trigg, pelting down Pilgrim Way towards them as if he had the devil at his heels. A second look revealed only Elspeth, following on at a leisurely pace, Pippin padding faithfully by her side. The transfer of the dog's affections was complete: she gave Rufus a kind of acknowledging bark before returning her gaze to her new mistress. Both children were partially clad in towels, though Elspeth had contrived to turn hers into a robe of sorts, and she'd obviously won at last the battle of the pigtails, her hair in damp black streamers round her face. She looked like a tiny, regal copy of her mother. Archie gave her a wave of greeting, and leaned down to stop Jebediah before he could plough past them into the flood. "Evening, young fellow. Where are you off to?"

"Ma sent me."

"To do what, for heaven's sake?"

"I'm not to say. It's because of the arkinologists."

"Arkinologists... Are they here to build us an ark? God knows we could use one."

"No. They're here for them dead witches."

"Too bloody cryptic for me," Archie said, turning the boy around and wading back into the shallows. He deposited him on dry ground and intercepted Elspeth, who clambered into his arms with an eerie cackle of delight. "Well, if it isn't my little monkey... What's been going on, Miss? Why are you two running around the lanes dressed in towels, and what's an arkinologist?"

She looked disappointed by his ignorance. "One of *him*, Archibald," she said, poking a finger at Rufus. "Only lots of them."

"Don't say *him* like that. It's not polite. Say *Dr Denby*, and don't call me Archibald. Do you mean some archaeologists arrived?"

"That's what I said, Archibald. Then the river came, and they all ran out of the Maidens' Dance, and now they're living with you, just like me and Alice and Captain Meredith. Oh, and Hester Trigg and Jebediah, too."

Archie cast a glance of wide-eyed horror over his shoulder at Rufus. "Looks like you were right. Why me?"

"You're everyone's port in a storm, Archie." Rufus took a couple of long strides to catch up. Jebediah, caught between agitation and a wild, yearning jealousy of Elspeth, suddenly grabbed at his hand. Awkwardly Rufus let him hang on to it. "Surely Caroline can't have sent anyone down from the museum yet."

"I don't know. She's not the type to let the grass grow under her feet."

"I just didn't think she'd be that excited by that kind of grass." He stamped some of the water out of his gumboots. "Why is Jebediah holding my hand?"

"You could always ask him yourself," Archie said in amusement. "He's just a little boy, despite his kleptomania and delinquent tendencies, and I suppose he's had a frightening time of it. Is that right, Jebediah?"

Jebediah nodded so hard that he almost fell over. "It were dark, and thunder and rain. And the water come all in the door. And my ma, she didn't want to leave. She was up in her room, crying and saying *horrible, horrible*, like she do all the time now. But Mrs Nettles and that other one—that witch as *isn't* dead—they come with Billy Prescott and they made her. Billy and Mildred is living with you now, too."

"Hellfire and bloody brimstone."

"Bad to swear, Vicar!"

"I apologise. Now, why did your ma send you back out into the flood? You can't get to the inn yet—the ground floor's still under water."

"She said for me to try, and to get rid of them papers she took out from the floorboards in my room."

"What papers? Why?"

"I dunno, do I? Because of the arkinologists!"

"Good grief. I can see we're not going to get to the bottom of this through you two." Archie spared a hand from the clinging little girl and heaved open the rectory gate. Light was spilling out of the house from all the windows and the open door. He ushered Rufus and Jebediah ahead of him past the drooping yellow roses, which showered them with wet petals and made his heart leap with joy to be coming home with his lover, even in these circumstances. The feeling was almost like Christmas. "I think it's the one thing I'll regret," he said, setting Elspeth down on the path. "That men like us can't have kids, I mean."

Rufus turned to him, a poignant figure outlined in light. Jebediah was still attached to him like a limpet. "Didn't you and Celia ever..."

"We wanted to. I think it was our only reason for all those conjugal duties. Celia never spoke about it, but I know she was sorry nothing ever happened."

"I'm sorry too. Don't give up on the situation, Archie. I know some women who would... well, help us out, if ever it came to that."

Archie raised his brows in wonder. "Really?"

"I do. You ought to be a father."

"You're a whole new world to me, you know." He shooed the two children inside, then looked beyond them. A figure had emerged from the shifting crowd in the hallway. It took him a moment to recognise Rosemary, barefoot and smiling as she was, dressed in Land Girl breeches she must have borrowed from Alice. "Oh, hello. You made it to us, then?"

"Just in time." She stopped in front of him shyly, then gave her brother an awkward hug. "I used the car to help evacuate the houses nearest the river. I'm afraid I broke it down in the process. Goodness knows what the brigadier will say."

"I don't think you have to worry about the brigadier anymore. I'll explain later. Who on earth are all these people?"

"They're from the Royal Museum. Rufus, your boss sent them down straight away when she saw your report." She'd been humbled, but not stripped of her ambitions: her eyes had kindled with pride. "I *knew* it wouldn't be some ordinary old church you were investigating. There's four of them—top men, and they're very excited. They were meant to stay at the inn up the road, but they got there just before the flood, and I brought them here. I hope that's all right, Reverend... er, Mr Thorne."

"Just call me Archie. And yes, of course it's all right. I'd better see Mrs Nettles, though—goodness knows how she's managing to feed everyone."

"Oh, that's all been organised." Rosemary bridled again, clearly delighted with her social advancement in Droyton. "Lady Birch has sorted it all out, and she asked me *personally* to help her, in such a natural way. She sent to Brighton to get absolutely tons of food for everyone, money no object. Isn't she marvellous?"

Rufus's mouth had quirked up, reflecting Archie's doubts over how marvellous Rosemary would have found Drusilla in her nightdress, with bits of river weed still tangled in her hair. "She is marvellous, yes. I'm glad you're here, Rosie."

"Oh, so am I. It was all Reverend... Archie's idea." Her face shadowed. "I feel so bad for trying to get you to Colditch, Rufus. I admit I did it because of the brigadier, but I didn't know what he meant to do to you until it was too late. Please believe that."

He made an admirable effort at pretence. Archie was glad that he failed: loving her was one thing, but trust had to be out of the question. "Your brother's had a tough time," he said, not hiding an edge of reproof. "I know you'll have a lot to talk about, but first he's got to go and get out of his wet things. Have a hot bath while you're up there, Rufus, and help yourself to any of the rector's clothes that you need."

"Hadn't I better go and talk to my arkinologists first?"

"They can wait." Archie jerked a thumb at the stairs, enjoying a first touch of lover's authority, as well as Rufus's reaction: feigned annoyance, and a wholly real flush of pleasure. Rosemary saw it too, and stared at the carpet. Well, she would have to get used to it. "Go on, Dr Denby. Quick march. Rosemary, you'd better show me what's going on in this house. I'll start with the kitchen."

She set off gratefully ahead of him. They squeezed past two tweed-jacketed gentlemen earnestly conferring in the hallway—Caroline's experts, no doubt, passing back and forth pages Archie recognised from Rufus's report. They nodded civilly to Rosemary but ignored Archie completely, probably taking him for a visiting plumber in his working-man's coat, his throat fearfully, gloriously unencumbered. Mrs Nettles let loose a cry of joy as he pushed open the kitchen door, and came rushing through a cloud of savoury steam to greet him. "You're back! Did you get Dr Denby?"

"I got him, Maria."

"Thank God. Don't tell me the two of you rode through this flood on your bike."

"No. We came down by train and then waded. What chaos I left you to deal with!"

"Oh, nonsense. All these things take is a little bit of management and money."

"I can see they've been managed. Where on earth did the money come from, though?"

"Miss Hazelgrove—Lady Birch, that is—doesn't want it talked about, but between us we've been doing fine. I trust you didn't mind us holding open house."

"I'd have done it myself, if I'd been here."

"Well, that's what I thought, Reverend." She raised a hand to the open neck of his jersey, and touched him lightly on the throat. "Is this... on account of the necessities of your journey? A disguise of sorts?"

"No, Maria. It's a little bit more than that."

"Ah. Then there'll be changes at Droyton, and some folks as never appreciated what it was to have a good vicar may *well* look back in sorrow and regret."

"Thank you." He tried for a smile, although the place the dog-collar had once shielded was aching. "I hope all the changes won't be sorrowful. No matter what happens, I'm certain my successor will need and value you."

"We'll see about that, Reverend... sir. For now, I'd better keep busy."

"You do have your hands full. Can I help?"

"Only by stopping out of the way. I have Billy and Mildred, both of them well used to running an establishment, and—can you believe it, Mrs Spence? Lady Birch herself is washing up for me." She had measured the length of Rosemary's foot: the poor little snob lit up with delight at the sight of a real-life Ladyship up to her elbows in soapsuds, and darted off to help. "About two dozen houses were flooded out, sir. We'll bed as many as we can down here, and one wing of Birch Hall is decent enough to take the overspill, though they'll be camping out in there, poor souls."

"I'm sure they'll be fine." Archie raised a hand and returned Drusilla's soapy salute. "Thank you so much, both of you. Er... Dr Winborn isn't here amongst your refugees, is he?"

The good woman bristled. "Certainly not. The news about what he did got out—not from me, because I knew you wouldn't like that, in spite of everything—and he made himself scarce."

"Oh, dear." Archie rubbed his brow. "I always found the other-cheek business hard, even when I was turning it professionally. I'd better find out what's happened to him, though."

"There's no need. He left before the storm came. His house is all closed up, just like old poacher Jakes and Bobby's."

"Good riddance to the three of them, I suppose, though it seems strange and sad to think that way. The badness of men never ceases to surprise me."

"Even after the war, sir?"

"Ah, we were all out there for the express purpose of killing one another. It felt...impersonal, somehow. Grim, but not sordid."

"Yes. I understand."

"But while I'm enquiring after the enemy, is Mrs Trigg about the place? I met Jebediah in the lane, and he didn't give a very good account of her."

"I'm sure I don't know what ails the woman. She hasn't stirred from her room, and I'd have thought she'd be in her element here, bossing everyone around and poking her nose into your domestic arrangements."

"I'll go and talk to her. Where have you put her?"

"Out of harm's way at the far end of the south corridor. Where she won't be offended by Alice and the captain."

"Oh, yes. I almost forgot about our lovebirds. Will I still have to cover Elspeth's ears whenever she goes upstairs?"

"As if the poor child could hear anything, with all her hair draggling down like that! No, the birds have left the nest for a while. They've gone to help dig a culvert ditch and get some of this water drained." She tried hard to pull a face of disapproval, but broke into a smile instead. "About time, too. Disgraceful!"

***

Archie's route to the south corridor took him past the foot of the attic stairs. He came to a halt, grabbing at the newel post. Something had caught his eye: a flicker of white cloth across the landing above him. He stood and watched.

A moment later, Rufus's head appeared around the edge of the archway. A hand, an arm, a naked shoulder. He was dressed in nothing but a towel. His brutal Colditch haircut was up in wet spikes. He said nothing, but his expression softened, and Archie forgot Mrs Trigg with blinding totality.

In the attic room, he found him waiting by the bed. The sleeping goddess and box containing the war medals were on the counterpane where Archie had dropped them. Rufus looked up as Archie pushed the door wide. "Is everything all right downstairs?"

"Fine. Maria and Drusilla are running the kitchen like a Red Cross operation. I'm almost afraid for them—women like that, I mean, and Alice, too. Most of the men I know won't have the least idea how to cope with strong, independent females."

"They'll treat them as monsters, or competition, I suppose." He smiled faintly. "Or maybe we'll learn to be friends. It makes me think of the murals in the church—the man and the woman reaching for one another, not touching. Finding a kind of balance."

"It's a good vision. Are *you* all right?"

Rufus touched the box. "I didn't realise I'd left these here," he said. "The goddess, yes. I knew you'd take care of her. But these... I suppose I was trying to get rid of them."

Archie closed the door. Now that he was here, he was shy. He might have misread that grey-eyed look from the top of the stairs. He and Rufus hadn't shared four safe walls since their last time together here, and Rufus had been to hell and back since then. "I'm sorry I went through your things. It took me the longest time to work out where you must have gone, and I was looking for a clue."

"I ran away from you. I was afraid you wouldn't let me go, and I thought that I had to. Or that you'd follow me and carry me away, which..."

"Which is exactly what happened."

"Yes. I should've known you wouldn't be that easy to shake off." He smiled uneasily, touching the black box. "I remember getting these now. It doesn't feel any less unreal."

Archie came to join him by the bed. He picked up the box and opened it. "I know you didn't want to go to war. But once you were there, you conducted yourself like the honourable gentleman you are. Would you like me to put these away for you?"

"Please. If I knew you had them, I could maybe forget them again, but in a good way."

Archie slipped the box into his jacket's inner pocket. "It's done. With regard to shaking me off, though—that *is* easy. All you have to do is say the word. I was on my way to find out what's wrong with our poor Mrs Trigg. Should I do that, and leave you to get dressed?"

Rufus glanced at the window. The sky was brightening, afternoon sunlight breaking the clouds like a promise of returning summer, endless afternoons on dappled grass beneath the lindens. Despite these beauties, he went and drew the curtains. "I'll always be this way," he said roughly, turning to Archie. "If you won't be shaken off, you'll have to be this way too. Forever and ever."

Archie caught his breath. "Forever and ever, Rufus?"

"You heard me."

Archie went to the door. He'd never been concerned about the lack of keys at the rectory. He'd never had anything to hide. Now he understood the difference between a petty shielding of personal affairs and goods and the need to preserve a great treasure, a diamond that could be broken back to coal dust by the weight of the world. It was damnable to hide, but hiding Rufus—hiding *with* Rufus, deep in the heart of everything—would become the dearest object of his life. Forever and ever, if Rufus would have it so. He picked up the chair by the writing desk and wedged it under the doorhandle. "There."

"Don't you feel trapped?"

"Not with you. With you, a purer freedom than anything I've ever known."

Rufus dropped the towel from around his waist. Archie almost heard fear and inhibition hit the ground with it, everything Rufus had had to learn for himself and pass on to his lover before they took this desperate punt on a shared life. The fragments broke on impact, sending up firework sparks. Rufus strode across the room and met Archie halfway. He clambered into his arms, breaking into laughter when Archie grabbed him by the backside and hoisted him up. "I want you," he rasped against his ear. "I missed you so much, even when I couldn't remember who the hell you were."

He was still damp from his bath, his skin warm as a greenhouse nectarine's and just as fine. Archie wanted to bite him for his juice. So much life left in him, for all the searing horrors he'd passed through! His bones were too near the surface, ribs heaving under Archie's hands. "I missed you too, dear Rufus. Can I take you to bed? Do we have time?"

"Come with me to the window. I know what I said, but..." He struggled down, grabbed Archie by the hand and towed him across the room. Tugged at the curtain fabric, releasing a cloud of dust from the ancient velvet, then jerked it aside. "The sunlight's so beautiful. And who's going to see us up here?"

"Nobody, unless Mrs T decides to do a fly-by on her broom."

A bad moment for a wisecrack. Rufus gave a helpless snort. "Idiot," he said reproachfully. "Now you've put me off my stride. And I wouldn't make jokes about the Droyton witches, not with Drusilla Hazelgrove in your kitchen."

"You're right. I apologise to all the fine witches of Droyton. Please say we can get you back into your stride."

"Oh, yes. Hold me just like that, and..." He caught his breath and went suddenly still. "Archie, wait."

"What is it? Have I hurt you?"

"No, just... Just wait. All the witches of Droyton." He wriggled round and hitched up onto the window sill, an utterly distracting vision to Archie, who held his shoulders and listened as best he could. "Think about Jebediah's pronouncements. Piles of dead witches under the church."

"Jebediah's been hearing his mother's chapel rhetoric. Any woman in this village who doesn't turn out for Hosea Evans on a Sunday is liable to get called a witch."

"And how long do you suppose that's been going on? You said it yourself—the ancient enmity."

"I did?"

"Yes. Your brain is fogged with lust, you bloody lovely reprobate, but listen to me for just one minute more. Triggs on one side and Nettles on the other, like heraldic beasts on a shield."

"I remember. Drusilla between them, or somebody like her."

"And I've been thinking—ever since I got here, I suppose, somewhere in the back of my head—about the Maidens'."

"The pub?"

"The Maidens' Dance, Archie. The dance. I've got to get down to the church."

"What? Why?"

"I can't explain. I just... The river here burst its banks. The church is on the floodplain, isn't it?"

"Yes, but it's on a mound. It ought to be safe."

"Not the tunnels underneath. I have to take the team Caroline sent and go there right now."

Archie surveyed him. Rufus had come to him damaged, flung into his arms out of a world of impossible hostility and pain. But he'd once led his country's finest minds in the most exciting and challenging archaeological ventures of the day. "Will you still need me," Archie wondered aloud, unable to help it, "when you're all better? When you're Dr Denby of the Royal Museum again?"

"I'm not sure that fine fellow ever really existed." Tears blurred the new lights in Rufus's eyes. "As for the other thing... I'm beginning to feel as if I'm all better now. And I couldn't need you more." He put his arms around Archie's neck, spread his thighs. "My friend, who came to fetch me out of hell. I didn't really know what it meant to have a lover until I met you. To have one or to be one."

"Oh, God. Are you sure we have to dash off?"

"Yes, and—now I come to think about it—I don't have any condoms, so I'm postponing our slow, delicious fuck over this window sill for now. But don't you find that once you've come a certain way, it's very inconvenient to stop?"

Archie shuddered in the grip of a hunger so sharp he almost cried out. "Very inconvenient. But I can."

"Of course, my perfect gentleman. You don't have to, though. Just let go with me now."

Archie leaned into him. He hardly knew himself: this bold man he'd become, thrusting up to drive his cock hard and fast against Rufus's. He grunted in joy as Rufus raised his thighs to clasp and embrace him: choked in shocked pleasure when questing fingers found the entrance to his body and pressed and rubbed. "Yes. That."

"A little bit. For more, we'll need the cooking oil."

"But I like it. I think I want it."

"There's no biological reason why you shouldn't, apart from... the lubrication." Rufus threw one hand back to brace against the sill, tipped his hips up to meet and return Archie's rhythm. "Oh God, I feel like I'm going to die of you. I'll fuck you, I swear, and you can fuck me, and the world can go..."

"Fuck itself?" Archie supplied, tasting the new word like delicious, dirty fruit. His cock slipped on sweat and he heaved up into the hot crease behind his lover's balls. "Ah. *Can't* stop now. I'm there."

"Don't stop. Don't..."

Rufus reached up and clung to him. He pressed his brow to Archie's shoulder, and Archie kissed his scalp, tracing the chaos of scars. Ecstasy snatched them both up, helpless as fish from a lake: an eagle-climax that could have borne them off forever, as far as Archie was concerned. "Please," he whispered in the aftermath, stroking Rufus's sweat-damped spine, propping them both against the impulse to fold up on the floor. "Please tell me there'll be time for us. For *this.*"

Rufus flattened a hand against his chest and looked up. He nodded exhaustedly. "Please God. Lots of this. In sunshine, with the windows open wide."

"In a bed, maybe?"

"Yes. And by a riverside, or in the orchard, and..."

"On a beach, definitely." Archie gave it thought. "Maybe not Cleethorpes."

"No, you clown." Rufus shook with laughter. "Sabros, perhaps, though I never thought I'd want to go back there again. There's a cove at the foot of the cliffs, completely deserted. The water's warm, and so clear you can see little coloured fish darting about. I'd like to take you there." His face cleared to a loving, absolute sobriety. "Oh, Archie. You and I both know—everyone who went to war knows—the one thing none of us can be sure of is *time*. But however much I have, long or short—it's yours."

Archie caught his breath. He laid one hand to Rufus's cheek. "That may be... the sweetest thing I've ever heard."

"Pretty romantic, eh?"

"Extremely."

"Good." Rufus grinned, looked ten sudden years younger, and made a grab for his shirt. "Because it's back to business, right now. We've got to go."

Chapter Ten

Too late. Despite the brisk run down the stairs, despite the bright promptitude of Rufus's archaeologists, striding to meet him in the library as he recognised them and called them by their names. Archie had stood in wonder as they'd clustered around him. His authority over them was friendly, easy, and he'd spared barely five minutes to recount for them his theories concerning the church, the Droytons great and small. He'd taken the goddess from his pocket and handed her quickly around them, gently cutting off their questions and exclamations. *Not now*, he'd said, and turned to Drusilla, who'd inexplicably been waiting in the hall he and Archie had come down, holding Elspeth by the hand, both of them dressed in outlandish waterproofs, Pippin at her side. *Not now. We have to go.*

And still it had been too late. Archie stood with him at the end of Pilgrim Way, lightly holding his arm. He wasn't sure which of them most needed the comfort of the touch. The archaeologists stared glumly. Rain dripped off the beech and oak trees and splashed into the puddles in the lane, and on the floodplain, newborn sunlight plucked out every detail of the destruction of Droyton church. "It was the Horshams, wasn't it?" Archie said grimly at last. "Those damn roof tiles."

Rufus seemed to emerge from a trance. "Not just those. The tunnels must have undermined the place long ago. When the flood collapsed them, the weight from above must have been too much."

The church now occupied an island. The low-lying meadow around it had become a gleaming moat, the track from the lane a causeway. The archaeologist standing nearest to Rufus—a lean, grey-haired fellow whose face Archie recognised from the *Review*—looked up, clearly grief-stricken. "I'm terribly sorry, Denby. What an inestimable loss."

"Thank you, Professor Wright. It ought to have occurred to me that this might happen."

"Or to any of us." He was clutching a handful of mimeographed sheets whose contents Archie also recognised. Regretfully he traced the shape of Rufus's sketch of the mural wall, which had fallen outward and vanished into the flood. "We all had access to your report. I'd have given a great deal to have seen these paintings."

"Don't forget the photographs," Archie said. Rufus obviously had: he and Wright turned to him, brightening. "We had a professional chap up from Lewes. Haven't seen the pictures yet, but he was there for hours, wasn't he?"

"Yes, and I asked him particularly to capture as much detail of the murals as he could. No substitute for the real thing, but..."

"No, no. Photographs are marvellous." Wright rubbed his hands. "Given the extent of the destruction, I wonder if we should rely on those, rather than venturing across to the site itself."

"Well, it may be dangerous over there. But I..." Rufus pushed his hands into his pockets. "I have to go. I think Drusilla does, too."

She had kept to the outside of the group. Elspeth was still at her side, with a little air of being in attendance. The child's desperation had left her, the fears that had led her to run about among new adults, anxiously probing for signs of madness or imminent death. She stepped forward when her mother did, clutching Pippin's collar, and smiled up at Rufus and Archie. "I have to come with you."

"I don't know about that." Archie suddenly noticed Maria, who must have followed the group in uncharacteristic silence, and was gazing solemnly across at the ruined church. "You'd better stay with Mrs Nettles, monkey."

"No," Drusilla said. "Andrasta must come. Maria Nettles, too, and you, Thorne, and Denby. All those who've been friends to our kind."

"Have we, Drusilla?"

"Unwittingly, sometimes, but faithfully. Yes." She raised her head at the sound of splashing footsteps in the lane. "Ah, and Alice Winborn, restored to the house of love. That's as it should be, my dear. Come here."

Alice was towing David Meredith by the hand. They both were dressed in muddy raincoats and waders, and Archie couldn't tell which of them was blushing the more vividly at Drusilla's welcome. "Drusilla," Alice gasped. "We just got back to the house, and Rosemary told us what happened to the church. Is there anything we can do?"

"Why, yes. You, at any rate, though the captain may accompany you. Ours is a hard task, and we shouldn't deprive ourselves of comfort."

"I don't understand." She didn't look as if she needed to: was quietly ablaze with happiness. She planted a kiss on Drusilla's cheek, then to Archie's astonishment, turned and did the same to him. "Never mind. Archie, I'm so glad to see you. And as for you..." She let go Meredith's hand and threw both arms around Rufus. "Bless you forever. You brought him back to me."

"What?" Rufus patted her, startled laughter shaking him. "No, no. I just bumped into him at the station."

"Maybe, but he's told me—the absolute *fool*—that he'd have turned around and gone straight back if you hadn't told him I was here, and on pain of death to find me." She lowered her voice. "You have your own magic, and I hope one day you'll forgive what my family's done to you. I don't know how to ever repay you, except that... well, one day you and Archie will have to join me and David in our house of love, if ever we can get jobs and afford to buy one."

"I'm sure you will."

"And then we'll come and visit the two of you in yours."

"Good Lord, Alice."

"Sorry. And it took me such a long time to work out, as well! No wonder Archie didn't want to marry me—how could I possibly compete?" She patted Rufus's face and stepped back. Her beauty was extraordinary, Archie thought, like the shift from spring into summer, a promise fulfilled. "Can we help in any way? Is there anything to be salvaged?"

"I doubt that, but we are going over to have a look. It could be dangerous, so—"

"We'll enjoy it all the more. Won't we?"

She leaned her shoulder against Captain Meredith's, her eyes bright with compassion for all the men who'd returned, and were expected somehow to take up normal lives in their fields and their offices again. Archie knew that the promise of physical peril would be a lifelong clarion call to him. He couldn't have remained the vicar of Droyton Parva. If he'd tried, he'd have drowned in his own damaged lungs.

They felt blissfully clear just now, deep enough to breathe for the whole world, but the top of the causeway was barely three inches above the water line, and the rain-fuelled levels in the floodplain would rise still further before they would fall. "All right," he said. "As Dr Denby points out, there might be danger here. You gentlemen from the museum have a work remit, and the church is my responsibility, so I have to go. Drusilla, Maria, Alice, Captain Meredith—will you consider staying behind?" He surveyed the ring of stubborn faces around him, then shrugged. "Follow on behind me, then, if we're ready. Drusilla?"

She nodded serenely. "We aren't yet all assembled, Thorne, but very well. Lead on."

He wondered who else she expected. What Rufus expected for that matter, in the wake of the destruction of the church, because surely all his theories had gone down with the ship. It wasn't the time to ask. Predictably he'd come to walk at Archie's side across the causeway, not permitting Archie to take a single dangerous step without him, but his focus was inward, a firm self-containment that didn't alter until he reached the other side. The dog overtook them and went racing ahead into the ruins. Then he flickered Archie a quick, odd smile, ran up the steps and stood where the south porch had been. "There were two very fine oak doors, early medieval," he said, addressing his archaeologists, who gathered on the bottom step to listen to him, like distinguished baby birds. "Their loss would be a shame, but perhaps they'll turn up in a ditch somewhere. It's of much less significance than... Well. Come up and see."

He waited until Wright and the others had climbed up to join him, then gestured south to the place where George Mount raised its strange peak. "Reverend Thorne showed me this. You can only see that odd-looking crest from this one place. And once you're up there, you can only see the church from one particular spot, too."

Professor Wright beamed. "Ah, intervisibility, eh? A dashed sight more convincing than your absurd ley-line theories, Ramsey, but—"

"Have to stop you there, old chap," Ramsey interrupted. "Watkins has been misinterpreted. It's hardly the poor fellow's fault—or mine—if his followers ascribed mystical energies to the perfectly reasonable system of landscape alignments he proposed. Don't you think—"

"Gentlemen," Rufus interposed reluctantly. "Have any of you had the chance to look at the painting in the library at the rectory?"

"Certainly have. Wright and I were arguing about it earlier. I say Iron Age hillfort, but he's with you on the idea of some kind of labyrinthine carving reflected in the name of the village. We both agree it was a stroke of etymological brilliance on your part, Denby, to make the connection."

Wright was nodding enthusiastically. "And my opposition to the idea is jolly fragile, I have to say. It's a fine notion, the link between a little Droyton labyrinth here and a great one up on the hill. Regardless of what we find up there, though, I'm afraid your proof here at ground level—the tunnels you described—must surely be gone."

Rufus turned to survey the tumbled ruins behind him. Archie climbed the steps and took up position at his side, glad he'd done so when Rufus shifted to lean imperceptibly against him. "Yes, completely gone," he said, folding his arms over his chest. "As a professional, I'm deeply sorry. But even that's of less significance than... Drusilla, are you there?"

She made her stately way up the steps, Elspeth trotting after. "We are here, Denby."

"It's hard for me to explain this. There's literally nothing set in stone, not anymore, and all I have is a theory. What would you be willing to tell us about your connection here, and the history of the other—the women who went before you?"

She shaded her eyes. A warm breeze was stirring her hair, and the surface of the waters, and plumes of drying dust from the strange shapes in the mud at the centre of Droyton church. "I will tell everything, now that the others are coming. The river bears us all to the same place—do you see?"

Archie looked round. His unseemly love of machines made him focus first of all on the motor car bumping to a halt on the causeway, not the people it contained. A Hillman, elderly but in good condition... Hadn't Caroline told him in one of her recent letters that she was going to buy one of those, to get Mildred out of the city at the weekends? "Rufus," he said, as the driver's door opened. "I do believe that's my cousin."

"I do believe you're right. Together with..." Rufus too squinted against the sun. "Together with my sister. And to complete the set—good grief, that's Mrs Trigg getting out of the back. Yours is a strange river, Drusilla."

Drusilla took off her bright souwester hat and waved it like a flag. "Indeed. Poor Hester."

In the lane, Rosemary pointed, and she and Caroline began to pick out a cautious track towards the church. Mrs Trigg stood by the car for a moment, then followed slowly, as if reeled in by a heavy chain. Archie and Rufus went to meet them, threading the group of puzzled onlookers. "Caroline," Archie called, reaching out to help her over the last muddy stretch of the causeway. She was dressed in her usual quiet blues, the utility jacket and skirt that became her spare frame so well. "This is an unexpected pleasure. Welcome to Droyton."

"Or what's left of it. Oh, dear, Archie—what happened to your church?"

"The revenge of an apocalyptic God, I'm sure some would say. A flood, in other words."

"The place is virtually gone. Is everyone all right?"

"No casualties reported. You must have arrived to chaos at the house."

"Rather. I'd thought to beg a night's accommodation of you, but you seem to have your hands full. I had a day off, and I thought I'd motor down and see what all the fuss was about, not to mention..." She stepped onto the stonework with evident relief. "Not to mention that I wanted to know the outcome of your mission."

"Yes. I was going to write to you tonight."

"There's no need now." She smiled at Rufus. "Good to see you again, Dr Denby. Your work on the remains here has been splendid, though I dearly wish it hadn't all been washed away. Your sister here was kind enough to give me directions."

Rosemary caught up with her and came to a breathless halt. Archie could read her like a book by now, and she was obviously torn between Caroline's rank—a deputy director!—and the shock of finding a woman in the role. Mrs Trigg had been easier for her to figure out, and had been left behind to plod through the mud as best she could. "It was my pleasure, ma'am—er, Miss Taylor," Rosemary said, glancing with pride at the tweed-suited experts gathered around Rufus. "This other person—landlady of the inn, I recall from my last visit—insisted on coming with us, but I'm not sure why—the closer we got, the more she cried. She's still crying now."

Somebody certainly jogged God's elbow when He was pouring out the milk of human kindness between you and your brother. Archie bit back the observation. Rufus and Drusilla had broken away from the group and were striding to intercept the poor landlady, whose world had so mysteriously ended with the disgrace of her son. Speaking of whom... "Mrs Trigg," Archie said, helping manoeuvre her to safety, "I'm pleased you came to join us, but where's Jebediah?"

She raised a woebegone face. "I made him go and get 'em. The papers."

"What? Oh, yes, he was talking about some papers when we met him in the lane. It's still flooded up there, though. Is he all right?"

"Oh, yes. He'll always thrive, that 'un."

"Not if he drowns." Archie exchanged a worried look with Rufus. "We'd better go and find him."

"No, no." Mournfully Mrs Trigg laid a hand to her bosom, where something rustled. "He come back all right, and Mildred and Billy is drying him out by the fire. Brought the papers, he did. Horrible—oh, horrible."

"Good Lord, Mrs Trigg—*what* is so horrible?" Together he and Rufus helped her up to the top of the steps, where she seemed to want to be despite the shivers racking her sturdy frame. "Nobody really blames your poor lad for what he did, you know. And if something else is worrying you, wouldn't it be better if you just said it out? Or if it would help to talk to me in private—"

"You would, wouldn't you?" She lurched to face him, making Rufus twitch and close a restraining grasp on her arm. "For all you're a high-Church vicar, as Hosea Evans says is little better than a papist priest, you'd hear my confession, chapel woman as I am. You'd *absolve* me."

"No. I'd try and help you find ways to make reparation, so you could absolve yourself."

"I can't. Too horrible."

"Come and speak to me, then. As a friend, not your vicar. Whenever you like."

Drusilla reached past him and seized Mrs Trigg by the hand. "No. Hester, I'm afraid it must be now."

Rufus and Archie turned. Drusilla was watching the other woman with a painful intensity. For a moment Mrs Trigg held back, as if despite everything she would seize back her old territory here, the little bit of ground where she'd set up her castle and home. Then all remains of bumptious life drained out of her. Her shoulders sagged, and she allowed Drusilla to lead her into the ruins of the church.

Rosemary began to follow, then hesitated, frowning at the sight of the pub landlady on the aristocrat's arm. Elspeth trotted over to tug at her sleeve. "Come on, sister Rose."

"Why, you funny little thing. I'm Dr Denby's sister, not yours." On an impulse, Rosemary bent down and scooped Elspeth up into her arms. "Look at this untidy hair! And what on earth are you wearing underneath your raincoat? Are those robes of some sort?"

"My best ones."

"Your mummy's been letting you play in her dress-up box, I think."

"Will you let *your* little baby do that?"

Rosemary shivered. "My baby was a little boy. Boys don't play dress-up with their mummy's clothes."

"Not *that* little baby, sister Rose."

Alice Winborn swooped in before Rosemary could drop the child. She lowered Elspeth to the ground by the armpits. "You're an unnatural imp," she said without rancour. "Don't take any notice of her, Mrs Spence."

"No. No, of course not." Rosemary walked on, but her face was an unreadable blank, and when Mrs Nettles came within reach, she grabbed her outstretched hand. "That can't be, though. That can't be."

"Ah, they make their own way into the world sometimes," Mrs Nettles said gently. "Sometimes they're a wonder, and sometimes the sorrow of their coming is too great, and then there's ways—old ways, and kindly ones—to alter the path."

"Don't talk like that. Don't."

"No. No more I should, in the presence of men who make laws to put women in jail for such kindly old ways." She looked around the scattered archaeologists, who were staring in more or less incomprehension. "Begging your pardon, gentlemen, and nothing personal meant, but such is the present nature of the world. Hold on to me, Mrs Spence, and don't fear. Now, Drusilla—my dear lady—is the time right?"

"The time, the place, seven sisters come to witness." Drusilla had halted at the place where the aisle had used to be, as if waiting, and one by one they clustered round her—Alice, Mrs Trigg, Maria, Rosemary, the child. "Caroline Thorne, who sent Denby here to begin this ending—come, if you will. Join us."

Caroline cleared her throat. She was the soul of rationality, Archie knew, and preferred her archaeological mysteries served up on a platter of hard evidence. "I sent Dr Denby to investigate the church, that's all. Most of his evidence is gone, but if there is anything left, I think he and his colleagues should go ahead of anyone else to assess it." She turned, hands on hips, to frown at her team. "I'm not at all sure why they haven't made a start. Gentlemen?"

Archie knew. He held his tongue. He and Rufus had come to a dead halt on the outside edge of the fallen church wall, and not one of the archaeologists had taken a step further. Fear could act like an infection, he knew, so he kept a quarantine silence. It was Wright who spoke up eventually: shifting uncomfortably, reaching to scratch at his brow. "Well, it's the strangest thing to admit, Miss Taylor, but I don't quite feel as if I can. How about you, Ramsey?"

"Same, old fellow, though it's seldom we agree about anything. Most frightful case of the horrors."

Caroline's eyebrows climbed. "What on earth do you mean?"

"Look at the dog, Miss Taylor. Look."

Pippin had ceased her aimless lope around the ruins and come to a stop at the exact place the altar had covered. There was no sign of the hole beneath it, but she sat down, lowered her head, and tucked up one paw. Her hackles rose. A dismal sound escaped her, a cross between a howl and a moan. "Good heavens," Wright said uneasily. "I've seen dogs do that in London—after a raid, you know. The rescue crews would bring the beasts along to see if they needed to keep digging. After they'd brought out everyone left alive, and it was just the..."

"Just the bodies," Rufus finished for him, finding a brief, reassuring smile. "The dog used to be mine. And she's just a mutt, not trained for anything, but she's female. That's it, isn't it, Drusilla? The reason why we can't come closer, and you can?"

"Yes," Drusilla replied. For the first time since her awakening, her voice was unsteady, and she put one hand on the dog's head and the other on Elspeth's, caressing both. Tears suddenly spilled down her cheeks. "Because of the maidens. The poor maidens. Oh, Hester, please—tell their tale."

Chapter Eleven

"It was papers, you see. Papers, in Jebediah's room. When Lady Birch—Miss Hazelgrove as was—told me to look there for the other things my wretched boy had took, I lifted up the floorboards, and there they were, in a sheepskin pouch half worn away by rats and time. Papers left behind, and I wish to God the rats had eaten them whole."

Archie had taken a seat on the remains of the west wall. He'd felt a strong desire to be sitting when Mrs Trigg unfolded her story, as if the earth were dragging already at his bones. He was deeply glad of Rufus's presence at his side, hand on his shoulder, the touch unconcealed. "Who left them behind, Mrs Trigg? Do you know?"

"I know. I know. My granddad used to tell the story from his grandfather before him, and laugh at it too, old beast that he was. I thought it a fireside tale, Reverend Thorne—a thing to frighten children. I thought the man in the story a bogeyman, like Hob the Devil or Tom Hop-o'-My-Thumb. You know how children's minds work. But this man's name was Hopkins."

"Hopkins? What did he do?"

"The Droyton inn's been held by my family for centuries. A Trigg I was born, and a Trigg I married, foolishly having taken my cousin in wedlock. I'm no war widow, Dr Denby, and I swear I'm sorry for the lie—Zachariah died of drink, just like the rest of his sottish family. Only I wanted you to think well of me, when you first arrived—do you see?"

"I do think well of you," Rufus said quietly. "You're not like your family. None of them would have come here and told the truth."

"No. I've always known the story. But a story's one thing, and proof's another, and the proof's been..." She reached into her coat and withdrew a moth-eaten pouch. "The proof's been burning my heart out. The inn wasn't always called the Maidens' Dance. It was called the Troy Town, and our pub sign—uncanny thing, as I always wanted to take down—was something to do with that. People used to come here, you see, hundreds of years ago, to see that hill what's called George Mount these days, and to see the church, and... what lay beneath it."

"What did lie there? Do you know?"

"Only from the story. I never ventured into such a heathen place. But these people—pilgrims, I suppose you'd call them— came by their hundreds, because under the church there was a maze you couldn't get lost in, and..." She paused for breath, shivering. "And miracles took place there."

Archie glanced up at Rufus, who gave him a nod of permission. "Miracles, Mrs Trigg?"

"All kinds of superstitious rot, Reverend. Healings, transformations. They said it was a place you went into, and when you came out, whatever things about you needed to change would be changed. It would... turn you around."

"Caer Droea," Archie said softly. "All right. What happened then?"

"I can't tell you. I can only read it."

"From the papers you have there?"

"From a paper of my own, as I sat up night after night writing down, to make the words out clear for myself so I could understand. So I could try *not* to understand, try to make it not true."

"Do you want me to read it for you, Hester?"

"No. I have to do it myself." She straightened up, unfolding a sheet of modern foolscap. Drusilla came to stand by her shoulder, and she painfully began. *"In the year of Our Lord sixteen hundred and thirty nine, the following history took place in the village of Droytown-the-Less.* Is it right, Lady Birch? The old words were hard to make out."

"Yes, it's right. Go on."

"I, Joshua Revelation Trigg, keeper of the Troy Town Inn, record it at behest of Pastor Gorringe, guardian of the pure souls of Droytown, and scourge of the unconverted. I write it to be placed in evidence against the wicked women here on trial for the vile crime of witchcraft, discovered as they are by the zeal and energies of our honoured guest here residing, Reverend Master Hopkins, appointed by God and by Parliament to hunt them out."

"Oh, Christ," Archie said, startling the gathered archaeologists. *"Matthew* Hopkins."

Dr Ramsey turned to him, white as a cod. "Hopkins the witch-finder?"

"Witch-finder General, self-appointed. Nothing to do with Parliament at all, or God, for that matter. What was he doing here?"

"Well, there's a theory that he spent time with the Puritan colony at Salem in Massachusetts. If he was returning from there to Essex—"

"Nonsense, Ramsey," Wright broke in. "He'd have disembarked at Bristol. Why would he detour to a speck on the map like this?"

"Ah, but what if he disembarked at Southampton? Brighton and Lewes would have been natural stops on his route home. It's an early date for him—he didn't get stuck into those three hundred poor old girls in East Anglia until the 1640s—but still, if he got wind of any wrongdoing in Droyton..."

"He did. He did get wind of it." Mrs Trigg had crushed her paper into a wrinkled tube in her agitation. She pointed the tube first at Ramsey and then Wright, and both fell awkwardly silent. "He came here. I can't hardly read my own handwriting anymore, but Joshua Revelation says this. Will you listen?"

"They'll listen," Archie said firmly, holding up a hand to stop Wright's next interruption. "Go on, please, Hester."

"Full many years have passed in evil and corruption in these parts, the authority of certain godless, unbridled women going unquestioned, most particular the creature called by the people here Lady of Birch. Not one woman has she been but several, passing on her property and name by means most unnatural, each one choosing her successor as she pleaseth, without benefit of law, God or husband. None such hath ever attended the Sabbath-day service at our church, but instead has set herself in guardianship over certain antique remains beneath it, being tunnels, curiously carved into the earth, and matching in their shape and form the devil-made signs upon the hilltop called Droytown-the-Great. At these unholy places do flocks of the unwary gather, to the peril of their souls, aided and guided by the Lady of Birch, and such among the village women as she has seduced into her service, and most obscenely calls her maidens, as they call her priestess."

The breeze shifted, bringing the voice of the river close. There was a new note in it, a rushing urgency, and Pippin began to paw restively at the earth. Rufus scanned the water surrounding the church. "You'd better tell the rest quickly, Mrs Trigg. Hopkins got wind of this—this wickedness, and he came here, did he? He can only have been a young man at the time."

"Yes, sir. That's what Revelation says. He and Pastor Gorringe—ancestor of our old goat of a rector, he must have been—admired him greatly for his youth and force of personality." She turned a weary shade of grey, as if all her ghosts were catching up with her at once. "I'll go on. I'll tell it quick, in my own words, blazoned as they are in my mind, so deep that I'll never be rid of them. He came here, Matthew Hopkins did, and he taught the Droyton villagers that Lady Birch and her maidens were wicked. The times was harsh and bad—a civil war coming on, and famine and sickness everywhere. It's easy to turn people's minds in such dark days, isn't it? Just as it was a few years ago."

"Yes. Just as it was then."

"And this Hopkins, he would charge twenty shillings for each poor creature he convicted of witchcraft. And the parish here found the money for him, because he told the men who helped and aided him that he could seize the property of anyone he put to death, and he swore to divide it among them. And the Lady Birch of that time..."

"She was wealthy. An easy target." Rufus rubbed his eyes. "This at a time when tuppence a day was the average wage, gentlemen, and more than most people's life was worth to stand up to such a man. He swept like a scythe across East Anglia. And my guess is that he began his career right here."

"Did you know it was him?" Archie asked, reaching to touch his hand.

"No. I was just certain that someone or something had come here and turned a sacred place into an unholy one, a charnel house. That's what happened, isn't it, Mrs Trigg? That's what's so horrible."

She nodded miserably. "This man Hopkins set up what he called a court, with Gorringe and Revelation Trigg at the head of it. They dragged the Lady Birch in front of all the villagers, and not one of them raised a hand to help her—except for a woman called Sairey Nettles, who cast herself in front of the Lady and said it was her duty to preserve her and all who belonged to her. And Sairey Nettles in her turn was taken up, and accused, and tried for witchcraft. Ah, and the ways they did it! Tormenting the poor souls so they condemned themselves whether they cried out or kept silence—pricking them with pins—boiling up water, or lead, and pouring it into their—"

"Hester, stop!" Maria ran to her, took her by the shoulders and gave her a gentle shake. "So long ago, these sorrows. I feel them as if they were yesterday. Let them go down the river with the flood."

Mrs Trigg sobbed. "With all my heart! Forgive me and mine for our part in it."

"It wasn't *you*. Just as it wasn't me."

"And still it feels like yesterday, just as you say. The blood in my veins is that of Revelation Trigg, who told this man Hopkins to use the inn to carry out the sentence he passed on Lady Birch and all of her maidens. Dear God, he took nearly thirty of 'em all told, and he hanged them one after the other on a gibbet they'd set up in the courtyard. And old Revelation, he thought it a grand joke, for from that day onwards he called the Troy Town inn the Maidens' Dance. Oh, how they danced, Maria! How they danced!"

She dropped to her knees in the mud. Maria went down with her, clasping her in her arms as best she could. Drusilla Hazelgrove stood over them both, spreading her robes and her waterproofs to shield them from the wind. Silence spread in rippling shockwaves through the small crowd, and even the swallows—swooping back and forth, seeking their lost nests amongst the rafters—ceased their cries.

"So it was," Drusilla said hoarsely at length, turning to look at Rufus and Archie. "So it was that a sacred place became a charnel house, Denby, where no man can enter without fear. Witch-finder Hopkins buried both priestess and maidens in the tunnels beneath the church, to pollute the very earth they'd worshipped."

"All of them, Drusilla? Here?"

"Here. Hopkins broke our line—the chain of priestess guardians who'd found their way here to serve the labyrinth. Those who came after were weakened and confused. One of them painted the murals, to try and heal the breach—man reaching to woman, and woman to man—and one of them placed the sleeping goddess in the wall of the church, to keep the murdered maidens at peace." Suddenly she raised her head. Her eyes glowed with ferocity. "Imagine what they might have done otherwise! Step forward, sister Caroline, who understands the nature of human bones. Come, Alice, true of heart. Come, Rosemary, for the life in your belly is no-one's but your own. Come, all of you, and look at the mud at your feet, and bear witness."

Caroline was first to obey her. She stumbled forward and knelt, and to Archie's astonishment began to turn the earth over with her hands. "Caroline," he called, and tried to lurch to his feet, but Rufus held him back. "What is she doing?"

"She's finding the witches. Stay here."

"But she'll hurt herself, or... Aren't you worried about the site? She's never been nearer to a real dig than her desk in Bloomsbury."

"Rosie and Alice will help her." Rufus lowered his voice. "Let things happen, Archie, love. Let this be."

All three women were kneeling now in the mud at the centre of the church. Alice looked strong and fit for her task—Rosemary only bewildered, but nevertheless she was first to lift a great clump of grass and tangled roots and set it aside as if it weighed nothing. "Look," she breathed, less in horror than wonder. "Oh, look!"

Stiffly Caroline got up. "There are human remains here," she said, dryly and calmly as ever. Tears were streaming down her face. "The storm has caused a good deal of dismemberment, but I see several skulls, and the aggregate of other bones would indicate a mass burial. Two dozen inhumations at least. Dear God. What should we do?"

Professor Wright, who'd been staring open-mouthed for the last several minutes, came suddenly to life. "Why, the poor souls should be laid to rest," he declared. "What a hellish tale. Can't you arrange for their Christian reburial, Thorne?"

"No. No, I don't think I can." Now Archie did get to his feet. The river had found a new voice upstream. The moat around the church was stirring with silt-brown life, currents flexing like muscles beneath the surface. On the far side of the floodplain, amongst the tangle of willows and fallen oaks, a surge was building. "Drusilla, Maria, all of you—get back here. Onto the causeway, quick."

Mrs Trigg lifted her head. "We can't leave them," she wailed. "The poor maidens!"

"We *can* leave them," Drusilla said calmly, bending to help Maria lift her up. "Their story has been told now, dear Hester. We can leave them to the river."

And just like that, the standing wave of horror and repulsion that had been holding Archie back was gone. He seized a deep breath. The other men were animating too, shaking themselves, rubbing their eyes. Alice Winborn heard the river's new song and gave a warning cry. She scooped Elspeth up into one arm and grabbed Rosemary with the other. "Come on, everyone! We've got to go."

Archie ran to meet them. Peripherally he saw Rufus taking charge of Mrs Trigg, the archaeologists offering hands and gallant tweed-clad elbows all round. Together they made for the causeway. Archie stood back and counted them past him, every last one right down to the dog, who escorted Alice with ferocious vigilance. "Keep moving," he yelled over the increasing roar of the water. "Get to the bank, fast. The whole thing's about to go."

They were halfway up the slope of the floodplain when the surge hit. Alice, weighed down by the little girl, had begun to lag behind: Archie took the child and flung her bodily into Maria's waiting arms. He pushed Alice ahead of him onto the bank and felt the earth slip and crumble beneath his last stride.

The sweet feral stink of mud-laden water filled his lungs. The current snatched the ground from under him. He measured his length in the shallows—tried to scramble up, and was suddenly waist-deep.

An arm shot down out of heaven. It would always feel that way to Archie when his lover reached for him. "Here," Rufus gasped, getting a grip on his arm and his coat. "Hang on to me."

The archaeologists had combined forces to anchor Rufus on the bank. Alice and Rosemary reached in to pull, and Archie—laughing helplessly for some reason, in the wake of such sorrow and peril—crashed to his knees in the soaking grass, where Rufus caught him and held on. "Is everyone all right?"

"Yes," Rufus said shakily. "Including you, by the skin of your teeth."

"Including me." Archie shifted round, glad of Rufus's warm grasp. The exigencies of the moment excused it, and anyone who didn't like it—well, the river was deep, and accidents happened. Sternly Archie controlled himself. This was euphoria, the joys of rescuing and being rescued. He'd have to learn to live as Rufus taught him, safe in their chains and disguises, but at least he would live. Oh, how he'd live, at the side of such a man... "Rufus, what's Drusilla doing?"

"I've no idea."

She had taken up position on a promontory of the riverbank, a spur of mud and tangled roots spared by the flood. She put back the hood of her raincoat, and her hair streamed out in the wind. "So passes Caer Droea," she said, and although she barely raised her voice, the words rang out with an odd reverberation, making Archie's eardrums flutter. "So passes the turning castle, the house of transformation—where lungs are healed, true natures revealed, the dead brought to life, and all things wrought to the next phase of their existence. So pass the maidens and the lady of Droyton Parva—hail and farewell, sisters, hail and farewell."

Rufus let Archie go. Slowly, watching the water, where island and causeway had now both vanished, dissolving in the flood, he went to join Drusilla. He reached inside his jacket and put the statue of the goddess into her hand. "This belongs to them."

Professor Wright jumped as if electrocuted. "Denby, no!" he yelled, and Archie heaved himself upright in time to stop him by main force. "What the devil are you doing?"

"The only thing I can, Wright. I'm sorry."

"You can't," Caroline rasped, clutching at Maria for support. "That artefact is priceless."

"I know. So were the women who died here. For the record, ma'am, I believe the entire island of Sabros to be a ceremonial labyrinth structure. It may warrant investigation."

"What does that have to do with—"

"Some things are lost, some found. That's all."

Drusilla cradled the little figure in her palm. She raised it to her lips, then flung it with all her strength into the water.

Chapter Twelve

A blazing morning in early June. Sunday, and the chapel bell in Droyton had rung with all its usual cracked vigour, even though no rival call to the faithful would ever toll out from the church on the floodplain again. Hosea Evans had drawn in a smaller congregation than usual, minus several of its leading lights. The new Anglican church—in the village this time, well away from the river—was still in the planning stages, her minister yet to be assigned.

Summer morning, rising to noon. Archie's faithful were out on the hill. Dusty heat blazed off the chalk, and in the shade of the oak trees that ringed the crest, Mrs Nettles and Drusilla were unpacking a picnic lunch of vast proportions. Hampers lay strewn about them, carried up from the rectory by many pairs of willing hands. George Mount, henceforward to be known as Droyton Magna, had been cleared by the Royal Museum for restoration, and the work was underway, under close supervision from Caroline Taylor's archaeologists.

Already thin slices of turf were building up on the outskirts of the rings. The vast banks and circles, newly exposed, were gleaming in the sun. Two dozen souls from the village had laid aside their Sunday rest and come to claim their labyrinth. "There,"

Mrs Nettles declared, shaking out a cloth to shield her array of sandwiches from flies. "That ought to feed everyone, just about."

Drusilla eyed the feast dubiously. Two big trestle tables had been set up, both of them covered with every kind of cake and scone the rectory kitchen could supply, and a range of cold meats worthy of one of Archie's butcher nights. "I agree, Maria," she said, "but these things are costly. Why didn't you come to me, as you've been gracious enough to do before, to discuss the price and how I might help?"

"Much more grace from me in that regard and I'd have bankrupted you, my lady. Besides, I..." She paused, and patted the pocket of her flowered apron. "I can afford it."

The apron was a new one. Drusilla raised an eyebrow. Without waiting for permission, she reached out and plucked an envelope from the rose-patterned pocket. Mrs Nettles stood by, watching benignly, while she extracted the papers and read. "The Reverend Gorringe appears to have died in Italy, and left you the rectory and all his considerable personal wealth, Maria."

"He has indeed. What beats me is, if he had so much personal wealth, why didn't he spend some of it in patching up his wretched house?"

"I don't pretend to understand all the legal language in which this letter is couched, but it would appear that his personal assets were tied up in trusts to prevent his squandering them. Which, given his nature, seems to have been a sensible precaution. Congratulations, my friend. To me this seems like justice done."

"Heaven knows what rumours it'll start. The gossip about me and the butcher was bad enough. That was a myth, you know."

"I know. But if it brought meat to the hungry souls of this village through the war years, who cares what it was?" Drusilla hefted a stoneware ale jar onto the table. "The gossip concerning me and Reverend Gorringe was *not* a myth, sadly."

"I did wonder. It seemed bad, even by his goatish standards, to prey upon a sick woman that way."

"You must bear in mind that to a certain extent I allowed it, sick as I was. I thought I would die, and there was no successor to the guardianship of Caer Droea. In the confusion of my mind, I felt I had to create one, and I could see only one way to do that."

"So you created Andrasta."

"With Gorringe's unwitting help. Continue to call the child Elspeth, Maria. She needs a grasp on the real world as well as her strange inheritance." Easing the cork out of the jar, Drusilla smiled. "Speaking of which, what will you do with yours? I hope in some small ways you'll still need me."

Mrs Nettles shaded her eyes to look at the workers on the hill. A cluster of tiny blue butterflies flickered skywards on an updraft, so many of them that they briefly shaded the sun. "I do believe *I'll* patch up the wretched house. The Reverend—our own Reverend, I mean—used to say there'd never be any shortage of waifs and strays. Dr Denby's sister wants to stay with us for now, and heaven knows she'll need help when her baby comes—she's still half out of her poor wits about how she conceived it."

"Maybe she can learn to accept that, as I did, and simply to love her child. She desperately wanted one."

"Yes, but it's not very proper, is it? She can't hardly sit with the ladies of the Mayfair tapestry circle and talk about that."

An undeniable chuckle escaped the high priestess. "Stop it, Maria. You still have Miss Winborn and the captain on your hands, don't you?"

"Yes, until she and David can find somewhere to live. And Alice wants to be married from the house."

"I can't blame her, given the shadow that's fallen on her uncle's."

"She's got a quaint notion about not being seen by the groom the day before, so you can help me by peeling David off her and stowing him away at Birch Hall." She shook her head, took the jar and began to pour out the shade-cooled ale into the waiting jugs. "I believe I'll run my rectory as a permanent hostel for lame ducks, fallen women and waifs. And I'll always need your help, my lady. Who knows who else may come?"

As if on cue, an engine began to purr. Drusilla and Mrs Nettles watched as an elegant motor car, made tiny by distance, gleamed and shimmered its way along the George Mount road, and came to a halt on the verge. "That's a nice one," Mrs Nettles said musingly. "I bet *he'd* have known what sort it was."

Drusilla nodded in sympathetic recognition of who *he* was, the place reserved in the housekeeper's mind for that man only. *Our own Reverend.* "I know little of such things," she said, "but it seems to me that the car may be outshone by the lady getting out of it."

Mrs Nettles propped her fists on her hips and gave a low whistle. "She'd outshine Rita Hayworth! Her young fella's not bad, either... Why, bless me. It's Giles!"

The young couple set off up the footpath. He was as beautifully dressed as his companion, his hair sleek, his shirt immaculate. He extended a courteous hand to aid her over the stile and she jumped down merrily into his arms, silk scarf flying. A few yards further up the track they both stopped and waved frantically. "I shouldn't be surprised if Giles had read the article in *The Times* and returned to help," Drusilla said, serenely waving back.

"They could use all the extra hands they can get up there. Do you think this big labyrinth will work like the little one did?"

"I don't know, Maria. But if it does..." She paused, her expression darkening. She'd stopped watching the progress of the Hollywood-glamorous pair, and had focussed on the footpath that wound its way up the flank of the hill from the Ashfield direction. At this height it was barely more than a sheep-track. A dusty figure was approaching the outer circle of the great chalk banks. His head was down, his whole demeanour crushed and weary. "If it does work wonders as the small one did, perhaps the miracles will be large in proportion. That is Dr Winborn, Maria. Please take him a jug of cold ale."

"Take him a..." Mrs Nettles lost a breath. "I'll take him the back of my hand, and I'll give it to him, too. The nerve of him, to show his face around Droyton again!"

"Nevertheless. Look at him."

Winborn stumbled to a halt at the base of the curved wall, the vast shape that guarded the interior. Billy Preston had appeared at the top of it. Billy's face became as grim as its cheerful lines would allow, but he caught his sister by the arm before she could hurl herself at the new arrival. She and Billy had been at work on the hill since dawn, not only permitted time off by Mrs Trigg but in that altered person's company. The inn was closed, for flood repairs and the breaking up of the courtyard's deadweight old cobbles for a garden. No-one had lifted the turf off the chalk banks more tenderly than Hester Trigg. She joined Billy and Mildred to stare down at Winborn, then lowered her gaze.

Alice and the captain emerged from the coils of the labyrinth. Both were flushed, Alice too occupied in brushing chalk dust off Meredith's back to notice her uncle at first.

When she did, she went as still as a deer in the forest. A mixture of disgust and pity twisted her features. Meredith took up a protective stance at her shoulder. Winborn crossed the remaining space between them painfully, as if using up his last strength. He looked from one to the other of them—the beautiful woman, and the lover whose heart even death had not induced her to sell out or betray. He sat down hard on a clump of turf and began to weep.

Mrs Nettles poured ale into the largest jug she had. She was about to set off with it when Elspeth and Jebediah came tearing out of the chalk walls. They were hand in hand, shrieking with laughter, the dog in hot pursuit. Jebediah's exultant yell carried like the cry of a buzzard on the air. "Ma! Ma, we done it, and we never got lost—we done the maze!"

"Technically it's a labyrinth," Drusilla murmured, watching in amusement while the children shot up the bank to Mrs Trigg, who scooped them off the ground on reflex and stood swaying beneath their weight, her face transformed with astonishment. "But I'd say that it's doing its work. A moment, Maria, before you take that to the doctor. There's something I want to say."

She drew Mrs Nettles a little way into the shade. The two stood together, watching the ordinary wonders of life unfolding on the hillside before them. "When I first came here," Drusilla said, "I was the most hopelessly lost of all the Caer Droea guardians. There was a maze inside me, not a labyrinth, and I would have wandered forever, had not Thorne and Denby found me. I dreamt last night that Denby was the man in the church-wall painting, holding out a hand to me."

Her eyes had filled with tears. Mrs Nettles tucked a comfortable hand through her arm. "Well, you're not lost now. You do look nice in your midnight-blue velvet, my lady, and relieving it with your big straw hat with ribbons and daisies was a very good idea. Where do you suppose they are at this moment— Dr Denby and the Reverend?"

"It's been more than a week, hasn't it?" She smiled, dabbed her eyes with the handkerchief Mrs Nettles had produced for her. "They'll be on Sabros by now."

Chapter Thirteen

The roar of a bike engine cut across the constant rasp and whisper of the sea. Rufus didn't look up from his sketch. Plenty of Sabrian workers got about on motorcycles. They did well, in tiny island streets designed for donkey carts. The six-truck Royal convoy had crept from the harbour inch by painful inch, kids and street vendors cheering as in-folded wing mirrors brushed white stucco walls.

The evening was deliciously hot. A wind from the north coast of Africa stirred the mosquito nets over the bed and made the blue-painted shutters rattle gently on their hinges. Rufus could smell fresh-caught fish on rooftop braziers, aromatic oils from the banks of myrtle growing downslope of the apartment house, and indefinable spices of excitement rising from the sandy dust. Bouzouki music skirred in through the windows, underlain by a faint throb of drums.

Another throaty roar, closer this time. Rufus closed his eyes and allowed himself a moment of hope. The hope thrust down a root, shot skywards, set seed and became a whole flourishing crop. Surrendering, he set the sketch down on the big olive-wood worktable, anchoring its four corners with stones.

Fine sand had found its way into every crease of his skin after a long day on site. He ran downstairs into the brightly tiled cube that served as a bathroom, stripped out of his day clothes and worked the rusty pump until water began to splash into the sink, which was big as a trough and probably once had been one. He stuck his head beneath the tap, came up gasping. His one luxury from England was a bar of soap he'd filched from the rectory— Archie's morning smell, which along with drying apples and fresh tobacco would forever melt the knees out from under him. He washed as best he could and stood up. To put on shirt and trousers again in such heat seemed ridiculous, so he shrugged into the long white djellaba Zadi had brought him from the market.

There was no mirror. He could only judge from his shadow on the wall whether or not he looked absurd. There was his upright shape, the long straight fall of the fabric neither revealing nor concealing. It didn't matter. The garment was simply a sane, comfortable thing to wear in a hot climate.

There wasn't much else he could do by way of preparation. A signal across the rooftops would bring one of Zadi's housekeeping team with a basket of bread and the catch of the day packed in ice. Wine was cooling in the cellar. Rufus took a breath. The sound of the motorbike was focussed now, distinct, closing the space between the road to the village and the apartment building where the Sabrian ministry was hosting its visitors. Slowing to a percussive backfire halt directly outside.

Rufus pulled open the front door. At the foot of the steps, Archie was dismounting from the Norton. He and Rufus had wanted to sail out together, but Archie's obligations had kept him in England for a week, shuttling back and forth between Droyton and London. Rufus had tried to wait for him, but Caroline Taylor—newly promoted to museum director, and throwing her weight about accordingly—wouldn't hear of it. If Dr Denby wished to lead the largest foreign expedition of the decade, he would have to be aboard the specially commissioned vessel departing from Portsmouth three days after the opening up of the Droyton Magna hilltop, and no questions asked.

Rufus hadn't asked any. He'd gone, promoted back to all his former Royal glories and more—Dr Denby of Sabros, hailed by a banner headline in *The Times*. He'd worked like a demon for the best part of a second week, and slept alone in the wide, netted bed, staring at the reflection of his dreams in sea-lit moon patterns on the ceiling. His heart was thudding, his vision threatened by tears and dust. Archie slung his one rucksack over his shoulder, raced up the steps to meet him. He scanned his face anxiously. "Are you all right?"

"Yes. I wasn't sure you'd get here today, that's all. And I've missed you, and..."

"Dear fellow. For God's sake come inside."

Archie slammed the door after them. He looked around the big first-floor room that served as kitchen, living space and bedchamber. "This is wonderful."

"Not really. At least—by local standards it's very good indeed, but..."

"It's perfect. A bed, a view straight to heaven, and..." He paused, long enough for Rufus to take his rucksack and stand gazing at him in dry-mouthed yearning and love. "And a feature unique to this part of the world, as far as I'm aware."

Rufus was slow. His lonely week had been filled with artefacts, soil stratification and the treasures of the dead. "What's that?"

"You, of course. So handsome in your... What is that thing called?"

"A djellaba," Rufus said happily, walking into his arms. "It's called a djellaba. I had Zadi get one for you too."

"You did?"

"Mm. Yours has long black stripes. I thought it would suit you. Oh, God, it's good to see you." Rufus squeezed a laughing grunt out of him and reluctantly let him go: the window not filled with the heavenly sea view gave onto a prosaic street, busy at this hour with passersby and carts. "Did you find the bike all right?"

"Waiting for me on the harbourside, polished and tanked up. Thank you for sneaking her out here for me."

"No sneaking involved—I listed her as vital expedition kit. She'll be really useful for getting around the site. How was your journey?"

"Long. I dreamed every night you were there. I'm afraid my cabin mate knew quite a lot about you by the time we docked in Crete—quite a lot about me, too."

"You could've had your own cabin. I told you that."

"You did. But I can't just *accept* things from you. I have to..."

"Hush." Rufus got hold of his hand. "All you have to accept for now is your new djellaba."

"Well, I admit I'd kill for a change of clothes. It's boiling here. Where is this marvellous garment?"

"In the wardrobe by the bed." Rufus let him go for long enough to close the street-side shutters, then steered him across the room. Together they divested him of his heavy jacket and trousers—clerical black, because after twenty years in the trade, he simply didn't possess any off-duty clothes.

A letter fell out of his pocket onto the tiled floor. "Ah. That was waiting for me at the harbour, too."

"Didn't you open it?"

"I couldn't spare the time. I just wanted to get home to you."

Home. Rufus shivered at the word. That was the best description for the restless sorrow that had kept him awake beneath the mosquito nets—homesickness, cured instantly and completely by his lover's arrival. Archie was home. "Now that you're here," he said carefully, keeping his voice steady, "do you want to look at it? We can read it together."

"You know who it's from, don't you?"

"Your bishop in Ashfield."

"I don't warrant quite such a luminary as that. The archdeacon. Whatever he says will come *ex cathedra*, though, yes."

"He came to see you at the rectory on the Tuesday after I left, didn't he? How did that go?"

"Well, I tried civil tactics at first. I told him I'd lost my faith, and didn't consider myself a fit person to look after the spiritual welfare of my flock at Droyton. Rather stupidly, I'd thought that would clinch the argument. Who wants a godless vicar?"

"I don't know. I've met plenty of godly ones who were so much less qualified than you. Did he try to hang on to you?"

"He told me that technically speaking I couldn't resign, that I was a clergyman forever, even if I chose not to fulfil the role. I knew that already, though it does seem stupid—like insisting on calling a man a bricklayer when he's sworn off ever laying bricks."

"You told him that?"

"In more or less those exact words." Archie sat down naked on the bed. He took the robe Rufus had handed him and spread it out over his lap. He ran an admiring hand over the long black stripes. "This is very nice. Your first gift to me."

"The first of many. What did the archdeacon say?"

"He said, *nonsense, man! It's up to you to propagate faith in others, no matter what troubles befall you in your own petty existence.*"

"Oh, dear."

"So I wrote to him that evening, telling him there were more cogent personal reasons why I shouldn't run a Church of England ministry anymore. I should imagine that this letter is his response."

He broke the seal and began to read. Rufus sat down beside him, putting an arm around the broad, pale-skinned shoulders that would burn so readily if he wasn't careful. Rufus intended to take the greatest care of him. "Is it very bad?"

"Well, I'm out." He managed a sickly smile. "I never thought I'd be able to see a man's hair standing on end through his handwriting. Great big fella he is, too, the archdeacon—so much for muscular Christianity."

"What else?"

"The bishop agrees that I should resign my post, rather than remain there as an example of evil and a... a corruption to youth." The smile faded out. "I don't mind so much the example of evil. That sounds rather fun. But the other... He means choirboys, doesn't he? He thinks I'd hurt little kids."

"I don't know or care what the bloody, bloody bastard means." Rufus seized him and pushed him down onto the bed, djellaba, mosquito net and all. He covered him with his body, the only shield he could offer—inadequate, but still Archie grabbed him as if he would do. "They all think every queer man wants to hurt little kids. That's what they're taught, and they never try to learn any better. Oh, Archie—that's the world I've brought you into. Can you stand to live in it?"

"You *made* my world." Archie stroked his face. "You are my world, if I have to get downright soppy. I don't expect it to be perfect."

"But it will be, as far as I can make it."

"I know. I know. Still, I have to work at it too. Am *I* vital expedition kit, Rufus? What can I do?"

Rufus kissed the questions off his lips. "There'll be plenty. I'll want you at my side every minute you can spare. But even if I didn't, it's all right for the future to be uncertain, my love. When did you last have a holiday?"

"I'm not sure I ever did. Celia and I used to go on retreats to the Anglesey monastery, but... I went from college straight to ordination and my Brighton parish."

"It's about time, then. I'm on the museum payroll again, and I think your cousin's embarrassed about the mix-up over my parish stipend. I have more than enough for us both."

"How luxuriant. You handsome devil—I can see why the conventional world sees men like you as a temptation and a threat." He waited until Rufus stopped laughing. "I can't, though."

"Can't what?"

"Can't just lie back and enjoy your bounty. I'm not like... I'll have to work."

"You will. And if you're trying not to mention Henry, it's all right. I did love him, undeserving little sod as he was, but he's gone. And I like to shower my men with gifts, spoil them and keep them when they need to be kept, so you'll just have to get used to it."

Archie subsided onto the pillows as if he had every intention of trying. But running footsteps scraped on the steps outside, and Rufus jolted upright, pulling Archie's djellaba out of the tangle. "That door has no lock," he warned, grinning wryly. "Better see if your new outfit suits you, pronto."

Archie flung the garment over his head. "What do you think?"

Rufus spared time for a whistle and a onceover. "Right down to the ground."

"It's like you took my dog collar, flipped it through ninety degrees and turned it into a dress pattern. This really is a new world."

Laughing, Rufus headed for the door. Before he could open it, Professor Hargreaves burst into the room, hotly pursued by Zadi, the minister's nephew, now in charge of hosting and logistics for the whole Sabros dig. "Professor," Zadi gasped, making a grab at Hargreaves' belt to slow him up. "You should knock for Dr Denby."

Hargreaves rounded on him. "I beg your pardon?"

"You should knock, sir. English manners."

"Don't you dare lecture me on English manners, you—"

"Quentin, please." Rufus stepped between them. "Zadi's quite right. A knock on the door is nothing but common courtesy."

Hargreaves went through his usual colour changes, sunburn to puce and back. But times had changed at the Sabros dig, and after a moment he made an absurd mime of flinching back from Rufus, holding up his hands to shield his face. "Oh, if Bruiser Denby says so—the terror of the Royal Museum..."

Obligingly Rufus faked a punch at him, as he'd done in response to the joke twenty times since his arrival. This was his colleague's way of dealing with what had happened between them, and Rufus owed him a large debt of patience. "Zadi's just following the rules we set down ourselves. None of the doors to the private quarters here have locks."

"Well, archaeologists in my day didn't need 'em. In my day, we thought ourselves lucky to have a tent that zipped up, and..." Hargreaves blinked, his eyes adjusting from the blaze outside. "Good heavens, Rufus—is this the friend you were telling me about? Have the two of you gone native?"

To judge by Zadi's expression, Rufus and Archie made a pleasing sight in their robes. "Yes, this is my friend," Rufus said tranquilly. "Archibald Thorne, of Droyton Parva in Sussex. He'll be staying with me."

"One of the Alfriston Thornes?"

"I'm afraid not," Archie said, holding out a hand. "Just an undistinguished Brighton one."

"Well, I'm glad to make your acquaintance. But really, I'd have hoped a visiting Englishman would help uphold our civilised standards of dress, rather than allowing lax local standards to—"

"*Quentin.*" Yes, times had changed. Hargreaves and Denby were Quentin and Rufus to each other now. But this was Rufus's excavation, and the reins were in his hands. He drew himself up, reminded Hargreaves with a look that he was the archaeologist who had caused a priceless artefact to be thrown into a river, and been granted command of the Royal's most prestigious mission anyway. "Is it really any of your concern what my friends and I choose to wear?"

"No, of course not. But these things are practically frocks, you know. Wholly unsuitable."

Zadi broke into an undisguised grin. Poor Hargreaves was poached half to death in his tweeds, his shirt glued to him with sweat. "Very unsuitable, Hargreaves sayyid."

"No-one asked your opinion!"

"Please speak civilly to the Sabrian workers, Quentin." Rufus folded his arms. "Speaking of which, has our new archaeologist arrived?"

"Our new what?"

"The Sabrian lady from Chania College in Crete."

"You can't call her an archaeologist. She's only just graduated, and she's..." He paused, apparently only now realising the horror of it for himself. "She's a *woman.*"

"Our boss in London is a woman."

"It's one thing when they're four thousand miles away behind a desk. Quite another when they're here in the trenches with us! A fellow can't relieve himself against a wall without looking in twenty directions at once."

Rufus fought not to laugh. Archie wasn't helping, leaning against the wardrobe, watching Hargreaves with unconcealed amusement. "Well, you'll have to make the best of her. A newly qualified archaeologist is just as much an archaeologist as either of us, and she knows more than we ever will about this island. Her gender is neither here nor there. A more important question would be, is she happy?"

Hargreaves frowned tremendously. "Is she what?"

"Is she settled in her quarters, provided with all the equipment she needs? Is she being made welcome by the others?"

"Isn't it Zadi's job to see to all that?"

"Zadi has more than enough to do already. I'd like to ensure that he's happy, too. Are you happy, Zadi?"

The young man lit up like a Mediterranean sunrise. "Yes, I am. And you?"

"Very, thank you. Has your uncle arrived?"

"Yes, Denby sayyid."

"That's good. Archie, Zadi's uncle is Minister Belesh, the Sabrian representative in Athens. I'm afraid he may be less than happy because no-one has spoken to him yet to assure him that any further discoveries at this site will be presented to him and his team of experts, and on no account removed from Sabros unless by mutual agreement. Would you undertake the task of telling him that, Quentin?"

"I will, but..." Poor Hargreaves shuddered. "It's damned nonsense, you know. These backwater islands can't curate their own treasures."

"Maybe not, but Athens can. Why are we taking their things away from them? It's like bringing Stonehenge here because some stupid Englishmen left it out on a heath to erode away in the rain. Thank goodness the great treasure here is something we can't lift up and carry off with us."

"That's what I wanted to see you about. I'm sorry I came bursting in on you, but I'm afraid it wouldn't wait. A bunch of the natives—er, the Sabrian workers—downed tools yet again when we went to open up the tomb beyond the one where you..."

"Where I went off my head and attacked you," Rufus finished for him, holding out a hand. Hargreaves took it with kindly readiness, as if he'd only been waiting for the opportunity to forgive. "Let me guess. There's some sort of structure concealed in the sand beyond the tomb, and they don't want it touched."

"That's right. They were shouting that word of theirs again."

"Agapomenu?" Zadi suggested. "Was that the word, sayyid?"

Hargreaves glared at him, but caught Rufus's eye and cleared his throat. "Yes, thank you, Mr Zadi. And the blasted thing about it is that there *is* something there, an earth-built bank or a great curving wall of some kind. It seems too huge to be manmade, at least in that time period. If it underlies the tombs, it's got to be four thousand years old. I say, Rufus—Caroline Taylor said you'd had some kind of insight into this place, something connected with that Sussex church. I wish you'd tell a fellow what it's all about."

"Yes. It's about time I did. Forgive me for keeping you in the dark, but I had to get back here and test my theory before I could be sure."

"And that's what you've been doing this week, is it—testing your theory? Because the other chaps couldn't quite understand why you've been wandering about the site in your djellaba, without so much as a trowel in your hand."

"Sometimes what we're looking for isn't down there in the soil. It's in the hills around us, on the skyline, or... Well, here on Sabros, it's everything. Come and have a look."

He led Hargreaves to the table where he'd spread out his sketch. He'd had to tape together a dozen sheets of paper from his notebook in order to collate his observations from his week on the island, his hours spent walking the dunes and the shore.

Archie followed eagerly, making sure there was room for Zadi at the table too. "This is a beautiful drawing, Rufus."

"Thank you. I used to sketch at sites all the time, but I got too busy, and I started relying on photographs. Working at Droyton made me remember how good it was to connect with a place by drawing it—the different things I'd see." *I'd like to sketch you. Oh, the things I'd see then!* The message flashed between them, and Rufus had to look away. "Having said that, please tell me the photographs from the church came out well."

"Perfectly. I forwarded them on to Caroline at the museum."

"Good, good. This is a sketch of the whole excavation area. It's also, as you can see, a sketch of the island, or most of it—I've included the shoreline, running into and out of the outer circle as the land's eroded."

Hargreaves ran a fingertip along one intact sweep of the curve. "What do you mean, the outer circle?"

"Don't you see it yet? Earth-built banks, one inside the other, looping back and forth in concentric shapes. Some are intact, and the later Bronze Age cultures understood their sanctity without knowing what they were. They built their tombs in the spaces between them."

"In the tunnels?"

"That's right. They were tunnels by then—the sand had blown over, and layers of earth had formed on top. Maybe some of them were deliberately infilled to protect or hide the tombs. But, taken overall, enough remains are still visible—and the people here revere them so much—that I believe we've discovered—"

"Tir!" Zadi gave a shout of delight, and fetched Hargreaves a sudden wallop on the back. "Lavyrinthos! Can it be, Denby sayyid?"

"The excavation will take years, but I believe so. Yes."

"The labyrinth," Hargreaves breathed. He didn't appear to have noticed Zadi's gesture: was staring at the map as if the dunes had turned to Mycenaean gold, the sea to lapis lazuli. He swayed, and Zadi grabbed a chair for him to sit down in. "I don't believe it. I can't."

"You were the first to suggest it, Quentin. Don't you remember? I didn't listen, and I'm sorry. Whatever Evans discovered at Knossos, I'd guess that it had its roots and its source right here, a pattern of ancient sanctity that spread right across Europe."

"But what was the purpose of it?"

"Miracles. Regeneration." Rufus hesitated, recalling his return to life in the brigadier's hellish prison. "Waking the dead. Magic, maybe, or maybe nothing more than the things we have inside us anyway."

"Surely it was built to conceal some great treasure."

"It wouldn't have been much use—not to keep a Minotaur in, or treasure-hunters out. Oh, I'm certain we'll find riches enough, as we excavate more tombs from the tunnels, but this isn't precious-object archaeology anymore. The treasure here is the island, the earth itself. Can we restore it, do you think, without betraying the people who live here or tearing it apart?"

Hargreaves cupped his chin in his hands. When he looked up again, his face was clear of everything but a childlike wonder. "I'll try," he said wistfully. "But for heaven's sake, Rufus—how did you *know*?"

Chapter Fourteen

The view stretched out to heaven, and only heaven could look back. The fierce heats of the island day had subsided to a dusk as fragrant and delicate as the shadow-patterns of amaryllis leaves on the wall. When Rufus held his breath to listen, shouts and laughter came to him on the seaward breeze, skeined with music: word had gone out that the whole of Sabros was sacred ground, a cause for firelit celebration, songs and dancing until dawn.

The archaeologists' lodge occupied a promontory, and the southern window framed nothing but sea and sky. Not even a patch of beach below. The street-side shutters remained closed. Rufus was sure that Zadi would soon train his unruly guests in the art of knocking, but a chair wedged under the door handle had been a friend and protector before, and the brightly painted ladderback looked comfortable in its place, a strange guardian angel. "I wanted you to do this to me before," he said, his throat tight. "In a window half a world away, with the smell of drying apples and tobacco."

"And cobwebs and dusty curtains in your face." Archie came to stand beside him. "Is this better?"

"It's beautiful, but just now I'd take any window with you anywhere. Please just do it, Archie. I want you inside."

"Christ, I'm almost scared. What if I'm not any good at it?"

"Hush." Rufus kissed him, standing on his toes a little to brush his lips over the worry-creased brow. "It's not the be-all and end-all, despite what you might hear in certain men-only dives around London. If we don't like it, it's fine. Henry and I never did it like this."

"Didn't you?"

"No. He thought it was unhygienic. Undignified. And God knows it can be both, and men can give each other diseases just like men and women can, so..." Rufus took the lid off an earthenware jar on the window ledge. His hands were shaking. He'd offered Henry's name as a reassurance, but saying it had suddenly invoked a hundred miserable nights of trying to love him. Watching his cravings turn to disgust in the aftermath, his rush to the bathroom to wash away his sins. "Zadi really is invaluable, you know. I told him I had a gentleman friend arriving, and half an hour later he was back on the doorstep with these, discreetly wrapped. The condoms will protect both of us, and the lubricant—better than Maria's cooking oil, I hope—will make it easier."

Archie took the tube and packet from him. He set them aside, cupped Rufus's face in his hands and gave him a look which Rufus felt like benevolent X-rays, right through to the back of his skull. "Everything's all right," he said softly. "I want you at least as much as you want me. I want to learn how to fuck, even if it isn't the be-all and end-all."

"To add it to your repertoire?"

"That's right. And you'll think me the greatest idiot in the world, but I've never used one of these little rubber-johnny things before."

"Well, you were with Celia, and you both wanted a child. You have to wear one now because of me, not you. I wasn't always choosy about who I went with after Henry."

"Ah, Rufus, I'll wear anything for you. You just have to show me how it goes on."

The past melted away. Rufus experienced a moment of pure, surging happiness. "Yes, I'll show you. We'd better take what Quentin calls your frock off first."

"That'll be twice I've been defrocked."

Together they disrobed him. Then it was Rufus's turn, and by the time Archie had lifted the white cotton djellaba over his head, they were both erect, desperate with waiting. Quickly Rufus unwrapped one of the condoms. "You put it on over the tip, like this, then you roll it down."

He demonstrated. Archie fell back against the window ledge, gasping. "Ah, I see how they work. They feel so nice when your lover puts them on that you pop before you get near him."

"Oh, no. Don't you dare." Rufus grabbed the tube and briefly worsened Archie's dilemma by rubbing the lubricant up and down the length of his sheathed cock. "Hold on, or I'll call for Zadi to bring ice."

"He wants you, that lad. I could see it."

"Well, he could've had me once. Not anymore. I'm yours."

Archie turned him to face the window. The force of the movement unlocked Rufus's joints. He leaned on the ledge, propping himself on his elbows. Ozone and pine-pitchy woodsmoke filled his lungs. Tawny last light painted the skin of his hands and forearms: his chest and belly, and he rose up groaning, Archie's arm clamped around his waist. Archie's warm mouth descended on the side of his neck—butterfly kisses, then a gentle devouring, a distraction while his cock pressed in. "Am I in the right place?"

Rufus could hardly speak. "Exactly right. Yes." He pushed back to meet the penetration. "Go in deeper. Give me it all." He seized Archie's wrist, the glimmering sea beyond the arch of the window darkening to his vision. The movement inside him was huge and deep, beginning to bring on an ending he would have fought back if he could, but his muscles were squeezing helplessly around the hot shape inside. His rhythmic gasps joined with Archie's. "Harder, for God's sake. Can't bear much more."

"Am I... hurting you?"

"No, but I'm going to die if it goes on much longer. Oh, I can't. I can't."

Archie pounded into him. Rufus would have given a world to watch him, to see the hard-muscled jolts of his spine and backside as he thrust. His body's reaction to each stroke—the spasm and recoil—merged into one unendurable crush. He writhed to be free, but the only way out was up and up through tightening circles of pleasure. Then came a consuming heat-burst, a blaze that began in his balls and set off grenades in his spine and gut. A raw yell ripped out of him—another and another, until Archie bent him over the sill and he could bury his face in his arms.

His lover's living weight came down on him. Archie enfolded him in an embrace that sent all the demons of Rufus's life running screaming back to hell. Whatever the world threw at him from now on, it would have to get through that hold, that blessed sacred circle of his arms. Slowly, blinded by tears, he straightened up. Archie's spent cock slipped out of his body, and he turned to seize him, to ease the shock of this first separation and give him back all the shelter he was offering—to be the circle within and without him, their own endless labyrinth walls. "Archie, my God. Are you all right?"

"Yes. But I see why they used to call it dying. I never knew till now."

"Come here. Come here to me." Rufus helped him peel off the condom, heavy with the juices of his life. They scrambled together onto the wide ledge: settled in a warm, worn-out tangle of limbs. Rufus stared in wonder at the former vicar of Droyton—naked and undone, hair in a tumble on his brow. In his eyes, a dazed brilliance to rival the lights of the Summer Triangle, the Swan and the Eagle and the Lyre, just clear of the horizon now in the sudden southern dusk. "Breathe," Rufus ordered him huskily, stroking back strands of his damp fringe. "It really is advisable to breathe."

Archie hauled in and released a huge sigh. "I almost forgot."

"The odd thing is, I'd have sworn you'd be dying for a cigarette just now."

"Yes. If ever the occasion called for one... But I haven't felt the least need, Rufus, not since we first went into the tunnels at Droyton and you gave me the kiss of life." He looked up suddenly. "Is it possible that the labyrinth there really saved me? That you breathed into me, and somehow... cured my lungs?"

"Those are two questions," Rufus told him wryly. "Did the labyrinth save you, or did I?"

"Do you believe what you told Professor Hargreaves? That miracles happen in these places because of some kind of magic we have inside ourselves anyway?"

"I don't know what I believe. But if I *had* to speculate—and I won't be doing so in the *Archaeology Review* any time soon, because I want to keep my lovely new job—I'd go further. I'm not sure we need the labyrinth."

"Oh." Archie sat back against the crumbling plasterwork, taking this in. "All that magic—that power to heal and change—might just be part of us?"

"In combination with other people, or the strongest impulses from our own souls. Maybe I was able to help you because we both so desperately wanted you to stay alive, because we both knew even then that we'd found each other, and that meant everything."

"Yes. Everything. Did Alice somehow bring Captain Meredith back to life down there, when she realised she could never love anyone else?"

"That would be my insane theory, yes. If I had to speculate."

"And Giles—Gillian—her soul's strongest impulse was to bring the man inside her to life."

"That's right. Madness, isn't it?"

"Absolute nonsense. Ouch!" Archie slapped at his shoulder, where a couple of sixpence-sized red marks were already on the rise. "Damn bugs are biting me."

"They are rather a terror after dusk. I'll put some benzoin on you. They can't resist that beautiful white skin."

"Ah, is that the problem? I'm irresistible?"

"You'll tan after a few days here, and that'll toughen you up a bit. Yes, the problem is that you're irresistible, and for now there's mosquito nets all around the bed. Come with me."

***

Much later that evening, the Triangle stars risen high overhead, Archie and Rufus walked along the island shore. The breeze blew away the mosquitoes, and the waning moon threw down a burnished path from the horizon to their bare feet. The path moved with them, always inviting, and all the night was in motion—fishing boats dancing with the shift of the water, bonfires leaping among the dunes. Because the beach was quiet, and eccentric Englishmen were permitted a certain latitude in this last stronghold of the old gods, they walked arm-in-arm. Rufus had a letter in his free hand, delivered by one of the enthusiastic boys Zadi employed to rush about between the village and the lodging-house. Post from England arrived via ferry from Crete in unpredictable waves. Archie had received a postcard from Elspeth in the same delivery, beginning *Dear Archibald* and assuring him that, although he was sadly missed, Troy Town was in good hands, new pilgrims already coming down the Way to visit the great hill, and ending in a series of childish kisses that had brought tears to his eyes.

Rufus's mail was from his sister. He and Archie paused near one of the bonfires to make out her scrawl. "She's well, apart from some morning sickness," Rufus said. "I'm glad she's decided to keep the baby, although God knows how she must feel about it. Maybe we should adopt it." He glanced at the corner of the postcard protruding from Archie's djellaba pocket. "Maybe we'll adopt Elspeth, too."

Archie burst into laughter. "Why not Jebediah, while we're about it? We can't just run around adopting children willy-nilly, you lunatic. Even if the foster services would let us anywhere near 'em, you'll be globetrotting all over the world on archaeological adventures, and—"

"*We'll* be trotting. And I know. I just want *you* to know that we'll have kids someday, somehow, if that's what you want."

"Thank you." Archie stood in silence for a moment, watching the flames. "I wonder what the brigadier would have to say about his son's widow's queer brother adopting his illegitimate child."

"Bloody hell. There's a thought. But I'm not sure we're ever going to hear from him again."

"They still haven't found him?"

"Not a trace, Rosie says, though Corporal Berry is at home and minding the family shop and the rabbits. I'm truly beginning to think Drusilla blew him away."

"Well, good riddance. I hope she blew the old bastard back to his rightful home in hell."

"Some evil wind blew Dr Winborn back to Droyton, though. He's a changed man, apparently—helping Alice and Meredith make plans for their wedding, and asking very kindly after you."

"That's very nice, but bugger him, too."

Archie's rage was warmer than the fire. Rufus leaned into him, understand the source, drawing life and strength from it. "Does it feel good to be able to say such things, now you're not a vicar anymore?"

"Bloody good." Only a young Sabrian couple was still dancing round the fire, too lost in one another to pay attention to any love but their own, so Archie slipped an arm around Rufus's waist. "But then I think—here we are, in this new world. And we're at peace, or so the politicians tell us, even if that peace was won by dropping a bomb that... Christ, that turned people to shadows on the wall. All these children we're going to adopt, love—I don't want them growing up under that sword, and I'd do anything to prevent it. But how can I say I want real, lasting peace, when I don't have peace in my heart towards my neighbour? I swear to you, I'd snap Winborn over my knee like a twig if he was here."

"I know." Rufus took hold of his shoulders, turned him gently to look up into his face. "But I remember what you said in your last sermon. If we have to wait until we have peace in our hearts before we start working for it in the world, we'll never get anywhere. We just have to start with what we have."

Archie stared at him. They were standing in the lee of the outermost labyrinth wall. Any miracles that took place on this beach would have to happen on the strength of plain human magic, the ancient and joyous communion of loving hearts. "You are a true pacifist," Archie said huskily. "You went to war, and in your own way you fought Winborn and Brigadier bloody Spence to a standstill. But you are."

"Perhaps. Make no mistake, though, Archie—I'd fight for you."

Archie nodded. The young couple had come to a standstill, rocking in each other's arms. He reached out and brushed a hand over Rufus's temple, tender as he always would be with the injured place, forever marked by the battles he'd lived through.

But all the scars were gone.

from A Summer Night (to Geoffrey Hoyland)

Equal with colleagues in a ring
I sit on each calm evening
Enchanted as the flowers
The opening light draws out of hiding
With all its gradual dove-like pleading,
Its logic and its powers:

That later we, though parted then,
May still recall these evenings when
Fear gave his watch no look;
The lion griefs loped from the shade
And on our knees their muzzles laid,
And Death put down his book.

- WH Auden

About the Author

Harper Fox is the author of many critically acclaimed M/M Romance novels, including Stonewall Book Award-nominated *Scrap Metal* and *Brothers Of The Wild North Sea*, Publishers Weekly Best Book 2013. Her novels and novellas are powerfully sensual, with a dynamic of strongly developed characters finding love and a forever future—after an appropriate degree of turmoil. She loves to show the romance implicit in everyday life, and she writes a sharp action scene too.

To find out more about Harper and see updates on her current writing projects, please visit www.harperfox.net